Dear Reader

Welcome to the premiere editions of Harlequin Duets!

This new and exciting series is written by authors you love and published in a great new format. Have you ever finished reading a romance and wished you had another one you could start right away? Well, we have the answer for you. Each and every month there will be two Harlequin Duets books on sale, and each book will contain two complete brand-new novels. (You'll always have your backup read with you!)

Harlequin Duets features the best of romantic comedy. Our opening lineup is an exciting one: stories by Vicki Lewis Thompson, Christie Ridgway, Jacqueline Diamond and Bonnie Tucker. Wonderfully romantic and funny stories about cowboys, bridesmaids, babies and one very unusual hero, a supposed gangster.

Harlequin Duets—double your reading pleasure!

Sincerely,

Malle Vallik

Malle Vallik
Senior Editor

P.S. We'd love to hear what you think about Harlequin Duets! Drop us a line at:

Harlequin Duets
Harlequin Books
225 Duncan Mill Road
Don Mills, Ontario
M3B 3K9 Canada

"Don't kiss me, Quinn."

"Okay, I won't." He lowered his head.

"You are." Jo was quivering. "You're going to kiss me."

When his mouth found hers, she didn't think at all. She sure did feel, though—cool lips that quickly warmed against hers and shaped themselves into the soul of temptation in no time, a tongue that told her exactly what Quinn would be doing if they didn't have two layers of denim between their significant body parts. She liked everything about this kiss, even the mud that squished between them as he eased his chest down to press against her breasts.

The only thing she didn't like was that he stopped kissing her.

"More," she whispered.

Why, oh, why hadn't she made an effort to date before now?

Francesca stifled a groan. With a little more experience she'd be better able to interpret Brett's nuances tonight.

"Francesca?" Brett asked. "What're you thinking?"

"That I should be married with three kids." Then the waiting and the wondering would be over. She'd be settled and satisfied and—

Would have missed the chance at Brett Swenson.

"Then we wouldn't be having this date," he said, just as if he could read her mind.

"Is this what this is?" Francesca whispered. "A date?" In her jeans and her tennis shoes she was actually *dating* Brett Swenson?

"What would you call it?"

Something she should have used a curling iron for.

Something that warranted every feminine grace and womanly wile she'd ever heard or read about.

Something she'd wished for on every girlhood star...

HARLEQUIN DUETS

ISBN 0-373-44067-7

WITH A STETSON AND A SMILE
Copyright © 1999 by Vicki Lewis Thompson.

THE BRIDESMAID'S BET
Copyright © 1999 by Christie Ridgway.

VICKI LEWIS THOMPSON

With a Stetson and a Smile

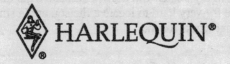

TORONTO • NEW YORK • LONDON
AMSTERDAM • PARIS • SYDNEY • HAMBURG
STOCKHOLM • ATHENS • TOKYO • MILAN • MADRID
PRAGUE • WARSAW • BUDAPEST • AUCKLAND

Dear Reader,

I'm so excited about being in the launch month for Harlequin Duets that I feel like cracking a bottle of champagne over the spine of the book. Actually, considering the Western flavor of my story, I'd better substitute a long-necked beer for the champagne.

By now it's no secret that I find cowboys...appealing. God bless 'em, these guys don't see the logic in wearing baggy jeans. I'm fascinated by men born to the saddle as well as city slickers who finally let the cowboy inside them come out to play. Quinn Monroe fits into the second category. He also fits into a pair of jeans like you wouldn't believe.

Maybe because I also started life as an Easterner, I relate to Quinn's culture shock when he makes the transition from Manhattan to Montana. I was ten when my family moved to Arizona, and I still remember the jolt of trading cozy landscapes for majestic vistas. But I acclimated fast, and now I feel hemmed in if I can't see at least fifty miles in all directions.

Fortunately, within that fifty-mile radius, I can always spot a goodly number of lean-hipped, broad-shouldered, square-jawed cowboys to serve as role models for the heroes in my books. Out here in Arizona a gal doesn't have to try very hard to locate a Stetson and a smile. And that works for me.

Enjoy!

Vicki Lewis Thompson

Vicki Lewis Thompson

For my sister Karen Santa Maria, and our first-ever
horseback ride many moons ago at
the River Road Stable.

MANHATTAN
MAVERICKS

Not quite home on the range

A SNAKE was loose in the cab.

Quinn swerved around a horse-drawn carriage parked in front of Tavern on the Green, whipped over to the curb and slammed on the brakes. He was out of the door and halfway across the street before he knew it. After several deep breaths, he finally worked up the courage to edge toward the car and jerk open the back door. Then he crept around to the passenger side and quickly opened both curbside doors.

He hated snakes. Come to think of it, he wasn't fond of lizards, either. One of the things he liked best about Manhattan was the absence of reptiles. If he'd known his fare was carrying snakes in that shoe box he wouldn't have picked him up. But the guy hadn't announced he was making a donation to the Central Park Zoo until they were almost there.

Quinn figured he'd been set up. It was too much of a coincidence that on the very day he'd accepted the challenge of driving one of Murray's cabs he'd be transporting snakes. Murray was convinced Wall Street had made Quinn too soft to handle a day driving cab, and it would be just like Murray to stack the deck and guarantee he'd win the bet.

Once Quinn had found out about the snakes, he'd almost gotten in a wreck twice on the way to the zoo. At last he'd let the guy off at the zoo entrance and pulled away with a huge sigh of relief. Then he'd looked down to find beady eyes staring at him from under the front seat. An escapee.

"Taxi!"

Quinn didn't turn around. He wasn't taking anybody anywhere until he got that snake out. The woman would have to find another cab.

"Taxi!"

Quinn realized she was coming over and turned to fend her off. "Sorry, I'm not..." He forgot what else he'd planned to say as he stared. Ogled. Lusted. Murray, always politically incorrect, would call her a babe. Tucked into a white silk shirt and red velvet jeans, with a red Stetson perched on glossy brown curls, she certainly produced a politically incorrect response in Quinn.

She adjusted her load of packages, which caused her silk blouse to shift and reveal a bit of cleavage. "I must get to the airport immediately."

"Airport?" Quinn struggled with the sad news that this fantasy cowgirl was leaving town.

"JFK. I'm in a hurry." She started toward the cab.

Watching her walk in those tight jeans and high-heeled boots was a treat. He also had a thing for long, curly brown hair after seeing *Pretty Woman* at an impressionable age. Taking this lady to the airport would be the highlight of his day—if it weren't for the reptile problem.

Quinn hated choices like this. The snake or the lady. "Uh, I'd better warn you about something. There's a snake in the cab."

She swung around. "Don't tell me you're one of those guys who keeps his pet boa constrictor near him at all times."

"No. My last fare left a snake. That's why I have all the doors open. I was trying—"

"Poisonous?"

Oh, God. He hadn't even thought about that. "How can you tell?"

"Folding fangs." She freed one hand and folded two fingers into her palm. Then she flicked them out, curving them to look like fangs. "They do that. Did this snake do that?"

"No." And if it had he would have fainted.

"Then let's go. On the way I'll coax him out for you."

"Oh, that won't be necessary."

"You look a little pale. You're not afraid of snakes, are you?"

"Me? Afraid of snakes? Nah. Not me." Quinn couldn't believe she could be so cool about the idea of a snake in the cab. She hadn't even asked what size it was. "I'm actually worried about the poor snake. He must be scared to death."

"I'm sure he is. Look, I really have to go. If I miss my flight my sperm will spoil."

Quinn almost swallowed his tongue. "Excuse me?" His voice broke like a sixteen-year-old's.

She rearranged her bundles and lifted a small cooler, the kind that could hold a six-pack. "Horse sperm."

Finally it dawned on Quinn that she, too, was part of this elaborate practical joke. "Okay, okay. You guys had your fun. First the snakes and now the horse sperm, just to throw old Quinn a curve. Murray's creative, I'll give him that. I'll bet that cooler contains the beer you're going to share with Murray while you celebrate winning the bet."

She looked confused. "Who's Murray?"

"Let me refresh your memory." He folded his arms and rocked on his heels. Now that he'd figured out what was going on he felt much better. "Murray's the guy you're in cahoots with, the one who owns the cab company, the guy who grew up next door to me in the Bronx, the guy who until today was my best friend, the guy I'm going to strangle once this shift is over.''

"I don't know any Murray."

"Oh, sure. What did you two do, follow me from the zoo? You've probably been following me ever since I picked up the guy with the snakes, who was also a plant. Am I getting warm?" He smiled. Yes, he was in control of the situation now.

She stared at him and shook her head. "You're a crazy man, and I probably shouldn't trust myself to a crazy man. But the thing is, I always have trouble getting a cab in this city. Now that I've captured one, I'm not letting it go, even if it is driven by a guy who's missing a few rails from his corral. I have horse sperm that must get to Montana today, so I'm going to ask you again, very nicely, if we can get into your little cab and drive to that big place outside of town where they keep all the airplanes. Can you do that for me?"

Quinn sighed. "Murray sure knows how to pick 'em. You're very good. Okay, kiddo. If you can stand a ride with a snake, I can stand it." He gestured toward the cab. "After you, ma'am."

"Thank goodness." She walked forward, put her packages in the back seat and closed the door. Then she climbed in the front.

Quinn closed the street-side back door and paused before he got in the cab. He really didn't want to climb in there with that snake, but he didn't want Murray to get the upper hand, either. Besides, if Murray was behind all this, the snake was harmless. And maybe it had already slithered out. He rested his hands on the roof of the cab and leaned down to peer inside. "It's customary for the fare to sit in the back."

"I've never liked that custom," she said. "It seems downright unfriendly. Out west we—"

"Oh, yeah. That's right. You're from the wild and woolly west. Central Park West, most likely."

"Listen, could you continue weaving your fantasies while we drive? I'm running out of time to chat."

Quinn surveyed the floor in the front. "Did you, uh, notice the snake by any chance?"

"No, but if I sit up here I can protect you better."

That did it. Damned if he'd let this woman insinuate that he was a wuss. He slid into the seat with all the confidence he could muster. "A little snake doesn't bother me. I just wouldn't want you to be startled."

"I've faced timber rattlers with bodies as thick as your forearm."

Quinn laughed as he started the car. "That's a good line. Next you'll be telling me about the grizzly bear who lives in the hills up above your ranch."

"Actually there are two."

"Oh, I'll bet there are." Quinn pulled into traffic, noticing as he did that she filled the cab with a nice fragrance. "So what name are you going by for this caper?"

"The name I always go by. My own. Jo Fletcher."

"Short for Josephine?" Quinn didn't believe for a minute that was her name, but he decided to play along and see what sort of whopper she and Murray had dreamed up. It also took his mind off the snake.

"Well, yes. After my great-aunt Josephine. Which is why she left me the ranch, I guess. Well, that and the fact I'm the only member of the family who knows diddly about horses."

"You and Murray must have stayed up nights concocting this story. I'm impressed. Ticked off, but impressed. The guy will do anything to win a bet."

"I don't know anybody named Murray and I certainly don't know anything about a bet."

Quinn gave her a superior smile. "Right."

She cocked her head and looked at him strangely. "Did anybody ever tell you that you look exactly like Brian Hastings, the movie star? Even the smile."

"Only a couple of million people."

"Ah. So you get that a lot."

"Yeah. I'm pretty sick of it, which is probably why Murray asked you to bring it up, just to needle me."

"I don't know Murray. But if you're sensitive about the Brian Hastings thing, we can drop the subject. It's just that you really do look like him."

He swerved around a delivery van. The job took reflexes he hadn't used in years, and he liked knowing they were still there. "But I'm taller than Hastings. You can't tell that on the screen because they use camera angles to make him look tall, and he stands on a box if he has a tall costar."

"I'd heard that he was on the short side. So what? People are too hung up on how tall a guy is. Being taller doesn't make you a better man."

"I didn't say that."

"You sort of did, Quinn."

"Aha!" He thought he had her this time. His name had popped right out of that luscious red mouth of hers. "How do you explain the fact that you know my name? Wiggle out of that little slip, if you can." He liked the mental picture of Jo wiggling. At least Murray had provided a beautiful woman as part of the joke. Quinn wondered if she was dating anybody.

"You told me your name."

"Did not."

"Did, too. You said, 'just trying to throw old Quinn a curve.'"

"Oh."

"Anyway, I loved Brian Hastings in *The Drifter*. Did you see that?"

"Nope. I pretty much don't go to his movies. I pretty

much boycott them, as a matter of fact." Two kids in purple hair jaywalked in front of him, and he gave them the horn. Except for the box of snakes, he'd had fun today. More fun than he'd been having recently planning investment strategies, to be honest.

"But why don't you go to Hastings' movies?" Jo asked. "He's a good actor, and now he's into directing. I think he's very talented."

Quinn recognized that tone of adulation. "Meaning you think he's sexy."

"Well, yes, I do. What, are you jealous because women find him sexy? Is that why you don't go to his movies?"

"No, I'm not jealous." It was more as if the guy had usurped his identity.

"Then why boycott his movies?"

"Think about it. I show up at a Brian Hastings movie looking like Brian Hastings. I've had women throw themselves into my arms, rip off pieces of my clothing, follow me for blocks."

"Poor baby."

"You think it would be fun, don't you?" He pulled over to let a fire engine roar past, siren screaming. "It's not fun. And besides that, they're not after me, Quinn Monroe, investment banker. They're after Brian Hastings, Hollywood star. So it means nothing."

"Investment banker? You must not be very good at it if you have to drive cab on the side."

Quinn glanced at her. She acted as if she had no idea he'd agreed to drive cab for one day on a dare. She just sat there gazing at him with an innocent look in those big brown eyes that would be hard to fake. For the first time he wondered if she was legit. "Either you're an incredible actress or you're telling the truth about this ranch in Montana."

"I can't act my way out of a paper bag."

"Would you be willing to show me your driver's license?"

"No, I would not."

He nodded, smiling. "Just as I thought. Your driver's license isn't from Montana, is it? I'll bet your name isn't even Josephine Fletcher."

"All right! I'll show you the damned license." She unzipped her purse and pulled out her wallet. "But you have to promise not to laugh at my picture. I look like an escaped convict." She flipped the wallet open and held it up.

He stopped at a red light and glanced at the license. Josephine Fletcher stared at him from the picture, unsmiling, grim, even, but still beautiful. The license had been issued by the Montana Department of Transportation.

JO WATCHED amazement spread over Quinn's face as he glanced from her to the license and back again. He really was a cutie, with his laser-blue eyes and movie-star looks. She flipped the wallet closed and stuffed it in her purse. "Is that proof enough, or would you like to see my maxed-out Visa card, too?"

"If you're really Jo Fletcher, then I guess you have horse sperm in that cooler."

"Of course I do! Do you think I'd make up a thing like that?"

"If you were part of Murray's big plan, you would."

"But I'm not." They crossed the Queensboro Bridge, linking Manhattan with Long Island, and Jo glanced at the skyline. She might never fly here again, which was why she'd stocked up on extra souvenirs for Emmy Lou. No use crying over it now, though. She turned to Quinn. "Since I've proven I'm not part of some intricate plot, would you kindly tell me who this Murray person is?"

"My best friend since the second grade and the owner of a fleet of cabs. He's convinced I've turned into a stuffed shirt who couldn't handle a day in one of his cabs, so finally I bet him I could. When the guy showed up with a shoe box full of snakes I wondered if Murray had somehow engineered that. A cooler full of horse sperm was so outrageous I decided you were also in on the campaign to rattle me and make me lose the bet."

"I see." Jo had caught a glimpse of the little snake twice. It was just a harmless garter snake, but she'd suspected from the beginning of this adventure that snakes sent Quinn into a panic. She'd decided to try to catch the snake with a minimum of fuss so he wouldn't wreck the cab. Then she'd suggest they let it go in one of the open fields near the airport.

"Now it's your turn," Quinn said. "What's with the horse sperm?"

"It belongs to my friend Cassie's stallion, Sir Lust-a-Lot. Cassie was my college roommate, and I worked at her family's stable in upstate New York after graduation. Then I inherited the ranch, and we established a spring tradition—I take the red-eye to New York, shop all morning, meet Cassie for lunch at Tavern on the Green and leave with the sperm."

"Are you telling me you don't have horse sperm in Montana?"

"Sure, we do, but this is a connection with Cassie, and besides, Sir Lust-a-Lot has extremely viable sperm. Good little swimmers. My mares get pregnant like *that*." She snapped her fingers for emphasis, then glimpsed the snake easing out from under her seat. She kept an eye on it and said nothing.

"Is that what you raise on your ranch? Horses?"

"No. We try to raise cattle." Jo sighed as she was reminded of her heavy debt load, most of it accumulated since she'd inherited the Bar None. She might be good with horses, but she was financially challenged. She should have followed Josephine's advice and taken more accounting courses, but they'd given her a migraine, and she'd really had no idea Josephine would will her the ranch. "We lost quite a chunk of the herd this past winter. I'm already behind on my payments to the bank, so I'm not sure what the future holds."

"I guess it's tough to be a small ranching operation these days."

"It is tough. And when the ranch is such a little gem and has been entrusted into your care by your favorite great-aunt, you'd do almost anything to keep it going." She glanced at him. "I'm sorry you're not Brian Hastings. One of his advance men came by the ranch last fall and said they were looking for a location for his next film. If you were Brian Hastings, I'd fall to my knees and beg you to use the ranch in your movie."

He smiled at her. "And if I were Brian Hastings, I would use your ranch in my next movie."

"Thanks." She really liked that smile of his. Actually she thought it was sexier than Brian's, but she probably shouldn't say so. They were only going to be sharing a cab ride, after all. No point in starting anything, especially with a guy whose roots were in New York City. Despite her money problems, she'd discovered a kinship with Montana. Even losing the ranch might not force her to leave. But she intended to find a way to keep the Bar None. Somehow.

"I take it you haven't heard any more from the Hastings organization?"

"Nope. But I shamelessly told the bank that the movie deal was a sure thing. It's kept them off my back temporarily, but if Brian Hastings never shows, the bank will start demanding money again."

"I don't know if it's a good idea to stake everything on the whim of a movie star," Quinn said.

"Probably not." Jo watched the snake ease out a little

more and poised herself to lean down and snatch it. To distract Quinn from what she was doing, she kept talking. "Considering the shaky condition of my finances I shouldn't have made the sperm run this year, but Cassie's decided to geld Sir Lust-a-Lot this spring, so this is my last chance to breed my mares to him, unless we get into freezing sperm, which is too complicated and expensive for me."

"Gelding. Is that where they cut off—"

"Let's just say he'll lose the ability to be a family man."

"Why would she do that?"

"Because he's a pain in the butt and useless as a saddle horse. Gelding should mellow him out. I don't blame her. She's the one who has to put up with his testosterone fits, not me."

"So you're carrying Sir Lust-a-Lot's last stand?"

Jo laughed. "I guess you could say that. The sperm's packed in dry ice, and it's always stayed fresh for the plane flight home, but I don't want to miss that plane and risk having it go bad."

Quinn stepped on the gas. "Then let's make sure you don't." He started weaving through traffic like a man on a mission.

Jo smiled. Some men took castration of male animals personally. Apparently Quinn was one of those who did. Maybe that was a good thing, because as long as he was thinking about Sir Lust-a-Lot's fate he might forget about the snake, which was almost within her reach. "So you're really an investment banker?" She leaned slowly down, straining slightly against the seat belt.

"Yeah, I really am."

She made a grab for the snake and missed. "Damn!"

"Sorry I'm not something more exciting, like a movie star."

"It's not that." She tossed her hat in the back seat and

unbuckled her seat belt as the snake moved quickly to Quinn's side of the car. "Slow the car, get in the right-hand lane and hold still."

"Oh, God. The snake." Quinn eased his foot off the gas.

"Yep. He's just a little guy, which makes him harder to catch." She got to her knees on the floor of the passenger side and reached toward Quinn's ankle.

"He's down there? Right by my foot?"

"Don't be afraid. He won't hurt you."

"I'm not afraid, dammit! I'm just…" He paused and made a strangled sound. "What's that?"

"Hold still. He's trying to climb up your leg."

"Up my *leg?* What for?"

"Maybe it's a girl snake, and she's curious." Jo clamped an arm around Quinn's thigh, noting he had great muscles, and reached under his pants leg.

"Oh, my God. What's happening?"

"Don't look down here! Watch where you're going, Quinn!"

"Holy sh—" Quinn's voice was drowned out by the loud thunk of metal against metal.

2

JO CLUTCHED Quinn's thigh to keep from being thrown against the dashboard as the cab lurched from the impact. The jolt dislodged the small snake, and she grabbed it behind its head. "Got him!"

"Jo!" Gasping, he clutched her shoulder. "God, I'm sorry. Are you okay?"

"I think so." She released his thigh and pushed herself upright. "See?" She dangled the snake in front of him. "Real small."

Quinn didn't look so good. In fact, he was breathing hard and looked ready to pass out.

"Quinn, are you hurt?"

"No." He kept staring at the snake. When someone started knocking on his window, he reached around and rolled it down without taking his eyes off the snake.

A man peered into the cab. "We got a problem here, buddy. You want to call the police?"

"Uh, sure." Quinn didn't move.

Jo figured if she didn't get the snake out of the cab he would stay frozen in that position forever. She looked around and discovered they weren't far from JFK. The vacant lot beside the expressway would have to do. She glanced at the man looking in the window. "Sir, I'm going to take this snake over to that field. In the meantime, Quinn, you can call the police and also call me another cab."

Quinn nodded, but he didn't take his attention off the wiggling snake in her hand.

Keeping a firm hold on it, Jo climbed onto the seat and opened the passenger door. As she got out she called to Quinn over her shoulder. "Move my stuff over to the other cab while I'm gone, okay? I don't want to miss that plane!"

She climbed the knee-high metal railing beside the road and sidestepped down an embankment. "After all this I want to get you far enough away from the road that you won't get run over," she said to the snake. "This looks like a good field. There ought to be plenty of bugs, and when you're bigger you might even find a mouse or two."

After hiking about thirty yards through clumps of wild grass, she slowly lowered the snake to the ground. "There you go. Stay away from the road. Have a good life."

The snake darted away without so much as a thank-you. But Jo felt immensely better as she walked toward the road. Holding the snake had been like a moment from home, where she'd learned to appreciate all creatures. She'd grown up in a city—her father and stepmother still lived in Chicago—but cities were no longer home to her. Maybe they hadn't been for a long time. Her summers with Aunt Josephine at the Bar None had probably ruined her for city life by the time she was ten.

When she reached the expressway, the police and a second cab had arrived on the scene. Quinn was standing beside the damaged cab waving his arms and looking upset. Even upset he looked damned good—broad shoulders, lean hips. He really was attractive, she thought. Too bad he lived in New York. She climbed the railing and walked to the group.

The man whose car Quinn had hit glanced at her suspiciously before turning to the police officer. "There was something kinky going on in that vehicle, I tell you. I was riding along next to them, and they were going really slow, so I got curious and went slow. Then they started swerving all over the road, and then she got down and put her face in his lap, if you get my meaning."

"She was trying to get a snake out of my pants!" Quinn bellowed.

The man glanced at the officer. "So who drives to the airport with a snake in his pants?"

"Nobody!" Quinn's jaw worked. "I'm sure my friend Murray is behind this snake thing. He probably paid the guy with the snakes."

The officer cleared his throat and gazed at Jo. "Would you like to tell us your version?"

She glanced at her watch and gauged the distance to the airport. "I would love to, but I'm warning you that unless I catch my plane, my sperm will spoil."

Quinn groaned.

Jo realized she should have phrased the sentence differently as soon as it left her mouth. "I was referring to horse sperm, Officer, which I am transporting, with all the necessary health department papers, to Montana. Quinn's previous passenger left a snake in his cab, and I was indeed trying to catch it when the incident occurred. I just released the little fellow in that field over there."

Quinn stepped forward. "Look, she really had nothing to do with the accident. I'll vouch for that. The cab company will assume all liability for this." He turned to the owner of the other car. "The sperm she's carrying is from a stallion that's being castrated, maybe right this minute. She has to get on that plane to Montana so the poor horse can have one last shot at immortality, okay?"

The man's belligerent expression evaporated. "Oh, well, in that case..." He turned to the officer. "Never mind the kinky thing. Just a routine fender bender. I'm sure the cab company will handle everything. This poor slob should be fired, though."

"I'm sure I will be," Quinn said.

"So I'm free to go?" Jo asked.

"After I get some basic information," the officer said.

Jo gave him what he needed and turned to Quinn. "I guess this means you lose your bet with Murray."

"Afraid so. Jo, I'm sorry about this. It's just that—"

"You're petrified of snakes."

He flashed her a little-boy grin. "Yep."

"There are worse flaws," Jo said. "Listen, I gotta go. Is all my stuff in the other cab?"

"Bill transferred it as soon as he pulled up. I think he consolidated a few things so it'd be easier to carry up to the gate."

"That was nice of him."

Quinn stuck out his hand. "Good luck with the ranch."

"Thanks." She liked the feel of his hand—warm, strong, secure. "Good luck with Murray." With a smile she released his hand and hurried to the waiting cab.

Approximately thirty-five minutes later, as she was checking into the gate, she realized that the cooler of horse sperm was nowhere to be seen.

QUINN didn't find the cooler of horse sperm on the floor of the back seat until the tow truck arrived. Just before the cab was winched on the flatbed, Quinn put in a quick call to Bill and had him pick him up.

Bill grinned as Quinn climbed into the cab. "You're lucky you caught me. I was next in line for a fare at the airport."

"You're lucky I caught you, too." Quinn held up the cooler. "You forgot to transfer this. It belongs to Jo, the woman you just took to the airport. We have to try and catch her before she boards that plane."

Bill gunned the engine and zipped into a break in traffic. "I thought that was your lunch, man!"

"It's sperm from a stallion that is probably being castrated even as we speak."

"Get outta here!"

"I know it sounds crazy, but she came to New York to pick this up and take it back so she can give it to her mares in Montana."

Bill shook his head. "Me, I don't believe in those methods. I know a guy who donated to a sperm bank. Now what fun is that?"

"Don't know. Never tried it."

"Me, neither." Bill glanced at Quinn. "How do you figure they do it with stallions?"

Quinn had been wondering the same thing ever since Jo had convinced him she was really transporting horse sperm. "Let's not even go there. Listen, drop me at the airline where you let her off."

"Good luck, but I really don't think you can make it. She was running behind. She thanked me for getting her packages all organized, and I guess she thought the cooler was in one of the bags."

"Yeah, well, it's been a crazy day."

"No kidding. Everybody knows about your little brush with the law, by the way. Murray's busting a gut laughing."

"I knew it! I knew he was behind that snake thing."

"No, he wasn't, swear to God! He said he couldn't have planned a better day for you if he'd tried." Bill maneuvered next to the curb. "Should I wait?"

"Nope."

"Yeah, but if you don't catch her, what are you gonna do? You can't follow her to Montana."

Quinn stared at Bill as he considered the idea for the first time. He hadn't planned his next step if he missed the plane, but he'd been mostly to blame for this whole mess, and Jo would be bitterly disappointed to lose Sir Lust-a-

Lot's sperm on top of all her financial problems. He didn't like to think about her being bitterly disappointed, especially if it was his doing. And it wasn't as if he couldn't get away from the office for a few days…. "Sure, I can," he said.

DRIVING a back road miles from Bozeman, Quinn felt as small as a flea on the back of a woolly mammoth. The headlights of his rental car cast the only light for miles around, not counting the moon and stars overhead. The mountains loomed threateningly around him, pitch-black except for a pale topping of moonlit snow. There was so much *space* in Montana. If his rental car broke down, he could imagine waiting for days before another vehicle came down this two-lane highway.

Belatedly he wished he'd brought food and water, a sleeping bag, a…a *rifle*. He'd never shot a gun in his life, but this was the sort of country that seemed to require firearms. And it was Jo's country. His estimation of her grit and determination rose with every bend in the increasingly lonely road.

He hoped to God he was on the right lonely road. While he'd waited for his flight he'd asked his secretary to call every chamber of commerce in Montana until she found somebody who recognized the name Bar None. Fortunately she'd hit pay dirt within the first half hour of phoning. Unfortunately it was located near a town named Ugly Bug, on the banks of Ugly Bug Creek. After snakes and lizards, Quinn listed bugs as his third least favorite creature.

If he was on the right road he might miss the turnoff to the ranch, but at least he'd eventually get to Ugly Bug. If he was on the wrong road he'd probably drive until he ran out of gas, and then a bear would eat him.

He'd always been fascinated with the West, but he realized that his picture of it had been highly romanticized.

Cowboys around a campfire, the comradery of a roundup, card games in the local saloon. His image of the West had been cozy, quaint and not nearly big enough. This country was enormous.

He rounded another bend and saw a spark of light nestled in a valley. Checking his odometer, he decided it could be coming from the Bar None. Maybe he'd defied the odds and found the place. Maybe they wouldn't find his bleached bones lying beside a dried-up watering hole.

A few more bends in the road, and sure enough, on his right stood a big wooden gate. Two upright poles supported a crossbeam, and from that dangled a sign. Quinn couldn't read it in the dark, but he'd bet it said Bar None.

He shone his car's headlights on the gate and got out to open it. The thing was wired together instead of padlocked, which was fortunate for him. The barbed wire fence on either side of the gate wasn't something he wanted to tangle with. He drove through and went back to hook the gate closed again.

Driving slowly down the dirt road toward the cluster of lights he assumed was the ranch, he noticed dark shapes scattered across the moonlit landscape. Either cows or bears, he concluded. He remembered Jo mentioning timber rattlers with bodies as thick as his forearm, and he shuddered. With luck, none of those would be hanging around the front porch of her house tonight.

Finally he arrived at a cluster of buildings and corrals. With his limited knowledge, he figured the two-story white clapboard one was the main house, the rust-colored structure was a barn and the third, also rust-colored, was probably a bunkhouse. Light spilled from the ranch-house windows onto the front porch with its wide swing and two rocking chairs.

The whole arrangement was right out of a Brian Hastings movie. Cowboys were making a comeback these days, and

Hastings was cashing in on the new craze. Quinn hoped to hell Hastings would contract with Jo for the use of her ranch. Any woman who could keep her cool under fire the way Jo had today deserved a break.

Taking the cooler from the passenger seat, Quinn got out and closed the car door. A plump woman of about forty opened the door and peered out. Such a thing would never happen in the city, Quinn thought, remembering his triple-locked apartment door.

He smiled at the woman. "Hello, I'm—"

"Glory, hallelujah." The woman gazed at him as if she were witnessing the second coming.

Quinn figured she must have recognized the cooler he carried, but even so he was a little taken aback at the woman's worshipful expression. "Hey, glad to be of service. It's the least I could do, under the circumstances."

"You know about our circumstances?"

"Some of it. Listen, is Jo around? I'm—"

"I know who you are." The woman's grin put big dimples in both cheeks. "And I'm tickled spitless to see you. We'd about given up hope. Come in, come in. I'm Emmy Lou, the housekeeper. Have you eaten? I can warm up the leftover chicken."

It was a most gratifying welcome. Quinn decided he'd done the right thing. "Chicken sounds wonderful." He followed the woman into a small entry hall. "I figured Jo would be worried. I came as soon as I could."

"Jo has been worried, all right. Poor woman takes her responsibilities very seriously, although between you and me, I think she needs someone to give her good financial advice. Maybe you could recommend someone. But the main thing is, you're here. I wasn't sure you'd show up."

"Well, a lot is at stake. And a stud deserves to have his last shot count."

"Last shot?" Emmy Lou's smile was coy as she looked him up and down. "I hardly think so."

"Well, that's what Jo said this would be."

"How rude of her!" She peered at him. "When did you discuss this with Jo?"

"In New York." Quinn was becoming a little confused by the conversation.

"That little dickens. I need to have a talk with that girl. She may be getting a little too big for her britches."

Quinn thought Jo fit her britches just fine.

"Anyway, you're here now." Emmy Lou led him into a country kitchen filled with the scent of chicken and baked apples.

Quinn's mouth watered.

"Sit yourself down and take a load off," the woman said. "I'll run and fetch Jo. She's upstairs. She'll be *so* glad to see you."

"Okay." Quinn felt extremely pleased with himself. Maybe this sperm-delivery trip would improve his image after his sorry performance with the snake this afternoon. And if Jo truly needed financial advice, maybe he could help her there, too. He set the cooler on the floor beside his chair. After Jo got over the shock of seeing him, he'd bring it out as a special surprise. He wondered how she'd react. Maybe she'd hug him in gratitude. That was a nice prospect.

Emmy Lou left the kitchen and walked down the hall. "Jo!" she called up the stairs. "You'll never guess who's here!"

Quinn smiled with pleasure. Despite the snake, he must have made a decent impression on Jo if she'd told her housekeeper all about him. He'd planned to head straight back for New York, but with this kind of welcome he might be convinced to stay a little longer.

Jo CAME to the head of the stairs. "Who?"

Grinning like a politician at a barbecue, Emmy Lou motioned her down, and Jo descended the stairs, eyebrows lifted.

When Jo was two steps away, Emmy Lou leaned forward and delivered her news in a stage whisper. *"Brian Hastings."*

"You're kidding." Jo's heart rate kicked up a notch.

"Nope. Sitting right in my kitchen."

Technically it was Jo's kitchen, but she didn't correct Emmy Lou. If possession was nine-tenths of the law, Emmy Lou owned the kitchen. "He just showed up at the door? Nobody's with him?"

"He probably enjoys getting off by himself once in a while, away from all those screaming women. Why, I decided I wouldn't even ask him for a button off his shirt. At least not yet."

"Go slow on the button thing." Jo glanced toward the kitchen, and her chest tightened. As much as she'd prayed for this moment, she realized she'd never negotiated a movie contract. It probably wasn't a job for someone with math anxiety, either. She'd have to concentrate really hard and make sure she counted the zeros, although she had no idea how many there should be when someone wanted to rent your ranch. Lots, she hoped.

"It's really going to happen, Jo." Emmy Lou's voice trembled with excitement. "The Bar None will rocket to stardom, and we'll be able to pay the bank. Not to mention having Brian Hastings around for weeks. Do you think I should ask him for a part in the movie yet?"

"No!" Jo whispered. "And don't you ask about that darned button, either! This might still be a preliminary visit. We might have made the shortlist or something." She ran her fingers through her hair and glanced at the torn jeans and old T-shirt she wore. She could either meet a famous movie star looking like this or go upstairs and change, which would keep a famous movie star waiting. She decided to go with the outfit she had on and headed for the kitchen. A man used to starlets probably wouldn't give an ordinary woman a second look no matter what she had on.

She paused outside the kitchen door and took a deep breath. He was only a man, she reminded herself. But herself wouldn't listen. Her heart was leaping like a rodeo bronc at the idea of coming face-to-face with the very person commonly referred to as the sexiest man alive. And she couldn't blow this interview. The future of her ranch might depend on the impression she made in the next minute.

Closing her eyes, she counted to ten. Then she walked into the room.

Quinn Monroe smiled at her. "Surprise."

"Damn! It's you!"

His smile faded.

"Josephine Sarah Fletcher!" Emmy Lou said. "Is that any way to treat Mr. Hastings? Apologize this instant!"

"I'm sorry," Jo said. "In more ways than one. Emmy Lou, this isn't Brian Hastings."

"What do you mean, he isn't Brian Hastings? You're talking to a woman who saw *The Drifter* fourteen times! And *this*—" she gestured dramatically toward Quinn "—is Brian Hastings."

Quinn winced. "As a matter of fact—"

"I would know this man anywhere." Emmy Lou marched over to Quinn and took his face firmly in her hand. She lifted his chin. "Look at those sensuous lips." She brought his chin down again. "Look into those intense blue eyes. And the profile!" She whipped Quinn's head abruptly to one side. "There! Are you trying to tell me that's not the profile of Brian Hastings, love god?"

Jo sighed. "That's the profile of Quinn Monroe, investment banker. I couldn't say whether he's a love god or not.''

"Only on alternate Thursdays,'' Quinn said.

Emmy Lou frowned and turned his head until she could look into his eyes. She fluffed his hair and stared at him some more. "Smile for me.''

"I can't. You're digging your thumb into my cheek.''

Emmy Lou released him. "Now smile.''

Quinn obliged.

"You see? It's the Brian Hastings I'm-too-sexy-for-my-shirt smile! Only in real life it's even better.'' She patted him on the cheek. "You should make more public appearances. You look good close up. Not all actors do.''

While Emmy Lou was talking, Jo's brain began working overtime. She was fascinated with the housekeeper's conviction that Quinn had to be Brian Hastings, despite Jo and Quinn denying it. Fascinated and intrigued. She might have been convinced herself if she hadn't seen him driving a cab, but logic had told her that Brian Hastings wouldn't get his kicks driving a cab in New York City.

"I'm here to deliver the sperm,'' Quinn said.

Emmy Lou gasped. "Young man, I know Hollywood's filled with sin and debauchery, but you're in Montana now, and we don't talk like that out here. You work up to that—a few dates, a few stolen kisses, a little fondling. And the term is *making love,* not *delivering sperm.*''

"You brought it?'' Jo asked. Now that was something to be happy about.

Quinn reached beside his chair and lifted the cooler onto the table. "I figured you might still be able to salvage it if I caught the next flight to Bozeman. So I just came. On the spur of the moment.''

"That's really...amazing. Thank you, Quinn. Let me stick it in the refrigerator.'' Jo's disappointment that Brian Hastings wasn't here to rent her ranch dimmed as she realized what a sacrifice Quinn had made. After putting the cooler inside the refrigerator she turned to Emmy Lou. "Remember the cabdriver who was afraid of snakes? This is him. I just forgot to tell you he looks like Brian Hastings."

Emmy Lou crossed her arms and surveyed Quinn. "Maybe Brian Hastings went undercover in New York City in order to get away from the pressures of making movies."

Jo shook her head. "Give it up, Em. He's not Brian Hastings, and all the wishing in the world won't make it so. But he's done me a very big favor, and I appreciate it." She glanced at him nervously as she thought about what a plane ticket had probably cost him. "I need to reimburse you for your ticket."

"No, you don't. I'm the one who made you lose the sperm."

"True. Then at least let us put you up for the night."

"That would be great. And I'm...sort of hungry." He glanced at Emmy Lou. "Does the offer of chicken still stand even if I'm not Brian Hastings?"

"Of course! I feed any poor hungry soul who comes through that kitchen door, no matter who it is."

"Thanks, I think."

"But I still can't believe you're—what was the name?"

"Quinn Monroe."

"Any proof?"

"As a matter of fact, I have the chauffeur's license I had to get before I could drive one of Murray's cabs." Quinn reached in his back pocket and pulled out his wallet. Then he glanced at Jo. "But you have to promise not to laugh. The picture makes me look like an escaped convict."

"I'll bet it makes you look like Brian Hastings." Emmy Lou studied the license for a long time. Finally she handed it back to Quinn. "Okay, so you're not him, but you could pass for him any day of the week."

"Yeah, I know that."

Emmy Lou stood and headed for the refrigerator. "Come to think about it, I read that Brian Hastings is a vegetarian. Are you a vegetarian, too?"

"Nope. I'd be willing to bet there is almost nothing about me that is the same as Brian Hastings."

Emmy Lou shook her head. "What a shame."

"Now, Emmy Lou," Jo said. "You sound as if Brian Hastings sets the standard for all men. That's a little extreme."

Emmy Lou pulled some containers from the refrigerator. "Not for me."

Jo sat at the table and smiled at Quinn. "You'll have to excuse her. She's been a real fan for ten years."

"I'm pretty much used to it by now."

"I'm sure you are." *And if you're so used to it...* Jo couldn't help herself. A plan was forming—a daring, audacious plan. And it just might save her bacon.

3

JO DECIDED to wait until Quinn had some of Emmy Lou's home cooking in his stomach before she hit him with her proposition. Still, she could do some preliminary spadework. "Is there a problem with you being away from your office for another day or so?" she asked.

"Not a huge problem. My secretary knows where I am. I thought I'd call her in the morning and see if anything major is going on I need to deal with."

"What time is your flight?"

He hesitated. "I didn't book a return because I didn't know exactly how long it would take me to find you. I can take care of it in the morning."

Excitement built within her. "Have you ever been to Montana?"

"Nope. First trip."

"Then as long as you've come all this way, how about staying for a few days? Spring is a great time of year in this country. You arrived in the dark, so I'm sure you didn't get the full impact. We have wildflowers galore, and all the trees are greening up. It's beautiful."

He looked interested, but cautious. "I'd hate to inconvenience you."

"No problem!" Jo liked her plan more and more. It might save the ranch and give her more time with this guy, and that was a good thing. Physically he appealed to her, but more than that she was charmed by his humanness. He might be afraid of snakes, but he'd traveled all the way to

Montana to return a cooler of horse sperm. Although she wasn't bold enough to say so, Quinn interested her far more than the macho image projected by Brian Hastings.

Emmy Lou turned from the stove.

"Betsy and Clarise are fixing to foal any day now."

"The miracle of birth," Jo said. "How many Wall Street investment bankers have seen a mare bring a foal into the world?"

"Certainly not this investment banker," Quinn said.

"You just said he was afraid of snakes," Emmy Lou pointed out. "They're starting to come out now. It's snakes and more snakes this time of year."

Jo smiled at Quinn, who was looking doubtful at the mention of snakes. "Will you excuse me a minute?" She walked to the stove, put her arm around Emmy Lou and leaned down to murmur in her ear. "Will you work with me here? I have a stupendous idea. And besides, I think he's very cute."

"I can see that he's cute," Emmy Lou said under her breath, "but you need a greenhorn like him around like you need an alligator in the stock tank."

"Maybe I should go back to New York tomorrow, after all," Quinn said.

"Just taste Emmy Lou's cooking first," Jo said. "And then tell me if you wouldn't like to stay a few extra days. One bite of her chicken, and I promise she'll have you moaning in ecstasy."

QUINN COULD THINK of another scenario that would have him moaning in ecstasy. Not that Emmy Lou's cooking wasn't melt-in-his-mouth perfect, especially considering how hungry he was by the time he bit into her fried chicken, but it wasn't the housekeeper's skills at the stove that had him considering a stay on the ranch.

Of course there were the snakes to consider, and he still

worried about how the town of Ugly Bug got its name. Maybe he could just stay inside a lot. Jo awakened basic urges in him, and basic urges were best investigated inside, anyway. He'd started fantasizing what it would be like to hold her in his arms, kiss those cherry red lips, touch her soft skin. But her physical attributes weren't the only draw. He was also a sucker for a woman in distress.

At first he'd only been concerned with getting the horse sperm to her on time, but now that he'd seen the ranch, he couldn't help thinking what a shame it would be for her to lose it. He didn't know a damn thing about ranching, but he knew a fair amount about money management. If he stayed a few days he might be able to suggest some things that would get Jo out of the bind she was in.

He doubted that she'd accept a personal loan, and he didn't have enough liquid assets to make that sort of gesture, anyway. But he might be able to arrange a new bank loan with one of his contacts or find her some investors. He mainly wanted to loosen the grip of this local guy and set her on a better course than the one that seemed to be leading her into trouble.

But he'd have to hang around a while and win her trust. The minute he'd seen her walk through the kitchen door, no matter how disappointing her reaction had been, he'd been inclined to do just that.

While he ate, he answered Emmy Lou's questions about New York. She'd never been there and had a fixation on the place, apparently. She proudly trotted out all the souvenirs Jo had brought her over the years, and Quinn made a mental note to send her something special when he got back to the city.

Finally he finished off the chicken and potato salad and pushed away his plate with a sigh of contentment. "That was delicious. Thanks."

Apparently his knowledge of New York and his appreciation for her cooking had warmed up the housekeeper considerably. "You have to have a piece of apple pie to top it off," she said.

He grinned at her. "Twist my arm, Emmy Lou."

She flushed and put a hand over her heart. "Land sakes, but you look like Brian Hastings when you do that. Makes my heart go pitty-pat."

"Maybe it'll also make you serve him some of your famous pie," Jo said.

Quinn had noticed that Jo was being terrifically friendly and obliging. He'd love to think it was his manly charm causing her to be so nice, but he also had the feeling she might be fattening him up for the kill. He just wasn't sure what sort of kill.

"Would you like ice cream on top?" Emmy Lou asked as she popped the slice of pie in the microwave.

"Sure, why not?" A piece of pie à la mode wasn't going to turn him into a mush brain, he decided. He'd navigated the tricky world of high finance without getting his butt kicked. Surely he could handle whatever this pair of women had in mind.

Jo watched him eat the pie with far too much interest. And every time she caught his eye she smiled a secret sort of smile. Something was definitely up.

He glanced at her. "Want a bite?"

"Oh, no, thanks. I just love to see a man enjoy his food."

Quinn polished off the pie. "I'm afraid the show's over. But I have to say that was the best piece of apple pie I've ever had, and I've eaten at some pricey restaurants. They could serve this pie with pride at the Waldorf-Astoria."

Emmy Lou looked enraptured. "I would love to see the Waldorf."

"I've offered to take you on my sperm runs," Jo said.

"No, no, not like that. It would break my heart to fly in

and out on the same day. I want to see the lights, feel the city's pulse, breathe in the rich aromas.'' She closed her eyes and took a deep, dramatic breath.

"You might want to give the rich aromas a miss," Quinn said. "New York's rich aromas can be overwhelming, especially on garbage pickup day."

Emmy Lou grinned at Jo. "Spoken like a man who's never cleaned out a chicken coop. You'd better keep him away from shovel duty while he's here."

"I had no intention of putting him on shovel duty."

"Anyway," Emmy Lou said as she turned to Quinn. "I don't want to give anything a miss. I want to hear the noise, taste a hot pretzel, mingle with the crowd in Times Square, give my regards to Broadway. I don't want a tiny bite of the Big Apple." She spread her arms wide. "I want to have it all."

Quinn curbed his impulse to immediately invite her there as his guest. It would be a real kick to watch her revel in the sights and sounds of the city. But he had no business inviting Emmy Lou Whatever to New York. He didn't even know her last name. The sugar must be affecting his brain for him to even think of doing such a thing.

Jo leaned forward, her dark eyes sparkling. "So, Quinn, are you ready to extend your visit a few days? I think we're having pot roast tomorrow night."

Logic warned him to use caution. She was a little too eager. But his libido reacted to that sparkle in her eyes in a very primitive fashion. And he did love a good pot roast. "I think it could be arranged."

"What about your job?" Emmy Lou asked.

"I can keep in touch by phone. With the help of Erin, my secretary, I can probably take care of anything critical from here." Quinn began to anticipate what it might be like living in the same house with Jo, or more appropriately, sleeping in the same house with Jo.

"Great," Jo said. "Because I have the most amazing idea. As long as you're going to be here, what if you told everybody you were Brian Hastings?"

Quinn groaned and buried his face in his hands as his fantasies dissolved. There it was. The catch.

Emmy Lou clapped her hands together. "Josephine, you're brilliant."

Quinn took his hands away from his eyes and leaned toward Jo. Damn, but she was beautiful. And treacherous. He lowered his voice. "But you see, I'm not Brian Hastings."

"You could fool them. You fooled Emmy Lou. And if everyone around here thought Brian Hastings was visiting my ranch, I could hold off the bank a while longer."

With a sigh of deep regret he leaned back in his chair. Like too many of the women he'd known, she was only interested in him because he looked like a famous movie star. "And then what happens when Hastings never shows up? You're in the same fix as before."

"But by the end of the summer I'll have some money, and I can make a partial payment. I need to keep the bank at bay until then."

"There may be other ways around this. It's possible I could arrange for a line of credit from—"

"No!" She held up her hand like a traffic cop. "I don't want anyone else getting involved in my financial problems. If I go down, I'll go down alone."

"That's very noble but totally unnecessary. Jo, this is what I do for a living. I don't know why I didn't suggest consulting with you about it before, during the cab ride."

"Consulting?" She raised her eyebrows. "I'm sure you don't do that for free, Quinn."

"Not normally. But we could work something out."

"I'd rather struggle along on my own. If you'd just agree to be Brian Hastings for a week, that's all I ask."

"All?" Quinn stared at her. "The guy's a movie star and a director, so he knows the Hollywood scene inside and out. Besides that he's a worldwide sex symbol. Do you realize how intimidating that would be for an ordinary guy like me?"

"Nonsense," Emmy Lou said. "You can do the sex symbol part with both hands tied behind your back. Just give the ladies that killer grin, throw in a wink or two, and they'll drop like flies."

Maybe, Quinn thought, but he knew that when women found out for sure he wasn't really Brian Hastings they had a tendency to turn nasty, and he'd be in constant fear they'd find out. Besides that, he was sick of never being evaluated on his own merits, and he wanted no part of this scheme, no matter how nice it would be to spend time with Jo. As far as he was concerned, this wasn't the way to handle her money problems, either. It was only a Band-Aid when she needed a tourniquet.

"As for the movie lingo, we can fake that," Jo said. "Emmy Lou has seen every interview that Brian Hastings ever gave—Barbara Walters, Larry King, Oprah Winfrey. She can coach you on the show biz angle."

Quinn shook his head. "Sorry. The whole idea goes against the grain. I've hated being mistaken for Hastings, and I sure as hell don't want to deliberately bring that kind of chaos down on my head. Listen, Jo, don't reject my financial advice out of hand. I might be exactly who you need. I could—"

"No, thank you. I appreciate the offer, but I have no guarantee I'll come out of this with the ranch intact. I don't want to risk your good name."

"You won't ruin my good name, and even if you did, I'd rather involve myself that way than pawn myself off as some two-bit version of Hastings."

"You're not giving yourself credit. You'd be at least a four-bit version," Emmy Lou said.

"That's what you think." The more closely Quinn evaluated this stunt, the more impossible it sounded. "He's not only a Hollywood insider, he's a cowboy. I can't ride, I can't rope, and if you put boots and spurs on me I'd probably trip and fall down before I walked two feet into the local saloon. Let me do what I do best, which is manipulate money."

Jo looked sad but determined. "I can't let you get involved with my messy finances, Quinn. I just can't."

"And I have no interest in masquerading as Brian Hastings."

"Then I guess that's that," Jo said. "But you're welcome to stay."

He hated like hell to turn her down, but he could see that a few days at the Bar None would be a nightmare as people continued to mistake him for Hastings. He pushed back his chair. "Thanks, but I'd better leave first thing in the morning. In the rush of coming out here to deliver Sir Lust-a-Lot's last legacy I forgot about your Brian Hastings connection. Chances are everyone would react the way Emmy Lou did. I'd rather not put myself through that."

Jo nodded. "I understand. Emmy Lou, would you please show Quinn his room? I need to go out and check on Betsy and Clarise before bedtime."

"Come along, Quinn."

Under Emmy Lou's reproving glance, Quinn felt like a misbehaving schoolboy. He silently followed her up the stairs.

"I don't think it would kill you to do what Jo's asking," she said in a very schoolmarmish tone.

"That's because you've never been surrounded by a hoard of women who wanted to rip your clothes off."

Emmy Lou sniffed as she continued up the stairs. "I'm

sure you're exaggerating. Why, I thought you were Brian Hastings up until recently, and I never once considered ripping your clothes off. All I wanted was a button from your shirt.''

"See? It starts with the buttons. What harm's in that? Then we run out of buttons, so somebody wants a sleeve. Then somebody wants my belt. Then it's strip city. It only takes one person to start it off, and before I realize it I'm surrounded. I try to tell them they have the wrong guy, but do they listen? Not when they're in their Brian Hastings crazed mode. There are at least twenty women walking around this world with a button or a sleeve or a back pocket of my pants, and all of them think their souvenirs came from Brian Hastings.''

"And I suppose this all happened in New York?"

Quinn followed her down the hall. "That's where I live.''

Emmy Lou stopped in front of a doorway and turned to him. "Well, there you go. It's the too-many-rats-in-a-cage theory. They start eating their young or stripping their celebrities, whatever is handy. Out here we have room to stretch out. We're not so snappish.''

"You just admitted you wanted one of my buttons!"

"Well, not now! Who wants the button off the shirt of an investment banker?''

Quinn was irritated. He couldn't decide which was worse, the loss of privacy when he was mistaken for Hastings or the blow to his ego when women finally accepted that he was *only* Quinn Monroe, investment banker. "I don't understand what women want with those trophies, anyway. Do they mount that button and shine a spotlight on it? Do they frame that piece of sleeve? Do they arrange my back pocket in a vase on the coffee table? I don't get it.''

Emmy Lou cleared her throat and glanced at the ceiling.

"Some might sew the button on a piece of velvet and embroider the person's name under it and frame it. If that someone really had a button from Brian Hastings' shirt, that is."

"Like you, for instance? I suppose your wall is full of framed buttons."

"No, it isn't. We don't get many celebrities out this way. And it was just dumb luck that Georgina Mason was in the ice cream parlor when Robert Redford came in. She claims he gave her the button, but it would be like her to pop it right off his shirt when he wasn't looking."

Quinn couldn't help smiling. "That'd be hard to do."

"Not for Georgina. She's the sneaky type. And she's such a showoff—has that framed button over the fireplace, where the whole world can see it." Emmy Lou gestured toward the doorway. "So here's your room, Benedict Arnold."

"Emmy Lou, nobody would believe me after the first five minutes! In New York it's different, because there are no horses for me to fall off of or cows for me not to rope."

"Cattle. Brian Hastings wouldn't say *cows*."

"That's my point!"

"We could teach you. Jo and I could whip you into shape in no time."

"Forgive me if I don't relish the sound of that."

"Okay. Be a coward. Bathroom's across the hall. If you were staying I'd hunt you up a change of clothes down at the bunkhouse, but I guess that won't be necessary."

Quinn vowed he wouldn't be baited into saying something he'd deeply regret. "Why couldn't you just take one of my buttons and claim it came from Brian Hastings' shirt?"

Emmy Lou looked shocked. "Because it would be dishonest!"

"Dishonest? You and Jo want to tell the entire town of

Ugly Bug that I'm Brian Hastings, and you're worried about fudging on a button?''

Emmy Lou clucked her tongue in disapproval. "It's not worth lying just to spite Georgina Mason. But I'd lie from now until doomsday to save the Bar None for Jo." Her pointed stare indicated that she thought he should have the same missionary zeal. "Why, I—" She paused and cocked her head. "Somebody's downstairs with Jo."

Quinn heard the voices, too. Jo was talking to a guy, and from the sound of her voice, she wasn't too happy about the conversation.

"It's that Dick!" Emmy Lou said, almost spitting out the words.

"Would that be a first name or a description?"

Emmy Lou's eyes twinkled at him. "I do like you, Quinn."

"I like you, too."

"Dick Cassidy is Jo's ex. One of the worst things she ever did was marry him, and one of the best was to divorce him. All he wanted, besides the obvious, was access to Ugly Bug Creek so he could water his cattle."

Quinn didn't like thinking about some guy enjoying the obvious with Jo. "The creek the town's named after is on this ranch?"

"Yep. At least the best stretch of it, and none of it runs across the Cassidy ranch next door. He put her through hell during the divorce proceedings while he tried to hang on to that water. We can't prove it, but we think Dick had something to do with so many of the cattle dying last winter. I think he was stealing the hay she put out for them. Besides that, he might have made off with some money, but Jo's not the best bookkeeper in the world, so she's not sure."

Quinn's protective instincts surged to the fore. He tried

to tamp them down, knowing they'd get him into trouble. "So why did she even let him in the door?"

"Oh, he always has some good reason he has to be let in. Last time, he came to report a break in her fence line, which I think he created. The time before that, his truck had broken down on the main road. The code of the west says you help out your neighbors, so Jo helped him. I say he's finding excuses to nose around and see how bad Jo's hurting. He's already offered her a lowball figure for the ranch."

Quinn glanced through the door into his bedroom, taking note of sturdy oak furniture and what looked like a handmade quilt on the bed. "Okay, you've shown me where I'm sleeping." As the voices downstairs rose in volume, he glanced at Emmy Lou. "What do you say to a cup of coffee before I turn in?"

Emmy Lou beamed in approval. "I'd say that's a great idea." She led the way downstairs.

As they approached the kitchen, Quinn could make out the conversation much better.

"That section of fence was fine yesterday," Jo said, an edge to her voice. "Somebody's cutting that wire."

"Now who would do a thing like that? You think I want your bull trampling my cook's garden?"

"If it means I have to pay restitution for your specially ordered designer veggie plants, yeah, I think you'd love to have my bull running around in your cook's garden!"

Give him hell, Jo, Quinn thought. He stepped into the kitchen behind Emmy Lou, but the five-foot-something housekeeper didn't block his view of the proceedings. Dick Cassidy faced the door, while Jo stood rigidly with her back to it. Cassidy had soft, fleshy features that might have been cute when he was a kid and would look ridiculously juvenile in another ten years. Quinn hated him on sight.

Cassidy's reaction to Quinn was exactly the opposite,

however. His eyes widened, and he broke into a goofy grin. "Well, I'll be damned. You're a sly one, Jo."

Jo turned toward the door and caught sight of Quinn and Emmy Lou standing there. Then she glanced at Dick. "It's not what you think. This is—"

"As if you have to introduce the guy." Dick pushed past her and stuck out his hand. "Dick Cassidy. I live on the neighboring ranch. I'd like you to come over and take a look. You might even like it better than the Bar None. The buildings are newer, and we've been able to keep up with painting and such better than Jo has. Well, you have to excuse her. A woman alone can't be expected to stay on top of everything."

"I like the rustic look." Quinn even hated Cassidy's handshake, which felt clammy.

"Then we can sand some of that paint off!" Cassidy said. "You name it, and we'll do it."

"Dick, let me explain," Jo said. "I know what you think, but this is—"

"Brian Hastings, of course." Dick pumped his hand. "I've seen all your movies. Damn good flicks, if you ask me."

Quinn had about three seconds to decide whether he could live with himself if he allowed this sorry excuse for a man to continue to ride roughshod over Jo. He decided in two. "That's good to hear," he said. "Which one did you like the best?"

4

JO HAD NEVER felt so much like hugging a man in her life. Thank God for Dick, jerk that he was. Apparently his appearance had tipped the scales in her favor and made Quinn decide to help her.

"It'd be real hard to pick a favorite movie," Dick said. "Which one did you like the best?"

"Couldn't say. Never see my own films."

Emmy Lou hovered nearby. "Except for the daily rushes, of course. I'm sure you see those."

"Well, yeah." Quinn gestured vaguely. "The daily rushes and sometimes the weekly rushes, but I don't bother with the monthly rushes."

Dick stared at him. "Monthly rushes?"

"Hollywood!" Jo threw up her hands. "Who can keep up with the funny little terms they use? Hey, I don't know about the rest of you, but I crossed two time zones twice today and I've had no sleep for twenty-four hours, so if you don't mind, I think I'll turn in." She glanced at Quinn. "Brian? You look pretty bushed, yourself. I'm sure you'll find the guest bed comfy."

Dick's jaw dropped. "He's staying here?" He turned to Quinn. "But where are the rest of your people? Your what d'ya call it...entourage?"

Quinn flexed his shoulders and looked bored. "I sent 'em off to Bimini, told 'em to relax, catch some rays. I need to be here alone, get in character."

"Wow. I never knew you guys were so dedicated. That's

impressive, Brian. Is it okay if I call you Brian? You can call me Dick.''

"I sure will, Dick.''

"How many Oscars have you won, anyway?''

"You know, Dick, it's easy to lose track of things like that, after the first few.'' Quinn glanced quickly at Emmy Lou, who discreetly held up three fingers. "Three.''

"Dick, I hate to be rude.'' Jo linked her arm through Quinn's. "But Brian's so polite he'd stay here answering your questions all night, when he really needs to get some sleep. I've appointed myself as his personal watchdog, to make sure he takes care of himself. Stars become so involved in their art that they sometimes neglect the essentials, like food and sleep.''

She loved watching Dick try to hide his jealousy. He hated seeing her getting cozy with this movie star, but he also wanted to suck up to that same movie star. Jo hadn't counted on this little perk when she'd created her plan. It was a nice bonus.

The warmth of Quinn's body next to hers was a pleasant extra, too. She had an idea she'd enjoy working with him. He had lots to learn about being a Hollywood cowboy, and teaching him promised to be fun.

"Then I guess I'll be going,'' Dick said with obvious reluctance. He started toward the entry hall but paused. "Listen, I know people probably ask you this all the time, but seeing as how we're neighbors, in a manner of speaking, I was wondering if there'd be a part in this movie for me? I ride and rope real good.''

Quinn took his time giving Dick the once-over. Jo caught Emmy Lou's glance and had to turn away and bite her lip to keep from laughing.

Finally Quinn nodded. "There might be,'' he said.

"Hey, that would be great. I really—''

"If...'' Quinn said, and paused dramatically.

"If?"

"If you lose some of that flab. You're soft in the middle, Dick. Can't have that. I suggest lifting weights, an exercise bike, maybe a little jogging."

"Jogging? An exercise bike? Cowboys don't jog, and they sure as hell don't ride no exercise bike!"

Quinn shrugged. "Up to you. I'm just throwing out suggestions as to how you can become more acceptable for the role. You can do it or not."

Dick sighed. "Hell, I'll do it. I just hope none of my men see me. I'll be the laughingstock of the county. When will you start shooting?"

"When it's time."

"Huh?"

Jo choked back a burst of laughter.

"It's all about light, Dick," Quinn continued. "I have to wait until we have the perfect light. I'll know it when I see it. Might take months, might be in two weeks. Better buy that exercise bike and start jogging."

"Yeah. Guess so. Well, see you around, Brian."

"See you, Dick. Oh, and about your vegetable garden. Do you think, under the circumstances, that you could—"

"Hey, I don't really give a damn about the garden. I'm a meat and potatoes man, myself."

Quinn lifted an eyebrow. "And it shows. I'd suggest you switch to broccoli and carrots if you want to lose that spare tire."

Dick reddened. "I guess the cook can plant another garden. It was probably too early, anyway. No problem. Forget it, Jo."

"Don't worry. I will." Jo managed to contain herself until Dick closed the front door and headed toward his truck. Then she collapsed into a chair and clutched her stomach while she laughed until the tears came.

Emmy Lou joined her, stopping every now and then to pound on the table with glee.

Finally Jo glanced at Quinn, her voice choked with laughter. "You've just given me the best laugh I've had in months. Thank you."

He smiled. "You're welcome."

"If I ever get depressed, I'll just think of Dick pedaling away on that exercise bike to get rid of his spare tire. And forcing down broccoli."

Emmy Lou took off her glasses and wiped her eyes. "Or jogging in his boots. I'm sure that boy doesn't own a pair of running shoes." She chuckled. "Good thing Dick doesn't know any more about making movies than Quinn, here. Monthly rushes. I almost lost it." She shook her head. "Here's my first bit of advice, Quinn. Don't ad-lib. Before you go to bed I'll get you some of my back issues of *Premiere* magazine to study."

"I think your best bet is to keep me mostly out of sight. I can do mysterious."

"That's no fun!" Jo said. Then she gazed at him. "I really do appreciate this, you know. I realize you didn't want to do it."

"I still don't, but I couldn't resist going a couple of rounds with your ex. Don't take this personally, but if he's any indication, you have lousy taste in men."

"I like to think I was having an out-of-body experience when I agreed to marry him."

Jo felt a noble impulse coming. Try as she might, she couldn't sidetrack it. "Quinn, you can still leave tomorrow morning if you want. Now that at least one person believes you were here, I can use that to convince the bank the deal is on. I'll just say you were suddenly called away."

Quinn rubbed the back of his neck and stared into space. Finally he met her gaze. "I'll stay a few more days."

"Spoken like a true hero," Emmy Lou said.

Jo had to agree. And heroes had been in short supply in her life recently. As she looked into Quinn's eyes her heart took on a jerky rhythm she hadn't felt in a long, long time. She wondered if she was risking more than she realized, if in the process of trying to save her ranch she was in danger of losing her heart. "I promise we won't be too rough on you," she said.

"Oh, I can take rough." He grinned. "The way this is shaping up, I'm just hoping I make it through alive."

QUINN WOKE with a start. The house was dark, but somebody was knocking on a door across the hall, which must have been what woke Quinn in the first place.

"Jo!" called a man in a loud whisper.

Quinn threw the covers back and got out of bed. He'd heard that locking the house wasn't always done out here in the neighborly west, so maybe neighbor Dick was back. Maybe Dick didn't know the meaning of the term *ex-husband*. Jo was probably out like a light after being up so many hours straight. Emmy Lou slept in a bedroom downstairs, but this joker had obviously slipped right past her. Jo's safety was in Quinn's hands.

Treading softly, he opened his door as quietly as possible and peered into the hall. Sure enough, a man was opening Jo's bedroom door. Talk about nerve.

Quinn crept across the hall and through Jo's bedroom door just as the creep leaned over Jo. "Oh, no, you don't, lizard breath." Quinn launched himself at the intruder's knees.

The guy let out a screech, followed by a loud yell from Jo as both men tumbled into bed with her.

"Don't worry, Jo!" Quinn wrestled with the guy as best he could, considering it was very dark and he wasn't sure which arms and legs belonged to which person. "I've got him!"

"I think you've got me!" Jo yelled. "How many of you are there? Let go! Ouch!"

"Help!" cried the man, flailing wildly. "Help, murder, police!"

"Murder sounds like a great idea," Quinn said, gasping. He made a grab for where he thought the guy was and encountered warm bare skin. Wonderful soft skin. "Whoops. Sorry, Jo." He tried for the intruder again and caught the guy's leg.

"What in hell is going on?" Panting, Jo struggled away from both of them.

"I'm protecting your honor." Quinn got hold of the guy's belt as he tried to squirm off the bed. "And where do you think you're going, buster? What makes you think you can—oof!" Quinn lost his grip as the guy kicked him in the privates. Groaning, he sprawled across Jo's legs.

The overhead light flashed on. "Everybody freeze or I'll shoot!" Emmy Lou bellowed.

"Go ahead," Quinn said. "Put me out of my misery. But save a bullet for your friendly neighbor, here."

"Don't shoot, Emmy Lou!" the guy cried.

"She can't, Benny." Jo sounded thoroughly disgusted. "That shotgun's not even loaded."

"You're not supposed to tell anybody that," Emmy Lou said.

"It's okay to tell Benny," Jo said.

Quinn's pain subsided enough for him to lift his head and gaze at Jo. She wore a plaid flannel nightshirt, which had become sort of twisted around as he'd tried to save her, and the effect was rumpled and very sexy. "Who's Benny?"

"Me," the guy said.

Quinn raised himself on one arm and glanced to the other side of the bed where someone who was definitely not Dick lay half on, half off the bed, staring at Quinn apprehensively. "Who the hell are you?" Quinn asked.

The guy flinched. "Benny," he said again. "Emmy Lou, can I move now?"

"You can all move," Jo said. "I don't remember inviting a single one of you to join me in bed this evening."

"I thought Benny was Dick," Quinn said. "I was saving you."

"That's very sweet. But Benny is not Dick. Benny is my wrangler."

"And Fred's the foreman," Benny said. "He's got a beard."

"Thanks for the info," Quinn said. "If he happens to show up at your door tonight I'll know who he is."

Jo glanced at Benny. "So I've figured out that Quinn is here because you're here. But why are you—oh, my God!" She threw back the covers and jumped from the bed. "I'll bet it's Clarise!"

Benny nodded. "It's Clarise. Fred sent me. He said you told him to get you if it was time. I didn't know you had a movie star in your house."

"He's not a movie star, Benny. His name is Quinn. But I want to be with Clarise. Thank you for coming to get me."

Emmy Lou snapped into action. "Foaling time. I'll make coffee." Shouldering the shotgun, she headed downstairs.

"I'll go help Fred," Benny said. He glanced at Quinn. "You sure look like a movie star. Sorry I kicked you in the—"

"It's okay, Benny." Quinn had figured out the guy was somewhat of a lightweight in the brains department. Quinn almost felt bad for scaring him, except that he had a kick like a mule, which took the edge off Quinn's regret.

"I'll just go downstairs, okay?" Keeping a wary eye on

Quinn, Benny eased out the door and pounded down the stairs.

Quinn climbed off the bed, suddenly aware that he wore only his briefs. "I, uh, really thought—"

"I'm sorry he kicked you." Her gaze drifted to that part of his anatomy. "Are you...okay?"

"I'll live." In fact, as she continued to look him over, his injured parts became full of life.

"I imagine you will live, at that." She looked at him with amused tenderness. "You thought somebody was about to do me wrong, didn't you?"

"Yeah."

"So with no weapon, and having no idea what you might be up against, you came charging in here to protect me?"

"Yeah."

Her gaze warmed even more. "I haven't had a man risk his own safety for my sake in a long time. It feels nice."

His pulse started to hammer.

She sighed. "We'd both better put on some clothes. My mare is about to foal, and I want to be there."

He was encouraged by that sigh and the interest in her brown eyes. "Of course."

"It's worth seeing, Quinn."

"I wouldn't miss it for the world." With one last look into those wonderful eyes of hers, he turned and headed out of the room. "Meet you downstairs in two minutes."

THE BIRTH of a foal always stirred Jo's blood, but with Quinn leaning over the stall door in rapt attention, the event seemed more emotional than usual. No doubt she was still affected by their encounter in her bedroom. The picture of Quinn standing there in his briefs would stay with her a long time. She'd never realized bankers could look like that. About her only experience with bankers was Mr. Doobie at First National in Ugly Bug. She'd never seen him in his briefs, but she could imagine it wouldn't be pretty.

Quinn, on the other hand, had made her tremble and quicken with desire. If she hadn't had Clarise on her mind...

"Get ready. I think we're close," Fred said.

"We're ready," Jo said. She and Benny stood behind the mare's rump, available to help deliver the foal, if necessary. Fred stood by her head, stroking her neck and talking to her in the gentle way he had with all animals. Some people were intimidated by Fred's size, his bushy gray beard and his gruff manner. Jo had known him since she was a kid, and when she'd inherited the ranch from Aunt Josephine she'd been thrilled when Fred had offered to stay on.

Unfortunately, his arthritis made riding painful for him, which left certain ranch chores strictly to Jo and Benny. That was how she'd ended up accepting help and advice from Dick, who'd even loaned her a couple of his men during roundup. But there had been strings attached. Actually more like steel cables attached. She'd felt shackled by Dick for way too long. Having Quinn step in tonight and torque Dick around had soothed her soul.

A couple of times in the past half hour she'd glanced up and caught him watching her. She wondered if he could soothe other parts of her, too.

The thought filled her with trepidation, because of how Dick had made her feel about herself sexually. Dick's method of intimidation was to subtly belittle a woman until she began to doubt her worth. She'd divorced him before he could do a thorough job on her, but she still felt insecure about a few things. Like whether she was any good in bed.

Clarise snorted and shifted her hindquarters.

"Here it comes!" Benny said.

"Yep." Jo's heart pounded with excitement as the mucus-covered nose and forelegs of the foal poked out between Clarise's haunches. "Good girl, Clarise. Keep pushing."

The mare groaned and sank to her knees as more of the shimmery foal emerged.

Fred groaned, too, as he knelt beside her. "You and me both, Clarise. After this I'm having a shot of whiskey."

Jo watched anxiously as the process seemed to stall. She clutched Benny's arm. "Do you think she needs us to pull?"

"I think she's doin' fine. Just fine." Benny's eyes shone.

Jo loved Benny like the little brother she never had, even though he was a few years older than she was. His mental slowness made him seem forever young, but when it came to ranch duties, Benny knew his stuff.

Sure enough, Clarise gave another mighty heave, and the foal slipped out.

Benny leaned forward to clean its nose so it could breathe. "It's a colt," he announced proudly.

"Wow," Quinn murmured.

"Wow is right." Jo couldn't take her gaze away from the new baby.

"What do you do about the glop it came in?" Quinn asked.

"Watch," Jo said. "Do your thing, Clarise."

The mare turned and began to lick her baby clean.

"Ugh," Quinn said. "I'll never eat oysters Rockefeller again."

Jo laughed. "Yeah, I know. If human mothers had to do this, I'd probably opt out of having kids."

Benny gazed at her with worship in his gray eyes. "You'd make a real good mommy, Jo."

"Thanks, Benny." She gave him a smile.

"So when are you gonna be one?"

Fred snorted as he got slowly to his feet. "Benny, you ask too many questions."

Benny looked troubled. "I don't mean to. But it'd be fun to have some little kids around."

"Yeah, it would." Jo stretched her stiff muscles. Too many hours on a plane and not enough sleep had taken their toll. "But a mother needs a daddy."

Benny grinned and jerked a thumb at Quinn. "How about the movie star? I'll bet he'd do it."

5

QUINN had joined in the laughter following Benny's remark, but under cover of the joking that followed, he'd checked out Jo's pink cheeks and the sparkle in her eyes. He decided she didn't hate the idea, no matter how embarrassed she was.

He didn't hate the idea, either, which was amazing. As the child of divorced parents, he was wary of the whole marriage and fatherhood thing. He'd promised himself he'd live with a woman for a long time before he even proposed, and as for kids, he hadn't thought he wanted any.

Yet watching Jo serve as one of the midwives for her mare, he'd had some very unfamiliar yearnings. Murray had two kids, and he'd raved about the delivery room scene. Quinn hadn't been able to relate...until now. Maybe it was the sugar in the apple pie still affecting his brain, but he'd found himself wondering what it would be like to be a proud father at the moment of birth. He'd probably imagined Jo in the role of the mother because she was handy.

"Stand back, everybody," Fred said. "She's going to get that little fella on his feet."

"No way." Quinn surveyed the colt's spindly legs and couldn't picture it. "I don't think he has the engineering for it yet."

"He has to," Jo said. "It's the only way he can nurse."

"He's not up to it, I tell you." Quinn grew agitated as

the mare hauled herself to her feet. "Make her lie down and drag him to the right spot."

Jo walked to the stall door and stood near Quinn. "You can't interrupt nature like that," she said gently. "In the wild, a horse's survival depends on getting upright as soon as possible. This has been going on for centuries."

"Well, I don't like it." Quinn folded his arms across the top of the stall door and frowned as the mare started pushing the colt with her nose. "She's expecting too much, too soon."

"She's acting on instinct," Jo said.

"She's pushy, is what she is." Quinn breathed in the sweet scent of Jo's hair. It looked as mussed and tangled as it had in the bedroom. She probably hadn't bothered to comb it in her rush to get to the barn. When she shifted her weight, tendrils of it brushed his bare forearm. If he moved his hand a fraction, he'd be able to wind a lock around his finger.

But he didn't want such a tame experience. He wanted to grab handfuls of her hair and let the rich silkiness flow between his fingers. He wanted to comb her hair over her naked breasts so that she looked like a brunette version of Lady Godiva. He wanted—

"See? He's up."

"I'll be damned." To Quinn's astonishment, while he'd been fantasizing about a sensuous experience with Jo's hair, the colt had somehow balanced itself on those four matchstick legs and was sucking vigorously on his mother's teat. "He's going to fall, I tell you. You should prop something under him. A stepladder would probably work."

Emmy Lou walked over and patted Quinn's arm. "Relax. These folks know what they're doing. We've had lots of foals born on the Bar None, and not a one of them ever needed to be propped up with a stepladder. Now if you'll all excuse me, I'll bring us some coffee."

Benny turned from his inspection of the colt. "And chocolate chip cookies?"

"Of course. What would foaling be without a batch of my chocolate chip cookies? Before we came down here I took them out of the freezer."

"Good thing." Quinn grinned at her. "I can't stand a foaling without chocolate chip cookies, myself."

Emmy Lou gazed at him and sighed. "Are you *sure* you're not Brian Hastings?"

"Matter of fact, I am. Until somebody blows the whistle on me."

"That reminds me." Jo turned to Fred and Benny. "I need to let you two in on what's happening. In spite of what you might think, this man is not Brian Hastings."

Fred stuck a plug of tobacco under his lip. "Who's Brian Hastings?"

Quinn smiled. He'd found a friend.

Benny pointed to Quinn. "He is."

"No, he's not," Jo said.

"Makes no never mind to me." Fred put his can of tobacco in his back pocket. "He can be Donald Duck for all I care. A man's name's not important. It's how he conducts himself."

Jo glanced at Quinn. "Fred doesn't go to the movies, and he hates TV."

"I gathered."

She turned to Benny and Fred. "Remember when that guy came by the ranch last fall looking for a place to shoot a movie?"

Benny looked blank.

Fred scratched his beard and finally shook his head. "Guess he didn't make no impression on me."

"He was an advance man for Brian Hastings, who is the top box office draw in the country."

Fred spit tobacco juice into a can. "Whoop-de-doo."

Quinn was liking this guy more every minute.

"The thing is," Jo continued, "I told Mr. Doobie at the bank that Brian Hastings definitely would use the ranch, and we'd be able to make a big payment on our loan soon, so he gave me an extension. Only Brian Hastings hasn't ever come here."

"But he did," Benny said. "We were all in your bed together."

Fred almost swallowed his chaw. "What did you say?"

"Benny, this is not Brian Hastings. He just looks a lot like him." She glanced quickly at Fred, who had developed a dangerous gleam in his eye. "Now don't look like that, Fred. This very nice man is Quinn Monroe, from New York."

"I don't give a damn where he's from. He'd better stay the hell out of your bed. Benny, you and me need to have a talk. You ain't ever been to the big city, and these city slickers got some tricky ways about them. You gotta be on your guard."

Judging from Fred's expression, Quinn was afraid he'd just lost his new best friend. And if he valued his life, he'd shelve his fantasies about Jo. "I was only trying to save her," he said.

"Yes, that's true," Jo said. "He saw Benny coming into my room tonight, and he didn't know it was about Clarise. He thought Benny was Dick, up to no good. So he tackled him, and we all ended up rolling around on my bed until Emmy Lou arrived with the shotgun."

Fred glared at Quinn. "Likely story."

Quinn tried to salvage Fred's goodwill. "Would you believe I've agreed to impersonate this Brian Hastings character so the bank will get off Jo's back?"

Fred pointed a gnarled finger at Jo. "Don't you be getting too grateful, Josephine Sarah. You see what gratitude got you with a Dick Cassidy type."

Benny jumped into the conversation and pointed at Quinn. "But he's not a Dick," he said brightly.

Fred scowled at Benny. "Go up to the house and help Emmy Lou bring the coffee and cookies down."

"Okay." Benny opened the stall door, and Quinn stood aside to let him out. Benny peered at Quinn. "Who are you, anyway?"

"Benny, I'm losing track of that myself."

Benny nodded as if he understood the problem completely and sauntered out of the barn.

Jo turned to Fred. "I haven't wanted to worry you, but we're not in good financial shape."

"I could figure that out on my own. If I coulda done more riding this winter I mighta been able to catch Cassidy doing some of his dirty work. We shouldn'ta lost all them cattle. But the only way to catch him would be sneak up on horseback. The truck makes too much noise, and that's all I was using this past winter."

"I tried to catch him," Jo said. "Never could. But that's water over the dam. Right now Quinn is my best hope. If Mr. Doobie believes Quinn is Brian Hastings, then he won't heckle me for money. If I could get Doobie signed up as an extra in the movie, he might not ever heckle me again."

"So I'll sign him up," Quinn said.

Fred held up his hand. "Wait a minute. You're not a movie star or director or nothin', but you're gonna sign Doobie up for a movie?"

Quinn shrugged. "Sometimes movies don't get made. The money dries up. I don't know much about it, but I figure a lot can go wrong when you're trying to raise a few million dollars to make a picture."

Fred's eyes widened. "A few *million?*" He turned to Jo. "If this Hastings really rented the ranch, how much would you get?"

"I don't know. The important thing is that Doobie

doesn't know, either. He's willing to let my note ride until after the movie's shot.''

"But Hastings never came back.'' Fred shifted his wad of tobacco to his cheek. "There might never be a movie.''

"I know, but Quinn's agreed to buy me some time. So for the next few days, if anybody asks if Brian Hastings is staying on the Bar None, say yes.''

"I can do that, but this may be way too complicated for Benny to figure out.''

Jo nodded. "I realize that now, but I can't lie to Benny. If I'd told him Quinn was a movie star and Benny found out later it wasn't true, I'd feel awful.''

Fred patted her shoulder. "Yeah, we all feel that way about Benny. I'll see if I can explain it to him.''

"Oh, and Fred, I have a favor to ask.''

"Yeah?''

"The real Brian Hastings is a cowboy star. He knows how to ride and rope and everything. Quinn's the greenest greenhorn you'll ever run across.''

Quinn stood up straighter. "Hey, I wouldn't go that far.''

"I'm telling you, Fred, he doesn't have the foggiest idea about that stuff. He doesn't even have the right clothes. I'd like to turn him over to you for…'' She smiled at Quinn. "For cowboy school, I guess you'd call it.''

Quinn's stomach felt as if he'd eaten cement, and he didn't trust the gleam of relish that flashed in Fred's eyes. Didn't trust it one bit. Fred looked Quinn up and down like he might be sizing him for a coffin, Quinn thought.

Finally the big man spoke. "I think he'll fit into Benny's duds. As for the rest—'' He grinned, showing tobacco-stained teeth. "Leave him to me.''

A shiver of dread ran down Quinn's spine.

"Now if you'll keep an eye on Clarise, I'm gonna head down to the bunkhouse and get my whiskey.''

"Could you bring an extra glass?" Quinn asked. He had a feeling he needed some fortification.

Fred smiled again. "Real cowboys don't need no glass," he said. "They drink straight from the bottle."

After Fred left, Quinn leaned against the stall door, which still separated him from the delectable Jo. Jo the turncoat. "I thought you were going to teach me how to be a cowboy."

"I was." She looked disappointed. "I was really looking forward to it."

"You weren't the only one."

"But then, while Clarise was giving birth to her foal, I started thinking."

"Yeah, me, too."

"About what?"

"You first." This didn't seem like the time to tell her he'd started thinking how nice she'd look pregnant.

"Here's the deal." She moved a little closer to him. "I like you. I like you a lot."

"Is that why you're turning me over to Grizzly Adams? Because, gosh darn, you sure do like me?"

"Yes." She trailed a finger along his forearm. "Because if I did all the teaching I'm afraid we'd get involved."

"And what a disaster that would be." So what if her touch affected his breathing? He could work around that. The one bright spot in this whole episode had been wiped out, almost as if Fred had hit it dead center with a stream of tobacco juice.

"It would be a disaster." Jo's expression was sweet and serious as she continued to draw imaginary lines over his arm. "Now that you're going to be Brian Hastings, you have to play your part and hightail it out of town before anybody's the wiser. You can never set foot in these parts again. It'd be too risky."

He was beginning to get her point. He didn't like it, but

he was getting it. He captured her hand. She had strong hands, but warm and so soft. She must slather them with lotion to keep them that way, he thought. "And you're not the kind of woman who wants a fling with a guy who can never set foot in these parts again."

"I wish I could be, Quinn. If I could be that kind of woman, you'd be the very guy I'd choose to have a fling with."

"That's such a comfort." He brought her hand up to his lips and kissed her knuckles one by one.

Her eyes darkened to the color of chocolate. "Are you the kind of guy who would have a fling with a woman you could never see again?"

Under the glow of that gaze he began to fidget. He looked away. His conscience wasn't as clear on this score as hers apparently was. There was that time in Rio, when both he and the woman had known the relationship would go nowhere, yet they'd had a damned good time for a few days. And then there was the woman he'd met on the subway. She'd come to New York for a convention and had flown home to Paris three days later. Even though the time together had been great, neither of them had felt committed enough to uproot their lives to be with each other. Both times he'd suspected the women were pretending he was Brian Hastings, but that was another matter.

"I guess you are that kind of guy," Jo said quietly. She tried to pull her hand away.

He held it tight and met her gaze. "Okay, I'll admit I've been willing to do that in the past. Not often, but it's happened. I'll also go out on a limb and say that I wouldn't want that sort of arrangement with you."

"Because you think I would get hurt?"

He stroked the back of her hand with his thumb. "Because I think we could both get hurt."

Her gaze softened. "Thank you. You're a kind man, Quinn."

Not kind, he thought. Right now he wanted to come into that stall and push her down on the fragrant hay at her feet. "Just telling it like it is. I hadn't thought this through as completely as you have. You're right. Now that I'm going to impersonate Hastings, we really shouldn't let anything develop between us." He hated saying that, but it was true.

Jo sighed wistfully. "You sure look good with no clothes on, though."

Quinn's body tightened even more. "You sure felt good—whatever part of you I got a grip on when I was wrestling with Benny."

"My thigh. You grabbed my thigh."

"Mmm." Probably another spot she slathered lotion on. An ache began to build in the vicinity of his groin. He should end this conversation while he could still walk. "I said I was sorry. I wasn't really."

"That's okay." She sounded breathless. "Maybe we should get all these comments out in the open, now that we're not going to…do anything. I think you look lots sexier than Brian Hastings. It's just my personal opinion, of course."

"That's the opinion that counts." He kissed her palm and felt the shiver that ran up her arm. "I've been wishing I could run my fingers through your hair. I love your hair."

She drifted closer, until they would have been nestled against each other if they hadn't been separated by the stall door. "And I love your eyes." Her voice grew husky. "Such a deep blue. I've heard Brian Hastings wears contacts."

"How do you know I don't?"

"Do you?"

God, but he wanted to kiss her. "No. Do you?"

She shook her head. "No contacts, no capped teeth, no breast implants."

He glanced down and noticed she'd skipped putting on a bra under her T-shirt. Her nipples pushed at the soft material. He looked into her eyes. "I wanted to comb your hair over your naked breasts."

Her breath caught. "And I wanted to feel your chest muscles flex. Do you...work out?"

"Not much." Desire thickened his vocal cords. He sounded as if he had strep. "Mostly I go out to Murray's house on Long Island and help him with his projects." Only one project interested Quinn at the moment, and that was finding a quiet place where they could both get naked. "He's always adding a room or something."

"You can do handyman stuff?" Her breasts touched his chest as she leaned closer.

"Hey, I'm very macho." He ached to kiss her, but he didn't dare. Instead he ran a forefinger gently over her lower lip until she closed her eyes and sighed, surrendering to the caress. "Forget teaching me to ride and rope," he murmured. As he eased his finger between her slightly parted lips, his erection pressed against the rough wood of the stall door. "I'll impress the population of Ugly Bug by hammering a couple of boards together. Then for an encore I'll saw a plank in half."

"Coffee and cookies, anyone?"

Quinn and Jo leaped away from their respective sides of the stall door. Then Quinn quickly plastered himself to the door again, grimacing at the impact of the wood against the body parts most affected by Jo.

"Hi, there, Emmy Lou. Hey, Benny." Jo blushed furiously. "We were just—"

"Were they kissing?" Benny asked Emmy Lou.

"Not quite." Emmy Lou set a wooden tray on a leather trunk in the aisle between the rows of stalls.

"We were talking," Jo said.

Emmy Lou poured a mug of coffee and handed it over the stall door to Jo. "Honey, no explanation necessary. You already told me you thought he was cute." She filled a second mug and gave it to Quinn.

Quinn's embarrassment turned to delight. "She did?"

"I just meant in a general sense," Jo said, blushing.

"But you did say it."

"Yes, she really did." Emmy Lou patted him on the arm. "I think you're cute, too."

"Well, I don't think he's so damned cute," Fred said as he walked into the circle of light by the stall door carrying his bottle. "How're momma and baby doing?"

"Sleeping," Jo said.

Quinn glanced guiltily at the mare and foal. They could have been dancing the tango for all he knew. Once everyone had left he'd forgotten the horses and become completely immersed in Jo.

"Whatcha gonna name him?" Fred asked.

Jo gazed at the little foal curled up against his mother. "Well, if people hear that Brian Hastings was present for the birth, they'll expect this colt to be named Brian, probably."

"Aw," Fred said. "Don't do that. That don't sound like a horse name. And don't be calling him Hastings, either. That sounds like a butler."

"Then I guess I'll call him Stud-muffin," Jo said.

Fred groaned.

"I think it's clever," Emmy Lou said.

"What's it mean?" Benny asked.

"Never mind, Benny," Fred said. "So is that it, Jo?"

"That's it."

"Then if it's official, I can drink to it." He uncorked his bottle. "Here's to—" He grimaced. "Stud-muffin. Long may he live." He took a swig and wiped the top on his sleeve. Then with a rascal's glint in his eye, he handed the bottle to Quinn.

Quinn took it. "I'll bet you think I've never swigged whiskey from a bottle before, don't you?"

Fred nodded. "That would be my guess, city boy."

"You'd be wrong." It had been a few years, but he'd done it. Once. "Here's to Stud-muffin." Quinn took a big swallow from the bottle and choked, spilling coffee on himself in the process. The whiskey burned its way to his stomach. The coffee on his shirt seared his chest. He whimpered.

"Give me that!" Emmy Lou grabbed the bottle out of his hand and sniffed it. Then she glared at Fred. "What do you think you're doing, giving that boy some of your hundred-and-fifty-proof home brew? You want to kill him before he has a chance to do this Brian Hastings thing?"

"Jo said I was supposed to turn him into a cowboy!"

"She didn't tell you to turn him into a lush, now, did she?"

Fred stuck out his chin. "A real cowboy can hold his liquor!"

Quinn had recovered enough to set his coffee mug on the wooden tray. "Give me that bottle, Emmy Lou."

"Nope."

Quinn knew his smile could accomplish most anything with Emmy Lou, and he used it. "Come on, Em. Let a guy salvage his pride."

Jo leaned over the stall door. "Forget your pride, Quinn. That stuff would burn a hole right through the floor of this barn."

"You're all a bunch of pansies," Fred muttered.

Quinn motioned for the bottle. "Give it here."

"Don't drink it," Benny said. "It rots your innards."

Quinn glanced at Fred. "He's still standing."

"You can't go by him," Emmy Lou said. "His insides are galvanized steel."

"Emmy Lou. The bottle."

"Oh, give it to him," Jo said. "It's a guy thing. Might as well get it over with."

Emmy Lou surrendered the bottle with obvious reluctance. "Just so you know, we don't have a very up-to-date medical clinic in Ugly Bug."

"I won't need a medical clinic." Quinn met Fred's piercing gaze. Then he slowly raised the bottle to his lips and took another drink, a slightly smaller one this time. Damn, but it was strong. Tears sprang to his eyes, but he lowered the bottle and smiled at Fred. "Good stuff," he said hoarsely. "You make this yourself?" His whole chest was on fire.

"I do."

Quinn wiped the bottle on his sleeve and handed it back. "Thanks."

"Any time."

"I'll remember that." Quinn looked into Fred's eyes and was rewarded with a gleam of exactly what he'd been hoping for—respect.

6

Jo woke at six-thirty, which was late for her, and heard rain drumming on the roof. She flopped back on the pillow. Rain was good, making the hay grow that she'd use to feed her cattle next winter. If she still had the ranch next winter. But rain meant mud as she went about her chores. Mud wasn't so good.

Jo turned her head and looked at the picture of her great-aunt Josephine sitting on her dresser. Aunt Josephine had believed in past lives, and she claimed that Jo was a reincarnated pioneer woman, which Aunt Josephine said explained everything.

Jo's mother had died when she was thirteen, and her father had married a woman who didn't seem to like Jo much. Aunt Josephine had been Jo's salvation, and she'd dreamed of helping run the ranch someday. But her great-aunt had insisted she go to college instead of moving directly to the ranch after high school, and there Jo had met lovable, bossy Cassie.

Jo smiled. When Cassie got an idea in her head, most people went along, including Jo. So after graduation she'd worked with Cassie at her family's stables for a year, always thinking she could eventually join Aunt Josephine in Montana. Then an unexpected heart attack claimed her seemingly ageless great-aunt, and suddenly the Bar None belonged to Jo.

"Heels down! Back straight! Grab some mane! That's it!"

That sounds like Fred. Jo threw back the covers and hurried to the window. Her breath fogged the glass, and she rubbed a clear place to look through.

Sure enough, Fred had somebody up on Hyper, and from the way the rider was bouncing around Jo knew who it had to be. God, what had she done?

As she pulled on her jeans, she hopped one-legged to the window to see if Quinn was still aboard Hyper. Trust Fred to give him the acid test, just like he had with the whiskey. And in the rain, no less. Everything was slippery in the rain, including saddles.

Still buttoning her shirt, she took the stairs at a rapid clip.

Emmy Lou was in the kitchen frying bacon. "Fred came to get Quinn at five-thirty," she called as Jo headed for the door.

"Why the hell didn't Quinn tell Fred to get lost?" Jo clamped her hat on her head and grabbed a yellow slicker from a peg by the door.

"I think he wants to be your knight in shining armor," Emmy Lou said.

"I don't know what to do with one of those," Jo said. "I never had one before."

Emmy Lou came to the door. "You were on the right track last night in the barn."

Jo shook her head. "That would completely louse up the plan."

"Then maybe you need a new plan."

Jo flung open the door. "Can't think about that now. I have to go save Quinn before Fred breaks every bone in his gorgeous body."

She ran toward the corral, splashing through puddles along the way, but she wasn't in time. As she arrived, Hyper slid to an abrupt halt, haunches down, and Quinn popped right out of the saddle. The corral was a sea of mud, so there was no question he'd land in it. Fortunately it was butt-first instead of headfirst.

Jo stormed up to Fred, who was leaning against the top rail, the brim of his hat creating a mini waterfall in front of his face. He didn't turn. "Mornin', Jo."

Jo would never publicly chastize anyone who worked for her, but it took an effort for her to keep her voice down so Quinn couldn't hear her. "It's raining, Fred. A real trash mover."

"I did notice that."

Jo nodded. "Okay. I guess we'll move on to my next point. Quinn's riding Hyper."

"I noticed that, too."

"Why is he riding Hyper, Fred?"

"That was the horse he wanted."

"Of course he did!" Jo heard herself getting loud and lowered her voice. "That's the horse everybody wants, because he's beautiful. I'll bet you didn't tell him that horse is a spoiled brat, did you?"

"'Scuse me a minute, Jo." Fred made a megaphone of his hands. "Your hat's over yonder!" he called to Quinn. "Grip harder with your thighs next time."

"I don't want there to be a next time," Jo said.

Fred turned to her at last, a challenge in his gray eyes. "Wanna take over?"

"No, I want you to take it easy on him! At this rate he'll end up in the hospital, which is not fair considering he's only doing this as a favor to me."

"I don't think he'll end up in the hospital."

"No? I've already seen him take one tumble. The next one could be—"

"He's hit the mud four times already." Fred sounded proud of the fact.

"Four?"

"Whoops. Make that five."

Jo whipped around to take stock of the newest disaster. What she saw made her go cold. Quinn lay facedown in the muck. "God, Fred, you've killed him." Jo ducked through the rails of the corral and ran toward Quinn. "Are you okay? Please be okay!" She crouched beside him. At least he seemed to be breathing. "Quinn! Speak to me!"

Slowly he rolled to his back and glanced at her, his face grimy with mud. He grinned. "Well, damn. I thought I'd have this riding thing figured out before breakfast. It may take a little longer than that."

"Don't move." Jo wiped a glob of mud from his chin with a trembling hand. If he was really hurt she'd never forgive herself. "You may have a concussion. A broken back. Broken neck. Broken ribs."

"Nah. Besides, I can't just lie here. The way the rain's coming down, I'll drown."

Jo leaned closer, her conscience kicking her six ways to Sunday. "You don't have to do this," she said in an undertone. "I'll tell Fred I've changed my mind about having you impersonate Hastings. Go get cleaned up, have Emmy Lou's famous ranch breakfast and drive out of here."

His blue gaze, usually so easygoing, slowly took on the look of tempered steel. "Nope. Can't do it."

"Why not? Surely you're not trying to prove something to Fred. I could have throttled you last night with that stupid posturing about the whiskey."

Quinn smiled and eased to a sitting position. "It did taste a lot like the muck in this corral." He turned his face away and spit.

"Go back to New York, Quinn. Please."

He looked at her. "You don't want me around anymore?"

"I didn't say that."

"Then I'm staying." He jerked a thumb at Hyper. "Is it true that horse slept in your bed?"

So Fred had explained that she was the one who had spoiled Hyper. "He was tiny. Premature, and an orphan. So cute and lonesome. Fred told me I'd be sorry."

Quinn gave her a sly grin. "You said I was cute, and I'm feeling kinda lonesome."

She tried to ignore the leap in her pulse rate. "I don't make those mistakes anymore. You see how Hyper turned out." She stood. "Come on, I'll help you up, and we'll go inside."

He ignored her outstretched hand and got to his feet by himself. "I told you I'd do this, and I'll do it."

She noticed him wince and caught his arm. "You were never supposed to learn to become a real cowboy! I thought you could pick up a few things and fake it."

He leaned down and retrieved his muddy hat, obviously a loan from Benny. The mud-spattered jeans and shirt looked like Benny's, too, and the worn boots. Mud-spattered or clean, Benny had never looked so good in these clothes. Quinn might be a lousy rider, but he was born to dress in snug jeans and broad-shouldered Western shirts.

He settled the hat on his head and glanced at her. "There's something I forgot to tell you. Faking it isn't my style." He tipped his hat. "Excuse me, ma'am." There was a definite drawl in his voice. "I need to go catch your spoiled-rotten horse."

As he ambled away, Jo stared at him with her mouth open. "What's with the drawl? You're from New York! New Yorkers don't drawl."

Quinn laughed. "I bit my tongue on that last go-round. Drawling feels better than talking fast."

"And where'd you get that bowlegged walk? That's not your normal walk, either."

He kept going, headed for the dark bay standing in a corner of the corral. "I always wondered why cowboys walk this way. After banging around in that saddle a few times, I get it.''

"Quinn, stop this!"

He kept walking.

Jo stalked to Fred. "We have to make him quit."

"Now, Jo, have you ever known a cowboy you could talk out of something once he's set his mind to it?''

"Read my lips—*he's not a cowboy.*''

Fred shrugged. "I wouldn't be so sure. I thought he shouldn't ride this morning on account of the rain. But he wanted to.''

"You're kidding."

"Nope. He just asked if rain would be bad for the horse.''

"But you should have talked him out of riding Hyper."

"I tried. He said if he could ride Hyper he'd know he'd really learned how to ride. Said he'd keep at it until he could stay on. And look at that. Damned if he don't have old Hyper figured out.''

Jo gazed across the corral. Hyper started out with his usual crow hops, but Quinn gripped with his thighs and held on. Jo could tell that he was gripping with his thighs because of the way the wet denim moved. Not that she was looking at his thighs on purpose. And she was definitely not looking at the spot between his thighs, the place that had taken so much punishment from the saddle this morning. He'd probably appreciate an ice pack for that area. She cringed as Quinn's butt came partially off the saddle and slammed down again.

But, God, he had a great butt. And he was keeping it mostly in the saddle this time. He dug his heels into Hyper's ribs, and the gelding took off at a lope. Quinn's hat flew off, and for a second Jo thought Quinn would tumble into the mud again, but he corrected his position by using those spectacular thigh muscles.

As Hyper and Quinn rounded the curve of the corral, Quinn let out a whoop. "Coming through," he yelled. "I still can't steer worth a damn!"

Jo scrambled through the fence barely ahead of the thundering hooves.

"Yee-haw!" Quinn shouted as Hyper made another circuit, flinging mud everywhere.

Jo turned to stare at Fred. "Yee-haw?"

"We'll work on that," Fred said. "He probably thinks that's what you're supposed to say at a time like this. Can't expect him to get everything right at first. He's from New York."

Jo gazed at Quinn sailing around the corral in the rain, a big old grin on his face. "Let me get this straight. This whole circus this morning was Quinn's idea, not yours?"

"I've seen how you look at him, Jo. I wouldn't deliberately do the boy wrong."

Jo pulled her slicker closer around her. "I don't look at him any certain way."

"Okay. Whatever you say. And he don't look at you no certain way, either. I'm an old coot and I don't know what I'm talking about."

Jo sighed. "You sound like Emmy Lou."

"Well, she's an old lady, just like I'm an old coot. Our eyesight's no good, and besides, we can't remember what it's like to have them feelings, so don't pay us no mind."

Jo had a sudden flash of insight. She began putting together isolated incidents and finally decided she had a case. "Fred, are you sweet on Emmy Lou?"

The part of Fred's cheeks not covered with his bushy gray beard grew red. "Now what makes you say a darn fool thing like that? Emmy Lou and me have been working on this ranch together for years, been giving each other hell for years, too. We've known each other too long, and we're too danged sensible for such goings-on."

Jo grinned. "I'll be damned. You are sweet on her. Does she know?"

"She don't know because there's nothing to it!" Fred turned abruptly and made a megaphone of his hands again. "Hey, Quinn, how about finding the brake on that nag? I need me some breakfast!"

"You go ahead. I'll be fine."

"You will not be fine. Don't go getting cocky on me. In case you hadn't noticed, you're on a runaway horse. Hyper's got the bit in his teeth, and if you weren't in this here corral, he'd be taking you on a trip to the high country, and you wouldn't have any say about it at all."

"I'll bet I could stop this horse whenever I want."

Fred exchanged a glance with Jo and sighed. "Ain't that just like any other cowboy in the world? A little success, and he gets to bragging on himself."

"Fred, he's not a cowboy."

"He sure as hell acts like one." He raised his voice. "Let's see this control you've got over that horse, cowboy. And don't go jerking the reins and hurting his mouth. Go easy."

"Okay." Quinn started pulling as he rounded the curve coming toward Jo and Fred. Nothing happened. He frowned and pulled harder.

Fred folded his arms. "We're waiting on you, cowboy. Try yelling *whoa*."

Quinn put more muscle into it. "Whoa!" he yelled. When Hyper still didn't respond, he leaned back on the reins. "Dammit, stop!"

"I'll get him not to say *dammit, stop* when I mention the *yee-haw*," Fred said.

"Good idea. Look out, here he—"

Hyper slid to a stop right in front of Jo and Fred, spraying mud all over them.

"—comes," Jo finished, holding out her arms and surveying her yellow slicker, now polka-dotted with mud. At least her clothes were protected by the slicker. Fred would have to start over before he appeared at the ranch house.

"Wow. Just like a New York street sweeper." Quinn sat in the saddle staring at them. "Sorry about that."

Jo glanced at him and saw the sparkle of mischief in his blue eyes. "Funny, but you don't look sorry," she said.

"Oh, but I am." He leaned on the saddle horn and grinned at her.

Amazing, Jo thought. At this moment every obnoxious, sexy, devilish inch of him screamed out *cowboy*. But he wasn't quite cowboy enough to know he should keep his feet in the stirrups until he was ready to dismount.

Taking note of that, Jo slipped through the rails of the corral. "Let me help you get off that beast."

"Oh, that's okay." He patted the horse's neck. "Me and Hyper, we're getting along fine. You have to know how to deal with him. He just needs a firm hand."

"I'm sure you're right. What was I thinking? Thanks for telling me." She hoped Hyper remembered the trick she'd taught him when he was still a colt. She grabbed his reins and gave a soft, low whistle.

On cue Hyper reared, and Quinn slid neatly down the horse's rump into the mud.

"It's a good idea to keep your feet in the stirrups when you're sitting in the saddle," she said with a sweet-as-pie grin. "You never know what might happen if you don't." She led Hyper out the gate Fred held open.

"Good job," Fred said, smiling in approval as he took the reins from her. "I'll walk him a little and give him a rubdown." He glanced at Quinn, who still sat in the mud as if he couldn't quite believe he'd ended up there after his grand finish. "Come on down to the bunkhouse for a shower before breakfast, cowboy," he said. "You're not fit to sit at Emmy Lou's table looking like that." He walked Hyper toward the barn.

Quinn continued to sit in the mud with the rain pouring down on him.

Jo stood by the open gate. "Are you coming out?"

"You did that on purpose," he said, a note of surprise in his voice.

"Somebody had to. You were getting way too big for your britches." She stepped a little closer, hoping her little maneuver hadn't been too rough on him. "Are you okay?"

"What if I'm not?"

Instantly she regretted her impulsiveness. She hurried toward him. "Oh, Quinn, I didn't mean to hurt you. I only wanted to prick a hole in your pride before it got out of control." Anxiety twisted in her stomach. "Can you stand?"

"I don't know."

Dammit, why had she allowed herself that moment of revenge? "Where do you hurt?"

His head drooped. "All over. I don't think there's a single inch of me that doesn't hurt."

"Oh, Quinn." She dropped to her knees in the mud beside him and put her hand on his mud-caked shoulder. "Did you twist your ankle? Is that why you're afraid to stand up? What can I do?"

His head lifted slowly. She had the space of a heartbeat to see the wicked gleam in his eyes before he grabbed her and wrestled her to the mud. She shrieked and fought, but he unsnapped her slicker and started smearing mud down the front of her shirt.

"Stop that! I'll kill you, Quinn Monroe!"

"Devil woman," he said, laughing as he rolled with her in the muck. "How dare you make that horse rear? You turned him into a regular water slide."

"How dare you tell me how to handle him? Let me up!"

He pinned her to the ooze and proceeded to rub mud all over her. "Not until you're as covered with this goo as I am. Dump me in the dirt, will you?"

"You were getting too cocky!" Her breathing became labored as she struggled to free herself. Or maybe it was the other sensation, the one of having his hands all over her, that was causing her to gasp for breath.

"I deserved to be cocky." His chest heaved as he gulped in air. "I got up at the crack of dawn and busted my butt, literally, on that spoiled horse of yours. And, by God, I rode him."

"I think it was more like he took you for a ride!" She continued to squirm away from his touch, but her heart wasn't in it. In fact, the squish of the mud was beginning to feel sort of good. And she was feeling a bit warm and oozy inside as well as outside.

"That horse knew who was boss." His hand grazed her breast as if by accident. "I was in control the entire time."

"Were not."

"Was, too." He grabbed her wrists and held them as he rolled on top of her.

Surely she hadn't meant to make a cradle of her hips. Surely he hadn't meant to ease himself between her thighs. Surely neither of them had intended to end up in the perfect position for her to discover that he was fully aroused.

"Were not," she whispered, looking into his eyes.

"Was, too." His eyes darkened as his gaze searched hers. "Jo…"

Her heart beat like a rabbit's. "Don't kiss me, Quinn."

"Okay, I won't." He lowered his head.

"You are." She was quivering. "You're going to kiss me."

"No. Brian Hastings is going to kiss you. Think Brian Hastings."

When his mouth found hers, she didn't think at all. She

sure did feel, though—cool lips that quickly warmed against hers and shaped themselves into the soul of temptation in no time, a tongue that told her exactly what Quinn would be doing if they didn't have two layers of denim between their significant body parts. She liked everything about this kiss, even the mud that squished between them as he eased his chest to press against her breasts.

The only thing she didn't like was that he stopped kissing her.

"More," she whispered, keeping her eyes firmly closed.

"Can't."

"Can so."

"If I kiss you some more, I'm liable to unzip your jeans and start getting serious about this maneuver."

Reluctantly she opened her eyes. At least he looked as frustrated as she felt. "Oh, Quinn, what are we going to do?"

He gave her a crooked grin. "I'm moving to the bunkhouse."

7

"TARNATION, boy, don't they feed you in New York City?" Fred stared at Quinn as he served himself a second helping of biscuits and gravy.

"Not like this." Quinn dove in while Emmy Lou beamed. He'd never been a breakfast eater in New York. Coffee and toast did the trick. But he wasn't in New York anymore, and he polished off enough bacon, eggs, biscuits and gravy to make him embarrassed, except that everyone else ate almost as much. None of the people sitting around the table was plump except Emmy Lou, and on her it looked nice.

Nobody was rude enough to mention the ice pack Quinn had positioned against his crotch. Emmy Lou had noticed the way he was walking and had suggested it. After a few minutes the ache had gone away and he just felt numb down there, which was probably a good thing considering the direction his thoughts took every time he glanced across the table at Jo.

The topic of conversation turned to Quinn's impending move to the bunkhouse. Jo didn't say much, just got pinker and pinker as the discussion continued. Her hair was damp from her shower, and she wore no makeup. Quinn had always loved the stage in a relationship when a woman became comfortable enough to appear in front of him fresh from the shower without doing her hair or putting on makeup.

Of course this didn't count as a stage, because he wasn't

involved with Jo. Wouldn't be involved with Jo. Dammit. Maybe he should strap an ice pack permanently to his crotch.

"People will think it's terrible if we make Brian Hastings sleep in the bunkhouse," Emmy Lou said. "I think you should stay up at the house, Quinn. The bunkhouse is grungy."

"No, it ain't!" Fred said. "Just because I won't let you clean it every five minutes and put doilies around on whatever don't move, you—"

"It's a pit," Emmy Lou said to Quinn with a smile. "Fred and Benny act like it's their clubhouse or something. All I did was try to vacuum one day and rearrange a few things, and you'd think I'd burned the place to the ground."

"You Hoovered the ace of clubs out of my lucky deck of cards, woman!"

Emmy Lou leaned over and patted Quinn's hand. "Stay up at the house. Don't you agree he should, Jo?"

"Well, I—"

"Emmy Lou," Fred said, pointing at her. "Don't be forgetting that Jo's a divorcée."

"So what?" Emmy Lou said.

Fred acted as if he were explaining a simple fact to a three-year-old. "People think a certain way about divorcées. They'll think there's hanky-panky going on between him and Jo if he sleeps in the house."

And they would be right, Quinn thought. But it had nothing to do with her being divorced. Jo would tempt him single, divorced, even virginal.

"That might be the way your mind works, Fred," Emmy Lou said. "But everybody doesn't automatically think like that."

"Wanna bet?" Fred pointed at Emmy Lou. "Try hanging out in the Lazy Bones Saloon sometime."

Emmy Lou glared at him. "I've been meaning to try that.

But first you'd better teach me how to chew and spit. Honestly, Fred. As if I care about what a bunch of old booz—''

"Watch yourself, woman," Fred said.

Benny's eyes widened. "You're gonna learn to chew and spit, Emmy Lou?"

"Not really, Benny." Emmy Lou smiled at him. "I think it's a perfectly disgusting habit, don't you?"

Benny glanced uncertainly from Fred's scowl to Emmy Lou's smile. "I think…I want some more biscuits."

"Well done, Benny," Jo said. "It doesn't pay to get in the middle of a lovers' quarrel, you know." Then she looked stricken. "Oops. I didn't mean to say that. I really didn't. Must be the stress getting to me. I'm sorry."

Quinn stopped chewing as silence descended over the table. He looked at Jo, who sat gazing anxiously at Fred and Emmy Lou. Then he glanced at Fred, who had a murderous gleam in his eye, and Emmy Lou, who had turned the color of the tomatoes ripening on the windowsill.

Finally Emmy Lou cleared her throat. "I have no idea what you're talking about, Josephine." She stood and started collecting dishes. "I wouldn't take up with that old goat for all the tea in Japan."

"It's China!" Fred muttered. "And that goes double for me." He pulled his napkin from where he'd tucked it into his shirt and tossed it on the table. "I got chores to do."

"You don't have to hide it!" Jo cried. "I didn't mean to spill the beans and embarrass you both, but I think it's wonderful if you two have something going!"

"Me, too!" Benny said. "What do they have going, Jo?"

"Not a dad-blasted thing," Fred said. He started out of the kitchen just as the doorbell rang. "I'll get that."

Jo walked to the sink and put her arm around Emmy Lou. "Em, I'm sorry. I didn't even figure it out until this morning, and then—damn, I just opened my mouth and out it came.''

Emmy Lou squirted a large stream of dishwashing liquid in the sink and turned the faucet on full blast, creating mounds of foam. Then she began washing furiously. ''If that man said anything to you I'm going to hang him by his…thumbs.''

''No! It was just the way he made a certain comment, and I asked if you two were sweethearts, and he got all red, like you're doing now. Em, you and Fred are like parents to me. This feels perfect, the two of you in love.''

In her agitation Emmy Lou slopped water and soapsuds on the floor. ''Who said anything about love?''

''It's perfectly obvious, the way you two fight, that you're in love.''

Quinn sipped his coffee and watched in fascination. For so many years he'd lived by himself in Manhattan. Sure, he had buddies, and twice he'd had a live-in girlfriend for a few months, but aside from occasional trips to Murray's house, he hadn't been in a family setting in a long time. That's what this morning felt like, and he was loving the hell out of it.

Fred appeared in the kitchen doorway. ''It's that fool Doobie and his scrawny wife, Eloise. I parked them in the living room. I imagine they want to get a look at Brian Hastings.''

Quinn tensed. Last night's performance with Dick had been a reflex action, and Dick hadn't been inclined to be skeptical. Quinn remembered that Doobie was president of the local bank. In his experience, bankers were born skeptics. He glanced at Jo.

''It's up to you,'' she said. ''You don't have to see them. In fact, you don't have to see anybody. You can be as reclusive as you want.''

"Yeah, but this is your banker. I'm supposed to offer him a part in the movie, remember?"

"You don't have to." Ever since they'd squirmed together in the mud this morning she'd had a captivating shyness in her eyes whenever she looked at him.

Quinn smiled at her. Hell, didn't she know he'd do just about anything for her? Only a guy who was wrapped around a woman's little finger would voluntarily suggest that he move to the bunkhouse after she'd announced that they shouldn't become sexually involved.

"I'm sure we can find a part for him somewhere," he said. He'd never wished that he could be Brian Hastings, but at the moment he almost wanted to be, just so he'd have the power to shoot a movie here and help her cause. He set down his mug and pushed back his chair. "Come and introduce me." He stood up, and the ice pack dropped to the floor.

Jo blushed as she glanced at the ice pack and at his crotch. "Um, are you better?"

Quinn leaned down and picked up the ice pack. "Good as new."

"I'm glad. I mean, that's good. I mean..."

Fred coughed. "Maybe you should drop that particular topic, Jo."

"Good idea." Jo swallowed. "Come on, Quinn. Let's go meet my banker."

"I'll come in with some coffee and arsenic in a little bit." Emmy Lou continued washing dishes without turning.

Fred snorted with laughter. Then he snuck a look at Emmy Lou and glanced quickly away again. "Benny, you and me got stuff to do. Let's get a move on."

Emmy Lou kept her back to Fred while she washed and rinsed dishes with a vengeance. "I was hoping you men would clear out of my kitchen and let me get my pot roast in the oven," she said. "Can't accomplish a dad-blasted thing when you're underfoot."

Jo winked at Quinn.

He winked back and followed her out of the kitchen. "How long do you think it's been going on?" he said in a low voice.

"Probably years. I was just too wrapped up in my own problems to notice, but when Fred started talking this morning I got this flash, and all sorts of things began to click in my brain." She walked into the living room, where a skinny man and his wife sat on a worn leather sofa. "Mr. and Mrs. Doobie! May I introduce you to Brian Hastings?"

Doobie popped up from the sofa and came forward, hand outstretched, but Mrs. Doobie looked as if she might pass out.

Her mouth opened and closed several times, but she made no sound.

"Mr. Hastings," Doobie said in an unfortunately high voice. The few strands of long hair he'd combed over his bald head quivered as he pumped Quinn's hand vigorously. "This is quite an honor."

Definitely not a speaking part, Quinn thought. "I feel lucky to be here," he said. "This is the perfect location to film *The Brunette Wore Spurs.*" Yeah, that was a good title. Amazing what he could come up with on short notice.

Jo stared at him in astonishment. "That's a working title, right?" She gave him a slight nudge with her foot.

"Guess so. Works for me."

"It sounds a little like a film that would be in the adult section at the video store." Jo chuckled and nudged Quinn again. "But, as we all know, film titles get changed all the time."

"They do?" Quinn had never thought about that. "I mean, yes, they certainly do. Why, Julia told me—you all know Julia Roberts, right?"

Jo looked wary, but Doobie and his wife nodded enthusiastically.

"Well, Julia told me that *Pretty Woman* was almost called *Pretty Prostitute*. And the other day I was talking to Bob Redford, and he said that—"

"Coffee!" Emmy Lou announced. "Hello there, Doobies! So good to see you up so bright and early this morning. What do you think of our celebrity guest, Eloise?"

Eloise licked her thin lips and twisted her hands in her lap. "Mr. Hastings, was that really your fanny in that nude scene?"

"Eloise!" Doobie blanched.

Quinn gulped. He hadn't seen a Brian Hastings movie in years. He didn't know the guy had shot a nude-fanny scene. He wished he had known before he'd agreed to impersonate the guy.

"Of course it was him." Emmy Lou calmly poured coffee from a silver urn into a china teacup. "You think anyone else would have a tush that cute? Here you go, Eloise. Sugar and cream's on the coffee table there."

"I've always wondered," Eloise said. She took the coffee but continued to stare at Quinn as if she might ask him to strip down and prove it was his fanny in the scene. "The lighting wasn't very good. You were mostly in shadows."

Thank God, Quinn thought. Even though he hadn't been the one naked in front of the cameras and half the free world, he was pretending to be that guy. He hoped there had been *lots* of shadow.

Doobie turned to his wife. His face had gone from pale to quite pink. "You told me you closed your eyes at that part."

"I lied, Cuthbert."

"You know I don't approve of a married woman seeing another man's naked...parts."

Eloise sat up straighter. "And I've obeyed you all the

years of our marriage, until I found out there would be a nude scene in *Rogue's Reward*. When we saw it at the Lyric Theater I closed my eyes to please you, but I left them open a little slit, like this.'' She demonstrated her peeking technique. ''Then I bought the video,'' she added bravely.

''And watched that scene again without me?'' Doobie looked scandalized. ''Eloise, how could you?''

''Brian Hastings is the only man who could tempt me to break my vow to you, Cuthbert.'' Eloise gazed adoringly at Quinn. ''Two hundred and six times.''

Doobie made a little choking sound.

''Well, that certainly must be a record!'' Jo said brightly. ''I don't know how many people watch the same movie two hundred and six times. You should be very flattered, Brian.''

''Oh, I didn't watch the whole movie.'' Eloise took a dainty sip of her coffee. ''Only the nude-fanny scene. I keep the tape permanently rewound to that section.''

Quinn couldn't look at Doobie. The poor little man seemed about to have a fit, and Quinn couldn't say he blamed him. He wouldn't be too happy to discover such a fact about his wife, if he had one. He glanced at Jo. ''What did you think of that scene?''

''It was pretty hot, Brian. Some of your better work.'' She looked as if she might burst out laughing any minute.

He didn't think it was so damn funny, and he didn't much like the idea that she'd been drooling over Hastings' butt, too. ''Did you buy the video?''

She pressed her lips together, as if that was the only way she could keep from laughing. She shook her head.

''I did,'' Emmy Lou said. ''And since you never watch your own movies, you might like to take a look sometime.''

''Yeah. Yeah, I'd like to see that, uh, scene.''

"It's wonderful," Eloise said with a sigh. "All the girls think so."

"Girls?" Doobie squeaked. "What girls?"

"The Ugly Bug Garden Club. We always close the meeting with a showing of that scene."

"Oh, my God," Doobie wailed. "My wife's peddling porn in the sanctity of our home."

"Get a grip, Cuthbert," Emmy Lou said. "It's one scene, for crying out loud. And it's not pornography, it's art."

"We're all hoping you'll do another," Eloise said to Quinn. "Any chance of that in *The Brunette Wore Spurs?*"

"No."

"That's too bad." Eloise set down her cup and saucer. "Mr. Hastings, the ladies of the garden club would consider it a great honor if you would—"

"What?" Quinn wasn't aware he'd backed up until he bumped into a leather wing chair in the corner of the room.

"—speak to our group," Eloise said. "Goodness, what did you think I was going to ask?"

"Uh, nothing." Quinn cleared his throat and took a deep breath. "I'd love to do that, of course." Not. He couldn't imagine speaking to a bunch of women who ended every meeting ogling his bare butt. Or Hastings' bare butt, which nearly amounted to the same thing. "But I'll be pretty busy investigating the area and figuring out..." He racked his brain for what a filmmaker might need to know about a location. "I have to decide where we can plug in our lights."

Jo turned to him with a puzzled expression.

But he'd hit upon a way to work in something he knew about, which was home improvement, and he decided to go with it. "Yep, electricity's a big concern with these things. I look around at Jo's ranch, and I like what I see, but I have to ask myself, are there enough outlets? When you're filming, you can never have too many outlets."

"Or *generators*," Jo said, rolling her eyes.

"Well, there's that option, too," Quinn said casually. "Personally I like lots of outlets."

"So I guess the Brian Hastings town festival is out of the question," Doobie said, sounding relieved.

Jo turned to Doobie. "What Brian Hastings town festival?"

"Dick Cassidy brought it up last night when he was buying rounds of drinks at the Ugly Bug Saloon. I guess he's pretty set up about getting a part in the movie. Word got back to the town council, and the mayor asked me to come out this morning and ask about it, considering that I have a close relationship with Jo, here."

"Do you?" Quinn asked. From what he'd heard, Doobie could hardly wait to foreclose on the Bar None.

"Absolutely." Doobie smiled at Jo. "She's like the daughter I never had."

Eloise bounced out of her seat. "Cuthbert Doobie, you *have* a daughter, and she's given you nine lovely grandchildren. It's not her fault that none of her husbands have been able to hold a job."

Quinn decided it was time to stroke old Cuthbert's ego. "I've been thinking about something ever since I walked in here." He pointed a finger at the skinny banker. "You're the perfect Pierre."

Doobie blinked. "Pierre?"

"A French character in the movie. You have that same worldly look, that same sophistication."

Doobie preened. "Maybe so, but I don't speak French."

"No problem. It's not a speaking role."

"Then how do we know that he's sophisticated and worldly if he never says anything?"

"Trust me. The minute you walk in front of the camera, everyone will know the kind of person you are."

Doobie nodded and looked wise. "I see your point. Then certainly, I'll do it. How about a dance?"

Quinn's jaw dropped. "You want to dance with me, Cuthbert?"

"No, no." Doobie laughed, and his dentures slipped a little. "I meant we could have a dance, just a simple dance on Saturday night, instead of the town festival. Or say, even better, a small rodeo in the afternoon, followed by the dance. If you could possibly see your way clear to participate, the people of Ugly Bug would be very appreciative."

Quinn glanced at Jo, and she shrugged, letting him know it was up to him. A dance sounded relatively harmless. He was a decent dancer. But a rodeo would expose him as a fraud, for sure. "You don't want me to perform in the rodeo," he said. "The liability, you know. If I got hurt, the resulting suit would bankrupt the town."

"Oh! Then of course we don't want you to be *in* the rodeo. You can be the guest of honor."

"All right."

"Wonderful! Then—"

"Cuthbert, if we hold these events, we have to make a rule," Emmy Lou said. "Women are not allowed to grab at Brian's clothes or pinch his tush. No button popping, no pocket ripping. None of that."

"Certainly not!" Doobie looked offended at the very idea. "Well, then, I guess our mission is accomplished, Eloise. Come along."

Eloise didn't move. She stood gazing at Quinn, a dreamy smile on her face. "Save me a dance," she said.

"Sure."

"Oh, *thank you.*" She sighed and clasped her hands together. "I'll be counting the hours."

Doobie snorted and took his wife's arm. "Don't make such a big deal out of it, Eloise. It's just a dance."

"Just a dance? Just a *dance?* I think not, Cuthbert." She kept her gaze fastened on Quinn as her husband dragged her to the entry hall. "Why, dancing with Brian Hastings is more important than winning best garden of the year, more important than giving birth to our darling Primrose, more important than our *wedding night.* Which reminds me. I know you think you're a great—"

"Thanks for the coffee!" Doobie called as he hustled his wife out the door.

After they left Jo grinned at him. "You've done it again. First Dick, and now that weasel Doobie. Thanks, Quinn."

"I loved it, Eloise's tush fetish and all." Emmy Lou gathered coffee cups.

"Don't remind me about that part," Quinn said.

"Oh, she's harmless," Emmy Lou said. "But he's not. Can you believe he had the nerve to say you were like a daughter to him? Just last week when you asked for an extension on your loan he said you might as well sell out and go back east, where you belong. Quinn, you were magnificent." She smiled at him. "Brian Hastings couldn't have done it better. Well, he might not have spouted all that nonsense about electrical outlets, but otherwise, good job." She left the room carrying the tray.

"Doobie really said that to you last week?" Quinn wished he'd been a little rougher on the guy.

"Well, to be fair, I am pretty far behind on my payments."

"Listen, Jo, I—"

"Nope." She held up both hands. "I shouldn't have brought it up. Forget I said anything."

Quinn gazed at her. "If you say so." Quinn longed to get his hands on her books. Okay, he'd rather get his hands on her, but she'd put the skids on that program. But if he could look over her accounts and have her explain the ranching business to him, he knew he could help.

"Don't you need to call your office?"

"Guess I do."

"While you're doing that, I'll go down to the barn and check on Clarise and Stud-muffin. See you in a little while, then."

"Right." Quinn noticed she hadn't suggested he use her office phone, probably because she didn't want him in there, period. So he made his call on the phone in the hallway.

As he was hanging up, Jo came in and hooked her slicker on a peg by the door.

"Everything okay at the barn?" he asked.

"Great." She looked damp, pink and very kissable. "How's your office?"

"No problems. What's next on the schedule?"

Jo shook her damp hair. "It's still raining. I called the vet before breakfast, and she can't come out to inseminate Lullabelle and Missy until tomorrow." She looked at Quinn. "We're sort of at loose ends today."

"What do you usually do when it rains like this?"

"Oh, paperwork in my office."

Exactly, he thought. "Jo, don't be so damned stubborn. Let's go into your office and you can give me a rundown on your financial situation."

"Nope, nope, nope."

Emmy Lou appeared in the doorway with a tape in her hand. "Here's *Rogue's Revenge* anytime you want to take a peek. I have some others, but it sounded like this was the one you were interested in."

"Hey, we can watch that!" Jo seized the opportunity. "You really should see one of your—I mean, Brian's—movies and get an idea of his personal style before you show up at the rodeo and dance on Saturday."

He couldn't argue with her reasoning. And he'd be dumb to turn down a chance to sit on the sofa with her and watch a movie. "Okay. We can do that."

She walked into the living room and opened the oak cabinet that housed the television set. "Sit down, sit down. You're about to be able to see yourself without hordes of screaming women interfering with your viewing enjoyment."

"I can hardly wait." He wouldn't mind one particular woman interfering, he thought as he sat on the sofa.

After shoving the tape into the VCR, she picked up the remote and started toward the sofa.

Okay, he thought, wondering how close she'd sit.

At the last minute she veered toward a wing chair. "Maybe I'll sit over here, for good measure."

"Hey, Emmy Lou's right in the kitchen. What could happen?"

"I suppose you're right." She sat on the sofa, but put a good three feet between them.

The movie started, and Quinn had to admit it was eerie how much Hastings looked like him, except that he seemed completely at home in a Western setting. "He's a good rider."

"You'll be fine with a little more practice. If all you do is attend that rodeo and dance, you might not ever have to demonstrate your riding to anyone."

He looked at her. "You mean I tortured my privates for nothing?"

She glanced at his crotch, and her cheeks grew pink. Then she looked at the television screen. "Watch the movie, Quinn."

He'd rather watch her, but he dutifully turned his head toward the TV.

Emmy Lou appeared in the doorway pulling on a raincoat. "The pot roast's in the oven, and I have to run into town for a few groceries."

Jo grabbed the remote and hit the pause button. "Want some company?"

"No, thanks. I'm taking the truck and I need the space for the bags. I'll be back in a couple of hours."

Quinn's heart began to pound. *A couple of hours.* He glanced at Jo.

She got up and moved to the chair. "Just to be on the safe side," she said.

Quinn didn't think there was any safe side to this situation.

8

On her way to the chair, Jo glanced out the window and saw Fred climb in the truck with Emmy Lou. So that's what Emmy Lou had in mind, Jo thought with a smile.

"What's going on out there?" Quinn asked.

"Emmy Lou's taking Fred to town."

"No wonder she didn't want you along."

"Yeah." Still smiling, Jo sat in the chair and punched the remote to restart the movie.

"But Benny's still around?"

"Oh, sure, and he's great with the horses, if you were worried about Clarise and Stud-muffin being alone down there. And if Betsy goes into labor, I'm sure he'll come up and get us."

"Glad to hear it."

"Now watch the movie, Quinn." Her pulse wouldn't settle down. She didn't think for a minute that he was worried about who was watching Clarise and Stud-muffin or whether Benny would alert them when Betsy went into labor. He wanted to know exactly how alone they were and how much temptation lay before him.

She wasn't about to explain that although Betsy was due any day, she showed absolutely no signs of going into labor. Benny wasn't the type to pop into the house for no reason, and Jo was sure Fred had told him to stay in the barn and keep an eye on the new baby. The chances of Benny showing up before lunch were practically nonexistent. She knew how alone they were, and it made watching the movie very difficult.

"I don't sound exactly like Hastings," Quinn said after a while.

"No, you sound better." Whoops. She hadn't meant to say it like that.

"What do you mean, better?"

Now she'd done it. "I happen to like a deeper voice on a guy, that's all."

"Oh." He sounded pleased with her answer.

"I don't think it's a problem that your voice is a little deeper than his. Nobody's mentioned your voice being different. In fact, they're all so gaga they don't notice anything different. They're prepared to believe you're him."

"I guess so."

But Jo could already tell big differences, and the advantage was in Quinn's favor. His eyes were a deeper blue, and his mouth had a more sensuous curve to the lower lip. And she liked Quinn's hands better. The fingers were longer, the back of his hand broader. Of course that was probably because Quinn was taller, bigger all over. And then she wondered if he was bigger *all over*. Her mouth grew moist.

The movie was quickly approaching the famous scene in the mining shack, the one that had made Eloise Doobie break her promise that she wouldn't look at another man's naked parts. The heroine, played by superstar Cheryl Ramsey, had already taken refuge in the shack while a terrible storm raged. She was conveniently in the process of taking off her wet clothes by candlelight while sitting on a cot.

"He's going to show up, isn't he?" Quinn said.

"Yep." Jo was becoming embarrassingly aroused being in the same room with Quinn during this sexy movie. She was so glad she wasn't a man. The poor guys couldn't hide their sexual interest at all.

"We're getting down to it, aren't we?"

"Yep." She didn't dare look at Quinn to find out if his sexual interest was beginning to show, but she'd bet it was. She could hear him breathing, and he kept shifting on the seat cushions. She wondered if getting an erection was painful after the punishment of his morning ride. "Are you okay?"

"How do you mean?"

"Um, are you...uncomfortable?"

"Yeah." His voice was dry. "Any suggestions?"

"I could get another ice pack for your—"

"No, thanks."

Jo tried to concentrate on the movie instead of the state of Quinn's private parts. Cheryl Ramsey was quite beautiful and quite naked. Jo really didn't like Quinn looking at her, but it couldn't be helped.

Brian Hastings opened the door of the shack. The woman glanced up. The look that passed between the two of them made Jo quiver. Then, without saying a word, Hastings unbuttoned his shirt.

Jo remembered thinking he looked pretty damned good when she first saw the scene, but that was before she'd been treated to Quinn Monroe in his briefs last night. Still, watching Hastings peel off his shirt and reach for the buckle of his belt reminded her of the joy of watching a well-put-together man undress. Quinn had been right about Dick's physique—he was soft in the middle.

She gripped the remote as Hastings, standing partially in shadow with his back to the camera, took off his jeans and his underwear in one movement. No wonder the Ugly Bug Garden Club closed out their meeting with this scene, she thought, her gaze riveted to the screen. But she'd wager that Quinn's behind looked even better than this.

Hastings walked over to Cheryl and sank to his knees before her. That simple, knightly gesture was the sort of thing that had made Brian Hastings number one at the box office, in Jo's estimation. She held her breath as Hastings kissed Cheryl—her mouth, her throat, her breasts. Jo's breasts felt tight and feverish.

As the music swelled, Hastings guided Cheryl to the cot, and the soft light illuminated their bodies as he moved over her.

Jo moaned softly and gripped the remote.

The scene froze in place.

"Did you mean to do that?" Quinn's voice was strained.

"No!" Jo glanced at the remote and punched it, but her hand was shaking so much she kept missing the play button.

"Fast forward through that scene, dammit," Quinn ordered tightly.

"I'm trying!" She stood and pointed the remote at the VCR while she stabbed at the buttons with trembling fingers.

"I'll do it." Quinn half rose from his seat and made a grab for the remote in her hand.

"I've got it!" She backed up and stumbled. The remote flew out of her hand and plopped between the cushions of the sofa.

"Oh, for crying out loud." Breathing hard, Quinn dropped to one knee and started fumbling for the remote.

"I've got it, I've got it." Jo sat on the sofa and shoved her hand in the space.

He pushed her hand aside. "Get out of there and let me. This cushion is the deepest—" The VCR clicked and whirred.

"You must have hit something. I think it's rewinding!"

"We're sure as hell not going to see that again!"

"Whoops, now it's going forward. Whoops—"

"Move your tush so I can reach under here and—damn, but leather is slippery. You paused the tape on purpose just when they were doing it, didn't you? You're just like those garden club ladies.''

"No, I swear! It was an accident!"

"Quit jiggling around. Okay, I've got it." He leaned forward, and his cheek bumped her breast.

"Oh." She couldn't help it. She was on fire.

Quinn went very still. Slowly he lifted his head and looked into her eyes while the movie rewound behind him. "Don't look at me like that," he murmured.

"How?" She drifted closer to him as if pulled by an invisible string.

"Like you want me to rip your clothes off."

"Oh." She was breathing hard. "Okay, I won't." She closed her eyes.

"Dammit, that's worse. Open your eyes."

She did as he asked.

He groaned. "No help there."

As her gaze shifted to his sensuous mouth, she couldn't seem to help the downward tilt of her head, bringing her closer and closer. "It's because of the movie. We're just worked up because of the—"

"Speak for yourself." He cupped the back of her head and kissed her.

But she couldn't speak for herself when he kissed her like that. She couldn't even think for herself with her heart pounding so loud. Vaguely she heard a click and whirr as the movie surged to fast forward again. Quinn must have abandoned the remote, leaving it to fend for itself. As if she cared.

A girl couldn't be worried about remote controls when being kissed by a man who knew how to use his tongue the way Quinn did. When he started unbuttoning her blouse she let him do it. She even helped with a button or two. When he fumbled with the front catch of her bra she pushed his hand away and unhooked it herself.

After all, a man who could kiss like that would know what to do when presented with a woman's aching, needy breasts.

Quinn knew.

Jo arched her back and moaned as he showed her the full extent of his knowledge. After stroking her for several delicious moments, he slid up on the sofa and leaned her back over the armrest. She'd never been caressed so fully or with such murmured appreciation. She barely noticed as the movie switched from rewind to fast forward with every abandoned movement she made. She began to respond in other ways, becoming very moist at the point where the denim seam of her jeans started to pinch. The tender spot cried out for his attention.

He was panting by the time he kissed his way back to her mouth. He plunged his tongue in deep, letting her know what he wanted, and then slowly drew back. "I'm in agony," he said, gasping. "We need a decision, here. Either unzip my jeans or button your blouse."

She cradled her face in his hands. "I'm in agony, too."

His smile looked strained. "Yeah, but you weren't bouncing on a horse for an hour this morning."

"Oh! Poor Quinn."

"Poor Quinn is right." He slid his hands under her bottom and fit his erection tight against her. "I'm being tortured here, Jo."

"Oh, Quinn." She pressed closer.

He pushed back with a groan. With a whirr and click the VCR reversed direction.

She rocked against him and closed her eyes. *Whirr, click.* "I don't know if—"

"I know I'll be permanently impaired in another minute. God, Jo." He shoved harder. Another click from the remote was followed by a loud snap and a frantic spinning noise from the VCR.

Quinn turned his head toward the television. "What the hell?"

Jo stared at the snow on the screen. "I think we killed the movie."

"We didn't touch it!"

"But we bounced on the remote, Quinn. We pushed its little buttons, back and forth, back and forth, until snap! It came apart."

He gazed at her. "You are certainly pushing mine back and forth, back and forth, Josephine, and I am definitely ready to come apart."

She didn't let many people call her that, but she had a feeling Quinn had become one of the select few. "I'm getting scared, Quinn. This has the potential to be bigger than both of us."

"That's what the bulge in my jeans feels like."

"Do you want some ice?"

"No." He looked at her with frank admiration. "I want you. I want to take off your jeans, undo mine and finish what we started."

Her heart hammered as she pictured them doing exactly that. "I want you, too. So I guess there's only one solution."

His hand went to the buckle of his belt. "Live for today and to hell with tomorrow?" he suggested hopefully.

"No. I'll tell Dick and Mr. Doobie that you're not really Brian Hastings. I'll say we were playing a practical joke and they should forget the whole thing."

He sighed and took his hand away from his belt buckle. "Nope. Absolutely not. Those two would never let you forget it. Doobie would probably foreclose on this ranch immediately, and Dick would snap it up so he could have Ugly Bug Creek." Looking very much in pain, he eased slowly to the end of the couch.

"Quinn, I'm sorry." She pulled her blouse together, not

wanting to make his condition worse. Or hers. But his sounded more critical.

"No, you're right," he said. "It's either tell everybody the truth or stop fooling around." He sat on the end of couch and rested her booted feet on his knees. "Be careful with your feet. One of these pointed toes in the wrong place would probably kill me."

"Maybe I could find you some sweats. That would give you more room."

"And maybe I should just stay away from you and Brian Hastings movies. Can we replace the tape?"

"We could have bought a new one at the video store yesterday, no problem. Today—big problem. I'll bet now that the word's out on you there's not a Brian Hastings movie for sale in the entire town of Ugly Bug."

He shifted position and winced. "Then I'll just call my secretary and ask her to overnight a copy of the tape."

"That would be wonderful."

"Yeah, I can autograph it for Emmy Lou."

"Oh, my God. Autographs. We need to find a copy of his signature for you to practice on."

"Or sprain my writing hand."

"A fake sprain, you mean."

"Oh, no, I want a real sprain. Something major to take my mind off my...other problem."

"Quinn, we're not going to deliberately injure you. I'm sure Emmy Lou has something with his signature on it. You can practice. I can't believe I didn't think of autographs. The trouble is, I keep forgetting that you're supposed to be Brian Hastings."

"You do?" He turned to her, and his gaze was steady. "I thought that's what was going on just now. You had me confused with him."

"You thought that?" She tightened her grip on her blouse to keep it together. "You thought I was like those women who rip your clothes off because they think they're getting a piece of Brian Hastings? You thought I'd parked my brain somewhere?'' She *had* parked her brain somewhere, which explained her rash actions, but she'd never for a minute fantasized that Quinn was Brian Hastings. Quinn was powerful enough for any woman's fantasy.

''Well, we were watching one of his movies, and you were getting turned on.''

''So were you! Does that mean you imagined I was Cheryl Ramsey?'' she asked, suddenly worried.

''No.'' He propped a hand on the back of the sofa and leaned over her. ''It means that the movie inspired me to think of what we might be doing. Power of suggestion. And to be honest, when I'm in the same room with you I need very little of that. This movie was overkill.''

''So it wasn't seeing that beautiful naked woman that got you worked up?''

''Not by a long shot. It was the thought of seeing this beautiful naked woman.''

Her pulse raced as his gaze traveled over her. ''And for the record, it wasn't seeing Brian Hastings' butt that got me worked up, either,'' she said.

He looked into her eyes. ''Thank you.'' He gave her a wry smile. ''But I would have taken that. I want you so much I don't care who you think I am if you'll let me touch you.''

''Me, too,'' she murmured. ''I don't care if I'm substituting for a glamorous movie star.''

Desire flared in his eyes. ''You're not. She wouldn't be a fit substitute for you.''

''That's sweet. I don't believe it for a minute, but—''

He leaned closer, and his hand went to his belt again. ''Want proof?''

''Oh, Quinn, I—uh-oh, I hear the truck coming up the road.''

Quinn moved to his end of the sofa and grimaced as his jeans tightened across his crotch. "Better go upstairs and put yourself back together."

Jo sat up. Under her cushion the remote clicked again, and snow crackled on the television screen.

"Easy." Quinn gently lowered her feet to the floor. "Would it help if you stood up?"

"Yeah. I'll do that in a minute. Go on."

"I hate to leave you to explain the broken tape to Emmy Lou."

"I'm a big boy."

She couldn't resist. "So you said."

His gaze was challenging. "Looks like you'll have to take it on faith."

"Yep." Jo couldn't help glancing at his crotch and remembering what he'd felt like pressed against her. She had some idea of what she was giving up, which didn't make the sacrifice any easier. A little bit of knowledge could be a terrible thing, she thought as she stood on rubbery legs. "I'm sorry I put us in this position," she said, starting past Quinn. "It won't happen again."

He reached up and gripped her thigh. "I'm not sorry," he said, gazing at her. "I love this position."

"Okay, so do I."

He gave her thigh a squeeze. "If it happens again, I'll make no noble guarantees about my behavior. I'd take you on any terms. Any terms at all."

Warmth rushed through her. "I'll keep that in mind."

"See that you do." He released her.

She wanted to stay, wanted to make love to him more than she'd ever wanted that with any man. The slamming of the truck's door propelled her reluctantly up the stairs.

QUINN'S EMOTIONS were in a shambles, but he could pick one truth out of this mess. He should never make Jo choose between him and the Bar None. Maybe in a moment of sexual weakness she'd choose him and hate him forever for causing her to lose this ranch.

Emmy Lou made a lot of racket coming into the house. Quinn suspected she was giving notice in case he and Jo were in the middle of...exactly what they'd been in the middle of.

"I'm back!" the housekeeper announced in a loud voice as she closed the front door with a bang and bustled into the kitchen with a paper sack in each arm.

"Need any help?" Quinn called. He was almost in shape to render aid. Almost.

"I've got it, thanks." She sounded breathless.

Quinn flashed on an old memory—coming home from a hot date and discovering his mother still up watching a movie on television. He'd responded to her greeting in that same breathless way before hurrying to his bedroom to see whether his shirt was buttoned up wrong or he had lipstick smeared across his mouth. Sure enough, once Emmy Lou dumped her bags in the kitchen she scurried down the hall toward her bedroom. Apparently everyone had some repair work to do.

Quinn took his time standing, then turned his back to the door to adjust himself. He'd had uncomfortable erections before, but nothing to compare with the pain of being saddle sore and aroused at the same time. He had new respect for cowboys who could ride all day and make love all night. They must be tough in places he'd never considered needed toughening.

Finally he was able to crouch and lift the seat cushion to retrieve the remote. As he reached for it, he noticed a movement next to his foot. He leaped back, knocking over the coffee table in the process.

"What on earth is going on in here?" Emmy Lou appeared in the doorway, her plump cheeks flushed.

"Stay back!" Quinn glanced around for a weapon and settled on the shovel from the fireplace tool set. By the time he had it in his hand, the creature had scuttled under the sofa.

"What is it?" Emmy Lou put her hand to her throat. "A rattlesnake?"

"It's not a snake." Quinn's insides were flipping around, but he was the only man in a house with two vulnerable women. It was up to him to protect them.

"Then what is it, for heaven's sake?"

Quinn thought of Jo lying on the sofa, her soft skin exposed, and shuddered. Then he thought of what might have happened if he'd unzipped his jeans, and he nearly passed out.

"Quinn, tell me what you've found."

"I don't know." He gripped the shovel and raised it over his head as he crept slowly toward the sofa. "But it's a monster," he said, his voice quivering.

9

"A RAT?" Emmy Lou asked.

"You have rats out here, too?" Quinn wondered how anybody in Montana slept at night.

"Well, of course."

"Well, it's not a rat or a mouse. It had a bunch of legs."

"Oh, a bug." With a chuckle, Emmy Lou took off her shoe and walked to the sofa.

"Stay back!" Quinn warned. "I'm the man around here. I'll handle this."

"If you whack that bug with the fireplace shovel you'll spray soot from here to kingdom come. Put that thing down and I'll take care of this, whatever it is."

"It had fangs."

"Really? How many legs, exactly?"

"Too many."

"Probably a wolf spider," Emmy Lou said.

"A *wolf* spider?" Quinn's hands grew clammy. "It attacks wolves?"

"No, no." Emmy Lou looked as if she was trying hard not to laugh, for which Quinn was grateful. "They just look ferocious. They're not poisonous or anything, and they keep the other insects under control."

Quinn got a bad feeling in the pit of his stomach. "What other insects?"

Emmy Lou gazed at him, a twinkle in her eye. "You know, it's really sweet of you to offer to defend me, considering you're so scared of bugs."

"I'm not, either! That's no bug. Bugs are things like flies and mosquitoes and ladybugs. Moths, butterflies, caterpillars. This is…prehistoric."

Emmy Lou smiled. "How did you think the creek and town got named?"

"I tried not to think about it, if you must know." He had a horrifying thought. "You mean these things are *common* around here?"

"Sure. You get used to them." A wicked little gleam appeared in her eye. "You're more likely to find them down at the bunkhouse than up here."

Quinn caught his breath. For one wild minute he thought of reconsidering his sleeping arrangements. Then Jo appeared in the living room doorway, and he knew he'd have to stay in the bunkhouse, ugly bugs and all. She'd combed her hair and fastened her clothing so she looked perfectly proper, but he remembered all too well how she'd helped him unbutton her blouse. And how she'd unhooked her bra for him. And then lifted those spectacular breasts, pressing them into his waiting hands.

"What's going on?" Jo asked, gazing at the sofa cushion tossed aside, the coffee table capsized and the fireplace shovel in Quinn's hand. "Spring cleaning?"

"Sort of," Quinn said. "Don't come in here, Jo. Wolf spider."

"Really? Cool! Where is it?"

He couldn't believe her reaction. "Under the sofa," he said ominously. "You know, under the *sofa*." He wondered how long it would take her to realize the monster could have attacked while she was lying there exposed.

"Then let's move the sofa," Jo said, totally nonchalant about the whole thing.

"Don't, Jo. You'll faint when you see it. It's huge."

"They usually are," Jo said, walking toward the sofa.

"Suit yourself, Red Riding Hood." Quinn folded his

arms, but he kept hold of the fireplace shovel. "Move that sofa and take a look at that big old wolf spider. Don't blame me if you start screaming your head off. I warned you."

Emmy Lou started out of the room. "Hold on. I'll get a glass and see if we can catch it and put it outside."

Quinn almost dropped the shovel. "You're going to *what?*"

"Try to catch it. You know, put a glass down on top of it and then slide a piece of cardboard underneath."

"Are you crazy?"

"No. I've done it before."

Quinn rolled his eyes. "Then you'd better bring a punch bowl and a piece of plywood! We're not talking about Charlotte here, ladies. We're talking big. Very, very big. Spiderzilla."

Emmy Lou smiled at him. "I've discovered that men tend to exaggerate the size of things." She left the room.

Jo let out a very unladylike snort of laughter, and Quinn glared at her.

She tried to compose herself but was obviously having trouble. "Did you tell her about the tape?"

"Not yet. I—"

"Well, this should work." Emmy Lou came in holding a water glass and the back of a cereal box.

"For one leg," Quinn muttered darkly. "But if you women are determined to do this reckless thing, I'll ride shotgun. If it starts to attack, I'll be here."

"They don't attack," Jo said. "Okay, Em. I'll move the sofa just a bit, and you stand ready with that glass."

"Right."

"And I'll stand ready to whack it when you two run screaming out of the room," Quinn said, raising the shovel over his head.

Jo moved the sofa a few inches, and the spider ran right at Quinn.

The women didn't scream, but he was afraid he might have as he started banging the shovel everywhere, stirring up clouds of soot as the spider raced around the room.

"Quick, over by the door, Em!" Jo cried.

Emmy Lou pounced with her glass. "Got him!"

"Or her," Jo said. She crouched as Emmy Lou slid the cardboard under the glass and expertly flipped the whole thing over. "Nope, it's a him."

Quinn stared at the two women in horrified fascination. "How can you tell? And why would you want to?"

"Spiders are fascinating," Jo said. "His sex organs are right by his mouth, an arrangement certain people might envy. Want to see?"

"That's okay." Quinn was sweating like crazy. Sure enough, the monster fit in the glass, but he wouldn't have bet on it. "I'll take your word for it."

"This is a pretty big one," Emmy Lou said. "That body looks almost two inches across, so with the legs and all, it's—"

"Gigantic, like Quinn said," Jo finished, giving Quinn an understanding smile. "Bigger than his fist."

"I'll take him outside and let him go," Emmy Lou said.

Quinn tried to sound casual. "Uh, where would that be, exactly?"

"Out in my veggie garden. He'll like it there. He'll probably stay."

"Oh." He rolled his shoulders and made a mental note to never, ever offer to pick vegetables for Emmy Lou. "I'll, uh, pick up around here, then."

"I'll help," Jo said.

Quinn replaced the shovel in the fireplace tool holder and turned to find Jo looking at him with great tenderness.

"What?" he asked.

"It's just that you're so adorable," she said.

"Adorable?" He preferred words like *virile* and *manly*, himself. *Adorable* was for kids.

"A big strong man like you who's afraid of snakes and bugs," she said. "And trying so hard not to be. It's very sweet."

Quinn felt his face heat up. He set the coffee table on its feet to avoid looking at Jo. "I had an older cousin who used to tease me, shoving wiggly things in my face."

"Shame on him," Jo said.

"It was a girl," Quinn said, growing even redder.

"Then shame on her." She walked over to touch his arm. "But you know, it's possible to get over things like that."

"I doubt it. Been that way ever since I was four."

"You can desensitize yourself. It would be easy around this place, because you'll always be coming in contact with creepy-crawlies. Soon you'd barely notice them."

He glanced at her hand. His arm already tingled where he felt the light pressure of her fingers. He looked into her eyes. "Think that would work with you, too?" he asked in a low voice. "Because I'd sure love to try."

She jerked her hand away and stepped back.

"If the concept works, it should work for anything," he said, closing the gap between them. "Maybe if I kiss you enough, eventually I won't get so aroused when I do it."

Jo swallowed. "I don't think...we have that much time."

"I don't think we'd ever have that much time," he murmured.

"So," Emmy Lou said from the doorway, "how did you two enjoy the movie?"

Quinn cleared his throat and glanced at Jo. "I broke it."

"No, we broke it together." Jo turned toward Emmy Lou. "We're both to blame."

Emmy Lou looked confused. "Broke it?"

"Yeah," Quinn said. "The tape snapped. Don't worry. I'll have my secretary send a new copy right away."

"How much did you get to see before it broke?"

Jo tapped her chin. "Let's see. Was it before the train robbery? Or was it after that scene in the miner's shack?"

Quinn didn't dare look at her. "The miner's shack scene, I think. Anyway, a new tape's practically on the way. I'll make a—"

"Oh, don't buy me a new one." Emmy Lou blushed. "I know why it broke."

"You do?" He wondered if she'd somehow figured out what had been going on.

"It's all that pausing and rewinding."

"How did you know about that?" Quinn asked before he could stop himself.

Emmy Lou's eyes widened, and then she clapped a hand over her mouth. A smothered giggle slipped out anyway.

Jo's cheeks grew pink. "You mean *you* paused and rewound the tape a lot at that spot."

Emmy Lou nodded, her eyes bright. "Plus it was a rental tape I bought on sale at the video store. I'm sure it was already weak right there. I guess you two weakened it a little more."

Quinn's ego had suffered enough. First he was revealed as bugophobic, and now Emmy Lou thought he was some sort of voyeur who'd had to replay a nude scene over a hundred times to get his kicks. "It was by accident that we kept rewinding it," he said. "The remote fell between the sofa cushions, and..." He realized the quagmire he'd stepped in about the same time he caught the dismay in Jo's eyes.

"You know, that pot roast smells a little too good," Jo said. "Maybe you should check on it, Emmy Lou. I think you might need to turn down the heat."

Emmy Lou put her hands on her hips and glanced from

Jo to Quinn and back to Jo again. "I believe I could say the same thing to you."

"The thing is," Quinn began, determined to find a way out of this, "I lost my balance and—"

"Did I hear the dinner bell?" Fred asked, coming through the front door.

"We don't have a dinner bell," Emmy Lou said.

"Well, I didn't think we had one, but then I was out in the yard and I heard all this clanging and banging that sure sounded like a dinner bell. So I figured I'd just wash up and come in to find out if it was time for lunch yet."

"Why, as a matter of fact, it is," Jo said. "I'm starving. How about you, Quinn?"

"Starving," Quinn agreed.

Emmy Lou glanced at them both with a smile on her face. Then she picked up the remote, pointed it at the television and flicked off the power. "Then let's eat."

"What was that clanging sound, anyway?" Fred asked as they headed toward the kitchen.

Quinn wondered if Emmy Lou would tell on him. Fred could make his life a real hell if he knew about Quinn's fear of bugs and snakes.

"You must have heard me banging around with my cast iron pans. I got in the mood to rearrange them," Emmy Lou said.

And with that single statement, Emmy Lou won Quinn's loyalty forever.

THE RAIN LET UP that afternoon, and Jo spent the hours between lunch and dinner riding the fence line with Benny, checking for downed wire, while Fred kept watch on the new foal and taught Quinn something about roping. Jo wasn't pleased to admit it to herself, but she also spent the afternoon missing Quinn.

She wanted to be the one to teach him how to rope,

although that would be a disaster in the making, and she knew it. Whatever time she spent with Quinn was filled with danger, and she wanted to be with him twenty-four hours a day. She had a gigantic crush on the guy.

She had plenty of time to analyze why Quinn affected her so deeply, and she nearly had it nailed down. Any woman would be attracted to a guy who looked like Quinn, which explained the physical draw he had for her.

But what had really hooked her was his ability to make bold, generous gestures coupled with his very human weaknesses. He'd flown all the way from New York on impulse to return the horse sperm, yet he was so frightened of creepy crawlies he'd wrecked the cab. He'd gallantly decided to move to the bunkhouse to keep a safe distance between them, but when faced with temptation, he'd crumbled, just as she had. Crumbled in a very delicious way. She still tingled at the thought of those moments on the sofa.

"Say, what's that yonder?" Benny asked, pointing to a far hillside.

Jo squinted into the distance. "It looks like a man running."

"Then somethin's wrong," Benny said. "People don't run out in the middle of nowhere. Unless they lost their horse or somethin's after them."

"I'll check." Jo reached to her saddlebag and pulled out a scarred pair of binoculars that had belonged to Aunt Josephine. She focused on the small figure running up the hill and grinned. "It's Dick. I think he's jogging."

"Jogging? I wanna see."

Jo handed the binoculars to Benny and leaned over to rest her forearms on her saddle horn while she gazed at the tiny figure pumping madly up the hill. In jeans and boots. She loved it.

"I can't figure out what he's tryin' to catch. There ain't

no horse around, or cattle, neither.'' Benny seemed totally mystified by the concept of a man running for no visible reason.

"Actually he's trying to lose something."

"Ain't nothin' chasing him, neither. No bear or nothing." Benny continued to stare through the binoculars. "He looks plum possessed. I ain't never seen him so red in the face."

"Let me look again." Jo knew that revenge was a mean-spirited emotion, and she shouldn't be indulging in it. Well, she'd have to get saintly some other day. Watching Dick jog was too damn much fun to miss.

She adjusted the focus so she could see Dick's red face. He was panting like a freight engine, too. Unlike Benny, she'd seen him that red in the face before—during the divorce proceedings when the judge had upheld her right to fence off Ugly Bug Creek so Dick's herd couldn't water there as they had been during the two-year span of Dick and Jo's marriage. At that point old Dick was back to hauling water, and he hadn't liked it much.

"Do you reckon we should go over there?" Benny asked. "Somethin' could be wrong."

"I think something's finally right," Jo said. Her heart lifted at the knowledge that Dick could be bested that easily, and she vowed she'd no longer be his victim. "Thanks to Quinn Monroe."

"Are you sure that's his name?"

"Yes." Jo tucked the binoculars away. "That's his name. Did Fred explain our plan?"

"He tried, but I got mixed up. You know I get mixed up."

Jo's heart squeezed at the forlorn look on Benny's face. "I know you're the best wrangler a gal could have."

"I wish I was smarter."

"You're smart where it counts, Benny. Now let me try and explain this situation as best I can."

All the way home Jo did her best to untangle Benny's confusion regarding Quinn Monroe and Brian Hastings. She thought she'd succeeded until Benny asked if he could be in the movie.

"There may not be a movie, Benny."

"But Dick and Mr. Doobie are gonna be in it."

"Quinn was only pretending about the movie when he told them they could be in it."

"If there's a movie, I wanna be in it," Benny insisted stubbornly.

"Okay," Jo said at last. "If there's a movie, I'll do my best to get you in it."

"But I ain't running up no hill."

"No, Benny." Jo smiled again at the memory. "That's a special thing only Dick has to do."

Benny grinned. "He looked like a dork, didn't he?"

"Yep, he looked like a dork." Jo was in an extremely good mood as she rode toward the ranch buildings in the light of the setting sun.

And the catalyst for her good mood stood in an empty corral, twirling a loop over his head. With a beat-up Stetson shading his eyes, leather gloves on and a rope in his hand, he looked a lot like a cowboy. Jo's heart picked up the pace. She wondered if buried under all that Wall Street conditioning was a man who could learn to love wide-open spaces and tolerate bugs and snakes.

Then she remembered why that was a dumb thought. No matter how much Quinn adapted to life as a cowboy, he couldn't stick around, even if he had a notion to. The person everyone believed to be Brian Hastings couldn't very well take up permanent residence in Ugly Bug.

Fred was nowhere to be seen, and Jo decided he must have coached Quinn on the basics and left him to practice.

Quinn twirled the loop one more time, and with a snap of his wrist he let it go. It floated out in a beautiful arc and settled nicely over the post he had been aiming for.

"Yes!" he shouted, cinching it tight. "Finally!"

"Nice throw, cowboy," Jo called.

He glanced over, shoved his hat to the back of his head and grinned at her. "Thanks, ma'am."

Jo gulped. Damn, but he looked good. Almost like he belonged here. She nearly tripped dismounting because she couldn't stop staring at him. "Of course that post isn't moving," she said. "Most things don't stay still when you try to rope them."

"That's a fact."

He'd even started sounding like a cowboy, she thought.

"I'll put the horses up, if you want to go talk to Mr. Hastings," Benny said.

Jo groaned. Apparently she hadn't gotten through to Benny on this double identity deal. "No, that's Quinn over there, Benny."

"His name's Quinn Hastings?"

"No, it's—" She decided if she kept this up pretty soon she'd be as confused as Benny was. She handed the reins to him. "Never mind. Thanks for taking care of Cinnamon for me."

"No problem. I love it."

"And that's why you'll have a place here as long as I own the Bar None."

"I know." With a shy smile, Benny tipped his hat and led the horses away.

Benny was another reason she needed to hang on to the ranch, Jo thought. A new owner might only notice Benny's mental deficiencies and not give enough credit to his instinctive bond with the animals. And then there was Fred, who was getting too crippled with arthritis to do as much as he once had. If Fred was fired, then Emmy Lou would leave the ranch. All three of them depended on her to keep the place going.

Jo looked at the corral as Quinn neatly roped the post again. The golden light from the setting sun touched his broad shoulders as he coiled the rope for another try. He was learning that skill for her, just as he'd been determined to ride Hyper this morning so that he'd do a credible job as Brian Hastings. If she managed to hang on to the ranch, much of the credit would go to Quinn for agreeing to her wild idea.

He'd abandoned his own work so he could get saddle sore, plagued with giant spiders and probably mauled by the townspeople during Saturday's rodeo and dance. All to help out a lady in distress. Other than the satisfaction of a good deed, he wasn't getting anything out of the deal.

A girl should be grateful when a man put himself out like that, Jo thought as she watched Quinn form a loop and twirl it over his head. Unfortunately, gratitude had landed her in hot water once before, when she'd been stupid enough to think she owed Dick the favor of marrying him after all the help he'd given her running the Bar None. But Quinn wasn't asking for her hand in marriage or a chunk of the ranch. All he wanted was to make love to her.

God, that would be tough to take, she thought with a wry smile. But it wasn't the lovemaking part that worried her. That would be glorious. No, what kept her from rushing into his arms and into his bed was not the loving. It was the leaving.

10

QUINN had loved watching Jo ride in. She'd tied her hair back with a scarf and worn an old brown hat that gave her a rough-and-tumble tomboy look he thoroughly enjoyed. She sat straight in the saddle, her tummy in and her breasts thrust forward as she laughed and talked with Benny. Nice.

Years of riding had obviously made her feel completely at home in the saddle. He doubted she was the least bit worried about falling off. He'd spent a little more time on Hyper this afternoon, and he'd been constantly worried about falling off. With good reason. He had bruises on top of bruises.

Wondering if he'd ever achieve that relaxed look on a horse, he studied the way Jo sat and how she gripped with her thighs. Then he had to stop studying Jo. Focusing on her while her thighs were open and her hips rocked gently in response to the horse was not a good idea.

He'd really done himself in this time. He couldn't back out of his agreement because Jo might lose the ranch and he'd feel guilty for not helping her. Yet the longer he stayed at the Bar None the more desperately he wanted to make love to her. Tomorrow was the rodeo and dance, and by Sunday he'd probably need to hit the road. His head understood perfectly that he should keep his hands off of her until then. The rest of him wanted to argue.

Thinking about Jo had screwed up his usually excellent concentration on the task at hand. Consequently, as she'd returned to the ranch, he had yet to rope the post. Fred had told him not to quit until he lassoed that sucker at least once, and he'd begun to wonder if he'd be out here after dark with a flashlight, still trying after everyone else had turned in. He wanted to have some roping ability in case something came up during the rodeo, but he seemed to have no talent for it.

Then he had an inspiration. Squinting at the post, he imagined it was Jo standing there, daring him to throw a loop around her. The concept took some effort, because Jo had interesting curves that the post lacked and a waterfall of fragrant hair and...okay, so the concept took *tremendous* effort. But finally he stared at the post so long it became Jo—saucy as you please, head thrown back, a taunting look in her brown eyes, a smile on those full lips.

Quinn took a deep breath. Now this he could get into. Twirling the rope over his head, he concentrated on the image of settling a rope around those lovely shoulders and pulling Jo closer and closer and... Flick. He sent the rope sailing as he'd done a hundred times this afternoon. And he roped the post.

Better yet, Jo had seen him do it and had called out some encouragement. Of course she also had to mention that the post wasn't moving, a fact he knew very well. He had to perfect this stage before he could advance to moving targets.

He decided to try again. This time he added an embellishment and imagined Jo standing in the corral, impudent as hell, with no clothes on. He roped the post even more competently than before. Apparently all he needed was the appropriate goal. Smiling, he loosened the rope from around the post and coiled it again.

"Looks like you made some progress this afternoon."

Quinn turned to see Jo walking into the corral. In a few seconds she'd be the same distance from him as the post, but a little to the left of it.

"I'm learning." He built his loop and swung it over his head again. "It's harder than I thought it would be."

"Chances are nobody will expect you to perform tomorrow."

"I know, but I'd still like to have the basics down." He twirled the rope and thought about his next move. If he missed he'd look really stupid. So he wouldn't miss.

"I hate to tell you, but the basics won't do you much good if somebody wants you to demonstrate your roping skills. They'll expect you to rope something alive, not a post planted in the ground."

"Maybe all I need is a little more practice." He turned toward her, took a split second to gauge the distance and tossed the loop.

She stared at him, openmouthed, as the loop dropped over her head.

Using every new skill he'd gained, plus some instinct he didn't know he had, he pulled at exactly the right moment, and the rope tightened around her arms, pinning them to her body. With a quick movement he cinched it.

"Quinn!"

Keeping the line taught, he went hand over hand toward her, watching her intently the whole way. She did her best to look indignant, but the effect was spoiled by the eagerness in her eyes. Finally he stood next to her. "How's that?"

"Very clever, Monroe." Her breathing was quick, urgent. "You can let me go now."

"I guess I could." He kept the rope taut with one hand while he pulled the glove off his other hand with his teeth. He loved the way her eyes darkened and flashed as she watched him. He tucked the glove in his belt. "Then again, I've never roped a woman before. Shouldn't I get a prize for that?"

"I've never heard of one. In Montana the men don't generally go around roping women."

"Maybe they should try it." He'd acted on impulse, not realizing how secluded the corral was. Benny and Fred would have no reason to pass on their way to the house for dinner. "It gets the women hot." He took off her hat and set it on the post. Then he took off his and dropped it on top of hers.

"Does not."

He loosened the scarf from her hair, pulled it over her curls and stuffed it in his back pocket. "Does, too." He brushed his knuckles over her throat and down the V in her blouse, taking great satisfaction in the shiver he produced. "You want me to kiss you so bad you can hardly stand it."

"Listen to you." She sounded breathless. "One lucky toss and your head's swelled up like a balloon."

"That's not the only part of me swelling up, honey bunch." He tunneled his fingers through her hair and cupped the back of her head. "But I have the feeling you're getting mighty stirred up, too."

Her lips parted in anticipation. "Your macho routine doesn't do a thing for me."

He leaned closer, keeping his grip firm on the rope. "Oh, I think it does."

"Wrong," she whispered.

His lips hovered over hers. "Let's see," he said softly, and took his prize.

If every roping session ended with this sort of reward, he'd give up his banking career. He took everything her ripe mouth offered, and she was offering plenty. She wasn't just hot, she was steaming. He shifted the angle of his mouth, then shifted again, trying to get deeper, trying to touch the essence of her.

She responded with a hunger that took his breath away.

With a groan he tugged on the rope, snugging her against him. As he pressed his body to hers, he remembered how her hips had moved rhythmically as she rode in this afternoon. He remembered her passion this morning—the velvet of her breasts, the erotic taste of her. And he wondered if not making love to her, not ever making love to her, would drive him crazy.

Fear of that prompted him to finally lift his mouth from hers and loosen the rope. It dropped to the ground at her feet. "I've tried not to want you, Jo." He gasped for air. "It's not working."

She lifted her arms and wound them around his neck as she rested her head on his shoulder. "I've tried, too. I thought about you all afternoon."

"Good." He continued to cradle her head as he stroked her back with his gloved hand.

"Not good. This can go nowhere, as you very well realize. Unless, of course, I blow your cover."

"Don't do that. Just make love to me. I'm developing a condition."

"A condition?" She lifted her head to look into his eyes. "What condition?"

"Denim-tightis. It's fatal if left untreated."

A smile twitched at the corners of her mouth. "I offered you sweats."

"Cowboys don't wear sweats." He cupped her bottom and brought her tight against him. "They take care of the problem so their jeans fit right again."

Her voice grew husky. "Do you think it's that simple?"

"Probably not." His aching erection sought her heat. "My jeans may never fit when I'm around you. But it's worth a try. I really don't think Brian Hastings would wear sweats to a country dance, do you?"

"No." Amusement and desire flared in her eyes. But gradually her expression grew serious. "What I meant was that making love is not a simple solution to the problem in any sense. Just suppose we make love tonight.''

"I like supposing that." His heart hammered as he rocked gently against her hips. "Let's do suppose that. Let's seriously suppose that."

"Quinn, quit joking around. I'm—'' She paused and cleared the huskiness from her throat. "I'm trying to make a point."

"So am I. Going to bed may not be a permanent cure for my condition, but I'm willing to settle for symptomatic relief.''

"And then what? Tomorrow's Saturday."

"Fortunately followed by Saturday night." He leaned forward and nibbled on her earlobe. "Another opportunity to treat my potentially fatal problem." He ran his tongue around the pink inner shell of her ear.

She moaned. "The point is—''

"Yes?" He loved the way she turned into a rag doll in his arms, so supple, so willing. He considered scooping her up and carrying her into the barn, except that Benny and Fred might still be in there, and what he had in mind required privacy.

She took a deep breath and attempted to push him away, but it was only a halfhearted effort. Her words came out in a determined rush. "The point is that Saturday's your big coming-out party, which means it would be very advisable for you to leave on Sunday, before people get suspicious."

He had no wish to think about the leaving-on-Sunday part. "Tonight could be the granddaddy of all coming-out parties, with your participation."

"Quinn, will you stop thinking about your…problem and listen?"

"It's hard." He lifted his head and waggled his eyebrows at her. "Very hard."

Breathless laughter trembled on her lips. "Honestly, you

act as if you'd never been sexually frustrated before in your life. Has every woman except me tumbled directly into your bed?''

"Not by a long shot. But this is not mere sexual frustration. This is sexual torture. To be more specific, I could represent my previous sexual frustrations by, say, a gnat, and my present one by, say, a wolf spider.''

"Really?" She looked sort of pleased with the news.

"I'm afraid so."

"Why do you think that is?"

"I've asked myself the same thing, Josephine. I don't know. All I know is that if I'm forced to drive away from here on Sunday without ever making love to you, I might have to throw myself off the top of the Empire State Building.''

Her cheeks grew pink, and her eyes sparkled. "How you exaggerate. Besides, they've put up barriers so people can't throw themselves off the Empire State Building.''

"Then I'd have to tie a cement block to my feet and jump off the George Washington Bridge. And I'd probably land on a garbage scow and sink over my head into the muck, like Luke Skywalker in *Star Wars*, only I wouldn't ever come up again. I'll die covered in slime." He kneaded her firm bottom with his gloved hand. "I'm sure you don't want that on your conscience.''

"You sure know how to treat a girl, Quinn." Her chin had a saucy tilt, but her bedroom eyes gave her away. "First you rope her and then you whisper sweet nothings about garbage scows and slime.''

"It's a gift." He smiled. "Take pity on me, Jo. I'm a desperate man.''

"But this is all we'd ever have."

"I know." His smile faded. "And I know that's a problem for you. It could be a problem for me. If I could find the off switch on this obsession I'd use it. That was my plan, to shut down that part of me. Turns out I'm not as strong as I thought I was.''

"I need some time to think."

Quinn glanced around. Dusk was upon them. After dusk came night, and it might be the longest, most frustrating one of his life if Jo shut him down. She thought he was kidding about the Empire State Building and the George Washington Bridge. And he was, sort of. But he'd never wanted any woman like this, and he wasn't sure life would be worth living if he'd never know the ecstasy of holding Jo's warm, responsive and totally naked body in his arms. "How much time?"

"You can see my bedroom window from the bunk-house."

"I guess. I never checked."

"Well, take my word for it. You can. By eleven tonight everyone will be asleep."

"Not everyone."

"Everyone *else,* then. I'll turn my light out at ten-thirty. If I flash it twice at eleven, meet me at the barn. I'll bring a blanket."

"We're doing this outside?" Quinn got a quick picture of all sorts of creatures slithering around and decided he'd have to deal with it. "Hey, outside's fine. Outside's terrific. I love outside."

"I was thinking the hayloft."

That was only marginally better in Quinn's estimation, but he smiled, trying to demonstrate extreme confidence. "Fine. The hayloft it is. Sounds great. A roll in the hay. I'm there. I'm—"

"But if I don't flash my light twice, then that means I think it would be better if we stay with our original plan and not make love while you're here."

Quinn had temporarily forgotten that she hadn't com-mitted to the plan. The realization hit him like a medicine ball in the gut. "Oh." He was afraid he looked like an abandoned cocker spaniel as he gazed at her. This craving was turning him into a pathetic shadow of his former self. "Please flash."

"I still think we'd be making a terrible mistake, Quinn. You're thinking short-term."

"Very short. Like from now until eleven tonight. What if you fall asleep and forget?"

"No chance." She stood on tiptoe and brushed her lips across his. "Watch my window," she whispered. Then she eased out of his arms, retrieved her hat and headed in the direction of the house.

Quinn stood in the shadows and knew exactly how Samson must have felt when bewitched by Delilah. Marc Anthony when captivated by Cleopatra. A woman had never wielded this much power over him, had never turned him into a beggar.

He picked up the rope and walked away from the post. He could barely see it in the darkness, but that made his new technique easier. He hardly had to squint to mentally turn the post into Jo. *Rope me, and I'm yours for the night, cowboy.* He twirled the rope, let it sail and neatly roped the post.

SITTING ACROSS the table from Quinn and contemplating her decision regarding the evening ahead, Jo could barely eat Emmy Lou's delicious pot roast. Quinn appeared to have no trouble, though.

"You sure seem to be enjoying your meal," Jo commented with some irritation as he forked up a second helping of meat. She thought it was highly unfair that nothing ever seemed to take away a man's appetite, while women's stomachs were affected by every little bit of stress.

"I love pot roast." He gave her a dazzling smile before tucking into the meal once again.

Emmy Lou beamed from the end of the table. "It's a pleasure to watch you eat, Quinn."

Fred snorted. "Why, I'm covered with goose bumps at the sight, myself."

"You are?" Benny stared at him. "I don't see nothin'."

"Oh, Fred, you're just jealous," Emmy Lou said, "because you can't put away food the way you used to when you were younger."

"Who says I can't?" Fred held out his plate. "I'll take another helping of that pot roast."

"I'm not serving you seconds." Emmy Lou pushed his plate aside. "You'll be up all night with heartburn and you know it."

Quinn glanced up in alarm. "Yeah, and the rodeo and dance are tomorrow. I'm sure we all need a good night's rest."

"Oh, we certainly do," Jo said, covering a smile with her hand.

"I damn well know what's happening tomorrow, and I'll have another helping, Emmy Lou." Fred thrust his plate in her direction again.

Emmy Lou rolled her eyes. "Okay, you stubborn old goat." She placed more meat and vegetables on his plate. "Don't blame me when you're walking the floor at three in the morning."

Quinn gripped Fred's arm. "You know, Fred, I'll bet that would taste even better for lunch."

Fred glared at him. "Listen here, greenhorn. I was eating Emmy Lou's pot roast while you were still in diapers, so don't be telling me the time of day when I can enjoy it. Now take your mitts off my arm."

"Well, I'll tell you what, my eyes were bigger than my stomach." Quinn pushed his plate away. "I'm stuffed. Couldn't eat another bite. Just one more mouthful and I'd have heartburn for sure. I'm saving this for lunch. And you know, Fred, if we put cellophane over our plates, we could heat them in the microwave and save Emmy Lou the trouble of making us lunch tomorrow before we leave for the rodeo. What do you think of that?''

Fred shrugged. ''Suit yourself. Emmy Lou knows she don't have to bother about my lunch if she's too tired. I'm capable of building a sandwich.''

''Is that a fact?'' Emmy Lou gazed at him. ''I'm glad you told me, Fred. And when was the last time you built yourself a sandwich? When Nixon was president?''

Fred looked down the table and winked at her. ''I do believe Johnson was in the White House at the time. Now if you'll excuse me, I have a meal to eat.''

Now that she understood the true nature of it, Jo was fascinated by Fred and Emmy Lou's relationship, which could turn from gruff to lighthearted in a split second. She assumed that was the mark of an enduring partnership, but she'd never been around a couple who'd had such a long and apparently loving association. She hadn't known either set of grandparents well, and Aunt Josephine had stayed single all her life.

How sweet it would be to know someone that well, she thought with a pang of longing. Irrationally she thought of Quinn, the man she was destined to know for less than a week. Funny, but he was exactly the sort of man she could imagine creating a long-term partnership with. She could picture them thirty or forty years from now, sparring with each other the way Emmy Lou and Fred did, with a deep respect and love underlying every teasing word.

Love. Oh, my God. Jo glanced quickly at Quinn, as if he might have been able to read her thoughts. She couldn't love him. She hadn't known him long enough. She'd never met his family, his friends. She didn't know if he had a dog, or maybe a cat, or precisely what he did for a living, except that it had to do with money, a subject that had always confused her.

Of course she hadn't been thinking that she *did* love him, only that she *could* love him, in some other circumstance, after they'd become friends and spent lots of time in each other's company—years, maybe. Love was a tricky emotion. She'd talked herself into loving Dick, and that hadn't worked at all.

Now it seemed she was talking herself out of loving Quinn. She hoped that worked a little better. Quinn was definitely the wrong man for her to fall in love with, unless she wanted to give up her ranch and send Emmy Lou, Fred and Benny into the street. Good thing she'd had this little mental chat with herself, so she didn't allow her heart to do something really, really stupid.

"Who wants dessert?" Emmy Lou asked.

Quinn patted his flat stomach. "Couldn't possibly."

"What is it?" Benny asked.

"Cherry cobbler."

"I'll have some," Fred said, finishing the last of his pot roast. "Warm, with ice cream on top."

Emmy Lou shook her head. "Frederick, I do hope you have a good book to read, because you aren't going to be doing any sleeping tonight."

"Ah, I'll sleep like a baby," Fred said.

"Babies wake up constantly," Emmy Lou replied.

"I could run into town for some sleeping pills," Quinn said. "Or those tablets that fizz, or maybe that pink stuff that coats your stomach, or maybe it's white. I don't know. I'll buy it all. Whatever you need. I think sleep is important. Very important."

Fred gazed at him. "You seem mighty interested in getting me to sleep tonight. Any particular reason?"

Quinn reddened. "Just looking after your health, Fred."

Fred nodded, but there was a gleam of mischief in his eyes. "That's what I thought."

11

AFTER DINNER Jo excused herself from the table and headed for her study to figure out which bills she should pay and which ones she could stuff back in the shoe box. She'd never completely understood Josephine's bookkeeping system, so she'd come up with one of her own, but even she had to admit it wasn't adequate. She should have stuck with those accounting classes, but it was a little late to worry about that now.

The process of bill paying always left her stomach in knots, but it was her responsibility. After an hour of figuring and refiguring, she kept coming to the same conclusion. She needed some quick cash, and one of her best mares had produced an outstanding foal. She had to sell Clarise and Stud-muffin.

She wrote down the decision so it felt irreversible. Sherry, the vet who was coming out early the next morning to inseminate the mares with Sir Lust-a-Lot's sperm, had mentioned she had a buyer for Clarise once she'd foaled successfully. Sherry knew Jo's financial problems well—the vet had let bills slide many times in the past. Keeping Clarise and Stud-muffin was selfish and financially irresponsible, Jo decided, and she couldn't afford either behavior.

With the decision made she got up from her desk and paced the small room while she tried to come to grips with losing one of her favorite mares. Aunt Josephine had taught her not to get sentimentally attached to the cattle, but even tough-minded Josephine had hated selling a horse, including the ones who misbehaved or who were too old and swaybacked to carry a rider.

Someone tapped on her study door. Drawing an unsteady breath, she walked over and opened it.

Quinn took one look at her and reached out a hand to cup her cheek. "What is it?"

She forced a smile. "Nothing. Ranch business."

He combed her hair over her ear. "I thought you were probably in here wrestling with your finances. I wish you'd be willing to discuss the situation with me."

"I did." Her emotions lay close to the surface, and his gentle touch threatened to bring tears. She stepped out of reach. "I told you I needed to stall Doobie until September, when I could make another payment on my loan."

He allowed his hand to fall to his side, and there was a flash of hurt in his eyes. "I'm sure there's more to the problem than that." His glance flicked to the shoe box. "If you'd tell me what's going on, I might be able to help you work through it."

"Quinn, you can't be my financial adviser, even if I wanted you to, which I don't. You're leaving on Sunday."

"So what?" He motioned toward the telephone sitting on her desk. "That's the connection I have with my clients, for the most part."

She stared at him for several seconds. Then she lowered her voice. "Quinn, you can't have it both ways. You can't beg me to make love to you one minute and offer to provide long-distance financial counseling the next. The two just don't go together."

He studied her. Finally he shook his head. "You're right, dammit. If we make love tonight—"

"Shh." Jo glanced into the hall before pulling him inside the room and closing the door. "For heaven's sake. It's an old house. The walls have ears."

"Then let's stop talking." He pulled her into his arms and kissed her thoroughly. "Mmm. That's better," he said, lifting his head.

Well, at least he'd taken her mind off her troubles, she thought as warmth surged through her. "Are you..." She stopped to catch her breath. His kisses packed a wallop. "Are you trying to influence my eleven o'clock decision?"

He studied her face for several long seconds. "I don't know what I'm doing."

"Could have fooled me."

"I came in here to see if I could help you with your books."

She wound her arms around his waist and fit herself against the jut of his obvious erection. "Uh-huh."

"Honest. And now you tell me the only way I can possibly help is if we don't make love tonight." He stroked her cheeks with his thumbs. "You sure know how to hurt a guy."

"I don't want you to help me with the books." But he could help her forget that she'd soon be selling Clarise and Stud-muffin.

"You should want me to. I'm very good at it."

"Yeah, well, maybe I'm more interested in finding out what else you're very good at." She rubbed sensuously against him and kissed the hollow of his throat. What she'd never admit to him was that she was embarrassed to have him look at her books and discover they were in total disarray. A professional like Quinn would probably go into shock if he could see the mess she'd made. She'd rather shock a stranger, if it came to that.

No, she didn't want Quinn's financial advice, but if she'd allow him to, Quinn could certainly get her through this rough patch. By impersonating Hastings, he was postponing her financial crisis, and by making wonderful love to her he could make her forget her worries, at least for a little while, and that was worth quite a bit.

Quinn groaned. "Damn, but you make it tough to be noble." He took her by the shoulders and gently pushed her away. "But I'm going to give it a shot. Show me your ledgers."

She couldn't admit that she wasn't sure what ledgers were, exactly, so she reached for the top button of her blouse. "I'd much rather show you my—"

"No." He gripped her hand and closed his eyes. "I can't believe I'm stopping you from unbuttoning your blouse. I must be out of my mind." He held her hand tighter and opened his eyes to gaze at her intently. "Jo, this is for your own good. Forget sex."

"Have you been drinking?"

"Not yet. I may start on Fred's rotgut after this conversation. Listen, forget everything I said to you out in the corral. Think about your commitment to the ranch. I can help you keep that commitment. Use my services. Please." He released her hand and stepped away from her. Although a muscle in his jaw twitched as if the effort was costing him, he kept his arms at his sides.

He was magnificent, she thought. As much as he wanted her, he'd deny himself in order to help her achieve her goals. "Why are you doing this?" she murmured.

For a moment he looked confused. "Because I—because that's the best thing for you."

"But not for you," she said softly.

"My needs aren't as important as yours right now."

She wondered if he knew he was falling in love with her. Just as she was falling in love with him. Their relationship would be short and intense, but at least it would exist. She wasn't going to squander this chance at a moment of happiness for the possibility of straightening out some dry old ledgers, if she even had ledgers, which she doubted.

She took a long, shaky breath. "I absolutely refuse to allow you to get involved in my financial affairs," she said.

"Jo, don't—"

"But I'm looking forward to our brief but significant love affair. Never mind all that signaling nonsense. I'll be at the barn at eleven with a blanket. Now go on out to the bunkhouse before Emmy Lou begins to wonder what we're doing in here so long with the door closed."

He shook his head, but his ragged breathing indicated he was greatly tempted by her offer in spite of his noble intentions. "You're making a mistake. Please reconsider."

She shook her head. "You don't have to show up at the barn, though, if it would compromise your principles."

His laugh was dry as he gazed at her with fire in his eyes. "Sweetheart, I'm not that strong. I'll be there."

QUINN didn't intend to give up the idea of helping Jo create a workable financial plan before he left. But obviously the straightforward approach wasn't going to work. He'd have to be more devious.

He walked into the bunkhouse to find Benny and Fred playing a game of what Quinn used to call War when he was a kid. It was a simple game, the kind Benny could probably understand, and Quinn thought it was decent of Fred to play it with him.

Fred glanced up. "Hey, Quinn."

"Hey, Fred."

"Hi, Mr. Hastings," Benny said before returning his attention to the game.

Quinn decided not to correct Benny about his name. Instead he faked a huge yawn. Yawns were supposed to be contagious. "Aren't you guys tired?"

Benny yawned, right on cue. "Guess so. You tired, Fred?"

"Nope." He glanced at Quinn. "Go on to bed if you want. We'll be quiet."

"Okay, believe I will."

"I'm going to bed, too," Benny said.

Fred shrugged. "Okay. I'll play solitaire."

One down and one to go, Quinn thought as he sat on the bunk assigned to him and pulled off his borrowed boots. The bunkhouse reminded Quinn of the cabin he'd been assigned to at Camp Washogee twenty years ago. He experienced no nostalgia—for a kid who hated wiggly things, summer camp had been a nightmare.

The metal beds looked exactly the same as the ones at camp. There were four of them lined up against opposing walls, two on a side. A scarred dresser topped by a mirror was against the end wall between the beds.

A table and four captain's chairs took up most of the opposite end of the bunkhouse, and a door in the far wall opened into a small bathroom. Nails driven into the walls held jackets, hats, a rope or two and a bridle Fred was repairing in his spare time.

Fred wasn't working on the bridle at the moment, Quinn noticed as he shucked his pants and shirt and pulled back the blanket on his bed. Fred's belt was undone, and the guy looked uncomfortable. Emmy Lou obviously knew Fred's digestive system well.

Quinn's stomach felt fine, but the rest of him was a little beat-up. He groaned softly as he climbed into bed. Between bruises and sore muscles, he could be pretty well crippled by tomorrow, especially considering the activity he had planned for tonight. He took off his watch and set it on the windowsill next to the bed, where he could see the time by turning his head. An hour and a half before he was supposed to meet Jo.

His groin tightened. In less than two hours, assuming he could sneak past Fred, he'd have Jo in his arms. He wondered what she'd wear to their rendezvous and if she'd bother with items like underwear. Underwear could be very erotic, but getting it off might take up valuable time. Quinn decided he'd rather she didn't wear any.

Maybe he wouldn't wear any, either, although you had to be damn careful with the zipper in a case like that. Too careful, come to think of it. He'd wear his briefs. Considering how much he wanted Jo, he'd be shaking like a leaf, and sure as the world, he'd get something important caught in the zipper.

Then he wondered if he should wear his hat to the barn. Of course he didn't *need* that Stetson on his head, considering it would be dark and he was planning to climb to the hayloft and make love all night. But in another way he did need the hat. Wearing it made him feel more like a cowboy, and damned if that didn't seem to add a certain something to his self-confidence.

He also liked the idea that he'd meet Jo looking like a seasoned ranch hand, a devil-may-care stud of a wrangler. Maybe he ached all over from today's activities, maybe he couldn't sit a horse like a pro or rope a wild bull yet, but he could project the image darn well when he put on that Stetson. He knew because he'd checked it out in a mirror.

Yeah, he'd wear the hat, maybe even keep it on while he took his other clothes off. He hoped Jo would keep her outfit simple. A pair of pull-on shorts and a T-shirt sounded perfect to him. He could strip those off in no time, leaving Jo lying on the blanket, waiting....

And then Quinn went cold. He had no condoms. He had no reason to expect Jo to be using any form of birth control, and besides, a stud didn't show up at the appointed place with no protection for his lover. Dammit, what to do? Benny wouldn't have any, but Fred...Fred might. But he couldn't ask. He'd have to snoop, and if he hit pay dirt, he'd have to swipe. Normally he wasn't a swiper, but this was an unusual situation.

"You asleep, Mr. Hastings?" Benny whispered from across the room.

"Not yet, Benny."

"I can't sleep from thinking about the movie."

Quinn sighed. "I don't think there will be a movie, so just relax and go to sleep, okay?"

"I think there will be a movie. And I want to be in it."

"Benny, I'd give up the idea if I were you. Chances are—"

"Will you promise me, if there is a movie, I'll get to be in it?"

Quinn hated to make a promise like that to a guy as trusting as Benny. What if the real Brian Hastings showed up some day? What if the damned movie actually got made? Dick and Doobie could go hang, but Quinn didn't want Benny to be disappointed. "I don't think I can make that kind of promise."

"Yes, you can. Jo did."

"She did?" Quinn thought about that for a minute. All along he'd been hoping that Hastings would come back and make the movie so Jo would get the money. Yet he suddenly pictured Hastings hanging out at the Bar None, interacting with Jo and granting her favors like giving Benny a part in the movie. If Jo was attracted to Quinn, who was a poor woman's version of Hastings, then she'd probably fall head over heels for the real thing. Quinn felt a little sick to his stomach imagining Hastings putting the moves on Jo. With a guy like that, it would probably be an automatic reaction to a beautiful woman.

"So can I be in it?" Benny asked again.

"I guess so," Quinn replied, feeling depressed. "If there is a movie."

"There will be," Benny said with complete confidence.

Quinn grimaced. Damn, he really wanted that movie to be filmed at the Bar None, for Jo's sake. Of course he did. This morning she'd insisted that looking at Hastings' bare butt hadn't been the reason she'd jumped Quinn's bones. Quinn wanted to believe her, but Hastings was America's sexiest leading man. *People* magazine had said so. Quinn wondered why every single thing that would be good for Jo turned out to be the worst thing that could happen to him.

"Night, night." Benny yawned. "Sleep tight."

"Thanks, Ben."

"Don't let the bugs bite," Benny added in a sleepy voice.

Quinn stiffened. "What bugs?"

Benny's reply was barely audible. "Dunno. People just say that." Soon afterward he began to snore.

Quinn lay rigid as a corpse and tried not to think about wolf spiders as big as his fist creeping under his bed, on his bed. Finally he cleared his throat. "Fred?" he called softly.

"Yeah, Quinn."

"You get many of those wolf spiders in here?"

Fred chuckled. "Ugly sons of bitches, ain't they?"

"I guess."

"That's how the creek got named, they say. Then the town after that. I picture some old prospector waking up in the middle of the night with one of those suckers sitting right by his nose. Musta scared the crap outta him."

Quinn swallowed. "Yeah, probably. I bet you don't see them much anymore, though. Like in the bunkhouse and stuff."

"Oh, sure, we do. This place was built in nineteen-ten, and it's not real tight. We get all kinds of critters in here. Last week it was a small rattlesnake."

"No kidding?" Quinn realized his voice had squeaked and deliberately lowered it. "That's interesting."

"You're turning into a regular chatterbox, aren't you, Quinn? I thought you said you was real tired."

"I am. Good night." Quinn didn't want to discuss critters with Fred anymore. He lay there wondering what he was doing surrounded by poisonous snakes and ugly bugs. In Manhattan he could swim with the sharks, or face a bear market without blinking. In Manhattan he could be a hero.

But Jo wasn't in Manhattan. She was in Montana, and so, for the moment, he had to do his best to be a hero in Montana.

He stared at his watch and willed Fred to go to sleep. Not only did he want to slip out of the bunkhouse so he could meet Jo, he also wanted to spend the night somewhere besides a place with cracks big enough to drive a truck through, or at least a herd of wolf spiders.

After what seemed like eternity squared, Fred began to snore in his chair. Quinn leaned over and checked the floor before swinging his feet down. He dressed in record time but left his boots off. He took the blanket off the spare bed and rolled it up before arranging it under his own blanket to approximate the bulk of a person lying in the bed. Then he padded to the dresser.

The top two drawers belonged to Fred. Quinn figured the top drawer was his best bet. He eased it open and felt cautiously among the socks, briefs and T-shirts. Nothing. Finally, in a back corner, his fingers closed over some foil packets.

He counted four. Decided to take two. If and when Fred discovered the loss, he might chalk it up to losing track of his inventory. Feeling like a seventeen-year-old raiding his dad's supply, Quinn shoved the condoms in his pocket with a little prayer that they were the right size.

There was just enough light from the lamp on the table

for him to see a shadowy version of himself in the rippled old mirror over the dresser. He put on his Stetson, gave it a rakish tilt and headed out carrying his boots. He would have given his best Armani suit for a flashlight.

JO CHANGED clothes eleven times between ten o'clock and ten forty-five. Quinn was probably used to fancy lingerie and soft little dresses that came undone with a quick pull on an invisible tie. At least that was the way Jo imagined a Manhattan woman dressed for a late-night meeting with a lover.

She didn't have anything like that. Cotton underwear made sense when you lived in jeans and Western shirts. In winter she wore thermal long johns, even less romantic. She had exactly two dresses, one full-skirted for dancing and the other a sedate linen thing that buttoned up to her neck. Neither of them qualified for a secret rendezvous.

Dammit, when Quinn looked back on this episode she didn't want him to think of it as the night he spent with the hayseed. She rummaged through all her drawers, tossing things on the bed. Then she went through her closet one more time, swishing hangers along the rod in her impatience. At the far end of the closet she found a box she couldn't remember putting there. She opened it and started to laugh. Perfect.

In an abortive attempt to put some romance into her relationship with Dick, she'd bought herself red silk boxers and a chemise. But before she'd had a chance to try them out, Fred had seen Dick kissing a waitress at the Ugly Bug Tavern and forced him to confess he was having an affair. Jo had filed for divorce and had forgotten all about the sexy outfit.

The silk felt good against her bare skin. She'd have to wear something over the outfit, of course, or she'd freeze to death walking to the barn. The slicker hanging by the front door would work. She stood in front of the mirror and admired herself in the red silk while she imagined Quinn's reaction. Her breath quickened.

Smoothing the material over her breasts, she closed her eyes. She craved his touch so desperately it scared her. Maybe meeting him tonight wasn't the wisest thing she'd ever done, but logic wasn't in charge at the moment. Deep in her heart she knew that if she didn't make love to him before he went back to New York she would regret it for the rest of her life.

She slipped on a pair of sneakers and picked up a folded quilt before creeping downstairs. As she made certain to avoid the steps that squeaked, she shivered as much from excitement as the chill in the air. The house was dark and quiet as she made her way to the front door and took down the slicker. She picked up the flashlight they kept on the entry hall table and reached for the knob of the front door.

As she started to turn it, she felt resistance, as if…as if someone was turning the knob from the other side.

Heart pounding, she stepped away from the door. Maybe Quinn had become impatient and decided to come to the house to get her. After the incident with Benny, he knew they didn't lock doors at the Bar None.

The door opened, but the man silhouetted by the glow from the porch light wasn't Quinn. He squinted in the darkness. "Jo, is that you?"

Jo pulled the slicker tight around her and swallowed. "Hi, there, Fred."

12

JO DIDN'T KNOW who was more embarrassed, she or Fred. She was glad the light wasn't very good, because she was sure her face was bright red. They both started a sentence of explanation at the same time, then stopped and stared at each other.

"I, uh, thought I'd get something for my upset stomach," Fred said, his usual bluster completely gone.

"I...wanted to go check on Betsy." It was a transparent fib. She'd checked on Betsy two hours ago, and the mare had shown no signs of going into labor. Fred knew that as well as she did.

But he nodded as if that was a brilliant idea. "Sure."

"There's...there's probably some of that pink stuff in the downstairs bathroom," Jo said.

"I figured." He glanced at the blanket. "How long you planning to, uh, spend time with Betsy?"

"Well, I wasn't sure." He probably knew what the blanket was for, she decided, but she wondered what he thought of her slicker. It wasn't raining. "A couple of hours?"

"Sounds about right."

"Then I guess I'll be getting on down there." She had no idea if Quinn would be waiting. With Fred prowling around, Quinn might have decided to stay put until the coast was clear.

"Yeah, might as well get on down there. Check on Betsy," Fred said.

"Fred, you're blocking the door."

"Oh!" He came all the way into the house, and they sashayed around each other in the narrow hallway like two people do-si-doing at a square dance.

"See ya," Jo said as she hurried out of the house.

"Yep." Fred closed the door quietly behind her.

Once she was headed down the porch steps, Jo began to grin. Shoot, those folks had probably been carrying on like this for years. Josephine might have known about it but couldn't find a good way to inform her young grand-niece. Jo wondered why they'd never made their romance public and gotten married.

But she could guess. Fred might enjoy having Emmy Lou nearby, and she no doubt felt the same, but Jo couldn't picture Fred becoming domesticated enough to live in the house, which would probably mean giving up his chewing tobacco and his occasional trips to the Ugly Bug Saloon.

Jo swept the ground with her flashlight, checking for snakes. She didn't expect to find any. The nights were still too cold for them to be out and about at eleven o'clock. Finding nothing, she started around the house toward the barn and glanced quickly at the entrance lit by a dusk-to-dawn light.

No Quinn.

Although Jo told herself he was probably waiting until he was sure Fred wouldn't see him, her self-confidence slipped a notch. Maybe he'd reconsidered and wasn't coming, after all. Or even more humiliating, maybe he'd fallen asleep, his ardor for her forgotten once his head touched the pillow. She'd rather be rejected outright than forgotten like some dentist's appointment.

The more she considered it, the less she liked the idea of hanging around the front of the barn for God knew how long before Quinn decided to show up, assuming he would show up and wasn't sawing logs at this very minute. Quinn wasn't following the script. He was supposed to be so excited that he'd arrive early. Eager and nervous, he would then pace back and forth until the appointed time. When he first glimpsed her, he'd rush to meet her, and she would drop the quilt and flashlight (gracefully) and run to meet him, except the moment would be drawn out in slow motion, with appropriate background music.

Instead Quinn was late. He would arrive, if he arrived at all, to see her standing in the unflattering glare of the dusk-to-dawn light wearing her yellow slicker and clutching an old quilt. She probably looked like a refugee. Or a flasher.

On impulse she stepped into the shade of a large oak. When she saw him coming, she could hurry forward as if she'd just arrived, as if she'd lost track of the time and had suddenly realized that it was past eleven. Yes, that was a good line. She'd say she'd been reading a wonderful book and hadn't realized how late it was. That should put Mr. Quinn Monroe in his place.

Assuming he showed up at all.

If not she'd have to stay here for two hours because she'd subtly promised Fred she wouldn't interrupt him and Emmy Lou any sooner than that. From Jo's perspective Fred and Emmy Lou had the ideal relationship. It sure beat marriage, from what Jo had seen of that institution. She envied their comfortable, no-strings arrangement. This standing out in the cold waiting for some guy to meet you was for the birds.

She used to play in this tree when she was a kid, she remembered. The trunk branched off about three feet from the ground, providing a crotch that was a perfect place to put your foot and heave yourself into the tree for a good climbing experience. The oak had leafed out in the past couple of weeks, and it provided dense enough shade to camouflage her until Quinn arrived or…he didn't. If the rat didn't show, she'd find some way to get revenge.

Strong arms came around her from behind, and she yelped. The quilt and flashlight plopped to the ground.

"How come you didn't come over to the front of the barn, where you said you'd be?" Quinn murmured in her ear as he pulled her hard against him.

"Because you were late!" she whispered hoarsely, her heart going like crazy. "I decided to wait here until you managed to get yourself out of the bunkhouse!"

"I wasn't late." He nibbled her earlobe as he held her tight and began unsnapping her slicker with one hand.

"Were so." Even through the slicker she could feel his erection pressing against her, rock hard and ready.

"Was not. I stayed in the shadows so there was no chance Fred would see me. I watched you coming toward me and decided I'd wait until you got right to the door of the barn before I showed myself, in case anyone was watching." His teeth raked the lobe of her ear as he slipped his hand inside her slicker. "Except for some reason you changed your mind and decided to hide under this tree. So I had to come and get you."

She gasped as he reached under the silk chemise and cupped her breast. Cool air touched her skin through the open slicker. She should suggest they go into the barn, but his hand felt so good she didn't want to move just yet. In a minute they could move. He kneaded her breast with his strong fingers. In another minute. "I...met Fred coming in the house as I went out," she said.

Quinn's breath was warm against her ear, his voice husky and deep. "And what did you tell him?" He rubbed his thumb back and forth across her nipple until the ache inside her became almost unbearable. Perhaps it was knowing that they would finally make love tonight that had touched some basic chord, making her vibrate so she could barely stand.

"I told him I was...oh, Quinn, I can't think when you do that."

"That's okay." He continued to knead her breast while he slid his other hand beneath the elastic of her boxers. His words rasped in the darkness. "I don't really care what you told Fred." Boldly he tunneled his fingers through her moist curls. "I just—" He caught his breath as he probed deeper.

She moaned and leaned back in his arms.

"Ah, Jo." He caressed her with a gentle, rhythmic motion that soon had her quivering. "You're drenched, sweetheart," he whispered. "Why did you hide from me?"

This was crazy, she thought, letting him touch her this way with only the darkness to conceal them. But for the life of her she couldn't ask him to stop.

He kissed her neck, then nipped playfully as he slowed his strokes, drawing out the exquisite pleasure. "Why, Jo?"

She could barely breathe as she reached for the summit. Almost there. Just a little more. "Playing it...cool."

"Oh."

She could feel his smile against her skin as he paused, his finger lightly touching her throbbing flash point. She thought she'd go crazy. "But I'm not cool," she said, her words a breathless plea.

"No?"

She trembled on the brink of ecstasy. "Quinn, have mercy. Do something."

"Like this?" He pushed deep and pressed down on that aching, needy spot with the heel of his hand.

Her world came apart, and the rest of the world would have known all about it if he hadn't taken his other hand from her breast and gently covered her mouth, muffling her cry of release. She arched in his arms as the quakes took hold of her. She felt tumbled about like a pebble in the rapids of a stream, and through it all Quinn held her, supported her, whispered sweetly in her ear.

At last she shuddered and was still, drooping in his arms as she gasped for breath. "Wow."

"Good?" His voice sounded hoarse.

"Oh, yeah."

He eased his hand out of her boxers and slowly turned her to face him, holding her firmly by her shoulders as if he realized without his strong grip she'd fall flat on the ground. "I'm glad."

She gazed at him. "I feel as if I've had too much to drink."

"I know the feeling. I'm pretty high myself."

"Yeah, but you're still standing. You may have to carry me to the barn."

He gave her a lopsided grin. "I'm not sure I can walk that far." He guided her a couple of steps backward until she felt the trunk of the oak against her back. "Let's rest a minute before we decide." He took off his Stetson, hung it on a nearby twig and leaned down and covered her mouth with his.

She didn't find his kiss at all restful. One thrust of his tongue and the ache began to build again as if he hadn't just given her the most dramatic climax of her life. She'd never experienced lovemaking like this. There seemed to be no quenching the fire inside. When she thought it had burned itself out, Quinn breathed the embers to life again.

His hands found their way under her chemise, cupping her breasts, coaxing her nipples to quivering tautness. Then he lifted his mouth from hers, pushed the chemise up and leaned down to draw one nipple into his mouth. Without the tree's support she would have definitely crumpled to the hard ground as he lavished her breasts with attention.

She was guilty of pulling the chemise higher, so it wouldn't flutter down and get in his way. And she arched her back to make it easier for him to do all those marvelous things with his mouth and tongue that she remembered from their session on the couch.

"Oh, Quinn, I want you so much," she cried softly.

"Undo my jeans," he murmured against her tongue-dampened breasts.

"Here?"

"Right here, sweetheart. I need your hands on me in the worst way."

She gasped as he resumed fondling her. "Then you'll have to stop...doing that."

She wondered if he'd heard her, but he must have, because eventually he kissed his way to her throat and nuzzled the sensitive skin beneath her ear as he continued to stroke her breasts.

"And that," she said breathlessly.

"What can I do?" He squeezed her breasts gently. "I want to touch you. I need to touch you."

She moaned with pleasure. "But I can't concentrate when you touch me. So stop. Just stand there."

With a husky sigh he drew back and braced his hands on the tree's two main branches.

Taking a long, shaky breath, she leaned forward and unfastened his belt with trembling hands. As she started to ease the zipper over his rigid shaft, she looked into his shadowed face, her heart pounding with anticipation. "You're sure you want me...to do this here?"

"Oh, yes."

"But—"

His voice was tight with desire. "No one can see. I wouldn't have known you were under this tree if I hadn't watched you slip back here. And I'll never make it to the barn, Jo. I'd wreck myself trying."

She unzipped his jeans carefully. His harsh breathing drowned out the crickets as she followed his lead and slid her hand beneath the elastic of his briefs. Her hand closed around enough warm, rigid male to make any woman very happy. Her body reacted with an intense, hollow ache and a rush of moisture.

She caressed him and he groaned, but it was muffled, as if he'd clenched his teeth to keep from crying out. That low, desperate sound made her heady with her own power to please. And the quilt was almost within reach. "Stay here."

"I couldn't move if you shoved a stick of dynamite up my—"

"I'll be right back." She released him, ducked under his arm, grabbed the folded quilt and dropped it at his feet. "There."

"What are you doing?"

"This." She knelt on the quilt and wrapped her fingers around his sizable erection once again. Damn, he was impressive. And he was all hers. When she took him into her mouth, a massive shudder went through him.

"Jo...I didn't mean...that you...oh, Lord." He began to quiver.

She lifted her head and gazed at him while she stroked his sensitive tip with her thumb. "Want me to stop?" She barely recognized her voice, which had become throaty and seductive.

He struggled for breath. "No."

"Good." She replaced her thumb with her tongue. The more she loved him, the more insistently her body demanded his presence deep inside her. She'd never felt this way, as if the world wouldn't make sense anymore unless she received that elemental connection with this particular man. Only with this man.

Quinn gasped and trembled. "Jo. Jo, stop now. Please."

She took her time about releasing him and gave him one last sensuous stroke before rising to her feet. "I need you now," she said, her voice thick with longing. "Right here, right now. On the quilt, in the dirt, I don't care. Now, Quinn."

His laugh was shaky. "I hate it when you're indecisive. Get off the quilt a minute."

She stepped aside, and he picked up the quilt. She thought he'd spread it on the ground and pull her down with him, but instead he kept it folded and settled it into the crotch of the tree. Excitement rose in her, hot and wild.

He turned to her and guided her close to the tree. Then he slipped his thumbs under the elastic of her silk boxers. "I like these," he murmured, tugging them down. "But they gotta go."

Impatient and aching, she started to help him.

He pushed her hands away. "Oh, no. My job."

He went to his knees in front of her as he pulled the boxers down. He kissed her navel, flicking his tongue inside the indentation. Need shot through her, and she cried out.

"Shh," he whispered, drawing her boxers over her knees as he kissed her damp curls.

She could barely breathe from the pressure of wanting him, yet he was moving at a snail's pace. "Are you…going to make a big…production out of taking those off?" she asked.

"Yep." Steadying her with one hand, he grasped her ankle and lifted, so that she stepped out of one leg of the boxers. Then, before she quite realized his purpose, he'd cupped her behind and tilted her pelvis so that he could give her a very intimate kiss indeed.

She gasped, and her knees buckled as pleasure surged through her. She felt the quilt brush the small of her back. Trembling, she leaned weakly against the padded crotch of the tree as he had his way with her. She was helpless against the onslaught of his tongue as he urged her pulsing, tightening body to enjoy, enjoy, enjoy.

Gripping the rough branch arching beside her, she pressed the back of her other hand to her mouth as the explosion came, rocking her against the tree. Her muffled cry sounded like the keening of a wild creature—the wild creature he had set loose within her.

And she wanted him still. Even as the shock waves continued, she wanted him. She took her hand from her mouth. Her plea was choked with emotion, but he couldn't possibly mistake what she needed.

He didn't.

He eased her gently against the tree and steadied her with one hand as he reached in his pocket. She made a real effort and managed to stay upright when he released her so he could put on the condom. Slipping it over his erection, he made a noise low in his throat, as if even that contact challenged his control.

Then he was back, his hands under her bottom, lifting her to the wide crotch of the tree, holding her there. She braced her hands against the outstretched branches, leaned into the cradle of his cupped hands and opened her thighs.

With her slicker draped protectively around them, he stepped closer and probed gently, his breathing ragged. "Don't let me hurt you."

She moaned in frustration. "I want all of you, Quinn. Every last rigid inch."

He eased inside a little more. "Okay?"

Oh, he was big, but she wanted big. She wanted to be filled, at long last, with everything this man had to offer. She panted with need. "Not enough."

He pushed slightly deeper.

"More," she whispered.

He gave her a fraction more, but he was obviously holding back, obviously had a hangup about being too big.

"Oh, Quinn." In one swift motion she wrapped her legs around his hips and pulled him in tight. "Oh, *Quinn.*"

Apparently he couldn't control his growl of satisfaction, but then he went right back to being the soul of concern, although his voice was a little rough around the edges. "I'm hurting you."

"That was not hurt you heard in my voice," she said breathlessly. "That was heaven. My body is singing, Quinn, singing the praises of your big beautiful—"

"Okay. I get it." He covered her mouth with his.

His kiss might be all it would take, she thought, her heart pounding as he explored thoroughly with his tongue while still locked against her. He might not have to move that astounding equipment at all, since it filled her so totally, making contact in all the right places.

Then he began to move, and she decided moving might be a good thing. Moving might be a great thing. Moving might be a really spectacular thing.

He lifted his mouth from hers. "Ah, Jo. I've never…this is so good."

"So very good." She absorbed another soul-filling moment as he buried himself deep, eased back and pushed home again.

"As if this is what we're meant for." He nibbled at her lower lip.

"Oh, yes." She welcomed another thrust, treasuring each and every one.

"We fit." He kissed her chin, the hollow of her throat, all the while holding her steady as he eased his hips back and forth, bringing her joy with every stroke.

"Like a sword in a sheath." The quickening that had started with the first glorious full contact had intensified with each rhythmic motion. She wanted it to last forever, but knew they had only seconds to go, knew from the subtle way Quinn increased the pace, the slight change in his breathing.

Faster still. Exquisite friction. So right. There. Yes. Now. Quinn. Oh, Quinn. Love me. Love me, love me, love me.

He kissed her hard, forcing the cry into her throat, smothering the groan rumbling from his chest. Holding her tight and deeply impaled, he absorbed her convulsions and drank her whimpers of delight until his own release gripped him.

For the first time in her life, she felt the joy of another's climax as if it were her own. And as he shuddered helplessly in her arms, gasping her name, she knew that no matter how much heartbreak it brought her, she would never regret this night of loving Quinn.

13

QUINN had decided to make love this way because he'd figured that lying on the ground was just asking for interference from snakes and bugs. However, the experience had turned out to be much better than he could have imagined. He'd go so far as to say he'd never known anything to equal making love propped against an oak tree on a chilly spring night in Montana.

With Jo, he quickly added. Jo, the most perfect sexual partner he'd ever known. The funniest, sweetest, sexiest woman he'd ever known. He kissed her eyes, her cheeks, her hair. Gathering her close, he savored the recent ecstasy of being enclosed by her warmth.

If this wasn't love, then he didn't understand what love was all about. He not only wanted to spend the rest of the night with her, he wanted to spend days, months, years with her. "Maybe I could dye my hair blond," he murmured, nestling her head against his shoulder.

"What?" She roused herself and stared at him. "Quinn, you make love like no man I've ever known, but your after-the-loving conversation needs work. This is not the time to discuss hair treatments."

He chuckled, and as he gazed at her he felt as if someone had poured warm melted butter over his heart. Yeah, he probably loved her, loved her strong enough to last clear into doddering old age. "Or I could shave my head. That's popular these days."

"I'm not wild about that look, if you're really determined to discuss this now. And blond won't go with your skin tones as well as dark brown does. What's this about?''

"I'm trying to figure out how I could sneak back to see you again after I leave town. I think the blond hair would work. And maybe a mustache and glasses.''

She cupped his face in both hands. ''Let's just tell everybody you're not Hastings.''

"No. I can't let you do that.''

"Well, I can't let you dye your hair. Your friends and clients would wonder what on earth was going on. I don't want to be responsible for making you look dumb in front of everybody. Let's tell.''

"No. I'll dye my hair.''

"No.'' She combed her fingers through his hair. ''I love it this color. That's partly what makes your eyes look so incredibly blue—your skin is a nice bronze color.'' Her voice grew soft and wispy. ''The contrast is wonderful,'' she murmured, drawing him down to her waiting lips.

Incredibly he began to get hard again. He deepened the kiss and kneaded Jo's firm bottom, just to see where that would take him. Sure enough, it took him right back to where he'd been when he'd first lifted her to the perfect level for this activity. Maybe it was the wildness of making love to a woman sitting in the crotch of a tree that was causing him to feel randy as a seventeen-year-old who'd just lost his virginity. Or maybe it was simply Jo, the scent of her, the taste of her, the feel of her.

And judging from the way her breathing had changed and the hungry way she opened her mouth to his kiss, she also wanted him again, and that was another small miracle. Heart soaring, he gave thanks for his foresight and prepared to enter paradise a second time. How he loved the supple feel of her muscles beneath his palms as she moved in response to his thrusts.

He longed to see her face, but even though he lifted his head to gaze at her, the shadows were too deep. ''I wish I could look into your eyes,'' he murmured, his voice already rough and trembling, his climax hovering near.

"Do you?"

"Yes." He heard the quiver in her voice and knew she was on the edge, too. How quickly they could excite each other. Like lightning.

"Why?"

"Because." He pushed in again, listening for the catch in her breath that meant she was ready. When it came, he slowed, wanting to draw the moment out this time. "I want to see how your eyes change when you're close, like now."

"Are you…?"

"Yes." He drew back ever so slowly and slipped in with practically no force at all. Easy, easy. "Very close."

She trembled in his grip. "I want to see your eyes, too."

"It's too dark." He held back, but even his lazy strokes were going to get them there very soon, no matter how much he wanted to draw out the process.

"I know how your eyes look." She gasped as a tremor shook her. "Like blue flames."

"And yours are like warm chocolate." She was there, and he couldn't keep himself from going with her, moving faster, pushing deeper, trying to touch that part of her that would make her his. "So rich…so hot."

"Quinn." His name was a moan on her lips. "Kiss me, or the world will hear how I feel right now."

He took her mouth with some regret. Maybe the world shouldn't hear just yet, but he'd like to. When he carried her once more into the whirlwind, he wished he could listen as she moaned and cried out his name. He wanted all the sounds he'd helped create as she trembled in his arms.

Because those sounds might include the words, "I love you."

JO CLUNG to Quinn for many long moments, savoring the closeness and the incredible pleasure. But at last he eased back and lifted her gently to the ground. She leaned against the tree, feeling weak and just the slightest bit bowlegged, while he turned and got himself together.

When he turned back to her, he had picked up her silk boxers from the ground. "Want some help putting these on?" he said with a smile in his voice.

Incredibly, considering all she'd experienced, a shiver of desire went through her. "No, thank you." She took the boxers from him and put them on. If she let him help, he might begin to think she was insatiable. Which she might be, but she still didn't want him thinking she was. Besides, as it was she'd have trouble sitting a horse tomorrow. Much more of Quinn's loving and she'd be crippled. Happy, but crippled.

"Stay there," he said. "I think I heard Fred leave the house. I'll go make sure." Quinn left the shadow of the tree and crept around the house.

Once he was no longer holding her, kissing her, making her forget everything but his loving, she had the unwelcome chance to think about their situation. He sounded really serious about disguising himself so he could come back and see her. The trouble was, she didn't want him to be an occasional visitor, she wanted him to be a full-time, old-fashioned husband. There, she'd finally admitted it to herself.

She loved him, and not only because he was, as the saying went, hung like a horse. That was a nice bonus, but she'd fallen in love before she discovered that pleasant reality. She'd fallen in love with his courage, his generosity and his sense of fun. To have him drop in once in a while would break her heart.

It could very well break his, too. The man she loved wouldn't be happy with that arrangement for long, but he was an investment banker, not a cowboy. He might want her, in fact he obviously wanted her very much, but he didn't want this life-style full of creepy-crawlies, belligerent horses and saddle sores. She couldn't ask him to sacrifice his career to live with her in Montana, but if she didn't cut their relationship off right now, he might get in deep enough to consider such a move only to regret it later. She hated the thought of hurting him, but it was the only way.

Quinn walked to the tree. "He's gone back to the bunkhouse," he said. "The coast is clear." He slipped his arms beneath her slicker and pulled her close, resting his cheek against the top of her head. "But I don't want to let you go. Listen, maybe I could use colored contacts and glasses. And a beard."

She drew back and gazed at him. Maybe it was just as well she couldn't see his face in the darkness. That made it easier to say what must be said. "Forget the disguise idea, Quinn. It wouldn't work."

"That's what you think. You'd be amazed what facial hair can—"

"No, I mean it wouldn't work for me. I don't know if I'll ever find another man to love, but if I do, he needs to be somebody who belongs in this country, somebody I can share ranch life with. If you keep showing up, I'll naturally keep wanting you, but you belong in New York, not out on some remote Montana ranch. We both need to cut our losses, Quinn."

He gasped and stepped back as if she'd slapped him. He seemed to struggle with his breathing for a moment, and then he finally spoke. "Okay, if that's the way you see it." His voice was raw with hurt. "I guess I thought we'd created something worth hanging on to."

"I will hang on to it," she said softly. "I'll never forget this night as long as I live."

"But you never want another one?"

She braced herself against his agonized plea. "Not when it means I have to keep watching you head to New York when it's over. And you have to do that, Quinn. We both know it. That's what you're trained for, what you're used to."

He turned away from her. "Yeah. That's me. Wall Street or bust."

She touched his arm. "Please understand how much you mean to me. How much what we've shared means to me."

"Yeah." His voice was thick with sorrow.

Oh, God. If Quinn started getting emotional, so would she. She'd be bawling her eyes out in a minute if she didn't get out of there. "I'd better get back to the house."

"Okay."

She gave his arm one last squeeze, grabbed the blanket and ran to the house. The quick movement told her she would indeed be very sore tomorrow. But it would be nothing to equal the pain in her heart.

QUINN STOOD in the shadows feeling as if somebody had come after him with a bullwhip. He knew he wasn't much of a cowboy, but she didn't have to be so brutal about it. Apparently he was so bad that she never even considered he might someday be of use on this ranch. She thought he was so hopeless that even she and Fred couldn't teach him enough to make his sorry ass worth something around here.

Nope, she was sending him right back to New York where he belonged. And she would look for a real cowboy. Like Hastings. Quinn gritted his teeth. He'd never met Hastings, and the guy was probably a decent human being, but Quinn was really beginning to hate the bastard.

He started to the bunkhouse and tripped over something. He picked up the flashlight she'd dropped when he'd grabbed her from behind. Damn, but her breasts were silky, and her...no. He couldn't think about any of that or he'd go crazy.

He glanced at the flashlight and remembered seeing it on the table in the hallway. Maybe he should quietly return it so it wouldn't become a topic of discussion. Tomorrow would be weird enough without having to explain the mysterious roving flashlight.

When he reached the porch he took off his boots so he

wouldn't make noise. The unlocked door still amazed him, but with all the nocturnal comings and goings around the place, a key would be a nuisance. And he supposed being surrounded by all these acres of rangeland kept the threat of crime very low.

He stood in the darkened entryway and battled temptation. Despite what Jo had said, if he went up those stairs and climbed into her bed, she wouldn't refuse him. He might be out of condoms, but there were plenty of other ways to find mutual satisfaction, and his hunger for her still raged. But that plan wouldn't come to pass as long as he had a shred of pride left.

He started to set the flashlight on the small table by the door when another thought occurred to him. He had a flashlight, so he wouldn't have to turn on a lamp and risk having Fred or Benny notice it. Okay, so he wasn't a cowboy, but he was a hell of a good hand with figures. If Jo didn't lock her front door she sure as hell didn't lock her desk.

He had a few hours before daybreak. It might be enough time to work some magic with Jo's books.

QUINN DIDN'T show up for breakfast, which was fine with Jo. Despite the open kitchen window that Emmy Lou had raised to let in a warm spring breeze, the air was thick with tension as Emmy Lou and Fred exchanged looks, and Benny, clueless, chattered away about the day's events. Finally Fred suggested that Benny go polish the tack in preparation for the rodeo, and Benny breezed happily off to do his chores.

"I'll be getting down to the barn, myself." Jo pushed back her chair. "Sherry will be here for the insemination any minute." She'd never blushed when she'd talked about such matters before, but she blushed now. Dammit.

"Hold on a second, Jo," Fred said.

Jo sat down. "Listen, if it's about last night, that's none of my business. I'm happy for both of you. I—"

"It's about last night." Emmy Lou cradled her mug of

coffee. "But not what you think. We're not kids, and we won't ask for your permission. If our behavior isn't to your liking, then we'll hire on somewhere else, right, Fred?"

Fred stared at her. "You'd leave this place on account of me?"

"Amazing, isn't it?" Emmy Lou grinned. "Don't let it go to your head."

"I just never thought..." He shook his head, a smile lifting the corners of his gray mustache.

"We were going to broach another subject, weren't we, Fred?" Emmy Lou prompted.

"Yeah." Fred hunkered over his coffee. "Yeah, we were. Jo, you know we didn't think much of Dick."

Emmy Lou cleared her throat. "Except to imagine him swinging by his—"

"Em." Fred sent her a look of warning.

"I'll bet Jo's thought of that, too," Emmy Lou said a touch defensively.

"I have."

"Anyway," Fred continued, "we think you should hang on to this one."

"This one?"

"The greenhorn," Fred said. "He has heart, Jo. More'n Dick ever dreamed of. I know he can't ride a lick or rope worth a damn, but he's got guts, and that's what counts. We could teach him—at least, I think we could. He's not real talented, but he's determined. And I have to say I was impressed because he had sense enough to...uh, use protection last night." Fred gulped his coffee and choked.

Emmy Lou pounded on Fred's back while Jo sat there getting very red and wondering how Fred could possibly know such an intimate thing. Surely Quinn hadn't left evidence lying around.

Once Fred calmed down, Emmy Lou glanced at Jo. "Quinn borrowed from Fred's supply," she said gently. "Fred noticed because he was down to four, and two were missing."

"Oh, my God." Jo buried her face in her hands. "I can't believe I'm having this discussion with you two."

Fred still sounded a little wheezy, but he seemed to want to get his message across. "It ain't always easy to talk about. But Emmy Lou and me saw you make one mistake by takin' up with Dick, and we don't want to see you make another one by lettin' the greenhorn go."

Tears pushed at the back of Jo's eyes. "That's the sweetest, most considerate and wonderfully protective attitude, and I thank you both. But there's a tiny problem. Quinn doesn't want to live here and be a cowboy."

Fred looked astonished. "Why not?"

"Because he's a New York investment banker. He chose that, the same way you chose to work on ranches. He wouldn't mind coming to see me once in a while, but he's not interested in moving to the Bar None."

"He said that?" Fred scratched his head, still not comprehending.

"Not in those words, but it's very obvious. I think it's a bit too primitive for him."

"What's primitive?" Quinn asked from the doorway.

Jo glanced up and couldn't seem to remember what she'd been saying. He looked tired, but still gorgeous. Despite everything she'd told herself, she wanted to walk straight into his arms.

Fred stood. "I got business at the barn. Sherry'll be here soon."

"And I have to check on something in my garden," Emmy Lou said, leaving the table on Fred's heels. "There's coffee and toast and a few hash browns left. I'm sure Jo could scramble you some eggs." She hurried out of the room.

Quinn glanced after them as the front door closed. "I sure know how to clear a room."

"I need to get going, too." She pushed back her chair.

"Before you do, I have something to talk to you about."

"What?" Her heart began to pound. Maybe he wanted

to make some sacrifices so they could be together. She couldn't imagine how it would work, but then she didn't know exactly what investment bankers did. Maybe he could investment bank in Bozeman.

"Well, I—"

"Yo, Brian!" The shout came from the front yard.

Jo groaned. She did not feel like facing Dick this morning.

Quinn walked over to peer out the window. "He's riding a bike."

"You're kidding." Jo got up to look. Sure enough, Dick was riding back and forth in front of the porch on—Jo could hardly believe it—a pink girl's bike that was too small for him.

"Hey, Brian! Got a minute?" Dick called. "My heart rate's up, and I need to keep it elevated, buddy. It ain't time for my cooldown, or I'd stop riding and come on in. But I gotta talk to you."

"Coming!" Quinn called through the window. "I'd better go or he's liable to ride around out there forever."

"He might," Jo agreed. "He functions on about a sixth-grade level."

"Come with me?"

When he gave her that look she couldn't deny him anything. "Okay."

Quinn walked out on the porch, and Jo followed. "Nice bike, Dick," Quinn said.

"Found it at a garage sale. It'll do until the Nautilus equipment arrives."

"Nautilus?" Jo asked. "You're getting a home gym?"

"Sure am." Dick grinned at her as he pedaled across the yard, his knees sticking out awkwardly. "After people see me in this movie, I might be getting other offers. Gotta stay buff, you know. 'Course, I don't ride this thing where my men can see me."

"Of course not," Quinn said. "What's on your mind, Dick?"

"Me and Doobie got to thinkin'."

"There's a scary thought," Jo muttered.

"Yeah?" Quinn said. "About what?"

"We understand you can't be in the rodeo and all, on account of you being such a valuable property, but we figured it wouldn't hurt for you to lead off the grand parade."

Jo remembered Quinn's wild ride on Hyper and smelled disaster in the air. "Oh, you know, Dick, that's a wonderful idea, but Brian really shouldn't be on a horse right now."

"Why not?"

Jo thought quickly. "Well, he recently spent some time in the tropics and went swimming in questionable water that gave him a real bad case of jock itch."

"I'll do it," Quinn said, glaring at her. "I'm completely cured."

"Don't be a hero," she said, glaring back at him. "You know you're not a hundred percent."

"Close enough," Quinn said.

"You're sure?" Dick asked. "That's nasty stuff. I remember one time I got it, and I tell you, I scratched till I thought my—"

"I'll be fine," Quinn said. "Plan on me doing it."

"Great. Well, gotta get on down the road. Still got my lifting program to do. Until the Nautilus stuff comes I'm using a broomstick with a six-pack strapped on each end. Oh, and I drink a glass of raw eggs every morning."

Jo grimaced.

"Good idea," Quinn said.

"I thought so. See you." Dick pedaled off, humming the theme from *Rocky*.

Quinn gazed after him. "So you don't think I can ride well enough to lead the grand parade?"

"Maybe. Depending on the horse you choose. But you're taking a big chance, Quinn. I think you'd be better off if you—"

"Said my jock itch flared up again?" He sounded testy.

"I'm sorry. It was the first thing I thought of, and I couldn't very well say you were saddle sore, could I?"

"And what makes you think I am?"

"The way you walked out on this porch."

"You're walking with a certain amount of care yourself this morning," he said.

Her cheeks warmed.

"Will you be riding in this grand parade?" he asked.

"Yes. All of the contestants ride in it, and I always do the barrel racing event."

"Barrel racing, huh? And how will that feel after...last night?"

She couldn't look at him. "I admit that I'm a little tender."

"Then I guess we'll suffer together. Because I'm going to lead that grand parade regardless of my delicate condition."

"Okay, then I'd recommend riding Butternut. He's—"

"Thanks, but I'll pick my own horse."

Jo groaned. "Don't tell me."

"Yep. I'll be lookin' good. I'm riding Hyper."

14

HIS CROTCH hurt like hell. Quinn sat atop a restless Hyper at the entrance to the small rodeo arena outside Ugly Bug and wished he'd used the jock itch excuse, after all. But when Jo had automatically assumed he couldn't even lead a sedate little parade, he'd taken offense. He'd decided he had something to prove to her before he left on the red-eye tonight.

Besides, after watching people steer horses down Fifth Avenue during parades in New York City, he figured there was nothing to it. This would be even easier because it was contained inside a fence.

He hadn't counted on the fact that the leader had to carry an American flag big enough to wrap a body in. And he hadn't counted on wind.

Hyper jumped sideways with every snap and billow of the massive flag. And with each jump, Quinn was painfully reminded of his manly attributes. Jo was somewhere behind him in line, along with Benny, Dick and a bunch of other real cowboys and cowgirls. Mostly they'd behaved themselves, and only a couple had asked for autographs, which he'd politely postponed until after the parade. With luck he'd sprain his wrist in the next twenty minutes, because he'd never gotten around to practicing Hastings' signature.

The other residents of Ugly Bug, however, weren't behaving themselves. Whistling, stomping and calling out his name, or rather Hastings' name, they jammed the modest bleachers. Camera flashes popped constantly, even though it was the middle of the day. At least ten homemade signs waved in the crowd. The more conservative ones said things like Brian Hastings for President, or We Love You, Brian, but one held by a rowdy band of high-school-age girls was covered in huge lipstick kisses with red, glittery letters that spelled out Take Me, Brian! Take Me Now!

A couple of Western lawmen types had positioned themselves at either end of the bleachers. Quinn appreciated having them there, but if the mob decided to rush him, even Marshal Matt Dillon wouldn't be able to control this crowd.

Quinn swallowed. If he survived the parade, he was supposed to sit in a special section smack-dab in the center of those bleachers. The roped-off area already held Doobie and his tush-fixated wife, along with several other middle-aged couples. Jo had wangled a place in that section for Fred and Emmy Lou, thank God. Maybe they'd help protect him.

As Quinn waited for the gate to open, sweat dampened the black Western shirt with pearl buttons that Benny had insisted he wear. Benny had also donated his best black Stetson, and Fred had brought out silver spurs that winked in the sunlight. Hyper's coat shone like polished mahogany, and his mane and tail were braided with red ribbon. The horse looked great, just as Quinn had imagined. All Quinn had to do was stay on him.

A wizened old cowboy swung open the arena gate, and members of the Ugly Bug High School Band swung into a fast-paced march. Quinn mentally reviewed his instructions. Once around the arena, then straight up the middle to face the grandstands. The other riders would fan out on either side of him, forming a line facing the bleachers as the band played the national anthem. Then he'd lead the riders around to the exit. Taking a firm grip on the flag, he nudged Hyper in the ribs with Fred's silver spurs, and the crowd surged to its feet, applauding loudly.

With a piercing whinny, Hyper reared.

Quinn grabbed at the saddle horn with his free hand and

by some miracle hung on, but by the time Hyper's front feet hit the ground, the horse had the bit in his teeth.

Quinn felt the gelding's muscles bunch. "Whoa!" he yelled.

Hyper wasn't listening. He shot through the gate and in three strides was in a dead run. Quinn's hat sailed off, and he lost his stirrups, but he kept his grip on the flag, which streamed dramatically over his shoulder. The grandstands, filled with cheering people, passed in a blur, then passed in a blur again as Hyper turned the arena into his private racetrack.

As Quinn whizzed past the gate, the other riders waved their hats and whistled. Quinn would bet Jo wasn't whistling. And if Hyper kept up this merry-go-round much longer, she might even ride out and pull him to a stop. God, how humiliating.

"Whoa, dammit!" he yelled. He was afraid to let go of the saddle horn to pull back on the reins, and if he dropped the flag so he could grab the reins, then everyone would know he was involved in a major screwup instead of the dramatic flourish they were giving him credit for. Worse yet, they might begin to wonder if he was really Brian Hastings.

He tried to remember what Fred had taught him. Oh, yeah. Grip with your thighs. You could even steer with your thighs, assuming your thighs didn't feel as if somebody had set fire to them, which Quinn's pretty much did.

He gritted his teeth as he flashed by the stands again. Hyper was young and strong. He could probably run for quite a long time, especially when he had the impression he was being chased by an American flag. So Quinn couldn't hope the horse would get tired. And he definitely didn't want Jo to ride out and save him.

The only solution was to get the horse through the gate somehow. After that Hyper would probably continue to run, but maybe they'd get far enough away that Quinn could safely drop the flag and try to establish control. Then again, maybe he and Hyper would see a great deal of the Montana countryside together.

Quinn figured that if he shifted his weight and used his tortured thigh muscles, he might be able to get Hyper to swerve through the gate instead of sailing past it. Bracing himself against the pain, he started leaning and squeezing as Hyper went into the straightaway and headed in the direction of the gate. Twice before the horse had veered left and continued around the arena. Quinn vowed he wouldn't do it again.

Apparently Hyper didn't care where he ran as long as he could keep doing it. He stampeded right through the gate as riders waiting beside it scattered in front of his pounding hoofs. Ahead was the parking lot, and beyond that, open country.

Quinn hung on as Hyper veered headlong between rows of pickup trucks. Once out of the parking lot, Quinn figured he'd drop the flag and try to put an end to this wild ride. Then he heard hoofbeats behind him and looked over his shoulder. Sure enough, Jo was in hot pursuit, with Benny behind her. Maybe it was just as well, he thought. He was nearly at the edge of the lot, and he really didn't want to ride this nag all the way to Idaho.

As he faced forward again, a long white vehicle pulled across the empty space at the end of the lot. Quinn squinted, not quite believing what he saw. A limo? In Ugly Bug? Hyper didn't slow his pace as the limo stopped, blocking the horse's path.

Quinn dropped the flag and seized the reins in both hands. "Whoa, you sorry nag! Whoa, goddammit! You're gonna hit the car, you idiot horse!" When Hyper didn't respond, Quinn braced himself for one hell of a collision.

Instead, Hyper gathered himself and sailed gracefully over the limo. Unfortunately Quinn didn't make the trip with him. Falling sideways, he hit the roof of the limo and rolled down the windshield, coming to rest facedown on the hood.

In seconds, Jo was leaning over him. "Don't move! Did you hit your head? Where are you hurt? Oh, Quinn, speak to me!"

He was having trouble drawing a breath, but he was at least able to register the concern in her voice. Well, good. She cared for him a little. "Don't call me Quinn," he muttered. "I'm Brian Hastings."

"That's funny," said another voice. "So am I."

"NOT YET, you're not," Jo said, barely giving the man a glance as she leaned over Quinn, her chest tight with fear. So Brian Hastings was here. So what? "Talk to me, my darling. Does anything feel broken?"

"I don't think so. Where's Hyper?"

"Benny went after him."

"Boss, you need anything?" said the uniformed driver as he climbed out of the limo.

"Not right now, Sid," Hastings said. Then he turned to Jo. "What do you mean, *not yet?* I've been Brian Hastings ever since the studio changed my name from Bernard Hilzendeger. I made it legal ten years ago. Listen, do you want me to call 911?"

"Yes," said Jo.

"No," said Quinn. "I'm okay." He pushed himself slowly to his hands and knees. "But I dented the limo."

"It appears you did," Hastings said.

"Call 911," Jo said as she gazed into Quinn's beloved face. Fred had said the greenhorn had heart, and Fred sure knew what he was talking about. "He's in shock."

"No, don't call 911," Quinn said, looking at Hastings.

"My God." Hastings stared at Quinn. "It's like looking in a mirror."

"Don't you wish." Jo didn't spare the movie star a glance as she stroked Quinn's cheek. "I'm so sorry I put you through this, sweetheart. Please forgive me. I should have found a better way to raise the money than having you impersonate this guy. If you're seriously hurt I'll never forgive myself.''

"Hold it." Hastings frowned at Quinn. "You've been pretending to be me? Trading on my fame? Well, I hope you have a damned good lawyer, mister, because you have a lot more to worry about than a dented limo hood.''

Jo whirled toward him, glad to be able to focus her anger on someone besides herself. "Don't you dare threaten him! He nearly killed himself for me, and all because you wouldn't get off the dime!''

Hastings' square jaw dropped. "This is my fault?''

"It certainly is." She shook her finger in his handsome face. "Your advance man came by my ranch and was so enthusiastic he got my hopes up that you would actually use my ranch in your movie!''

Hastings adjusted his sunglasses. "Actually, I was thinking I'd—''

"But did you show up to close the deal?" Jo barreled on. "No, you did not. Well, you may have millions, but some of us struggle along from one payment to the next, trying to live the American dream, while our ex-husbands sabotage us at every turn.''

"But, you see, that's why I'm—''

"And then, when we finally find a decent guy who's willing to go that extra mile for us, willing to risk life and very attractive limb to make our dreams come true, along comes some millionaire movie star threatening to sue the pants off him!''

"And these aren't even my pants," Quinn added.

Hastings propped his hands on his hips and gazed at Quinn. Then he looked at Jo. "I still don't get it.''

Jo took a deep breath. "It's very simple. If my banker thought Brian Hastings was staying at my place, he'd assume the movie deal was on and that at some point in the future I'd be able to make a sizable payment on my loan so he wouldn't foreclose.''

"But then, if the movie never gets made…?''

"By this fall, especially if the price of beef goes up, I should be able to make a payment that will satisfy him."

"I have a couple of other ideas, too, Jo." Quinn climbed off the hood and came to stand beside her. "You don't have to sell Clarise and Stud-muffin. Instead you should shop around for a better insurance rate, for one thing. What you're paying is outrageous."

She turned to him, her eyes wide. "You snooped in my books?"

"Yeah, as a matter of fact, I did. I set up a basic book-keeping system you should have no trouble following, and in the process found some cost-saving—"

"I can't believe this!" Jo cringed at the thought that he'd seen the chaos of her financial affairs. "That is extremely private!"

"Dammit, Jo, it's my area of expertise. And I thought we'd arrived at a point where I could—"

"You think because of what happened in that tree you now have the right to invade my private financial records and make all sorts of recommendations? Well, let me tell you, Mr. Quinn Monroe, investment banker, that I—"

"Excuse me, Jo," Hastings said. "That is your name, right?"

"That's my name." Jo still glared at Quinn.

"Jo, I have a comment to make. I'm not sure what went on between you and this Hastings look-alike in the tree, but if he's willing to give you some free financial advice as a result, I suggest you take it. I hate to tell you what I pay my accountant, but it's worth every penny. I'm not good with numbers, and obviously, neither are you."

Jo lifted her chin. "I've been managing."

"Oh, yeah? Then what was that speech about the American dream and loan payments and sabotaging ex-husbands all about?"

"I got...carried away."

"Okay, but it's hard-won advice I'm passing out. And these guys hardly *ever* work for nothing. That tree experience must have been something else." Hastings folded his arms and glanced across the roof of the limo. "Here comes the horse you rode in on, Monroe."

Jo looked over to see Benny leading Hyper toward them. Then she glanced toward the arena and noticed a small contingent of people, led by Emmy Lou and Fred, coming toward them. She had to find a way to stall them until she figured out what to do.

Benny reined in his horse and stared at Quinn and Hastings. "Separated at birth," he said in an awed voice, shaking his head.

Jo hurried to him. "Not quite. Listen, Benny, I need you to do something for me. See Emmy Lou and Fred coming over here with all those people?"

Benny nodded.

"I want you to ride over and tell them that Brian Hastings has a big surprise planned, and everyone has to remain in their seats, or it will be ruined."

Benny frowned. "Okay. But the flag's on the ground."

Jo snatched it up, shook it off and handed it to him. Benny had always longed to carry that flag. "You take it back, Benny. You're the flag bearer and the messenger, okay? I'm counting on you."

Benny grinned. "You bet." He kicked his horse into a fast trot to make the flag ripple as he rode toward the approaching crowd, and Hyper followed docilely behind.

Jo heaved a sigh and turned to Quinn and Hastings. "Now, where were we?"

Hastings gazed at her. "I was about to ask if you want to negotiate the terms for my use of your ranch, or are you going to be smart and turn it over to Mr. Investment Banker, here?"

Jo's heartbeat quickened. "You really want the ranch?"

"Yep. I drove out there just now, and it's perfect. But nobody was home, so I came into town, saw all the commotion and decided to investigate."

Jo glanced from Hastings to Quinn. "That's great. Really

great. But we have this tiny problem.'' She looked at Hastings. ''People around here think Brian Hastings has already arrived.''

Hastings stroked his jaw and looked at Quinn. ''Think we could make the switch?''

''Maybe,'' Quinn said.

Jo shook her head. ''No way.''

''Why not?'' both men said at once.

''Because you really don't look anything alike,'' Jo said. ''Quinn's eyes are much bluer, and he's taller, and his shoulders are broader. His hair's thicker, and he's got that cute little freckle on his cheekbone, and everyone may not notice, but when he smiles, one of his eyeteeth is *slightly* crooked, which gives him a rakish air you can't get with caps.''

''I don't have caps,'' Hastings said stiffly. He glanced at Quinn. ''But maybe I need the name of your stylist. To be honest, I haven't been all that happy with Antoine recently.''

''My barber's in New York.''

''No problem. Maybe he'd like to relocate.''

Quinn's expression turned belligerent. ''If you're going to steal the first decent barber I've found in six years, I'm not telling you his name.''

''Guys. Could we get back on track? I don't think it will work to switch one of you for the other, so what else have we got?''

''We could say it was all a joke,'' Quinn said.

Jo looked doubtful. ''But you promised people parts in the movie.''

Hastings groaned. ''Oh, boy. Here we go. Not speaking parts, I hope?''

''No,'' Quinn said. ''I wasn't specific, except I told this one guy, Jo's banker, that he'd be perfect for this French character.''

Hastings shook his head. ''I'll get with the scriptwriters. The last thing I want is bad publicity because some local guy thought he'd be in the movie and he's not." He hesitated, as if afraid to ask the next question. "Did you...tell them what it was about?"

"No," Jo said.

"That's a relief."

"I only gave them the title," Quinn said.

"The title?"

"Yeah. *The Brunette Wore Spurs.*"

"Ye gods and little fishes. That's *awful.*"

Quinn looked hurt. "I sort of liked it."

Hastings gave him a disparaging look. "Which is why you're in investment banking and I'm in filmmaking. Okay, we can deal with that. I'll tell them we had some fun with that title, thought of turning this into a Mel Brooks type spoof, but the producers didn't think it would suit my image. You didn't know that when I sent you out to Ugly Bug."

"You sent me? Wait a minute, you didn't—"

"Work with me here, Monroe. I'm trying to get you out of trouble, sport. Now, picture this." Hastings glanced around to make sure they weren't being overheard. "I met you in New York. That's where you're from, right?"

"Yep."

Hastings nodded. "Good. I go there all the time. So I met you and noticed the striking resemblance." He sent Jo a challenging look, but she only shrugged. "I've been looking for a stand-in, so I asked you if you were interested. You agreed to give it a try, so I sent you to Ugly Bug as a test, to see if people would believe you were me. It worked. I'm ready to hire you."

"But I don't want the job."

"I'm not really offering you the job! Hell, you probably can't even act!" Hastings shook his head. "Damn, but bankers can be literal. So I offer you the job, you turn it down, and we go on from there. Do you love it?"

Quinn nodded. "It might work."

"Might work?" Hastings threw his hands in the air. "It's

brilliant! Improv at its finest! It's so hard to get any honest appreciation these days.''

"I appreciate it," Jo said. "You've just found a way to save my reputation in Ugly Bug. Thank you.''

"That reminds me," Hastings said. "Where'd that dumb name come from?''

"You don't even want to know," Quinn said.

"Maybe not. We're sure not using it in the script, that's for sure. I even hate to put it in the credits, but I guess we'll have to.'' Hastings motioned to the limo. "Shall we?''

Jo eyed the limo dubiously. "Where are we going?''

Hastings smiled his perfect smile. "Straight into the arena, my friends. If there's one thing Brian Hastings knows how to do, it's make an entrance.''

Jo glanced at Quinn. "You'll have to go some to top the last one.''

15

QUINN WATCHED Hastings maneuver his way through the rodeo festivities and the dance that evening, and by the end of it he had to admit Hastings was a hell of a guy. He handled crazed fans with a finesse Quinn envied, but of course he'd had plenty of practice. For the first time Quinn understood that being a star in the spotlight required boundless energy. Hastings was on the go constantly from the moment he stepped out of the limo in the middle of the rodeo arena to his late-night tour of the Bar None ranch buildings.

Quinn used the time Jo and Fred were showing Hastings around to change into his city clothes and lay his borrowed ones in a neat pile on his bunk. He hadn't told anyone about reserving a seat on the red-eye, figuring he'd make his goodbyes short and sweet when the time came. Finally he walked to the house, where a light shone from the kitchen window and he could see people gathered around Emmy Lou's table, probably swapping stories of the day and sampling one of her pies.

Quinn felt very sorry for himself. Not long ago he'd sat in that kitchen enjoying the same treatment Hastings was getting, being fed like a king and hailed as Jo's savior. Now she had a new hero. Come to think of it, she'd never really needed Quinn. Salvation had arrived only a few days after he was pressed into service. If Hastings hadn't turned out to be an understanding guy, Quinn's presence even might have ruined the movie deal. He'd been worse than useless—he'd been in the way.

At least he wouldn't make the mistake of hanging around. He walked up the steps to the porch just as Jo came out the front door.

"There you are! I've been wondering where you—" She paused and surveyed his outfit. "Why are you dressed like that?"

"I'm taking the red-eye, Jo."

"Tonight?" Her face paled. "You're leaving right now?"

He nodded. "I was coming in to say goodbye to everyone."

"I see." She swallowed. "Well, let me say, while we're out here by ourselves, that I'm very grateful for all you've done." She twisted her hands in front of her. "I can't...thank you enough."

Gratitude, he thought, was beggar's wages. He wanted love from her, not a polite thank-you. But she needed a cowboy to love. "It turns out I didn't do a damn thing. Hastings was on his way."

"We didn't know that. You stepped into the breach, Quinn. I'll never forget...that."

He figured she would forget it, and him, eventually. He wasn't part of her world and never could be. But standing here and not reaching for her, no matter how dumb the gesture would be, was the most difficult thing he'd ever done.

"I, um, guess you need to come in so you can get going," she said.

"Yeah." His voice was husky with sadness.

"I'll...I'll be right down. I need to...check on something." She turned and fled, letting the screen door bang after her as she ran upstairs.

With a heavy sigh Quinn walked into the house and entered the cheerful kitchen, the kitchen he'd never see again.

Conversation stopped, and Fred glanced up from his plate. "Where've you been, boy? I know how you crave Emmy Lou's cooking."

"It's been one of the best things about this trip," Quinn said, smiling at Emmy Lou. "Thank you for feeding me so well."

Emmy Lou frowned. "That sounded like a goodbye thank-you, to me."

"And you got your own clothes on for a change," Benny said.

"I'm catching the red-eye for New York tonight," Quinn said.

Benny leaped from his chair. "I'll be right back. Don't leave yet."

"I've got a few minutes left," Quinn said. Funny how emotional he felt at this moment. Like he was leaving his own family.

"Does Jo know?" Emmy Lou asked.

"Yeah. I met her on the porch."

"So that's why she pounded up those stairs like a skunk was after her," Fred said.

Quinn cleared his throat. "I wanted to say that you've been great, all of you." He glanced at Hastings, who sat at the table with his chauffeur, Sid. Hastings had a button missing from his shirt. Emmy Lou had scored her trophy, after all. "You, too, Brian," Quinn said. "You could have nailed me for this little stunt. Thanks for letting it go."

Hastings grinned and leaned back in his chair. "Hey, I love a challenge. Figuring out how to explain you to the good folks of Ugly Bug was the most fun I've had in years. Just don't go trying to be me anymore, okay?"

Quinn returned his smile. "I never wanted to be you in the first place."

"You *didn't*?" Hastings pretended great shock. "Who wouldn't want that?"

"I sure as hell wouldn't," Fred said. He got up to come over and shake Quinn's hand. "It's been a pleasure."

Quinn's conscience nagged him about the swiped condoms. "Uh, Fred, I—you might notice sometime that you—"

"I already did." Fred winked at him. "Forget it."

Not likely, considering what I used them for. Quinn nodded. "Thanks."

Emmy Lou pulled Quinn into a big hug. "Come back, you hear?"

"I...we'll see."

Emmy Lou stood back and gazed at him with tears in her eyes. "How about a button off your shirt?"

Quinn laughed in surprise. "I'm no celebrity."

"You are to me. I've never known a New York investment banker before. Can I have one?"

Quinn shrugged, more touched by the request than he wanted her to know. "Why not?" He stood patiently while she found some scissors and snipped off the button nearest his collar.

Then she patted his chest. "I mean it. Come back."

He was sure she knew that wasn't going to happen, or she wouldn't be fighting tears. "I'll try."

Benny came charging into the kitchen, his black Stetson in his hand. He shoved it at Quinn. "Here."

"Benny, I couldn't take this. It's your best hat."

"It looked good on you today. Well, until Hyper started running and it fell off. Wear it in New York. Go on. Take it."

Quinn recognized the gift as a gesture of friendship that meant as much to Benny as it did to Quinn. "Thank you. I'll wear it with pride." God, it would be tough leaving these people. He put on the hat and adjusted the brim while

Benny beamed at him. Another couple of minutes and Quinn was afraid he'd be bawling. "Well, folks, I'd better get on the road."

"I'll walk you out," Hastings said, pushing back his chair.

Uh-oh. Quinn wondered if Hastings was as laid-back as he'd seemed about the impersonation thing. Maybe he wanted Quinn to sign an affidavit promising never to repeat the stunt. Or maybe he was planning to press charges after all. "Okay."

After a last round of goodbyes, handshakes and hugs from Emmy Lou, Quinn walked to his rental car with Hastings, his eyes moist. It took him a few seconds before he trusted himself to speak. "So, what's on your mind?" he asked as they reached the car.

"The more appropriate question is, what's on yours?"

Quinn stood by the driver's side of the sedan and turned to Hastings. "What do you mean?"

"Are you really as stupid as you're acting right now, or do you have some master plan you're not telling anyone?"

Quinn stared at him.

Hastings sighed and shook his head. "So you're stupid. So stupid you're going to leave that woman, even though she loves you to pieces."

"Jo?"

"No, Meg Ryan." Hastings snorted. "Yes, Jo! Lord love a duck, but you're dense. I was thinking of hiring you for a couple of financial deals I'm working on, but if this is how you are, forget it. Jo is crazy about you. Genuine crazy, not the starstruck stuff I get most of the time. She loves you deep down to the bone. A guy finds that maybe once in a lifetime, if he's lucky, and you're walking away from it. You're an idiot, Monroe."

"She wants a cowboy. She said so."

"Oh, my God. So be a cowboy."

"I'm no good at it."

"Trust me, she won't care. All you really need to pull it off is a Stetson and a smile. Benny just gave you the Stetson, and according to Jo, and I quote—" Hastings slipped into falsetto "—when he smiles, one of his eyeteeth is slightly crooked, which gives him a rakish air." Hastings rolled his eyes. "That's love talking, sport. L-U-V, love. She looks at you as if you're the most expensive thing on the menu, something she'd give anything to have, but she's afraid she doesn't have the money to pay for."

Quinn's brain whirled as he wondered if he dared believe what Hastings was saying. "But if she really wants me—"

"She's scared to say, because of your big important job. Are you married to that hotshot position in New York, or could you see yourself moving to Montana? Montana's not so far from California, and if you can convince me you have at least a few brain cells working, I could probably scare you up some Hollywood clients. They're flaky, but they're rich. But then, you're flaky. It should work out."

"I'm not flaky."

"Oh, sure. I've heard enough to think otherwise. You hop on a plane to bring the lady horse sperm, and then you parade around here pretending to be a big star when you're clueless about the film industry, and then you climb on some spoiled-rotten horse and go tearing around a rodeo arena in front of the good people of Ugly Bug when you can't even ride, let alone ride and carry a flag. I'm gonna hook you up with Steve Martin. You two are soul mates."

"You've got me pegged wrong." Maybe he used to be like that when he was growing up in the Bronx with Murray, but he'd changed.

Hastings grinned at him. "Have it your way. I've spent years studying how character is revealed, and I know this cold. You're a wild man. I'm not even going to ask what went on in that tree, but news flash, Quinn, baby—tight-assed guys don't make love in trees.''

''I was just trying to stay away from snakes!''

''Are you kidding? Snakes can climb trees!''

Quinn could have lived without that factoid. ''Okay, okay. What do you think I should do?''

''I have to tell you? Put away your car keys and go upstairs!''

''But everybody's in the house. It's an old house. I don't want—''

''I see your point. Okay. Especially considering your wild streak. Sid and I will take everybody for a moonlit limo ride. I can give you an hour, maybe an hour and a half. But if you can't get your business done in under sixty minutes, you're not the banker for me.''

Jo KNEW she was being cowardly, but she couldn't go back downstairs and watch Quinn leave. Besides, no amount of makeup or eyedrops would be able to disguise that she'd been crying buckets. She'd closed her door and muffled the sound with pillows so they wouldn't be able to hear her downstairs, but with all those people in the house talking and laughing, they probably couldn't hear her, anyway.

Through her sobs she listened to everyone filing out of the house. No doubt they'd all gone to wave goodbye as Quinn drove away. He'd been a popular guest. The sound of a car engine drifted up to her window, and a fresh wave of tears engulfed her. He was really gone.

When she heard her bedroom door open, she moaned. ''Go away, Em. And don't tell me I'm stupid to cry over him.'' She sniffed. ''I already know that.''

Footsteps approached the bed.

''Please, Emmy Lou. There are some things a girl has to get through alone. I should never have allowed myself to care about him, but I did, so now I get to pay the consequences.''

The bed sagged.

"Dammit, Emmy Lou. I don't need mothering, I need—'' She lifted her head and stared into Quinn's blue, blue eyes.

"Loving?'' he murmured, smoothing her tousled hair from her damp cheeks.

She buried her face in the pillow, mortified that he'd heard her babble about him and especially that he saw her like this, weeping like a dope because he'd left. "What are you doing here?'' she mumbled into the pillow. "You'll miss your flight.''

"Guess so.'' He stroked her hair.

"Why are you wearing Benny's hat?''

"He gave it to me. He likes me.''

"Well, I don't. And don't you dare stay here because you feel sorry for me! I'm not crying over you, anyway.''

"You're not?'' He kicked off his shoes, took off his hat and scooted down next to her on the bed. "Then what are you crying for?''

"None of your beeswax.''

He curved his arm around her waist. "I haven't heard that since fourth grade.''

"Don't touch me, either.''

"Why?'' He nestled closer and pushed her hair back so he could nibble at her ear. "Because I have cooties?''

"Exactly.'' She didn't want to like his arm around her, or his warm breath on her ear. Maybe he wasn't leaving tonight, but he would leave tomorrow. And she'd have to go through this all over again.

"But you like bugs.''

Apparently she'd cried so hard she'd sapped her strength. That was the only explanation for why she allowed him to roll her onto her back. And before she knew it, he'd plastered himself on top of her. And her stupid body was getting all hot and bothered about it, too. "Go away." The words came out in a croak.

"No." He began to kiss her eyes and her cheeks.

"Don't kiss me. I probably look like hell."

He grinned. "No, you don't. Just a little red and puffy."

"You missed your plane just so you could tell me that? What a guy."

His grin faded. "No, I didn't miss my plane so I could tell you that. I missed my plane so I could tell you this. I love you."

The world stopped. She stared at him, her mouth open.

"Breathe, Jo."

She gasped.

"That's it. Now keep breathing. In, out, in, out. That's a good girl."

She struggled to do as he asked, but it wasn't easy. "Sorry," she said in a strained voice. "But that's not the sort of thing I hear every day."

He gazed at her with loving concern. "I sure hope not."

She looked into his eyes. She'd suspected he was falling in love with her, but she'd never in a million years expected him to say so. "Why are you telling me this?" she asked.

"In hopes I could get you to say the same thing back to me."

"And then what?"

He nudged her gently with his arousal. "We have an hour before the group comes back from their moonlit limo ride."

"No."

The light in his eyes dulled. "No, you don't love me?"

"Yes, I love you, but no, we won't be frolicking in the sheets for the next hour."

The gleam returned to his eyes. "Why not?"

"Because this love talk is bad enough, but if you throw

in a session with your talented and very large equipment, I won't be able to survive your leaving tomorrow, that's why."

He leaned down and brushed his lips across hers. "Which means I have to stay."

Her breath caught at that sweet contact. "Don't be ridiculous. You can't stay. You'll ruin your career."

"My career will be fine." He feathered a light kiss on her mouth. "I'm just afraid I'll be in the way around here. I can handle your ledgers like no one you've ever seen, but as you know, I can't ride and I can't rope and I'm scared of snakes and big ugly bugs."

"You think I care about that?"

He lifted his head to gaze at her. "I thought you did, yeah. I thought I wasn't cowboy enough for you."

"Oh, *Quinn*." She pulled his head down and proceeded to kiss him until the press of his arousal became very prominent indeed.

Gasping, he levered himself away from her. "Is that a yes?"

"I don't recall you asking a question."

"I didn't? Damn. Okay, let's make it a two-parter. First part—will you marry me? And second part—can we get rid of these clothes and get to it before that limo pulls up in front of the house?"

She smiled at him, her heart brimming with happiness. "Here's a one-part answer to your two-part question. Yes."

"Hallelujah." Quinn began unbuttoning her blouse at a furious pace.

"Oh, Quinn, we haven't talked about children!"

"Do we have to right now?" He tugged off her jeans and panties in one motion. "We only have about forty-four minutes left." He pulled his shirt over his head without unbuttoning it.

"We certainly do have to talk about children, unless you

came prepared for this encounter, which I seriously doubt, because I happen to know Fred's supply was nearly exhausted last night.''

Quinn paused, his pants half off. ''He told you I swiped?''

''Yes, and he's about out by now. So, are we having kids or not?''

''That's up to you.'' Quinn pulled a foil-wrapped square from his pocket before letting the slacks fall to the floor.

''Are you taking Fred's last one?''

''Nope. He has a backup stash. And this time I didn't have to swipe it. He offered.''

Jo's cheeks heated. ''So everybody knows what we're doing up here?''

''Pretty much. So what'll it be?'' He leaned down and wiggled the packet in front of her face. ''I happen to like kids, myself.''

Jo's embarrassment lost out to a powerful surge of desire. ''I like kids, too,'' she said, her voice husky.

Quinn straightened, tossed the packet over his shoulder and took off his briefs.

Jo looked at him standing before her in all his glory. He was perfect, but one little detail would make him even more perfect. ''Quinn, do me a favor?''

''Anything.''

She picked up the Stetson from where he'd laid it on the bedside table. ''Humor me and put this on.''

Quinn chuckled as he took the hat. He set it on his head and pulled it low over his eyes. ''Damned if Hastings wasn't right.''

''About what?''

''Nothing, sweetheart. Nothing at all.'' Then he smiled that heart-stopping smile, the one that made her knees weak and her pulse race.

Her heart brimming with happiness, Jo opened her arms. ''Come here, you big, beautiful cowboy.''

CHRISTIE RIDGWAY

The Bridesmaid's Bet

TORONTO • NEW YORK • LONDON
AMSTERDAM • PARIS • SYDNEY • HAMBURG
STOCKHOLM • ATHENS • TOKYO • MILAN • MADRID
PRAGUE • WARSAW • BUDAPEST • AUCKLAND

Dear Reader,

I'm a little sister. And like many of us, I spun my share of romantic daydreams about my brother's friends. One day, I imagined, they'd see beyond the braces and the knobby knees to the beautiful woman within.

I hate to say it never happened. As a matter of fact, even though I'm married and I've given my brother two nephews, I'm not sure *he* even realizes I've grown up. But for Francesca Milano, the heroine of *The Bridesmaid's Bet,* it's another story. Everyone is seeing her differently: her father, her four older brothers and particularly her brothers' friend, attorney Brett Swenson.

Of course, as every younger sister knows, there's that teeny tiny problem with overprotectiveness. Francesca has four brothers who've practiced it all their lives, and now Brett thinks he needs to protect her from falling in love. Too bad for him, it's too late...or is it really such a bad thing after all when Brett's the one Francesca loves?

I'm thrilled that Francesca and Brett's story is part of the first Harlequin Duets. I hope that you enjoy it as well as every wonderful, romantic and fun story to come. I enjoy hearing from readers and you can write to me at P.O. Box 3803, La Mesa, CA 91944.

All the best,

Christie Ridgway

Christie Ridgway

In loving memory of Judy Veisel.

1

FRANCESCA MILANO tugged her black baseball cap more firmly over her hair and stared narrowly across the kitchen at her older brother Carlo. "I spent yesterday in a bridesmaid's dress—looking like a cross between Scarlett O'Hara and something out of *Saturday Night Fever,* mind you—and now you're saying I owe you money?"

Carlo's cool expression didn't change. The fingers at the end of his outstretched palm even wiggled impatiently. "Fifty bucks."

Still reeling from her hours in puce-colored polyester over a ruffled petticoat, Francesca opened the back door to her father's apartment to let in a little air. The breeze cleared the smell of the meat-maniac pizza that was filling the stomachs of Pop and her other brothers as they watched baseball on the living room TV.

Carlo raised his eyebrows. "Stop stalling, Franny."

She did, anyway, inspecting the short fingernails she'd recently given up biting. "Who would guess that Nicky would catch the garter?" The oldest of her four brothers seemed the most firmly entrenched bachelor.

"I did," Carlo said. "The matrimony bug has bitten him bad."

Francesca frowned. Nicky *had* nearly tackled the teenager in front of him to secure the thing. But she couldn't see him *married*. "Bet he thought it would get him a shot at the maid of honor."

Carlo shook his head. "You're close to welshing on one bet already, little sister. Pay up."

She pursed her lips. At twenty-eight, Carlo was closest to her age of twenty-four and usually the kindest. "Carlo, please," she pleaded, attempting to play on his big brother heart strings—she hadn't grown up as the only female in a household of men for nothing. "I'm supposed to be going shopping with Elise later."

He went still. Then he grimaced and stretched his hand out farther. "The fifty. I'll probably need it for Nicky's wedding present."

Francesca waved the thought away. "Nicky! If we're talking weddings, I think it's my turn."

Carlo's eyes widened and his hand dropped. "Your turn for *what?*"

Francesca hadn't planned on voicing the thought, but at least Carlo was distracted from the fifty dollars she wished she didn't owe him. "Last month I was a bridesmaid, yesterday Corinne Costello dressed me up in ruffles and got married, and my best friend Elise is saying 'I do' next month. I've *got* to be up next."

"You've *got* to be kidding."

Annoyed, Francesca thrust her hands in the pockets of her jeans. "Why not me?"

Carlo rolled his eyes. "Beyond the absurdity of you

actually wishing yourself into romance-hell, there's the small fact that you haven't dated in—what?—years?''

Maybe that small fact merely underscored that it must be her turn. "I'm going to change all that," she said stubbornly.

Crossing his arms over his chest, Carlo shook his head.

"I am!" Francesca insisted.

"Tell you what, then," he said, a calculating smile crossing his face. "I have another bet for you."

Despite Carlo's crafty smile, a little thrill rushed through Francesca. Another thing growing up with brothers did was give a woman a honed sense of competition. "Double or nothing?"

"Yeah. A hundred bucks says you can't do it."

"Do what?" she asked warily. No telling what Carlo, who had been unpleasantly moody the past couple of months, had up his sleeve. But she liked the idea of a chance to recoup her cash.

"I'll bet you can't get yourself a hot matrimonial prospect by—" he paused, then snapped his fingers "—by your next stint as bridesmaid."

Francesca grimaced. "What kind of bet is this, Carlo?"

His expression hardened. "Maybe you're right. Maybe it's time...maybe we gotta get ourselves a life."

The "*we* gotta" was interesting. She stared at him.

"Sheesh," he said. "Forget it. Just hand over my fifty."

"No, wait!" Thinking, Francesca clicked her nails against the tile countertop. "I don't have to pay you now?"

"Nope. But you owe me a hundred when you don't have somebody to bring to Elise's wedding at the end of the month."

That rankled. The assumption she'd lose did not sit well with a woman who had been scrambling to keep up with her four older brothers for the past twenty-four years. "Let me get this straight. A steady man in my life by Elise's wedding cancels my debt?"

Carlo nodded. And his confident smirk filled Francesca with determination.

LITTLE FRANNY MILANO on a manhunt? On the other side of the open kitchen door, Brett Swenson stood, stunned by the idea.

Of course, she must have gone from little girl to woman in the twelve years since he'd left, but still Brett couldn't resist the decades-old habit of rescuing her from sibling skullduggery.

To prevent them from finalizing their bet, Brett rapped on the doorjamb. Carlo, whom he could see clearly in profile, immediately swung his way, a grin breaking over his face.

"Brett, you old dog! You made it!"

Brett reached out to shake the other man's hand. "And ready to move in. I just stopped by to say hi and get the keys."

"Brett? Keys?" Franny said, breaking in.

Brett turned her way, for the first time getting a glimpse. She hadn't grown much. Still slight, and her features were shaded by the deep bill of a baseball cap. He let out a satisfied sigh. With all of life's unpredictability, this one thing hadn't changed. Tomboy Franny. Still the scrappy little sister he'd never had.

"Franny," he said, bending slightly and peering under the hat, trying to get a clearer look at what growing up had done to her.

She looked away from him quickly, to cock her head at her brother. "What's going on?"

Carlo grinned. "Didn't I tell you? Brett is back in San Diego. I ran into him at the D.A.'s office. He's in Apartment 7 until he decides where he wants to live permanently."

A bouncy ponytail swung from behind her ball cap as she shook her head. "Pop didn't mention anything to me."

Carlo shrugged. "You've been occupied with wedding stuff." He rubbed his palms together. "Which reminds me, Franny—"

"Do I smell pizza?" Brett interrupted, his impulse to stop their wager resurging. He remembered another Milano bet made years ago. Francesca's brothers had laid odds on how long their tag-along sister would cry once they ditched her for a boys-only bike expedition to the park.

Unable to stomach the thought of the little girl's tears,

Brett returned for her alone. After drying her grubby, tear-streaked face, she'd ridden with the dignity of a tiny tomboy princess, carefully balanced on the handlebars of his stingray bicycle.

Now she jabbed her thumb in the direction of another door, "They're all in Pop's living room—Nicky, Joe and Tony, downing a double order of a double-meat, double-cheese."

Brett almost smiled as another unfamiliar rush of all's-right-with-the-world flooded him. The decision to return to his hometown had been the right one. Eighteen months had passed since Patricia's death, and it was time to restart his life.

The Milanos were just the family to help him do it. The four Milano brothers had been like his own growing up. And Franny...

"About what we were discussing, Carlo," she said.

...had been much too young to date! "How old are you now?" he blurted out, trying to turn the conversation again.

She slanted him a look from underneath the brim of the cap, then shifted her gaze to Carlo. "Old enough to get what I want when I want it. You're on, big brother."

"CARLO'S LOST IT," Francesca's best friend, Elise, said, stopping in the department store aisle to finger a paisley scarf. "And what's wrong with you? Why'd you agree to such a bet?"

Francesca made herself touch the scarf, too. She really

had no interest in the slinky, slippery thing, but she'd promised herself to start taking some clues from Elise. Her friend, engaged to be married in a month, had also never been short of boyfriends during their growing-up years. "I agreed because the bet will finally make me do something about it."

"About what?"

"About getting that life Carlo mentioned."

Elise swung around and squinted her eyes, her gaze sweeping over Francesca. "I've been saying you need one for years."

"I know, I know. It's just—"

"That you work for your dad. That your dad manages a bunch of apartments mainly filled with senior citizens. That you don't have much opportunity to meet men. That you don't know how to attract them. That you don't know how to dress." Elise hadn't stopped for a breath, but she drew one in now. "Do I need to go on?"

Francesca smiled in apology. "What about Aunt Elizabetta? Don't I always use her as an excuse, too?"

Elise nodded, and a delicate waft of her perfume drifted by Francesca. "How could I have forgotten? And you don't have another woman to show you the ropes. Since your mother died when you were two, your only female relative is Aunt Elizabetta, otherwise known as Sister Josephine Mary of the Good Shepherd Convent."

Francesca slapped a glass display case. "That's about the size of it."

"Well if you ask me," Elise said. "It's a bunch of

hooey. I've begged since we were fourteen to do something with you.''

Elise wore her blond hair in a short, waved bob, and even in jeans and a white blouse—like now—she looked polished and pretty. Francesca sniffed again. And Elise always wore perfume.

Francesca sighed and looked down at her own clothes. Levi's. Size Carlo-at-age-thirteen. She couldn't remember if her T-shirt was a hand-me-down, too, but it advertised auto parts. Her usual ball cap was in the car, but she'd pulled her hair into a simple ponytail.

One sneaker had a hole in the toe and the lace of the other had broken twice and was knotted in two places. ''Maybe I should save myself some grief and give Carlo the hundred dollars now.''

Elise picked up another scarf from the display to hold it below Francesca's chin. ''Bite your tongue! You just pry open your purse, pull out a credit card and I'll do the rest.'' She frowned. ''Do you like the color rose?''

Rose? What exact shade was ''rose'' and how was it different from pink? ''Elise…''

''Didn't you say you wanted to get a life?''

Francesca *had* said it. She *did* want to get a life. Yesterday, standing at the altar and wearing a dress—even an ugly one—for the first time in forever had made her feel womanly and lonely all at once. ''I want to primp for a candlelight dinner and have a man open a door for me and feel my heart flutter when he takes my hand,'' she whispered.

And speaking of heart flutters... Francesca took a breath. "Guess who's back in town?" He strode into her mind's eye just like he'd walked through the door to her father's kitchen, tall and lean with dark blond hair and those memorable, startlingly blue eyes.

Elise was inspecting the label on the square of silk. "Brett Swenson."

"You know!"

"David heard from somebody in their old gang. He's joined the district attorney's office."

Elise's fiancé, David, had run with the same crowd as her brothers and Brett. Francesca swallowed and casually inspected her nails. "Why do you think he's back?"

"For love."

"What?" Francesca's voice squeaked.

Elise raised her eyebrows. "Don't you think? To recover from it. When that car killed Patricia she wore Brett's engagement ring on her finger."

Right, Francesca reminded herself. And a grieving Brett was as far from her reach as he'd been when she was a moony twelve-year-old and he a university-bound high school senior.

With a sigh she grabbed the scarf from Elise and held it up to her face herself. She looked around for a mirror. The color rose. Did she like it? She didn't know, but she had to start somewhere.

"Why am I doing this?" she murmured, briefly giving in to doubt.

"Because you want to fall in love," Elise said firmly.

No point denying it.

With iron resolve, Francesca relegated Brett Swenson to the mental pile of unsuitable males in her life labeled "Brothers and Others."

"Fall in love?" she repeated, nodding. "With all the trimmings."

BRETT TOSSED a quasi-cold bottle of beer across his new—if temporary—living room into Carlo's cupped hands. At the baseball game's seventh-inning stretch and with the San Diego Padres well ahead, Carlo, his three brothers and their father had helped Brett unload his Jeep and the trailer he'd towed from San Francisco. Brett's Apartment 7 was next door to Carlo's own apartment, and Carlo lived next door to Franny who was next door to her father. All four were in one of the complexes owned and managed by the Milano family. Actually, according to Carlo, managed by Franny and her father.

The oldest Milano brother, Nicky, was an attorney in private practice. Tony worked construction. Joe Milano was a street cop and Carlo a police detective. At thirty, Brett fell somewhere in the midst of their stair-step ages, but it was Carlo he'd always been closest to and would have professional dealings with now that he'd joined the county district attorney's office.

"I owe you guys one," Brett said, twisting the top off his own brown bottle. The other four men had already left.

Carlo drank from his beer and grimaced. "You owe

me a cold one." He lifted the bottle and inspected the label. "We should have stocked the fridge first instead of last."

"Yeah." Brett took a swallow. "I'll make it up to all of you by springing for dinner next weekend." He paused. "Franny, too."

Brett didn't know what made him bring up her name. Well, yeah, he did. That bet still bugged him. Maybe Carlo would confess the whole thing. Explain his reasoning.

Instead, the other man grunted.

Grabbing from the kitchen counter a shoebox with "Mail" scrawled along the side, Brett tried again. "An invitation came before I left San Francisco." He shook the box. "David Lee and Elise Cummings, huh? Getting married?" Apparently that wedding was the deadline for Carlo and Franny's wager.

Carlo closed his eyes and took another long swallow of beer. "Right." His voice was low and hoarse. Then he dropped onto Brett's couch and used the remote to switch on the TV.

Brett narrowed his eyes and stared at his friend. "You okay, bud?"

Carlo stared at the TV screen and grunted again.

That was answer enough for Brett. For some reason, Carlo's habitual good humor had slipped away, and it didn't look like he was going to explain why. Brett shrugged. He had his own share of dark moods and didn't talk much about what bothered him either.

None of which shed light on the bet with Franny.

Hell, why did it bother him? She was two times older than his last memory of her at twelve. And even though he'd only caught a glimpse beneath that dark-brimmed hat she wore, she was doubtless a grown woman. He didn't have one excuse for insinuating himself into her business, unless seeing himself as a kind of brother counted.

And since she had four of the real McCoys already, she could do without him. Anyway, since Patricia's death, he'd steered clear of female entanglements. No sense in compromising his self-made vow now.

Even with someone he merely regarded as a little sister.

THE TWILIGHT AIR smelled of pork roast and potatoes when Brett encountered Franny in the apartment complex's parking lot. She clutched some shopping bags to her body and the handles of others ringed her arms from wrists to elbows. Her hat shaded her eyes again.

A brother would have let a sister struggle onward by herself.

Brett divested her of what he could.

A small smile crossed her face and gleamed in the near darkness. "My hero!" she said lightly, then led the way to her apartment, unlocking the door and flipping on the entry hall light. On a nearby hook, she hung her baseball cap.

Brett halted, blinking. "Franny?" For an instant, he thought he'd followed the wrong woman home.

He could see her clearly now. The dark hair that had been in a ponytail earlier in the day now brushed her shoulders. The stuff's shine was so glossy he thought maybe he could see his reflection. More glossiness, wispy layers of it, framed a face that was so like he remembered—and yet so different.

Her half smile faltered. "It's me. A new hairstyle today, but me."

But it wasn't. The Franny that Brett held in his memory had been a little squirt with big dark eyes and a baby nose. This Franny—Francesca—still had the big dark eyes. She still had the cute little nose. But now she had cheekbones and warm golden skin and a mouth with full, lush lips that looked ripe and ready for kissing.

Damn. He stood there, arms full of packages, and couldn't think of one rational thing to say.

She saved him by turning away and leading him toward the living room. He preferred this view of her. In loose jeans and a T-shirt she looked like the girl he remembered.

She threw him a quick look over her shoulder and cleared her throat. "I never really welcomed you back today, did I?"

No, she'd hightailed it out of her father's kitchen nearly the moment he'd entered it. "You said you had someplace to go."

She gestured toward an easy chair and he dropped the bags he'd been carrying onto its seat.

"I had some work to do," she said. "Shopping."

He almost smiled. Few women would think of shopping as "work." Then he figured she was working on winning that bet.

He didn't like how that bothered him. Hadn't he decided not to get involved? "I better head out," he said abruptly, taking a step toward the front door.

His quick movement upset the pile of packages on the easy chair. A wide-mouthed shopping bag slid off the top, spilling several tissue-wrapped items and a small box onto the floor.

They both bent to gather them up. She looked at him over the disarray of clothes, a little smile playing over that brand-new mouth of hers. "Remember the time you took me to the mall?"

And suddenly he did. She'd wanted something new to wear to her first sixth-grade dance. Her brothers had groaned and moaned until Brett had volunteered to give her a ride. And then somehow she'd coerced him into actually *shopping,* in claustrophobia-inducing stores that smelled like bubblegum and hairspray. What a sucker he'd been for her.

Now she stood, rubbing her hands against her pants in a nervous gesture. "Do you, uh, have something important to do right now?"

Caution made him shuffle back a step. "I need to go. I'm supposed to—" Looking into her big brown eyes, he couldn't think of anything he was supposed to do except continue looking.

Her eyebrows rose toward her fringe of bangs. "Really? Darn. I was hoping I could show you what I bought today. Get your opinion. I made a major dent in my credit card and I'm a little nervous about it."

Brett nearly groaned. He was supposed to be keeping his distance. "Why me?"

She smiled. "Because you're perfect. An interested, disinterested party."

He shook his head as if to clear it. "What's that mean, exactly?"

"That I can persuade you to stay, and when I ask if you like something, no matter what you think you'll say yes." That smile of hers widened into a grin.

Something hot shot through Brett. "Maybe I should get Carlo." For both their sakes. "Or Nicky. I think he's still at your dad's. Or all three of them."

Franny frowned. "If even one of the men in my family had an ounce of good taste, do you think I'd look like this?"

She held her arms away from her body, and as instructed, Brett looked. As he'd noticed before, she wore jeans and a T-shirt.

"What? You look fine." He tried to find an apt word. "Useful."

"Useful," she repeated. She turned her back and began restacking her purchases. "Like I could change a tire if I had to?"

She was pretty small for torquing lug nuts off a hub, but he didn't want to insult her. "Ready to go bowling, maybe."

She groaned. "That bad?"

Brett realized he'd said something wrong. Franny must not like to bowl anymore, though she'd gone dozens of times with them when she was a kid. "A tire," he said hastily. "You look like you could definitely change a tire."

Franny sighed. "I think I'm convinced every penny was worth it."

Though he hadn't wanted to get involved, he hadn't wanted to hurt her feelings, either. "I'll go now," he said, taking a few more steps back.

She was already unwrapping the tissue from the first item on the stack. With a flick of her wrist, something skimpy and soft unfurled. Before he made it to the doorway, she turned and held it up against her. "What do you think of this?"

He froze. Plastered against Franny's body was a sleeveless sweater of some sort of soft rose-colored knit fabric.

"Cashmere," she said. "Do you like the color?"

It matched the color in her cheeks, and her lips were shaded just one tone darker. She pressed her palm against her stomach, pinning the little thing even closer to her form, showing the sweet curve of her breasts and accenting the slimness of her waist.

Franny had a top half that was two handfuls of temptation.

Brett immediately wanted to kick himself. This was *Franny*. He regarded her as a *sister*.

Not anymore, a little devil inside him whispered.

Yes, he insisted in return. After Patricia's death he wasn't in the running for anything else.

Franny must have taken his silence as approval, because she started dropping bags to the floor and tossing new clothes across the couch. Short skirts and tight tops in a rainbow of pinks and blues.

The last bag floated to the floor. "Well?" she said.

Well, he wished he'd left twenty minutes ago.

"Wait! Wait! Don't say anything yet!" She dug through one last bag to pull out a perfume atomizer. One spritz filled the room with a scent that was light but seductive. Spicy and sweet. He imagined it warmed by Franny's smooth skin.

"What do you think? As a man, I mean? Does it, uh, entice you?"

"Entice *me?*" The thought had a dangerous appeal.

She flushed. "Not you, of course. I didn't mean—I'm sorry if that offended you. I know that Patricia's death— that you—"

"It's okay."

The color on her cheeks receded. "What I'm asking is what you think. I'm usually a jeans-and-sweatshirt kind of woman. Will I look good in this stuff?"

He knew she was really asking if, wearing it, she'd

find a man—some man who could win her that bet. And after what must be major wear and tear to her credit card's magnetic strip, she probably hadn't enough left to come up with Carlo's hundred bucks. Still, Brett didn't like the idea of Franny shedding her jeans and putting on a skirt for anyone but—

For *anyone.*

The whole thing was none of his business, though.

And sure, Carlo was a jerk for pulling the stunt, but Franny looked more than a little excited by the whole bet idea.

He didn't like that, either.

"Well?" she said impatiently. "Give it to me straight."

He shook his head, eyeing the cavalcade of sexiness strewn across the couch cushions. "I'm just sorry for whoever you unleash this on."

Her smile was brilliant. "Thank you, Brett. Thank you." Her expression turned impish. "You can witness it for yourself tomorrow night."

Oh, no. The last thing he wanted to do was that. He was staying out of the Milano family business. Franny's business.

"We're going out together. Carlo, Nicky, all of us. David Lee and Elise, too."

She would have her brothers there to watch over her. "I don't think—"

"I'm going to wear this." She plucked a skimpy, stretchy dress out of the pile. It was violet. Something that winked like stars dotted the fabric. The short skirt swung as she held it up.

Of course, it had been one of her brothers who had started this whole, dangerous mess. "Tomorrow night I—"

"Haven't another thing to do. Come on. It'll be good for you to go out, Brett."

"N—"

She touched his arm. He couldn't think for a moment. It had been so long since a woman had touched him. More than eighteen months and four days.

"Come with me," Franny said.

She should have said "us," he thought. Then he could have refused. But the "me" made him think of her out alone at night in the violet-and-stars dress that would mold her breasts and swish around her thighs.

"Yes," he said.

2

STALLED by the large crowd filtering through the entry to the country club's banquet room, Francesca tried to separate the notes of the light rock pouring out the door from those of the country band playing on a nearby patio. Then the logjam ahead broke up and she followed the rest of her group inside. The charity fund-raiser— sponsored by two radio stations and some local businesses including the accounting firm Elise's David worked for—was packed, and Francesca was instantly separated from the others. On tiptoe to see over the shoulders of those around her, she finally located her brothers Nicky and Joe, who had already commandeered a couple of tables for the eight in their party.

Francesca skirted the dance floor and took the last seat available, squeezing herself in between Brett and Carlo. Judging by their stiff expressions, they weren't going to be the cheeriest of table mates.

She sighed. Carlo's mood mystified her, but she took some responsibility for Brett's. From all reports, he continued to deeply mourn his fiancée and longtime love, Patricia, who had died so tragically. Maybe twisting his arm to come along tonight hadn't been such a good idea.

Elise's fiancé, David, and Nicky were grousing about the lack of cocktail waitresses. From the other table Elise sent Francesca a significant look and then rolled her eyes in the direction of a group of men by the bar that was set up on the other side of the room.

Right. She wasn't here to fix Brett, but to fix herself up with a man who could win her that bet at the end of the month.

Elise had suggested going to this event as a way to launch Francesca into circulation. In case she felt insecure wearing a new dress, makeup and high heels, she had family and friends as a comfortable homebase. Leaning forward, Francesca put her elbow on the table and her chin in her hand to survey the guys Elise had pointed out.

The right age and not drunk. Two excellent starting points.

"Can I get you something to drink?" Brett's voice made her start. "We've given up on the waitress."

"Oh, um, sure. A glass of red wine would be great," Francesca said, reaching for her purse.

Brett grinned, his sudden smile startling her. "Don't worry about it. Carlo's buying."

She smiled back as both men stood. Carlo had a list of drink orders scribbled on a crumpled cocktail napkin.

Brett followed Carlo, and Francesca peered through the crowd to watch the two as they waited at the bar. Carlo had the dark Italian good looks shared by all the Milano brothers, a handsomeness completely familiar to

Francesca. But Brett was like a different species. He was over six feet, lean and hard looking. His hair was dark blond, his face high-cheekboned. He wore soft jeans and a short-sleeved sports shirt. Its searing color matched the Scandinavian blue of his eyes.

"Mooning over somebody already?" Elise had slipped into the seat vacated by Carlo. "Which one?"

"The least likely candi*date*," Francesca murmured.

"Huh?" Elise leaned closer. "Who?"

Francesca decided against confessing. "I'm not mooning, I'm moaning. *Pantyhose.*"

The return of Carlo and Brett spared Francesca any more probing. After ordering her to "Get to work," Elise returned to her fiancé. Francesca nodded and obediently shifted her attention to the single men beyond the confines of their tables.

It took half a glass of wine to realize she had something else to moan about, though. As one of only two women with six guys, and wedged between the two most forbidding, Francesca realized single men didn't seem much inclined to approach her.

The chairs were half-mooned around the tables to face the band. When her brother Nicky left his seat to grab another beer, Francesca squeezed out of her chair and took Nicky's. At one end of the moon shape, Nicky's spot put her closer to the dance floor and without anyone on her left. Two tables away, a cute guy in khaki pants caught her eye. A thrill zinged through Francesca. She smiled quickly then looked away, hoping he'd come over to chat or ask her to dance.

Maybe this finding a date stuff wasn't so hard!

She focused on her wineglass, but from the corner of her eye kept tabs on Khaki Pants. He pushed out his chair and slowly stood. Francesca's heart started beating faster. And faster, when his tasseled loafers turned in her direction.

Should she look up? Smile? Pretend she didn't see him until he was right in front of her?

"Here you go, Brett." Nicky had returned, a beer in each hand. Brett rose to take the beer and they remained standing on either side of her, hovering like skyscrapers blocking the sun. Between their imposing bodies, Francesca caught sight of the tasseled loafers turning away.

Nicky bent down. "I think I just saved you from dancing with a dweeb. A guy was heading in this direction."

Francesca glared at him. "I can say no to my own dweebs, thank you very much."

Nicky blinked. "Not on my watch, little sister."

Francesca frowned and thought she saw satisfaction cross Brett's face. Certainly that was a thumb's-up Joe sent Nicky's way.

Francesca gritted her teeth. Her brothers' interference was a problem she hadn't anticipated. But they were not going to cause her to lose this bet or this chance to get a life. Catching sight of Khaki Pants in line at the bar, Francesca left the table and determinedly headed that way herself. She would order a diet cola and hope for a chance to speak to the potential dwee—date.

As she threaded through the tables, the headline band was introduced and the audience went from rockin' to raucous. A pulsing bass line buzzed through the soles of her feet, and a renewed determination infused Francesca. She wanted to dance with Khaki.

The bartender filled her order and she moved close to the dance floor, sipping her drink. Her gaze slid toward Khaki Pants, and he smiled at her. Heart starting to flutter, she smiled back. He sidled closer. The band was so loud he'd have to get very close to begin a conversation.

He was still three steps away when her brothers Joe and Tony pounced. Joe took her glass from her hand. Tony pulled her onto the dance floor and immediately spun her to the corner farthest from Khaki. Francesca gave the stranger a mournful, squiggly fingered farewell. He'd already turned away.

When the dance ended, Tony linked his arm with hers and dragged her back to their tables. "I'm not fifteen, Tony," she said through clenched teeth. "Cut me some slack."

Tony pretended he didn't hear and from somewhere dredged up enough gentlemanly manners to pull out a chair and insert her at the table—once again between Carlo and Brett.

If weeping wouldn't have run her brand-new mascara, Francesca might have resorted to it.

Instead, she stared morosely at her half-full glass of

wine and barely touched cola. She might as well give up and go home. Once out of the stretchy knit dress and into comfy sweats, she'd pop a satisfying bag of Orville's finest in her microwave.

Of course, her habit of doing that had led her to this very, dateless moment.

Irritation rose, and she glanced around at her handsome and complacent siblings. Maybe she should just tell her brothers to lay off!

Right. If they listened to her, Joe wouldn't have bought his last girlfriend a car tune-up for Christmas, and Tony wouldn't be permanently tattooed with the name of the woman he'd loved, then lost.

Then there was the possibility of enlisting their help.

She sighed. As if that wouldn't be a total disaster. Consider the one mushy Valentine she'd received in the third grade. Her brothers' idea of fostering a budding romance had been to glower at poor Wesley Burdett for two months and to tease her unmercifully for two *years*.

Only Brett had been able to shut them—

Brett.

Beside her, his beer hit the tabletop with a *clack*. Francesca looked at him—a plan instantly crystallizing.

"I want to dance," she announced loudly across their two tables.

With matching grimaces, her brothers looked at each other expectantly, obviously hoping another would volunteer for sister duty. Only Tony, who had already sacrificed himself, appeared unmoved by her request.

"To *country*," she added.

All four Milano men groaned in pain, as if she'd stated there'd be no cheesecake for Sunday night dessert. They *hated* country music.

Perfect.

She looked over at Brett. "*You* will dance with me, won't you?"

She restrained the smile breaking over her face. He didn't have any choice but to agree, as all four of her brothers sighed with relief, the saps.

Francesca's smile widened. With Brett as escort, she'd make a break for the potential-man-crowded patio where she could conduct her search in sibling-free peace.

A TWINGE OF GUILT pinged Francesca as Brett followed her through the packed room. He probably didn't feel much like dancing, and she'd had no opportunity yet to let him in on her little plan. Of course, she wouldn't tell him the humiliating truth—that she'd made a bet with her big brother to force herself out of the house to look for a man—but she'd make it clear that she only needed his help to escape the overprotective Milanos.

She wasn't expecting him to take her into his arms.

Shivers ran down her spine, a reaction she chalked up to the fresh air breezing through the open door as they neared it.

Once outside in the darkness, Francesca hesitated on the lit pathway that led toward the country-western band.

Another couple brushed by them, hurrying in the direction of the patio. "I love this song," the woman said to the man she tugged along with her. "Come dance with me, honey. Hold me."

Francesca didn't move.

"You okay?" Behind her, Brett's voice tickled her nerve endings.

She remained still, frozen by a thought that was adolescent and silly and about as likely to happen as a twelve-year-old's romantic daydream about an older boy.

If Brett danced with her, if he held her...if he even touched her...she might stop breathing.

The certainty of the thought was scary. It was as if it had been simmering in the back of her mind since the moment he'd entered her father's kitchen yesterday.

She couldn't risk going toward the dance floor just yet.

To the *clickety-clack* of her new high heels, she rushed in the opposite direction of the patio and the country band and stumbled upon a small courtyard surrounded by rose bushes and low trees strung with white fairy lights. At the center she halted beside a sundial set on a waist-high pedestal.

Brett had followed her. "Franny?" His voice was puzzled.

As she turned to face him, the breeze blew, rustling up a faint scent of roses and chilling Francesca's stockinged legs. Her short dress ruffled against her thighs.

Any notion of giving him some vague excuse for not

wanting to dance with him or of making a lame joke about her two left feet evaporated. Brett was staring at her legs. And then his gaze moved up, over her body, a man's gaze of appreciation.

Goose bumps sped over her skin, fast as a kid with a baseball mitt running away from a broken window.

From between his teeth came the sound of a light, sweet wolf whistle and he shook his head slowly. "Franny—no—*Francesca.* What happened to you? Where'd you go?"

She couldn't think of anything to say.

He moved closer and she retreated, the small of her back pressed against the pedestal. "You've been in my head all these years," he said. "A little urchin with brown eyes and a stubborn chin." He shook his head again. "You weren't supposed to change."

Another spurt of breeze blew by, flattening her dress against her body. "You've been gone a long time, Brett." She swallowed, trying to ease the croak in her voice.

"That long?"

She swallowed again. "Long enough for me to grow up."

He was silent a minute, then he laughed ruefully. "Doesn't seem like your brothers have accepted that."

"No," she agreed.

"So then why should I?"

She stared at her feet, unfamiliar in their pointy-toed high heels. *Because I want you to see me as a woman.*

Her teeth came down on her tongue to stop the silly, adolescent-daydream words.

"Francesca…"

He was moving closer again, and she tried to move back, but one of her heels caught on the pedestal base behind her and she lost her balance. Brett made like he was going to catch her and, desperate to keep free of his touch, she twisted, her hand grabbing the metal pointer of the sundial to keep herself upright.

It bit sharply into her hand. "Ouch!"

"What happened?" He reached for her fingers, but she whirled away in time.

"Nothing. Just a little cut." And a large dose of embarrassment, she thought. See her as a woman? Brett was seeing her as a klutz.

"Let's go get some disinfectant for that."

"No way!" Francesca made a wide circle around him and headed toward the main path. "I hate the stuff. Stings like the dickens. I'll run water over it in the ladies' room."

He was following her again and she avoided looking at him by walking briskly to remain in the lead.

His voice stopped her outside a door marked Women. "Francesca," he said.

"Yes?" She swung around slowly.

Fairy lights were strung in the trees here, too, and they backlit Brett, dazzling her. "You grew up beautiful," he said.

Her knees melted. The throbbing of her cut hand suddenly triple-timed to match the startled beating of her heart. And Francesca realized it took less than Brett's touch to rob her of air.

ON THE LARGE PATIO hosting the country-western band, Brett kept an eye on Francesca from a table placed deep in the shadows of bordering shrubbery. He nursed a beer, his gaze not leaving her as she attempted the intricate steps of a line dance.

She turned the wrong way, laughed, then pushed that gleaming hair of hers out of her eyes. In the dimly lit dance area, the stars on her dress winked like a thousand shiny enticements.

Just as he'd imagined the evening before, the dress displayed her body in a way that boyish jeans and over-size T-shirts couldn't. Rounded and slender in all the right places, Francesca was built like a womanly gym-nast—taut muscles and full breasts.

As if responding to his thought, two men moved from another line to take up places beside her. Brett gripped his beer hard.

He was going to keep his distance.

After she'd tended to her hand—he'd scrounged a bandage from the club personnel—she'd avoided his gaze while telling him she didn't want that dance after all. Her reasons had been less than clear, but he'd let her off the hook without a fight.

Though she didn't know it, he was aware of her bet

with Carlo. She was looking for a hot prospect and needed freedom from her brothers to accomplish it.

But not freedom from him.

No, he'd assigned himself the task of watching over her for the evening. Any man who was going to get Francesca was going to have to pass muster with him first.

One of the men beside her bent toward her ear. She looked up at him and smiled, her eyes shadowed and mysterious. The ends of her smooth dark hair brushed against her star-strewn dress, and now the second man leaned toward her.

Brett's gut burned. Damn. She was innocent and gorgeous and he wanted to keep her safe.

"Hi." In front of him, a feminine voice intruded. A tall blonde slid onto the chair opposite him. "Taken?"

He shook his head. From the corner of his eye, he checked out Francesca again. Flanked by the two men, she was still gamely attempting the dance.

"Having a good time tonight?" The blonde's long fall of hair reminded him of Patricia.

His insides twisted, but he forced out a brief smile. "Sure."

"I just got dumped," the woman said. The last half of her glass—the olived toothpick made it look like a martini—went down in one gulp.

The big-beat country song ended and Francesca was clapping. So were the men beside her, both smiling down at her.

Brett glued his gaze on them. The blonde beside him was still talking.

"He was a rat, but a generous rat. You know. Flowers. Jewelry." Her other ringed hand moved, and Brett realized she held a second drink. Her black, highly arched eyebrows rose. "You want one?" She gestured toward her glass. "Vodka martini."

"No, thanks." The first guy who had spoken to Francesca, long haired and tight jeaned, bent close. Brett kept his eyes on him as Francesca nodded, then smiled another time.

"As I was saying." The blonde across from him again. "He really had me going. He said all the right words. Made all the right moves. Gave me a *diamond*."

Brett kept his mouth shut. He couldn't believe this lady was confiding in him. He'd never been the girl's-best-friend type.

Francesca did another smile-nod-smile as the long-haired one leaned toward her and talked.

The woman beside Brett downed her next martini in two gulps, and he figured it was the vodka and vermouth that had chosen him as her confidant. "So tell me," she said, her voice insistent. "You're a man. Why would he do it?"

Brett stared at the blonde. Men *did* disappoint women. That guy could do a number on Francesca. Some other man she met tonight might break her heart.

Could? Might? *Hah!* It was practically a certainty.

God and he knew life didn't run smoothly, even if you had beauty and youth on your side.

The thought panicked him. He glanced over to check on Francesca. The long-haired man bent even nearer her ear. More smiles were exchanged.

Brett's hand tightened on his sweating bottle of beer. The band hadn't started their next song, so the patio wasn't noisy enough to warrant the other man's closeness.

"Who's she?" With a three-olive toothpick, the blonde gestured toward the dance area. "The woman you can't keep your eyes off."

"A friend." How annoyed would Francesca be if he wandered over?

She laughed. "Yeah, and the rat's going to give up his cheese and come back to me."

It was Francesca who was laughing now. She put her hand on the sleeve of the guy talking with her. He grinned and covered her fingers with his.

Brett stood. He would just introduce himself. Let this potential rat know that Francesca had people looking out for her. Just as he took a step forward, the rat gave Francesca a two-fingered salute and strode away. The other man who'd been hanging by her trailed behind.

Brett could relax now. Could resume his seat across from the blonde and take her drunken meandering as a reminder of how risky love was.

Or...

He could take a step forward in a suddenly formed

plan he had for Francesca. The one where it was he who helped her win Carlo's bet.

Why not? For her pride, or the money or both, Francesca was determined to win that bet by the day of Elise and David's wedding. But that deadline could lead a naive young woman to trouble or pain.

The band started up something slow and country. Brett imagined Francesca in the long-haired rat's embrace, his big hands on her body.

Brett found himself striding toward her. Standing at the edge of the dance floor, she didn't see him coming. He grabbed that hand that had been touching the rat and pulled her into the circle of dancers.

Then he pulled her into the circle of his arms.

God. Her dark and grown-up eyes stared up at him, and he wanted to answer all the questions they asked.

He'd say anything to make her smile.

"You looked…" As if she could be hurt on this manhunt. As if he could step in like he'd done all those years ago and make everything better.

And then he stopped thinking and started registering how Francesca felt in his embrace. He took in a deep breath and that perfume she'd tested on him the night before entered his lungs.

His body hardened.

It didn't surprise him. Over a year and a half had passed since he'd held a woman. But he didn't want to scare Francesca by a purely natural reawakening of physical response, so he edged away from her.

It seemed to him she sighed.

Keeping her inches away, he shuffled his feet to the slow beat of the music.

He took in another breath of that sweet and spicy perfume. It joined with another warm scent—her skin, he guessed—and suddenly his head dizzied with the mix of the fragrance and the flashing stars on her spangly dress.

"Francesca." Like a man with handfuls of unexpected treasure, he stared down at her, amazed.

She looked up, her eyes going wide at what she saw on his face. And what *did* she see? Arousal, surprise, that odd resurgence of the all's-right-with-the-world feeling?

His hand rested on her shoulder and the soft ends of her hair slid across his knuckles, sending more sparklers of sensation up his arm.

"Why are you doing this, Brett?" she asked.

Dancing? Feeling? "Because I want to take you out," he answered. "What do you say?"

3

ELISE PULLED a paper napkin from the dispenser on Francesca's kitchen table and wiped her hands free of sandwich crumbs. "Well," Elise said impatiently. "What *did* you say?"

Francesca gathered up their plates and turned toward the sink. "What should I have said?"

"Francesca..."

"Okay, okay." Francesca surrendered the secret she'd been hugging to herself for the past fifteen hours. "When Brett asked me if I'd go out, I said yes."

Elise stared at her, her chin sagging in obvious surprise. "Francesca Milano dating Brett Swenson?"

Maybe she should take her best friend's disbelief as an insult, but to be honest, Francesca had been just as startled by the notion herself. "It sort of popped out of my mouth," she explained. "My head was thinking 'no way,' but my—"

"Good sense must have gone to Tahiti!"

"Elise..."

"Francesca..." Elise sank back in her chair in an attitude of despair. "You've got to know better than this."

With quick movements, Francesca loaded her dishwasher. Yes, she'd known the idea of tomboy Francesca on a date with gorgeous Brett Swenson bordered on the impossible, but she'd been dizzied. Those fairy lights. The intensity of Brett's blue eyes. The strength of his arms around her and the almost painful flutter of her heart when his hands had brushed her skin.

She'd thought if he touched her she'd lose her breath. Instead she'd lost her head.

Swallowing, she turned toward Elise slowly. "I know it's like the peacock and the mud hen, but..."

Elise shook her head. "That's not what I mean at all!" Frowning, she jabbed her finger in Francesca's direction. "You keep forgetting to look in the mirror."

"But—"

"But nothing. Brett Swenson or any man would be lucky to have you. Problem is, Brett Swenson isn't looking to have anyone."

Now why should those words make her ache? "I know," Francesca answered honestly. "But he did ask."

Elise worried her lower lip. "Which bothers me. But I *am* glad you're under no delusions."

Not delusional. Not even hopeful. Just... "I know I could have refused." It had even crossed her mind for half a millisecond.

"But?" Elise prompted. "Because you also know you shouldn't be wasting your time with nonpotentials."

Right. There was that bet at the end of the month. Her

need to win the guy gamble. And that other need she had, deep inside, to finally, finally fall in love.

"But—" Francesca didn't know the reason she'd agreed herself, so she tried making it up as she went along. "But maybe I figured we both needed an easing-in."

Elise raised her blond eyebrows in perfect arches.

Francesca felt the beginnings of a cold sweat. "Hey, with my dismal dating scorecard, I could use the practice," she said quickly. "And Brett, maybe Brett wants to dip a toe back into the dating pool."

Elise crossed her arms over her chest. "As long as it's just a toe."

"C'mon." Francesca smiled. "I have four brothers singing that song. Just be happy I'm going out instead of sitting at home with my cat and reruns of 'Happy Days.'"

Her best friend rubbed a crimson-tipped finger over her nose. "You are pretty pitiful."

"See? Now help me find something to wear tonight."

Clapping her hands together, Elise popped out of the chair. "Oh! Closet combing. My favorite. Where's he taking you?"

Francesca stopped herself in the act of biting off her thumbnail. "He left it up to me. I chose the fun center."

Elise looked ready for another heart attack. "The fun center? Pee-wee golf? Bumper boats? Those machines that go ding-ding-ding? That kind of fun center?"

"Pinball machines, Elise. And yes, that kind of fun

center." Francesca braced herself for her friend's next explosion at her unconventional choice.

"*Whew.*" Wiping her brow dramatically, Elise dropped back to the seat of her chair. "You should have told me that in the first place. I can't tell you how relieved I am."

It was Francesca's turn for bewilderment. "Huh?"

"Sweetie," Elise said. "You had me worried for a bit there, about Brett breaking your heart. But you are a smart girl."

Francesca was really glad to hear that, of course, but she couldn't suppress her second "Huh?"

"The fun center's no date," Elise proclaimed. "That's just a boys' night out."

BOYS' NIGHT OUT. Elise's comment echoed as Francesca stared at her reflection. With a tiny groan of regret she pulled off her baseball cap and tossed it on the bed. Jeans, tennies and an "I Stop For Roadkill" sweatshirt were statement enough.

The statement being: Boys' night out.

Because the minute Elise said it and the more Francesca thought about it, that was probably what Brett meant to suggest anyway. Yeah, yeah, he'd said she'd "grown up beautiful" and all, but that didn't guarantee he'd asked her out on a *date* date.

Heck, the poor man was new to town and lived just a few doors down. He probably wanted company. He'd probably tried Nicky, Tony, Joe and Carlo first. Pop even. But Tuesday nights the men in her family all had commitments—jaycee meetings, basketball leagues, Pop hit the bingo game down at the local church and always took at least one of her brothers and three or four of their senior residents with him.

Only Francesca had been available to "date" tonight.

Good thing she'd suggested the fun center—the first thing that had popped into her mind—instead of a dead giveaway like an ocean-view restaurant or a picnic bonfire on the beach.

Yeah, she and Brett, just two good buddies, were going to spend the evening playing games.

Kid games, not man-woman games.

And in her tennies, second-best jeans and the sweatshirt Nicky had given her for Christmas, she'd make clear she understood her good-friend, just-one-of-the-boys status. Thinking again, she made a grab for the ball cap. An additional reminder wasn't a bad idea.

Tugging it over her hair, she looked straight into her reflected gaze and vowed not to make the mistake of considering this a real date.

Then the doorbell rang. With a final deep breath, she jogged toward her front door and pulled it open as she pasted on her best and friendliest smile.

To feel it slide right from her lips.

She tried resurrecting it, she honestly did, but Brett looked so *good.*

Feet in suede hikers, long legs in denim, then a soft

yellow sports shirt. Her gaze traveled upward, taking in his wide grin and Scandinavian eyes.

Young Italian women must be susceptible to blue.

With effort, she curved up the corners of her mouth. "Hey, pal." *Friends. One of the boys.*

His eyes laughed a little. "Back at ya."

On the way to the parking lot they easily dispensed with the how-was-your-day stuff. At his Jeep, though, she was startled to find herself wrestling with him for the door handle.

On her side. The passenger side.

It took a moment to realize he was opening the door for her. Like a real, honest-to-goodness date.

She swallowed. "Oh, you don't—"

"I do." Brett put his hand beneath her elbow to boost her into the high seat.

As he shut the door and circled to his side, Francesca rubbed at the goose bumps on her arms and tried to think. Something wasn't quite right here.

Too soon, he was behind the steering wheel. In the closed confines of the car Francesca breathed in his scent, just a hint of citrusy soap. Her brothers all used something orange and antibacterial that made them smell...sanitized. Closing her eyes, she sniffed again in appreciation.

"Francesca?"

She snapped to attention to find Brett looking at her expectantly.

She stared back, mystified. What had she forgotten? "Uh," she responded, exhibiting her high IQ.

Brett grinned, then reached across her for the shoulder harness. He buckled her in like he would a child...or a woman.

"Uh," she said again.

He raised his eyebrows.

Opening the car door for her, helping her into her seat, buckling the seat belt. She couldn't see Brett doing those things for Carlo. Not considerations you'd give to one of the boys. Or if you did, one of the boys might just slug you.

She licked her lips, wondering where she'd gone wrong. *Was* this a date? Clearing her throat, she tentatively tested the theory.

"I guess," she started, then cleared her throat again. "I guess you know that my brothers are all busy tonight."

If he could catalog their activities, she would know he'd asked them out first.

His sandy eyebrows came together, and a gleam entered his eyes. "Francesca." His tone was mildly shocked and mostly amused. "You're not trying to tell me no one will be waiting up for you tonight, are you?"

Francesca nearly swallowed her tongue. "No! Yes!" Those double negative questions always tripped her up. "I didn't mean anything by it." Her cheeks burned. "Nothing at all."

She quickly averted her gaze to his hands, focusing

on his long, capable fingers, which then turned the key to start the car. As the engine vroomed to life, vibrations hummed against her toes, curled tightly against the soles of her shoes.

Her fingers were curled tightly too, meshed with each other in a tense bundle beneath "Roadkill" on her sweatshirt.

Forcing out a long breath of air, she commanded herself to relax. She'd feel better once she knew for sure Brett's expectations for the evening.

He turned out of the parking lot and she tried again to pin down the situation. In a roundabout way, of course. "I think we'll have a good time at the fun center, don't you?" she said brightly.

If he agreed enthusiastically, it signified boys' night out.

He shrugged.

A shrug! What did a shrug mean?

Francesca stifled a groan. Why, oh, why hadn't she made an effort to date before now? With a little more experience she'd be better able to interpret these nuances. One of her hands crept over her eyes.

"Francesca?" He sounded slightly worried. "What's the matter? What're you thinking?"

"That I should be married with three kids." Then the waiting and the wondering would be over. She'd be settled and satisfied and—

Would have missed the chance at Brett Swenson.

"Then we wouldn't be having this date," he said, just as if he could read her mind.

"Is that what this is?" Francesca whispered. "A date?" In her jeans and her tennis shoes and her roadkill sweatshirt she was actually *dating* Brett Swenson?

"What would you call it?"

Something she should have used a curling iron for.

Something that warranted every feminine grace and womanly wile she'd ever heard or read about.

Something she'd wished for on every girlhood star.

A TALK-SHOW ROMANCE GURU insisted that a man enjoyed an evening most when his date made him feel like a king.

Francesca focused on the insight for the entire thirty steps from the car to the fun center entrance. But then an instinct kicked in—a primordial kill-or-be-killed instinct—honed over twenty-four years of being the smallest and youngest, constantly challenged by the older and stronger.

Not just a survival instinct, but a winning instinct.

So, without even thinking, she outscored Brett at pinball. Rammed him unmercifully with her bumper car. Beat him at air hockey.

Not until now, she thought, as she putted into the smiling, red mouth of the clown at the seventeenth and second-to-last hole of the miniature golf course, did Francesca remember her original intention to follow the guru's advice and give Brett the King treatment.

And their scores were tied.

Her cheeks burned in embarrassment as she considered the evening from Brett's point of view. If he'd actually wanted a date, she didn't know *what* she'd given him instead.

"You're suddenly quiet," he said as they waited for the group in front of them to finish the eighteenth hole. "Thinking of the old place?"

Suddenly quiet? Thinking of the old place? She wanted to bury her head in her hands. In between her triumphant exclaims of "Gotcha!" and promises like "I'm gonna whup you now!" she'd told Brett nearly every detail of her life—including the family decision to sell their childhood home and move into a set of apartments.

He gave a gentle tug to the end of her ponytail escaping from her ball cap. "Some memories are hard to let go of."

Great. Now she had him thinking of Patricia, the golden-haired beauty who had known how to date, how to talk to a man, how to make him feel like a king.

On the eighteenth "green" of indoor-outdoor carpeting, Brett let Francesca tee off first. The end of the hole was around a bend, and a good player would ricochet her ball off the dead end curb in front of her to send it toward the putting area. Instead, Francesca let loose a weak swing that caused the ball to stutter unremarkably down the pee-wee fairway.

He gave her a considering look, then stepped up and

made the shot that she'd wanted to. Because his ball was closest to the hole, he had to wait while she took two more ineffectual swings to get her ball within range.

Using the stubby pencil, Francesca kept track of her strokes with hash marks. Pursing her lips, she glued her gaze to the scorecard. "You're obviously the superior player," she said. "I don't have a chance."

He threw her another odd glance but didn't say anything, even as she struggled to make sure her ball hit the red revolving door of the miniature schoolhouse three times before letting it finally make it through to settle into the cup.

Brett made it in one.

She threw up her hands. "The winner!" she said. *The king.* Hoping she'd gotten this date thing right—better late than never—she smiled at him.

He didn't smile back.

Instead, he grabbed her hand and tugged her to the car. After opening her door and helping her in, he drove the short way home in silence.

BRETT PULLED into the last stall in the apartment parking lot. He turned off the car but kept his hands on the wheel, determined not to use them to throttle Francesca.

She cleared her throat nervously. "The security lights don't reach this space well. I'll have to do something about that."

"Tomorrow," Brett answered shortly. "I like the darkness now."

"You do?"

"I chose it for a reason."

"You did?"

"Because if you could see my face, Francesca, I'd scare you."

A hint of guilt crept into her voice. "You saw the mustard stain on your shirt? I'm really sorry. That corndog—"

"No." He was so mad he couldn't think clearly. And his anger was all muddled by the image of unholy and gorgeous glee on her face as she rammed him with her bumper car. Of her spectacular wins at air hockey and the little sizzle sound she'd made with her tongue against her teeth after licking her forefinger and then touching her skin.

"I'm hot," she'd said.

By God, she was, and so was the image of her cute little tush bent over the pinball machine. The memory burned a hole in his brain.

But then—

"Damn it, Francesca! Why'd you go all soft on me?" He couldn't restrain his irritation.

"I...I don't know what you mean," she said hesitantly.

"But you do. Admit it. You let me win at miniature golf."

Even in the darkness he could tell she squirmed on her seat. "No. You were just better—"

"I was *maybe* equal."

She tried again. "You can't know—"

"I know."

She sagged against the seatback.

He wasn't going to let her off the hook. "Why, Francesca?"

"I—" She lifted her hand, let it drop to her thigh. He heard her sigh. "You said it yourself. I wanted to go soft on you."

"To what purpose?"

"I don't know." She sighed again. "To make you feel like a king. To show you a good time. To be a real date."

Something inside Brett twisted into pretzel knots. Damn. She was a walking romantic tragedy just waiting to happen.

Another wave of anger rose. "Hell, Francesca. Tell me you know *not* to be showing guys a 'good time.' Tell me your brothers have taught you better than to make some man feel like a king." He was working up a real mood to kick some Milano-men butt.

Her head hit the back of the seat with a muted thud. "That's the whole problem! They've only taught me to how to *win* and nothing about how to *date*."

He thought he just might lose it. His hands started to shake and he gripped the steering wheel to stop them. *Thank God.* Thank God and the blasted universe that she hadn't made this nutty bet with Carlo months ago. Who would have protected her then?

"Francesca," he said, not surprised at all to find his voice hoarse. "What am I going to do with you?"

The little bit of laughter in *her* voice surprised him, though. "Not beat me at miniature golf next time?"

That pretzel knot inside him twisted tighter. He swallowed. "Exactly. Francesca, don't change *anything* about yourself when you're with a man, okay? Promise me?"

"Even my habit of dripping mustard?" She was trying to keep it light.

"Even that. Men don't care about mustard stains."

"Ain't that the truth." She sat up straight and swiveled his way. "I've lived with four brothers, remember?"

"I remember." And those four brothers and one loving father had created the female before him. An incredible mix of naïveté and beauty and go-for-it guts.

"Francesca." He said her name just because it rolled so sweetly off his tongue, and he let go of the steering wheel.

"I wanted tonight to be perfect," she said, a mournful note in her voice.

He smiled. With his forefinger, he reached out and traced the brim of her ballcap. "It was perfect. Seriously. I haven't had a good time like that in a long while. The 'Roadkill' sweatshirt capped it off for me."

She groaned. "Don't blame me. This was Nicky's Christmas gift."

"What? No perfume? No fuzzy sweaters for his little sister?"

She shook her head. "Nope. And the others gave me sweatsocks and cookbooks."

Something made him probe a little further. "No boy-friend to give you lacy naughty stuff?"

"Me?" A shocked, very feminine giggle floated through the car. "Who could imagine me in lacy and naughty?"

He could. The idea fired his blood to red-lace-teddy temperature. He gritted his teeth against the *bam-bam-bam* of his heating pulse.

"We should probably go in," he said tightly. Smart move. Safe move.

"Right." She hesitated. "Right."

Damn. He could read her hesitation in mile-high let-ters. A date should end with a kiss. A perfect date should end with a perfect kiss.

A chaste, first-date kind of kiss and here he was, burn-ing up thinking about her tush and lace teddies.

He ground his molars again. So it had been a long time since he'd been with a woman. That didn't mean he couldn't offer Francesca the kind of good-night that she deserved.

Sweet, warm. A simple thank-you for what had been pure fun and unexpected exhilaration.

"You're going to have to teach me that slick, air-hockey move you have," he said.

"I might," she said with mock haughtiness. "But what's in it for me?"

He smiled slowly. "I have a few moves of my own I could show you."

And then, so that she'd know what he had in mind, he put his forefinger to her hat brim again. He tipped it off her head. It tumbled away, falling against her shoulder and then to the floor of the car.

She bent forward.

"Leave it," he said.

She froze, and he slowly leaned toward her. *Simple. Chaste. Warm.*

His heart slammed against his ribs, like a warning to do this right. *Do it right for Francesca.*

He cupped her cheek with his palm, curling his fingers around her jaw and tilting her mouth up.

His blood was burning now, pounding along with his heartbeat in a steady path to his groin. He closed his eyes against the good ache and tried to think only of Francesca. Of her trust in him.

Simple. Chaste.

He brushed her lips. Like he might a maiden aunt or a little sister or a good friend.

But a teasing hint of her taste tempted him. Leaning closer, he pressed harder against her mouth.

And though he sensed it about to happen, and though he screamed *No!* in his mind, and though he could have moved away himself, he felt her lips part.

Her sweet, heated breath rushed over his lips.

Simple.

Simply nothing could stop him from taking more.

4

FRANCESCA TASTED like cotton candy. The kiss melted on Brett's tongue, pink and sweet. He should stop now. Pull away. But who had the willpower for just one taste of that fluffy stuff?

He pressed closer again, her mouth opened again, and he moved his tongue softly inside. Okay, so he'd have belted any other guy who made such a move on Francesca on a first date, but he couldn't resist. She inhaled a little startled gasp, and he tensed, ready to leave her, then her tongue met his, stroked against it as if she was joyfully discovering a brand new flavor of ice cream.

He went rock hard.

Not trusting himself, he dropped his hand from the golden smoothness of her skin. But on the way down, his fingers brushed her thigh, slender and firm, and he found he couldn't move. He laid his palm there but thought he'd better break the kiss.

He tried, really. But when he moved his tongue from her mouth she chased it into his. The maneuver seduced him. He gripped her thigh and the sound of another of her soft gasps lit a match to an already smoldering sexual burn.

Heat and instinct overtook him. He reclaimed the kiss, sliding into her mouth with a sure stroke and then exploring her teeth, her tongue, the response she made when he set up a thrusting rhythm.

She moaned, twisted to get closer to him, and he found his fingers dangerously close to the heat between her thighs. A hot chill ran up his arm toward his chest. Just millimeters and he could touch Francesca more intimately.

The thought hit him like a slap. Francesca! This was *Francesca* moaning against his mouth. *Francesca's* tense thigh beneath his fingers.

Francesca!

He snatched his hand from her and abruptly lifted away from her mouth. She stared at him, a dazed look on her face. Brett's shoulders and neck tensed.

Any minute now she'd realize what had happened to a simple good-night kiss. Any minute now awkwardness would descend and the dazzle on Francesca's face would disappear.

"Let me walk you to your door," Brett said quickly. Maybe he could get her there before embarrassment changed things between them, before the wetness of his kiss on her lips dried.

Because he wanted to go to bed remembering her just like this. Eyes dark and wide, mouth rosy and wet.

Hell, who needed sleep?

She jumped out of the car before he could make it around to her side. She practically ran to her apartment, pulling her house keys from her pocket even before reaching the door.

Halfway over the threshold, she paused. As she turned around, her hand came up. Maybe she was angry. Maybe she was going to slap him. Oh, he hoped she would.

But her face was unreadable and her palm felt cool as she laid it against his hot cheek. "I had fun, too," she said, then slipped inside and shut the door.

Fun? *Fun?* Brett worried about that term all the way back to his own apartment.

THE NEXT DAY Brett focused on work. He didn't let himself think of anything but briefs, cases and court appearances, and it was a good day. A very good day. Until Carlo Milano showed up in his office. Carlo, Francesca's big brother.

Francesca, whose mouth should come with caution signs.

Carlo peered at him beneath one raised brow. "You with me, Brett? You have time to talk?"

Oh, yeah. He was here as Carlo the police detective. They had business to discuss. Legal business. Unless Carlo was here to talk about Francesca. About how Brett had kissed her so damn silly that he hadn't slept more than forty minutes last night. But he didn't think his best friend would be wearing that faint smile if he had any knowledge of that.

Carlo waved a hand in front of Brett's face. "The

Rearden case? Yesterday you said you had some questions for me?''

Yesterday. Before Francesca's mouth had melted beneath his.

Brett stacked the papers he'd been looking over. "Right."

Carlo slouched in the chair across from Brett's desk. "You okay, bud? You look like you've been flattened by a steamroller."

Brett grimaced. "A steamroller." Yeah, she'd rolled right over his good intentions.

Shaking his head, Carlo narrowed his eyes. "A *female* steamroller. I recognize the look."

Brett wasn't going there with Francesca's brother. "Huh." He grunted noncommittally.

"You can tell me," Carlo said.

"Huh." Brett grunted again.

"Okay, okay." Carlo put up his hands. "I won't ask anymore. But after Patricia…" He cleared his throat. "Didn't you tell me you'd, uh, withdrawn from the fray?"

The fray. Relationships. Love. After Patricia's death Brett had mourned the girl he'd cared about since high school. And though his grieving had ended, he'd decided that he didn't want to involve himself like that again. Too much potential for pain.

"Brett?" Carlo grimaced. "Hey, hope I didn't say the wrong thing."

Brett waved away his friend's concern. "Don't worry about it."

"Then bear with me for another moment here. From what I see on your face I think you need to hear the same advice I've been giving myself."

Brett cocked an eyebrow.

"Lighten up."

"Lighten up?" Brett repeated, wondering what was weighing so heavily on Carlo's mind.

"Yeah. Two words to live by," he said, without adding any more.

"Lighten up." Rubbing his stiff neck, Brett took a moment to try out the concept. Lighten up.

Lighten up. Relief sluiced through him. Hell, he *had* been worried about nothing.

They'd exchanged a kiss. A hot kiss, but still just a kiss. There was no reason to attach any more importance to it. It needn't even change things between him and Francesca. If he kept his mind off her mouth and on winning that bet of hers, he could still help her.

Without anyone getting hurt.

BY THE TIME Brett made his way through the apartment's parking lot that evening, he'd completely expunged the kiss from his mind and was ready to proceed with his bet-winning plan. Busy tucking his cell phone in his pocket and juggling his briefcase, he tripped over Francesca. Literally tripped over her feet, sticking out from beneath her small red-and-white clunker of a pickup truck.

Her "Hey, watch it!" came out slightly muffled and characteristically direct.

He grinned. This Francesca was the same one who had trounced him in air hockey. Tomboy Francesca, who apparently could change oil like a pro, if the stacked quarts of oil beside the truck were any indication. This was the Francesca he could completely control his reaction to.

With the toe of his leather shoe he nudged one of her rubber-thonged feet. "Good evening to you, too."

Her legs stiffened. Not much, but just enough for him to guess she might be thinking about how the night before ended. Which, damn it, started him thinking about how the night before ended, too.

"Oh, hi," she called out.

She was wearing a paint-stained and holey pair of cutoff shorts. Below the fraying hem was the length of her legs. Curved, feminine, slightly tanned. Brett slid his gaze off the sweet line of her calf to focus on the scar on her knee. Ah, now *that* reminded him of the Francesca of the past. Relief again. He smiled.

"Good day?" he asked.

"Fine. Yours?" Her voice still sounded strained. Either she was having trouble unscrewing the oil drain plug or she was uncomfortable around him.

Because of the kiss.

He ignored the thought and shifted his briefcase to the other hand. "Listen. About last night—"

Beneath the car, something clattered to the ground.

"You okay?" he asked hastily.

"Fine! Completely fine!"

He'd planned on saying he'd had fun the night before and then asking her out again. But her voice sounded so odd. If he made her that uneasy, if they couldn't get past that wild burst of passion...

He stared at the bottom half of her, his back teeth grinding in frustration. What was the right thing to do? Retreat? Pursue? Damn, he hated making blind decisions, but he didn't have a clue what she was thinking when all he could see of her was thighs to toes.

"Francesca," he started.

Toes. Suddenly they snagged his attention. He leaned closer. Francesca had painted her toenails. A light pink, but painted all the same. And obviously she was no expert. The color was swiped across the edge of one little toe and smudged on another.

"What?" she said from beneath the truck.

"I—I—" Damn. The innocent and mussed nail polish tugged him so hard and in so many places he could hardly speak.

But he could hardly let her go so some guy could break her heart, either.

"I wondered if you're free for dinner this weekend," he said.

That got him a full look at her. She scooched from

beneath the engine, grease on her T-shirt, the drain plug dripping oil from her fingers to catch on the utilitarian plastic band of her digital watch. Her brown eyes were wide and she had another black streak across one cheek.

He could almost ignore the full rosiness of her mouth.

Yeah. They could go out again. Nobody would get hurt that way.

IN HER father's kitchen, Francesca wiped her palms against the butcher-style apron she wore over her new dress. Carlo breezed in and greedily eyed the pile of croutons that sat ready to garnish the green salad she'd made as part of their Saturday-night dinner of lasagna and garlic bread.

His fingers inched out, and she quickly slapped them back.

"Ow!" He threw her a wounded look. "Can you blame me? Those gotta be homemade. What, does Pop have the bishop on the guest list tonight?"

Francesca shook her head. "Just Pop and the five of us kids." She paused. "And Brett."

"Mmm." Carlo had turned to stick his head in the refrigerator and didn't seem the least perturbed by the news.

No, the "perturb" was all Francesca's and all stemmed from their date...and their kiss.

That kiss.

It should be a constitutional right for a woman to receive at least one kiss like that. A sweet-then-hot kiss from the one man she'd fantasized about her entire life. Some women would pick a movie star or sports celebrity as their fantasy men, but Francesca would choose Brett Swenson every time.

Anytime.

Which was where the whole situation got sticky. She couldn't go on expecting more kisses like that from Brett. Yes, he'd asked her out, then kissed her, then asked her out again. But was it because he was so attracted to her? More likely he'd done all of the above because he was lonely and still reeling from the shock of losing Patricia.

He wanted companionship.

And she'd always wanted him. But it was different now. No longer a twelve-year-old who lived for him to notice her, Francesca was a grown woman who had finally decided to start acting like one.

But though she might be slipping on high heels every once in a while, that didn't mean she'd reached Brett Swenson height. He was still beyond her reach. So when he'd asked her out that second time she'd closed her ears to every passionate impulse that urged her to scream "Yes!" and instead invited him to join the family tonight.

Francesca narrowed her gaze at Carlo, who looked like he was about to take a swig straight from the milk carton. Catching her look, he rolled his eyes and grabbed for a glass instead.

You had to be careful around men. Francesca knew

that. And the way she figured it, she'd be safer looking at Brett as just another one of her brothers.

Just another one of her brothers.

She did fine with the decision, all through the greeting him at Pop's front door—his eyes looked laser blue, but she valiantly ignored it—the accepting of the bottle of red wine he'd brought—she made sure his fingers didn't brush hers—and the sitting down to the meal—when to her brothers' astonishment Brett held out a chair to place her at the head of the table opposite her father.

Francesca even looked around with some satisfaction at her family of males—Brett included—as they sighed and grunted and moaned in appreciation over the hot dinner that she tried to provide for them once a week. On her right, Brett offered to serve her some salad, and she managed to see it as a brotherly gesture.

Then Pop broke into the clattering of serving spoons. "Franny, you've still got your apron on."

Automatically Francesca felt behind her for the bow at the small of her back and loosened it. But then she froze as all eyes turned her way. Usually she hated being caught at the dining table still in her apron. But usually she was wearing something equally practical underneath.

Tonight, though, she'd put on a dress that silver-tongued Elise had talked her into. And why she'd chosen tonight of all nights to debut the pink tropical-print thing, she really couldn't say. The men were all still looking at her. Five pairs of brown eyes. One pair of searing blue.

She laughed stiffly. "Oh, maybe I'll just keep—"

Smiling kindly, Brett slipped the apron's top loop over her head.

Six sets of eyebrows rose skyward. Six pairs of eyes focused chest high.

The apron slid from Brett's suddenly slack hand to the floor.

"*Franny*," somebody said.

Her brother Joe choked on his wine and grabbed desperately for a napkin.

Francesca wished they were kids again and the stuff would spew from his nose, because then everyone would look at Joe instead of her chest.

As it was, their stares compelled her to look down at herself. How bad could it be?

Pretty bad.

Elise had said the dress fit her like a glove. Well, yes. But the spaghetti-strapped, square-necked bodice fit like a glove because it pushed some essential body parts over the top. No more was exposed than any other twenty-something female showed on a regular basis, but it was *tons* more than Francesca had ever revealed.

For years the men in her family had treated her like a pesky, weakling little brother. But from the expressions on their faces it looked like they'd finally figured out she was female.

"*Geez*, Franny." Apparently Joe had managed to catch his breath and find his voice.

Tony looked incapable of saying anything.

Carlo was wearing that suspicious, interrogation face of his, eyes narrowed and one brow winging upward.

On her left, her brother Nicky took his cloth napkin and dropped it over her cleavage. The napkin held a moment then slid to her lap.

Francesca threw it back at him before daring to look at her father.

His expression unreadable, she tensed. Then she thought she saw his eyes water. He reached for the handkerchief in his back pocket and made a quick swipe across his face. Then he beamed.

"*Bella.* Beautiful. A beautiful woman just like your mama."

"A woman? Franny?" Tony hooted, obviously working up to an unmerciful tease.

Pop held up his hand. "You show your sister some respect." He sent all of her brothers a stern look. "Enough. Now eat."

Not until she heard the obedient scrape of forks against plates did Francesca slide a glance at Brett.

He hadn't picked up a single utensil. In fact, she doubted he'd moved since he'd dropped her apron on the floor beside her chair. She leaned over to retrieve it and found his hand there first. Their gazes met over the apron's striped denim.

"*Bella,*" he said softly.

Her mouth dried, and she licked her lips to wet them.

He followed the movement with his eyes. "*Bella* there, too."

For lack of a better response, Francesca smiled.

He smiled in return, then straightened.

To recover from the dazzling whiteness and the whispered word, Francesca gave herself another moment below table level. Then with a fortifying breath, she sat up and applied her attention to her plate.

Or tried to.

But from the corner of her eye she was continually distracted by Brett's tanned and capable hands. With her brothers, she never noticed how they held their knives, never noticed how often they took a sip of red wine, but she found herself fascinated by Brett's every move.

Gluing her gaze to her plate, she moved around lasagna and lettuce leaves, a giddiness in her stomach leaving no room for food. A gulp, then several more gulps of the full-bodied cabernet didn't seem to help. Warmth radiated out from her belly, and the wine gave her the guts to slide another look Brett's way.

He was staring at her.

The sounds at the table receded. Far in the background she heard the clatter of china. The bark of male laughter. A brother asking for more lasagna and another telling someone to pass the wine. It was the familiar music of her life and it faded to a mere buzz in comparison to the high-volume message coming out of Brett's eyes: *I like what I see.*

And though maybe she'd misinterpreted him, the exposed skin of her shoulders and chest tingled in response.

She knew the instant he noticed the chills. His knuckles turned white where he gripped his fork. His nostrils flared just the tiniest, the movement so sexual that Francesca's mouth went arid again and she blindly reached for her goblet to toss back the rest of her wine.

Licking a last drop from her bottom lip, she madly tried resurrecting her initial intention. *A brother, a brother, a brother!*

But how could a woman treat a man like a brother when he looked at her like she was a queen?

WHEN THE MEAL was finally over, Francesca found enough good sense to get away from the men by trading Tony, Joe and Nicky dish duty in return for a detailed cleaning of her truck the next afternoon. Back in the kitchen, with her voluminous apron rewrapped and wearing oversize yellow rubber gloves to protect her new manicure, Francesca regained her perspective and a fingernail hold on her control.

A dress didn't change anything. Gauche inside a gorgeous package was still just…gauche. And gauche couldn't sustain the interest of a man like Brett.

Any minute now he would take his leave or, if he settled in around Pop's TV like her brothers, then she could always slip back to her own apartment through the kitchen's back door. Away from Brett she'd feel more like herself.

She tried not to worry when Brett pushed through the

swinging kitchen door, bearing the last stack of plates in his hands.

Cautious, though, she kept her eyes on the water running into the kitchen sink. She pointed one yellow, floppy rubber fingertip in the direction of the counter. "Right there, please," she said cheerfully, fully expecting him to follow her direction and then make an immediate about-face to the living room.

Instead, he paused after depositing the dishes.

She felt him there, hovering, but she steadfastly refused to turn his way and continued sliding the rinsed plates into the small dishwasher.

Finally he spoke. "Where are the dish towels?"

Unable to stifle her amazement, Francesca spun around. "A man requesting dish towels? I should faint with shock!"

He grinned and sidled closer. "Goody. Then I'd have to catch you." His comic leer made her giggle.

And then it made her get nervous. "No, no, no," she protested. "You're the guest. No catching the cook or helping with the dishes."

He shook his head. "I'd deem it an honor."

Which one? Doing the dishes or putting his arms around her?

Francesca decided not to ask. And then she couldn't talk as he edged closer. She tried moving away, but the sink was at her back and the countertop pressed against her spine.

She held up her hands to warn him off, but in the big

yellow gloves they appeared clownlike instead of serious. With his thumb and forefinger he pinched one rubbery tip of each glove and drew them off her hands.

"You're done," he said.

Oh, she was. Done with the silly brother stuff. Done with thinking she could control her reaction to him. Done trying to stop her heart from pounding so darn hard that she couldn't hear anything but its beat in her ears.

She looked up into those blue, blue eyes of his. She saw her reflection there and thought, for the first time, she looked different. Really different. In Brett's eyes, Francesca saw herself as a woman, a woman with a sexy curve to her hair and a sensuous smile on her lips.

Her reflection boosted her confidence. Maybe this was what she looked like to him. Maybe this was who she was to him.

The idea gave her the courage to follow her desire.

As if he'd made her hands naked just for this, she slid both arms around his shoulders and touched her palms to the silky blond hair at the back of his head. She pulled him down for her kiss.

Maybe it didn't explode right away. She had to kind of slide her mouth over his hard cheek to locate his lips—but once she found his mouth the kiss ignited. She pressed against his lips harder. He pressed back.

He wasn't close enough to her. She tried dragging his solid body closer, but when that got her nowhere she moved forward to him. Her mouth opened against his, the woman she'd seen in his eyes giving him every bit of a woman's kiss. It was every bit a woman's instinct, too, that drove her to lean into him and entwine one leg around the back of his calf.

But then, just as the heat between them started to boil, it was very much a man's move—Carlo's move—that suddenly wrenched Brett away from her and planted a big brother's fist square against his jaw.

5

STUNNED, BRETT STOOD in Pop Milano's kitchen, breathing hard, and as much staggered by Francesca's kiss as he was by Carlo's fist. God, he might have laughed at the tableau the three of them made if his jaw wasn't throbbing like hell. Carlo, bellow-breathing like an enraged bull. Francesca, grown-up looking in her cut-to-there dress, but in wide-eyed innocence over what that dress—that *bella* dress—had wrought.

As for him—well, Brett guessed he was the villain of the piece.

Francesca moved first. *"Carlo!"* She planted her hands on her hips, and her dark eyes flashed fire in her brother's direction. "How *dare* you!"

He sputtered a bit, but what Carlo didn't dare was protest as Francesca grabbed Brett by the arm and dragged him out the kitchen's back door.

"Hey, hey!" Brett tried halting her momentum, but she sent him a quelling look and just tightened her grip on him. Well, he figured he owed her the first apology and so let her lead him in the direction of her apartment, the full skirt of her tropical print dress billowing behind her.

In seconds he was in her small kitchen beside a table the size of a TV dinner. She forced him to sit on a straight-backed chair with a no-nonsense shove against his shoulder. Before he could blink she—*splat!*—slapped a bag of frozen peas against his aching jaw.

"Oof!" He couldn't stifle an involuntary wince as he held the bag there.

All the starch went out of her. "Oh!" Her shoulders drooped and she dropped into the chair beside his. "I'm sorry. I'm so mad at Carlo that I was taking it out on you."

The frozen peas crunched against each other as he spoke. "Listen Francesca, I should be the one to apologize."

Her eyes widened in surprise. "No—"

"Yes. It's natural for your brothers to want to protect you." He didn't add that he felt the impulse in spades himself. "I shouldn't have put you in an, uh, uncomfortable position."

Color flagged her golden cheekbones. "Wait a minute—"

"I'm just saying that you shouldn't be mad at Carlo. And I hope you'll accept *my* apology for, well, *compromising* you in your father's kitchen."

"Hold it!" That fire had returned to her eyes and it looked hot enough to make instant green pea casserole. "Are you telling me that you're sorry for kissing me?"

"Well, uh, yeah."

She slapped her palms against the tabletop. "Well that

just about does it.'' Her full upper lip curled in disgust. ''I can't even get getting-caught right!''

Get getting-caught right? ''Francesca?''

She ignored him, instead rising from her chair to pace away from him. ''Other women are caught kissing when they're fourteen. It finally happens to me and you ruin it!''

He'd ruined it? Brett moved the frozen peas to his forehead thinking the cold might clear his confusion. Nope, no help. ''I ruined it, you said?''

She continued striding away from him. ''Of course you did!''

''Uh, Francesca?''

She reached the sink and spun around, breathing so hard he found he couldn't look away from the smooth skin of her cleavage, rising at dangerous levels over the top of her dress. She glowered at him. ''What?''

He tossed the peas on the table. ''When we were…'caught,' exactly what did I do wrong?''

''The fist in the face aside—'' she crossed her arms over her chest, pushing up her breasts more fateful inches ''—I'd think you'd be embarrassed, still aroused maybe, but not apologetic!''

As if she could see he utterly lacked a clue, she frowned and blew out a long breath of frustrated air. ''Brett, for the first time in my entire life I was doing something womanly and a little bit…wild and you've taken the glory out of it!''

What did that make? Five or six hundred times she'd

poleaxed him today? The low-cut dress and every breath she took in the sexy thing, that whopper of a kiss, this whole "glory" business.

He shook his head. "Francesca, what am I going to do with you?"

She pursed her lips as if deciding how to respond. Then she said, "I kind of hoped we were doing it." Pink color flooded her face. "Before Carlo came in, I mean."

Well, hell. A woman dressed like an exotic, tropical temptation. The recent memory of the best-tasting kisses of his life.

He was a marshmallow when it came to Francesca.

She must have seen it on his face, because she crossed the kitchen floor in two speedy heartbeats. One forefinger trailed gently over his jaw. "Let me kiss it?"

He pulled her onto his lap.

Fragrant and small, she nestled easily against his chest and looped her arms around his neck. Then she smiled at him.

He cleared his throat. "So you think you can make it better?"

Her smile went from womanly to wicked. "I know I can," she said.

That's when he stopped thinking. His heart slammed against his chest, his lungs struggled for oxygen, and he pretty much figured he needed Francesca to save him.

Her mouth began the rescue mission.

As promised, she touched the injured part of his face first, but it wasn't the kind of twinge he expected when she flattened her tongue against his jawline. His thighs and groin tightened, and she rocked against his lap just as her lips found their way to his.

Like earlier in the kitchen, he let her control the kiss. Not because he wanted her to lead, but because he was afraid he might frighten her if *he* did. Her tongue experimented again, teasing the corners of his mouth, washing across his bottom lip.

He groaned when she tickled the seam between his lips, and he opened for her, but she ran away from a deeper kiss, moving her mouth to plant baby kisses up his other jawline in the direction of his ear.

She whispered to him, her breath sending waves of heat rolling across his skin. "Thank you, Brett," she said.

Thanks for the burning pleasure *she* gave *him?* His arms were circling her slender waist, and he didn't allow himself to explore her any further. "Francesca..."

"Shh." She placed two fingers over his mouth. "Don't say anything. Don't think anything. I need the experience."

He groaned again. Like a kitten flexing her claws, she wanted to see how deep she could dig. What kind of pleasure she could have.

She wanted experience, and she wanted it with him. If he didn't give in, who would she go to?

Don't think. The words echoed, and Brett couldn't resist drawing one of Francesca's fingers—still so conveniently placed against his lips—into his mouth.

She gasped. He saw her stiffen and then her eyes closed when he rubbed his tongue along the sensitive inner skin between her fingers. A flush brightened her cheeks, and he watched it deepen as he sucked, holding her small finger against the roof of his mouth with his tongue.

He took one of his arms from around her waist. He circled her wrist and drew her finger from his mouth. Her eyes opened, and he watched them closely as he directed her wet fingertip to her own skin, letting it paint a damp line on her fragile collarbone.

Her pupils dilated, and chills chased one another down her neck and into the low-cut bodice of her dress.

Brett could hear his own harsh breathing and he stilled, making an effort to slow down.

"Brett?" she whispered. Not a shred of doubt colored her voice, only the sweet demand of desire.

He smoothed his palm over her hair. "Francesca."

She frowned a little bit. "Kiss me some more, Brett."

He smiled. "I haven't kissed you at all."

Her frown deepened. "Well, whatever you call it, I want some more."

God, she made him laugh. "That sounds like an order."

"It is."

He laughed again. His tomboy princess. "Your wish is my command," he said, and then he brushed back the hair from her face and kissed her nose, her cheeks and then finally explored the dainty curl of one ear.

Her nails dug into his upper arms as he nipped on her earlobe, and the little pain mirrored the good ache in his groin. Beneath her hips he shifted a little in the chair, and she wiggled, too, until his arousal settled into the warm notch of her thighs.

He groaned.

Her eyelashes flew open. "Am I too heavy?"

He didn't want her going anywhere, so he ran a fingertip down the slope of her shoulder as distraction. "Not a chance," he said, and then his finger met the skinny strap of her dress and the strap slid off her shoulder.

They both froze.

Then Brett lifted his other hand to surf the line of her opposite shoulder. He flicked the strap there and it dropped down, too. Above the bodice of her dress the roundness of Francesca's breasts rose and fell with even quicker breaths.

"Kiss me, Brett," she demanded.

With a hand cupping each bare shoulder he did, and her mouth softened immediately, opening for him. He thrust inside, turned on so damn bad now with her bare skin against his palms, with her fragrance rising around him like a soft cloud of arousal.

She moaned when he lifted his mouth, and then again when he slid kiss after kiss against the skin of her neck.

Her hands moved across his back and she pulled impatiently at his shirt. But she tasted too good to abandon, so he kept kissing her neck and shoulders until she pulled his knit shirt free from his jeans and pushed it upward.

Her palms burned him wherever she touched—so, so good—and he pulled away just for the instant it took to throw off his shirt. Now she found his mouth and her hands explored his chest, teasing him with a light, wondering touch.

His blood burned, his groin tightened rock hard, and as she ran her little hands up his skin, his fingers found the back zipper of her dress. The rasp as he drew it down didn't register over the syncopated hoarseness of their breaths.

He curled his fingers into the neckline then thrust his tongue into Francesca's mouth just as he jerked the dress to her waist. With one more quick movement the naked, hot skin of her breasts met his chest.

"Brett."

He barely heard the sweet exclamation over the exhilarated scream of every nerve ending in his body. Francesca's breasts were round and swollen, and the hard nubs of her nipples pressed into him like the very best kind of torture.

He twisted his torso so they grazed each other's skin.

"Brett."

Francesca's eyes were secret-dark, the pupils dilated with desire. He pulled back, eager to hold the fullness of her breasts in his hand, to taste the hard nipples. She watched him, her face completely trusting.

So trusting.

Damn, damn, *damn* trusting.

Wasn't this the very thing he was supposed to be protecting her from?

Closing his eyes and gritting his teeth, Brett made himself draw up her bodice. Made himself zip the damned enticing dress. Made himself lift her off his lap with only one more sweet, gentle kiss to her lips.

Made himself promise he'd never touch her like that again.

FRANCESCA FOUND herself thrust into the chair beside Brett's, still gasping for breath, her skin still tingling from his touch. Her dress was rezipped too, so she just blinked dizzily at him as he felt around for his shirt on the floor beneath him. He pulled it on, and a little sigh escaped her.

She thought he heard the sound, but he didn't look at her. Instead, he scrubbed his face with his hands and raked his fingers through his dark blond hair.

It had felt smooth and springy between her fingers. She sighed again.

His blue eyes cut her way. "Francesca..." He scrubbed his face again and inhaled a deep breath.

She watched his chest slowly rise and fall. It had been hard and hot beneath her hands and like...nothing she could describe when he'd rubbed it against her breasts. She allowed herself just one more sigh.

He groaned. "*Francesca.* You're not making this easy for me."

Well, good. It wasn't easy for her to come down from a desire high, either. Especially when it wasn't her idea.

Brett took another deep breath. "Okay. I'm going to say this and then get out of here. Francesca, I am very, very sor—"

"No!" She threw him a murderous look. "Don't you *dare* say that word."

"Francesca—"

"Don't." She shook her head for emphasis. "Or I'll put my fingers in my ears and hum 'The Star Spangled Banner.'" If he tried apologizing again her ego would shrivel to the size of a raisin. She didn't need that right now, not when she was still reeling from a passion she didn't even realize she had inside her.

She jumped up from her seat. "Let me make us some coffee instead."

Now *he* sighed. "If you're not going to let me talk, I should really be leaving."

"Talk? Who said we couldn't talk?"

He narrowed his eyes. "You're not going to hum or anything?"

She made her most serious face. "No humming, I promise. But I always reserve the right to break into song."

He laughed, and for the first time since they'd stopped kissing she saw him relax.

Good. She crossed to her small pantry to search for the coffee filters. The last thing she wanted—after an apology, that is—was for him to be tense around her.

Not when *she* really *did* want to sing and then shriek and then Snoopy-dance with joy.

Brett had kissed her and touched her and gone up in the same flames she had.

A woman who had doubted her ability to attract men—a woman who had dreamed about attracting *this* man since she was twelve years old—could only be ecstatic about that.

Scooping coffee grounds with a hand that still tremored, Francesca acknowledged that Brett might not be as thrilled as she. Most likely the last woman in his arms had been the beautiful love of his life, Patricia.

Certainly Francesca couldn't compare to her.

But if she let him back away right now she might never get another chance with him. It didn't take years of experience to realize that the moment he began seeing her as a woman was no time to let him get away.

So, MOMENTS LATER, with two oversize blue-and-yellow ceramic cups between them, Francesca smiled at Brett brightly. "There," she said. She took a sip of her milk-laced coffee, peeking at him over the brim. Time to talk. Get to know each other as adults. Work, books, movies. She'd even be willing to discuss sports teams if she had to.

He wrapped his palms around his cup. "About what just happened…"

Francesca almost choked on her coffee. As it was, she

had to swallow quickly and set the cup down with a clatter onto the matching saucer. "What?"

"We need to talk about it, Francesca."

"Oh, please." Her face warmed. "Could we do without the recriminations?"

Something passed over his face that looked like pain. "I don't know."

"Look, Brett. It happened, okay? It was good…"

His gorgeous mouth moved in a rueful grin. "So now let's forget about it?"

That wasn't exactly what she had in mind. Next he'd say they should make sure it never happened again.

He leaned forward. "Listen. I'm at a different place in my life, and—" He hesitated.

Terrific. Here came the "it should never happen again" part. Probably followed by a whole bunch of stuff about the wonderful Patricia. Francesca's heart twisted. She just couldn't bear hearing it right now.

She hopped up. "Speaking of different places in life. Wait'll you see what I have."

Bless him for indulging her avoidance. She scurried to the living room bookshelf and retrieved a photo album. She'd made one for each brother and then herself last Christmas, after finally going through the shoeboxes full of family pictures that no one had bothered sorting in over twenty years.

She laid the album on the table in front of Brett. "I think you show up more in the boys' albums, but I just *know* there are some photos of you in here."

Leaning against the wall behind him, she let Brett turn the pages. As the youngest of five children, there were few baby pictures of her. "Pop said we all looked the same when we wore only diapers and dimples," she told Brett, but he still got a chuckle over the one bare-behind-on-the-bearskin shot.

But his laughter quieted when he came across a photograph of Francesca's mother, Dina. Silently he traced the edges of the picture with one forefinger. Then he cleared his throat. "I remember her. Your mom."

From her position she could only see the side of Brett's face, but his cheek creased with a small smile. "She baked great chocolate chip cookies and made the best spaghetti I've ever tasted. And..." He stopped.

Francesca tried swallowing away the sticky lump in her throat. Her brothers and Pop rarely talked about their mom in front of her and she suspected it was because they didn't want her to know what she'd missed. "And?" she prompted. "Spaghetti and cookies and what else?"

"And your father was right. She was beautiful. Just like you."

Lucky she was leaning against the wall, or else she'd be a messy puddle at Brett's feet. She swallowed again. "Thank you," she whispered.

He acted as if he didn't hear her, going ahead to turn the pages of their childhood. He was present in a lot of the group shots: around the Milano Christmas tree, beside the grinning jack-o'-lanterns, in a baseball uniform on one of the many teams Pop had coached.

He pointed to one particularly unflattering shot of Francesca. "You haven't changed much."

She groaned. "Oh, yeah, that's me all right. With a Band-Aid on each knee and a prematurely missing tooth."

"Joe knocked it out with an elbow."

"How'd you remember?"

Brett shook his head. "Because I never heard anyone scream so loud in my life. Scared me to death. Your brothers scoured the grass for the tooth but I couldn't move."

She remembered as if it was yesterday. She'd been about five years old, and while everybody else was looking for the tooth, Brett had mopped up the blood and her tears. "You held my hand all afternoon," she said.

"And the other one I clapped over my ears." He gave her a self-deprecating grin.

He didn't want her to see him as a hero. But he'd been that for her when she was growing up. And somewhere between four and twelve she'd gone from hero worship to puppy love.

And somewhere in the past few days she'd gone to—

"Hey! This looks familiar."

Francesca peered over his shoulder. "Oh, yuck," she said. "My sixth-grade school picture." Braces, goofy hair in what some backward beautician had called a "pixie" cut. Francesca also sported a caged expression and one of Carlo's too-big shirts. "Poor Pop. He always tried to get me into dresses for picture day but I was slippier than an eel."

"Wait a minute," Brett said, lifting one hip off his chair to slide his billfold from his back pocket. "Guess what I have."

He shuffled through a wad of the stuff that gathered in wallets: receipts, credit and business cards. "Hah!" he finally exclaimed, and tossed something to the table-top.

That exact same sixth-grade photo of her. Except this one had a "Love, Francesca" written across the bottom and "To My Main Squeeze, Brett," across the top. The *i* in *main* was dotted with a heart.

He sent her a triumphant look. "That was my going-away-to-college present."

Francesca sat down in the chair beside Brett's, half embarrassed, half pleased that he'd kept it all these years. "My sincere apologies."

He frowned slightly as he tried to shove the remainder of the stuff back into his wallet. "I thought we weren't going to apolog—"

The stack got away from him and scattered over the table. Gas cards. ATM receipts. A studio shot of Brett's golden-haired Patricia landed inches from the photo capturing Francesca's preteen pain.

Her heart stopped beating.

"I thought I'd taken this out," he said quickly, reaching for Patricia's picture.

Francesca beat him to it. She cradled the photo in her hand, her heart restarting sluggishly as she registered the woman's smooth blond hair, toothpaste smile, the lace collar of her dress and perfectly manicured nails. "She was lovely."

"Yes," Brett said quietly.

Francesca gulped. "She was everything I always wanted to be, but didn't know how."

"I didn't even know you knew her."

Francesca shook her head. "I didn't, not really. But your senior year I went to the homecoming game with Pop and the brothers. I was just at the right age to be dazzled by the Homecoming Queen."

"Ah. But I would never have taken you for a Homecoming Queen wanna-be."

She didn't look at him. "Now that's where you're wrong. There's nothing I ever wanted to be more than a queen. Or a princess, even."

"You were the queen of the Milano household, that's for sure."

She threw him a disgusted look. "No. I wanted to be *real* royalty. Well, high school royalty. I wanted a crown and a corsage and at least once I wanted to ride in a limo with…"

"A prince?"

That would do. "Right." Not any old prince, though. She'd wanted Prince Brett.

"Francesca," he breathed her name softly, as if he didn't know what else to say.

She met his eyes. "Pretty silly, huh?"

He shrugged. "Just surprising."

She shrugged too. "Well, it was so surprising that not a bit of it ever happened. No crowns, no limos, not even one measly date to the prom." She slid Patricia's picture back toward Brett.

Instead of reinserting it into his wallet, he absent-mindedly shoved it in his back pocket. "I don't believe you didn't go to the prom."

"Nobody asked me. To help them tune up their car, yes. But to a dance? To a place I'd be required to wear a dress?" She shook her head. "I don't think it ever occurred to any boy I knew."

He smiled, reaching out to lightly touch her tropical print skirt. "Their loss."

She ducked their head. "I'm more suited to jeans," she mumbled.

There was a moment of silence, then Brett spoke. "Maybe," he said, chucking her under the chin. "But I like you just the way you are."

After a stunned moment, Francesca's temper ignited. He'd actually *chucked her under the chin!* She looked up, staring at the now-avuncular and slightly superior expression on his face. If she'd been twelve she would have landed him a facer to match Carlo's for the stupid gesture.

And then she absorbed what he'd said. *I like you just the way you are.*

Her temper flared higher. She wanted to scream. She wanted to cry. Punching sounded awfully good again.

Because "liking" wasn't the feeling she wanted from Brett, particularly not in that placating, almost-condescending way. Yes, as a testament from the man who had just an hour ago brought you closer to ecstasy than at any moment in your entire life, it was a mouthful of mere ashes.

6

BRETT TURNED into the apartment parking lot, burned out and ticked off after three fourteen-hour days on a case that had blown up in their faces when a witness recanted his testimony. He was not in a good mood and it turned even lousier when the first mug he should see once he exited his car was the one owned by the guy who had given him a face plant four days before.

Carlo.

Brett let out a sigh, then dropped his briefcase to the pavement. "If this is round two, let me just say that I've had a bad day and I'd be honored to take it out on your nose."

Carlo stepped into the circle of the security light illuminating the 10:00 p.m. darkness and shoved one big hand into the front pocket of his jeans. "Naw. I'm here to apologize." He rubbed the back of his neck with his free hand. "I've been a little edgy lately."

Brett bent to retrieve his briefcase. "Well, if we're offering up apologies, I guess I should—"

"Don't." Carlo shook his head. "Franny read me the riot act. She said the uh, situation was all her fault *and* made me promise not to let you apologize, either. She was adamant about that.''

That sounded like Francesca. The adamant-about-apologies part. But the kiss being all her fault? Well, maybe that one had been, but God knew that Brett was responsible for all the rest. All the rest that had severely impacted his ability to sleep the last few nights.

But he would stay away from her. What had started out as a white-knight impulse had escalated into a white-hot lust that he had no business feeling for Francesca. She deserved candy and flowers and forever, and he was incapable of promising that.

Brett looked over at Carlo. ''You up for a beer?'' This was the Milano he could afford to spend time with. From now on, Francesca was off-limits.

Carlo relaxed, as if the weight of the world was lifted from his shoulders. ''You just caught me leaving. I'm meeting Joe and Tony at the tavern for some beers and pool. Wanna come?''

Brett opened his mouth to answer. But then a car zoomed—too fast—into the parking lot and halted with a squeal of brakes. From a couple of cars away, Brett could see Francesca in the passenger seat, laughing at something the hot-rodder said.

Brett felt the beginnings of a burn in his gut. ''Who's that?'' he asked Carlo.

''Franny.''

Brett rolled his eyes in the other man's direction. ''I mean, *who* is that with her?''

Carlo shrugged. "I don't know. You coming with me, or what?"

Francesca was still laughing. She reached over the back of the seat and pulled something into her arms—it looked like clothes. Then she disappeared down into her seat. He couldn't even form in his head what she might be doing now, but that beginning of an ulcer started gnawing at his belly again.

Annoyed, he stared at Carlo. "It's okay for her to be with some stranger, but you throw a punch at *me?*"

"There's no kissing involved."

Well, B.S. Because as Brett watched she leaned over and bussed the guy on the cheek before jumping out of the car. Then, with her finger hooked over the hanger of some plastic-encased garment, she leaned into the car. Her cute little tush piked into the air, she chattered at the guy a mile a minute, probably charming him, making him smile, making him laugh, making him willing to do anything to win her that bet she'd made with Carlo.

That bet.

He nearly groaned out loud. There was still the problem of that bet. With Brett bowing out of her life, she'd be looking to fill the void and find a man.

"Brett?" Carlo sent him a puzzled look, as if he'd been calling his name several times.

With a final cheerful wave of her hand, Francesca dismissed her Daytona driver wanna-be. She disappeared in the direction of her apartment without even acknowledging her brother or Brett.

"Brett?" Carlo again. "Are you coming out for a drink or not?"

"Not," he said absently, following in Francesca's wake.

FRANCESCA FUMBLED with her keys. Darn Brett. Just catching a glimpse of him after four days could set her hands trembling. From where he had been standing in the parking lot with Carlo, she couldn't tell whether he was coming or going, but she wasn't taking any chances.

Get in the apartment in case he happened by!

She didn't want to see him. He'd shown up with plenty of regularity in her dreams the past few nights, and she was hoping that time apart from him would bring about The Cure.

The Cure. That's what Elise claimed Francesca needed. Not that she'd gone into great detail about what had happened between Brett and her, but just a few choice words and Elise had seemed to grasp the picture. And The Cure had been her solution.

Ah. The key finally fit in the lock just as she glimpsed Brett coming in her direction. She slipped inside the door and slammed it shut behind her. Nothing could have stopped her from peering out the peephole, though. And yep, there he was.

Blue-eyed, Scandinavian-beautiful Brett, all clean cheekbones and broad shoulders. Her heart started skipping around again and she forced herself away and toward the kitchen. Toward The Cure.

She carefully hung her third and thankfully last brides-maid's dress from the top of the pantry door. She'd have started The Cure this moment, but Elise swore it required a full evening, and Francesca was worn out after a final fitting of the dress and a night out with the other women of the wedding party.

Rubbing her palms against her jeans, she turned to contemplate the kitchen table and The Cure ingredients. The phone rang and Francesca absently picked it up.

"Who was that?" said the caller.

"Brett?" The sound of his voice sent a betraying set of chills down her spine. Francesca frowned at the phone. "How'd you get my number?"

"You're in the phone book."

"Oh." Sheesh, of course. Hearing his voice again made her silly. "That's right."

"No, that's wrong." Brett didn't sound like he had a good hold on his patience. "It's not even listed as 'F. Milano.' It says plain, old 'Francesca.'"

"That's me. Plain old Francesca."

He made a noise suspiciously like a snort.

"I gotta go, Brett." Francesca swung back in the di-rection of her Cure ingredients. When you needed to get a man off your mind, Elise had the answer. First you had to get him out of your sight and then you had to take The Cure. Francesca was pretty sure phone calls from said man were not part of the prescription.

"Just answer my question first."

From the table she retrieved Elise's handwritten list.

It had taken Francesca three stops and thirty dollars to fulfill the requirements, but if it worked, it was more than worth the cost.

"Who was that man?" Brett asked again, his voice surly.

Herbal face mask, check. Peach-pit exfoliating body cream, check. "What man?"

"The one who drove you home."

Hot-avocado oil hair treatment, this banana-scented stuff you put on the cuticles of your fingers and toes.

Francesca figured she knew how this Cure thing worked. It got men out of your life, all right. By turning you into a woman only a fruit-bat would love.

"You're not talking to me, Francesca."

Because I'm trying to forget about you. "A friend. He was a friend." From under the table she retrieved a little tube of cherry salve that was supposed to take years off your lips.

She'd settle for the removal of the memory of a few kisses.

"What are you doing tomorrow night?" Brett asked.

Francesca's shoulders slumped, and she collapsed into the chair beside the table. Not this again. "I'm busy," she said.

"With what?"

"I have plans." *Plans to take The Cure and rid you from my heart—no not heart—mind.*

"Plans with your 'friend'?"

Francesca felt her temper kindle. "To what purpose is this phone call?"

Now it was his turn to not answer.

"Are you checking up on me out of brotherly concern?" she said, exasperated. "Because if you are, I have more than my share of that overrated stuff."

Through the phone she heard him swallow. "I feel...differently from a brother."

Francesca's heart dropped to her stomach. She took a deep breath, hoping to lift it back into position. "Wh—" It took a moment to catch her breath. "What do you mean?"

"Hell, Francesca, I had you half-naked in my arms the other night. Surely you've got to know that wasn't *brotherly.*"

Francesca flung out a hand and knocked over the bottle of face mask. "Of course, of course." She squeezed shut her eyes, not wanting to remember how easily he brought the passion out in her.

He groaned softly, as if he was picturing the same thing. "It just seems...dangerous, Francesca."

Her mouth was dry. "Dangerous, how?"

"You—" He broke off.

"What?"

"It's so hot, so fast." He cleared his throat. "Just forget I said that."

She wouldn't forget it as long as she lived. Because it told her something. It told her that Mr. Scandinavian

Blue-Eyed Calm wasn't as in control as he'd seemed the other night.

Francesca's heart had flown back up to its rightful place and now was flapping around in her chest like a butterfly gone suddenly free. She gripped the edge of the table. "Why don't you come over, Brett?"

"What?"

"Right now. Come over and be with me." She wanted to see him. She knew, just *knew* he wanted to see her.

Silence stretched out across the line.

"Please," she cajoled, not caring a whit about her pride or any female don't-ask-first games that she'd heard her friends advise each other about all her life.

She'd been raised by men. "What do you say, Brett?" Straightforward, direct men, who'd taught her that those who don't ask, don't get. Even so, she held her breath, willing him to agree.

"I say no."

"No?" Embarrassment burned hot patches on her cheeks and the back of her neck. "You're rejecting me?" she whispered.

"No! *Not* rejecting you, Francesca, but—"

He was still talking as she hung up.

The phone rang again. She didn't answer. It rang some more. She wouldn't answer.

She was too busy lining up the bottles and potions of The Cure. Elise had promised it would work. Francesca wasn't so sure.

Maybe it was her Italian blood, but Francesca thought the whole process needed something.

She got out a cookbook. Her mother had baked chocolate chip cookies. And Francesca made cannolli that everybody swore kicked butt.

In the morning Elise brought over brownies. With the psychic connection that signified a true best friend, Elise just showed up at Francesca's door with a plate of the fudgy walnut squares *her* mother was famous for.

"She's sabotaging me!" Elise shrieked. Apparently their psychic link was on the blink because Francesca hadn't a clue what Elise was talking about, and Elise didn't seem to realize that Francesca was deep in the dumps herself.

Francesca led the way to the kitchen and automatically filled the teakettle. "Who and why?" she asked.

"The woman who made these tempting things, that's who! My mother who is paying for a wedding dress that isn't going to fit me after I down these brownies!"

Francesca patted her best friend on the shoulder and took the brownies away from her. "Don't eat them."

"Bridal jitters are worse than a bad case of PMS!" Elise said, grabbing back the plate. "I need this food."

"You don't," she said, pulling the plate away.

Elise wrestled the brownies back again. "Franny, you *know* sometimes we just gotta have the worst thing for us."

Francesca opened her mouth to respond, but her doorbell rang.

Afraid to leave Elise alone too long, Francesca ran to answer it. On her doorstep stood a delivery girl holding a vase containing a huge spray of pink wildflowers surrounding one perfect pink rose. Francesca blinked. "These can't be for me."

Elise came up behind her. "Of course they can, you ninny. Your name is on the delivery sheet. Now sign for them."

Stunned, Francesca obeyed, then shut the door and carried the flowers into the kitchen. The kettle was whistling, so she set the flowers down on the table and began to make tea.

Elise stared at her. "What are you doing? Don't you want to open the card?"

The card. Of course. Flowers came with a card and you opened it and it told you who they were from. It was just that she'd had little experience receiving flowers.

No experience, to be precise.

She wiped her hands on a dish towel and found the tiny card, perched on a plastic fork thing nestled amidst the arrangement. The tiny wildflowers trembled on their stalks as she tried to gently work the card free.

"Oh, come on!" Elise snatched the card out of the flowers and handed it over to Francesca. "Let's see what it says."

The little envelope was sealed. Even though she'd

given up biting her nails, Francesca couldn't get enough of a grip to open the flap. She bit her lip, looking for the best place to begin.

"Oh, my God!" Apparently those jitters really had hold of Elise. She took the envelope from Francesca and instantly ripped it open and pulled out the card. "Here."

"Sorry," it said. "Forgive me?" in a masculine slash.

Brett wanted her to forgive him. Before Francesca could decide if she did or not, the front bell rang again.

"I'll get it." Elise ran to the door and in seconds was back. "Another florist," she said. She thrust a small cool box into Francesca's hands.

Francesca slipped into a chair and set the white box on the tabletop. Conscious of the impatient Elise, she worked quicker now and opened the lid to find the most beautiful creation inside. More pink roses, one in full bloom and two half-opened blossoms, cunningly set with delicate bows of tulle ribbon and a circle of silver elastic.

"It's a wrist corsage," Elise said. "Who is sending you a wrist corsage? And *why* is someone sending you one?"

A corsage. Francesca touched the edge of the fragile ribbon. She'd never had one before. She'd always wanted one. She'd told Brett.

"Look." Elise pointed to another tiny card tucked into the box.

No envelope this time. "Be my date tonight?"

Francesca's heart clenched. The doorbell rang again.

"This is getting good." Elise ran for the door and was back in seconds. "No flowers this time. Just some generic delivery guy."

Another box, this one larger and wrapped in silver paper with a big pink bow. Francesca's palms started to sweat. She pushed it toward Elise. "You open it."

"No way. Just hurry up."

Francesca took a breath and tore into the paper. Then opened the lid of the box. And almost suffocated by forgetting to take a second breath.

The box was filled with silver-spangled tissue paper. And cushioned in the middle of it was a rhinestone tiara. The most sparkly, delicate and fantasy-fulfilling crown that Francesca had ever seen.

Even Elise was speechless.

Inside this box was a card too. "Be my princess tonight."

Both Elise and Francesca reached for a brownie at the same instant. Their eyes met as they both took huge, chocolaty bites.

"This is from Brett," Elise said around her mouthful.

Francesca nodded.

"Brett whom you're supposed to be taking The Cure from tonight."

Francesca nodded again.

Elise looked back at what had just been delivered. Francesca followed her gaze. Flowers, corsage, crown. They sighed together.

"Well?" Elise said, the question in her eyes.

Francesca held up her brownie. "You said it, Elise. Sometimes we just gotta have the worst thing for us."

BRETT KNOCKED on the Plexiglas shield to signal the limo driver to stop in the apartment parking lot. Then Brett exited the long white car.

He couldn't let Francesca feel he'd rejected her. God knew he'd caught her at a vulnerable time in her life, what with that stupid bet. He couldn't let himself pierce her heart when he was the one trying to protect it.

So he had to let her see that she attracted him. As dangerous as it could be, it seemed the right thing was to let her know he thought she was beautiful and desirable.

Tonight the plan was to give her everything she'd yearned for. The corsage, the crown, the ride in the limo. It didn't take a great intellect to see Francesca thought those were the things that would make her a woman.

Those and a man's desire.

That was the easy part. Tonight Brett would let her see what she did to him. He wouldn't go too far, but just far enough for her to know what power she had. And then he'd let her go.

He walked toward Francesca's apartment, promising himself to get this evening right. At midnight the princess would realize she really *was* one, and then she could move on to find her future prince.

FRANCESCA FIDGETED, impatient for Brett to pick her up. She inspected the contents of her purse, adjusted the strap of her new sandals, found a tissue to wipe the persistent dampness from her palms. Finally she returned to her bedroom to admire the sparkle of the tiara Brett had sent. It sat upon her pillow, winking at her in the fading light, as if it knew something that she didn't.

She wanted to get on with the date. Not that she had any idea why she was so anxious for it to begin. Without a clue as to how she wanted to behave toward Brett, or of what she expected or wanted from him, it might be better if their evening out was postponed until she had a plan.

Still, she paced quickly back to the living room. At the front door she went on tiptoe and put one eye to the peephole. No Brett, not yet. Unable to contain her anxiousness, she opened her front door and peeked down the walkway.

He was heading her way.

Francesca whipped back inside and slammed the front door, squeezing shut her eyes.

It didn't help. *God.* She could still see him, his image burned upon her retinas. Brett, wearing a black tuxedo that lightened the burnished gold of his hair and made his eyes the blue of the kind of wicked promises a good girl wasn't supposed to want.

And suddenly, in the wink of a rhinestone, Francesca didn't want to be a good girl anymore.

Her heart started thrumming against her breastbone.

To put a finer point on it, she wanted to be bad with Brett.

She gulped, stunned by the instant, unwavering certitude. Maybe it wasn't the best idea that she'd ever had. Maybe not the most logical goal. But the second she'd seen him in that tuxedo, she'd immediately leaped to the idea of lying naked in his arms, and there came a sense, a rightness that she'd never experienced before.

Call it woman's intuition.

And she'd wanted to feel womanly her entire life.

Her hands started to tremble.

Brett. Her first lover was going to be Brett. It *had* to be Brett.

She racked her brain for every hint, any scrap of advice she'd ever heard or read. How did she make this happen? How could she make this evening end the way she wanted?

She took one last look in the mirror beside the door, too late rethinking the sweet pink of her dress, the long time she'd spent treading the safe and narrow.

Could Brett be persuaded to walk her over to the wild side?

And did she have the nerve to try?

BRETT BUTTONED the jacket of his tuxedo, then knocked on Francesca's door. His lips curved as the door swung inward, then the smile dropped away as his jaw fell open.

Damn.

He'd never seen a sight more gorgeous. A woman more arousing.

In a dress of transparent pink layers, Francesca looked like a fairy. Somewhere beneath the filmy stuff was a tight-fitting sheath that accentuated her sculpted body and revealed inches of that cleavage that constantly surprised him.

Her hair was swept up in a dark knot, and one wavy tendril floated over her cheek and pointed in the direction of her pink, wet-looking mouth.

Damn. He thought he was going to die.

Clearing his throat, he tried to get a hold of himself. "Fr—" The sound came out hoarse. "Francesca," he finally said, clenching his fists to keep from reaching for her.

"Brett," she said softly, her little smile torture to him.

He tightened his fists again. Then suddenly it hit him. He didn't need to hold back. Tonight was all about *showing* her how she made him feel.

How she could make *any* man feel, he reminded himself.

He reached for her hand. It was warm and soft and the corsage on her wrist made her fingertips smell like roses. He flattened her palm against his cheek. "I don't believe it."

"Believe what?"

That she'd grown up. That she was here with him. That he could make it through tonight without going too far.

That he could *ever* let her go.

He shook his head to shake loose the thought. "The limo is waiting."

Her eyes widened. "No!"

He laughed. God, she enchanted him. "Of course. You said you wanted to ride in one."

She shut the door behind her, then stopped and looked at him suspiciously. "You're not taking me to a senior prom, are you? Because if you are I'll have to go back in and get my crown."

He laughed again. "No. That was just a...symbol. I thought we'd go to dinner and go dancing. Maybe ride around in the limo later."

She sighed dramatically. "A limo." She went on tiptoe to kiss his cheek. "Perfect."

That brief kiss zipped right into his bloodstream like a shot of whisky. He closed his eyes. If looking at her made him breathless, if her lips on his cheek made his blood heat, how would he survive the rest of the evening?

7

BRETT SURVIVED the evening with surprising ease, he discovered. Mostly because, unlike him, Francesca seemed completely unaffected by anything between them, fascinated instead by the limousine's accoutrements and the limousine driver himself.

She flipped through every TV channel, played several FM stations, inspected the crystal stemware, the appetizers, and refused a glass of chilled champagne. After the five minutes that took, she slid back the partition separating them from the driver and for the rest of the way to the restaurant quizzed the older man on how long he'd driven, whom he'd driven, and if he'd ever gotten lost.

Brett tried not to feel neglected. After all, this evening was about her. And she seemed to be having a good time, though slightly nervous. Through dinner she chattered away, entertaining him with wacky stories about apartment managing and the escapades of their mostly elderly tenants.

The limousine must have been a big hit for her, because after they ate she wanted to ride around in it instead of finding a dance club.

Bemused, Brett agreed. So much for the problems

he'd anticipated. Though he'd planned to show her his desire for her, he'd also worried that he might take it too far. As it was, she was treating him like one of the brothers she usually complained about.

She avoided his touch, avoided any kind of personal conversation. Back in the limo, she retreated to the farthest, darkest corner of the long seat. It was left to Brett to dim the interior lights and securely draw down the partition that gave them complete privacy.

Without asking, he poured her a glass of champagne. The limo smoothly rolled forward as he slid down her seat to hold it out to her.

Just as she leaned forward to reach for it, the limo took a quick corner, lurching her toward him.

There wasn't time for either one of them.

No time for her to catch herself.

No time for him to stop the champagne glass from falling to the carpeted floor.

No time for her to prevent herself from falling across him and no time for him to stop the instant hot reaction he had to Francesca lying across his lap.

He stared down at her dark and mysterious eyes. He watched her breasts rise and fall in a quick, involuntary breath.

And as if a switch had suddenly turned on, a high-voltage, sexual buzz filled the interior of the limo.

NERVOUS AS A DUCK in a pillow factory, all night long Francesca had babbled and forked food in her mouth and more than expressed her interest in the limousine, all because she didn't know how to let Brett know she wanted him.

That she meant to have him.

Thank goodness for that quick right turn. After a speedy mental promise to slip the limo driver a hefty tip, Francesca sank into the dizzying warmth of Brett's arms.

Heart accelerating, she tried to smile. "Well, hello."

There was blue fire in his eyes. "So you noticed I'm here."

Just every breath. Just every eyelash flutter and every movement of his long, strong fingers. "Yes," she said simply, still unsure how to proceed.

He pulled her closer against his chest. "Comfortable?" he asked.

She swallowed. *No.* She was edgy and nervous and she felt like she needed to shed her skin.

One of his forefingers traced the arch of her eyebrow. Heat shot from that single point of contact to radiate down her body.

"You're beautiful," he said, and there was something new and dark and exciting in his voice. "I want to kiss you."

"Oh?" she said quickly, her voice squeaking with nerves. *Oh?* She wanted to slap herself silly. What kind of response was "Oh?"

"What do you say?"

Say yes. Say please. Say take me. But her mouth

seemed to have a mind of its own. "I've never made out in a car," she said instead, all squeaky with anxiety again.

"No?" One of his eyebrows shot up, and he seemed calm, cool, collected, even amused. "It's highly over-rated."

"Coming from one who knows?"

He grinned. "I've been a teenager, remember?"

She made a face. "Don't forget I was one, too."

His smile faded and he lifted her closer to him. "Francesca, I wish…"

Her heart kicked into the next higher gear. "You wish?"

But he didn't answer. "What happened?" he said instead. "That tuneups and dresses problem again? Why *didn't* you ever make out in a car?"

At her shrug, his grip tightened on her shoulders. He pulled her up so she sat in his lap instead of across his legs. "I hate myself for this," he said, frowning. "But I'm glad you haven't."

The protective comment didn't rankle. For the first time she didn't feel she'd missed out, not when she hoped Brett might rectify the situation any instant.

"Brett?"

He was staring into her face. "Mmm?"

"Didn't you say you wanted to kiss me?"

He groaned. "Francesca…"

Her heart slowed down a bit. "I don't like the sound of that."

"Isn't knowing I want to enough?"

No. Only all of him would be enough.

"Francesca, don't look at me like that...." He groaned again, as if he was in real pain.

Francesca's heart skidded to a halt. She licked her lips. "Is this—is this about Patricia?" she asked hesitantly. Great. Here she'd been only thinking of herself. Was it painful for Brett to be in another woman's arms?

He shook his head. "This is about *you*, Francesca. I promise. Only about *you*."

"Okay, then." In relief, she bounced a little against his lap.

"Francesca." Another long groan.

Uncertain, she froze, but then she thought about what she was feeling beneath her backside. Not just hard male thighs, but...hard male.

Maybe they weren't so far from the wild side after all.

She swallowed, steeling herself to be as direct as she had to be. As she wanted to be. "Brett," she said softly. "Thank you. Thank you for tonight. You fulfilled my teenage fantasies."

He pulled back his head, as if he realized something more was coming. "And? But? Though? However?" he said, looking at her suspiciously.

Francesca drew in a breath. A little do-or-die impulse had been nurtured in her from the day she opened her eyes and met the gazes of her four older brothers. It roared to life now, breathing enough dragon fire to cinderize any princessy qualms.

Just tell him what you want, the impulse prodded. *Ask for it.* You might not always win, taking on a challenge, but where was the glory in playing it safe?

She wet her lips again and tried looking assured. Whenever you went, um, guts to the wall, you had to be confident. She ran one fingertip across his cheekbone and watched the muscle in his jaw tick in reaction. You could be devious, too, if you needed to.

She smoothed back his hair. "Come on, Brett. Just once. Kiss me."

He briefly closed his eyes, then gave in. His lips pushed hard against hers and then eased to seduce them soft and open. Her heartbeat slammed against her breast as she felt him enter her mouth with his tongue. Chills shivered down her skin, heat burned deep in her belly.

He lifted his head, his eyes a blazing-hot blue. "You're a witch," he said.

Maybe so. Because inside her, confidence built and the dragon roared, adding to the sexual fire that she didn't bother hiding anymore.

She touched his face again, even more determined. "Now that we've done the teenage stuff, I thought we could grow up," she said, her voice surprisingly steady as she laid it straight on the line. "I thought you might make love to me."

I THOUGHT YOU MIGHT make love to me.

Brett couldn't get the words out of his head, even though the minute she'd uttered them he'd slid her off his lap and instructed the driver to take them back to the apartment complex pronto.

She looked at him now, eyebrows raised, as if still waiting for him to answer the question.

He scrubbed a hand over his face. "Don't even think about it."

A little smile curved her lips. "If you're talking to me, it's *way* too late."

She bent over to retrieve the champagne flute that had fallen to the floor and set it in one of the built-in holders. Her hair had half fallen from its knot and trailed down her back. Smooth and silky, it curled against the sheer pink fabric, and he wanted to touch the stuff, then touch her skin, then do to her all the things she didn't know she was asking for when she'd said, *I thought you might make love to me.*

She took up a fresh glass. "Some champagne, please?" she said, holding it out to him. The chilled bottle was on his side of the limousine.

"No!" Somebody needed a clear head, and his was more than muddled.

She frowned and reached across him to grasp the bottle herself. "It's perfectly legal."

He pressed back against his seat so her arm wouldn't brush him. "Well you shouldn't be," he muttered.

Champagne glug-glugged into her glass. "I heard

that,'' she said, then lifted her glass in his direction. Her gaze captured his. "To us," she said.

He couldn't look away. Like static electricity, sex still crackled in the air, and he called himself every son-of-a-curse he could think of for starting on this path to disaster.

She took a swallow of champagne. It was the kind of swallow that loosened inhibitions, and he edged farther away from her.

"You haven't answered the question," she said.

"You couldn't have been serious." There. That said it all. That said they'd been playing around. Flirting. Enjoying a little male-female game that didn't need to go anywhere beyond the few kisses they'd shared.

He didn't let himself think of the sweet, heated taste of her mouth.

"I am serious."

He thought about jumping out of the car. Anything to end this conversation. He'd wanted to restore her confidence, not create a whopper of a problem for himself.

"Hah." He thought it sounded a little like a laugh.

"Hah?" She repeated, then drained her champagne. "Are you afraid you won't respect me in the morning?"

"I'm afraid I won't respect *me* in the morning," he muttered, then stopped, appalled at how that had sounded and by the stunned look on her face. "No, no, you don't understand. That didn't come out right."

He slid closer to her. He found himself taking the champagne glass from her and then holding her hands in his. "How could I...take this from you, Francesca?" He brought her fingers up to his mouth and kissed them, like a supplicant asking for royal favors.

He felt the fine tremble in her hands, and she shook her head. "Why can't it be something I *give* to you?"

"Francesca. Your family would kill me."

She stubbornly set her chin. "This is not about them. This is about *me*."

He sighed.

Then she withdrew her fingers from his. She turned sideways on the wide bench seat to face him fully and placed her hands on his shoulders. The small and warm touch roller-coasted to his toes.

"Who taught me to ride a bike?" she said.

He thought back. "I guess...I did."

"Who showed me how to make a kite tail and wind the string on a stick?"

He frowned. "Me."

"Who held my hand when I ice-skated the first time, and who made sure I didn't throw like a girl, and who taught me how to dive instead of belly flop?"

She'd tackled each new skill with a verve and intensity that he'd admired even as a teenager. She'd had a passion— Damn.

Passion.

Brett closed his eyes, but she kept talking, whispering like the temptation she was turning out to be.

"You, you, you," Francesca said. "You were there every time I needed to learn something new."

She wanted a teacher, a tutor, a mentor, in…sex. But she'd call it lovemaking and right there was the biggest sticking point.

Maybe she could read the objection on his face. "I'm not asking for forever, Brett. I'm asking you for tonight. I want this and I trust you. You'd never hurt me."

But he might. He could. And her passion would definitely burn him. His blood pumped hot and heavy, and the sight of her naked torso flashed through his mind. He could almost feel the plump heat of her breasts against him.

Setting his back teeth, he took hold of her hands again and drew them off his shoulders. He cradled her fingers in his own. That's what he was supposed to be doing. Sheltering her, protecting her, not remembering the taste of her skin or the responsive catch of her breath.

The limo rolled to a stop. Brett looked out the window and realized they'd made it back to the apartments. Just in time. He'd say no as gently as he could, and she wouldn't have a chance to work those wiles of hers on him again.

He opened his mouth.

But she spoke first. "Think about it, Brett. If it's not you, it *will* be someone else."

At the words, the burn in his blood and his belly turned to red fire in his brain.

Scruples fled. Reasons not to involve himself retreated. Every rational thought receded, and everything but Francesca turned hazy dark.

He slipped his hands from her fingers to handcuff one of her wrists. He pulled her from the car, dug money from his pocket and tossed it at the driver. Walking as quickly as he could, he led her in the direction of his apartment. One part of his brain realized she was almost running to keep up.

The rest of his brain just wanted to be alone with her as soon as possible.

In seconds they were inside. In an instant he'd slammed shut the door. He didn't bother with the lights. Surrounded by inky blackness he pushed Francesca back against the door and dove for the dark heat of her mouth.

He thought he heard her gasp, but he didn't let up. He pressed harder, pressed forward, pushing his tongue into her mouth and taking her taste into himself.

If it's not you it will be someone else.

When he couldn't breathe, he lifted his head and breathed raggedly. "Well?" he said hoarsely. "Sex isn't kites and bike rides. I can't be gentle with you, Francesca. Not every moment. Not even if I wanted to."

He closed his eyes, and his heartbeat pounded like flashes of fire against his eyelids.

If it's not you it will be someone else.

His breaths moved harshly in and out of his lungs. "It's now or never, Francesca." He stepped away from her, every muscle in his body granite hard. "Your call."

Only one more quick breath passed. Then she came against him, her arms around his neck, her mouth hot against his throat. "Now," she said, her voice strained with what he recognized as passion. His skin shuddered in response. "Please, Brett. Now."

DESPITE her big brave words and the tingling desire in her body, an armada of goose bumps set sail down Francesca's spine. She'd expected Brett to be a tender and gentle lover, but he was hot and hard, and she was a little afraid she couldn't keep up with him.

She bit down on her lower lip, but then he was there instead, seducing her with a heavy, heated kiss. Her limbs went soft, and she locked her arms around his neck to stay upright.

"That's right," he said, his voice hoarse and deep. "Lean against me, honey. I want to feel you."

Francesca shuddered in response, and he trailed his mouth down her neck. He kissed her there, too, and she almost fainted at the sweet, slight burn of his whiskers.

His mouth returned to her lips. "Kiss me back," he murmured to her, but she couldn't. She couldn't kiss or say his name or even breathe, because his fingers found the zipper at the back of her dress and in seconds he'd opened it and peeled the dress from her shoulders. The fabric pooled at her feet and he dragged her out of the tangle of its folds by stepping back.

"Let me feel you," he said again, his voice harsh, his hands hot and hurried as they trailed down her shoulders to her wrists. She still wore a strapless bra and panties and yet Brett's touch was so knowing, so intimate, so *impatient* that her heart sped up again and she gasped for air.

He took her mouth again but she wrenched her face away because she needed still more time to breathe. His heart pounded insistently against her chest, and when he lifted her against him, pushing her hips against his so his arousal pressed against the notch at her thighs, she felt a sob rise.

He didn't seem to notice her panic. He twisted his head and thrust his tongue into her mouth and she stiffened, instinctively pushing away from him with her hands.

He didn't seem to notice that, either, instead grinding his pelvis against hers and kissing her neck.

"Brett."

Tears stung the corners of her eyes and a real sob tore through her throat. "Brett, *please*. Stop."

Instantly he drew his hips away from hers. Instantly his hands softened and loosened. "Have you had enough?" he asked quietly.

"Uh…" She blinked in confusion and a now-extraneous tear burned a path down her cheek. "Wh-what?"

He moved completely away from her, and she followed the sound of his voice toward his living room couch. "Have you had enough?" he repeated.

With the back of her hand she wiped her face dry. "I…I don't get it."

"Damn it, Francesca." His voice sounded strained.

"You must be careful what you ask for. Be careful *who* you ask for."

She came several steps forward. "Are you saying I should be afraid of you?"

"No. Yes." In the darkness she could barely make out the wave of his hand. "Maybe this is one of those things that come with the experience of prom dates and making out in cars. You've just got to learn to be more careful about offering yourself."

A flush of embarrassment heated her cheeks. "So that—" she pointed toward the door "—that was about teaching me a lesson?"

"You wanted to learn, didn't you?" he said flatly. "And if not from me, from someone else. Well, that's what somebody else might offer you."

Francesca had never been a cryer and didn't think that now would be a good time to start, but she felt a new sting of tears nonetheless. "You scared me." In the darkness she stared at Brett accusingly. "You really scared me."

Silence welled in his side of the room. Then his voice sounded, hard and cool. "That was the whole point, Francesca."

Anger moved in to replace the tears, and Francesca welcomed it. She stomped over to her dress and stepped inside, then wriggled to pull it over her hips. "Well, thank you very much, but I'm not an idiot."

From his side of the room there was a grumble.

She sent a murderous glare his way. "I'm *not* acting

like one. An idiot *would* go to any man when she wanted to make love for the first time. An idiot *would* have found a way when she was sixteen or eighteen or twenty or anytime before now, if all she wanted was to have sex.''

She heard his quick intake of breath.

"Well, I'm smarter than that. I'm smart enough to wait until I'm ready. I'm smart enough to pick a man that I…care about. A man who makes my skin quiver and my bones melt and who I *thought* I could count on to make me feel beautiful. To make *it* beautiful.''

She struggled with the zipper that seemed stuck somewhere at the small of her back. "If you ask *me* Brett, the only stupid one around here is *you*.''

The zipper wouldn't budge. She wanted to stamp her foot in frustration, but that would take precious seconds away from a timely exit. She just had to get this dress on! Arms behind her, she worked at the dress, feeling the shoulder straps slide down her naked shoulders.

The light beside the couch blazed on.

She stood there, caught in its glare, half angry, half teary and half-dressed. Three halves, she thought hysterically. That can't be right.

"Francesca.''

She didn't want to look at him. She didn't want to see any smugness or superiority on his face. The zipper moved an inch, stuck again.

"Francesca, please. Look at me.''

She breathed out her nose impatiently. "What?" she said, reluctantly sliding her gaze in his direction.

The light from the lamp colored his hair gold, and he'd tossed off his jacket and tie. His white shirt was open at the throat, and his blue eyes took hold of hers and wouldn't let go. "I'm sorry," he said. "I screwed up and I'm sorry."

Her hands froze on the zipper. He had an expression on his face she'd never seen before. His cheekbones pushed starkly against his skin and his eyes were wide and serious. "I don't know if I wished you hadn't grown up or I'm down-on-my-knees grateful you did or…" He shook his head. "I just can't seem to get this right."

He rose from the couch and walked toward her. "Let me help you, honey." With achingly gentle hands he turned her so her back was to him. She let go of the zipper and he eased it up, past her hips, her waist, the middle of her back.

"There," he said. "All done."

She didn't turn around.

He didn't move.

And then he touched his mouth to her shoulder. Gently. A butterfly's kiss that made Francesca's nipples harden and warmth pool instantly between her legs.

Oh.

He rested his cheek against the top of her head and pulled her back against him. His shirtfront was scratchy and hot, and her skin rose in goose bumps to meet it.

"Let me, Francesca?" His voice was soft and hoarse at the same time. "Let me try again?"

8

BENEATH HIS HANDS Brett felt Francesca tremble. He'd made her afraid and he hated himself for it. She was beautiful and sweet and fragile, and if he didn't restore her faith in him he wouldn't forgive himself.

He kissed the side of her neck, gently, softly, closing his eyes to the seductive scent of her perfume, remembering how she'd tried it out on him that first night.

For better or worse, she wanted him. And the only thought he could focus on now was making sure it was better. The best.

"Francesca?" he murmured against her skin. "Let me have another chance?"

The stiffness slowly flowed out of her body. "Admit you're an idiot," she said.

"I'm an idiot." He sucked lightly on the side of her neck.

Her voice came fainter. "And you were wrong."

"I'm often wrong." He breathed against her temple and she shivered.

"And...and..." She leaned back lightly against him and shivered again. "I'm nervous."

He squeezed her shoulders, half relieved, half disappointed. "Then why don't we say good-night."

"*No!*" Her body straightened and she took a quick breath. "Sorry. Sorry. Just feeling a bit skittish."

"Are you sure—"

"I'm sure!"

Brett pressed his fingers against her shoulders, kneading the tight muscles. "Then just relax. Think of tonight as…"

"As what?" Her muscles remained tensed. "A rite of passage? An initiation rite?"

"Yeah," he said softly and smiled. "To probably the world's biggest club."

She didn't laugh.

Brett continued massaging her shoulders. If she was determined to go through with this, he was determined to make it worthwhile. No mechanical, let's-get-it-over-with act for Francesca.

"Speaking of clubs." He put his mouth against her ear. "Remember when you wanted to join our Boys Only Club?"

Her lips curved up. "My brothers refused. They would have broken your legs if they knew you let me into that rickety clubhouse you built in our backyard."

Brett wondered briefly what punishment they'd enact if they knew what he was doing now, then pushed the thought away. "That's right," he said. "I took you out there and showed you the place."

Her body leaned back against his. "In the middle of the night."

"I bet it wasn't much later than nine, but okay."

Francesca shook her head and her hair tickled his chin. "You said it had to be pitch-black."

Brett slid a glance in the direction of the living room lamp. "I did, didn't I?" In an instant he strode to the light, turned it off and returned to Francesca. "I remember now. You'd been bugging me about it all day. I said we had to wait until dark."

In the blackness inside his apartment, he heard her breathing quicken. Then he knelt by her feet.

"What are you doing?"

"Don't you remember?" he said, circling her ankle to lift one foot. "So we wouldn't get caught creeping out of the house you had to take off your shoes."

She didn't protest. Having taken both her shoes off, he stood. Then he reached around her back, the tab of the zipper cool against the hot skin of his fingers.

Francesca jerked. "Wh-what?"

He pulled it down. "Someone might hear the rustle of your clothes," he said matter-of-factly, the escapade of the past turning into another kind of game entirely. "We better take them off."

The *bzzzip* of the zipper opening sounded loud and harsh in the darkness. Brett's pulse started a sledgehammer beat, and he swallowed hard as the dress fell away from her. He leaned down to kiss the side of her neck, stroking the spot with his tongue.

She moaned.

"Shh," he said, moving upward toward her ear. "We have to be very, very quiet."

At her sides, he laced their fingers and just leaned into her, letting her become accustomed to the heat and hardness of his body.

"What about your clothes?" she whispered. Strained tension remained in her voice.

He ignored the question and instead lifted her light form into his arms. "The grass is wet on the way to the clubhouse. And because you're afraid of slugs—"

"I am *not* afraid of slugs!"

"And because you're afraid of frogs—"

"Frogs, either!"

Smiling, he turned toward the short hallway. "And because you're a kind young woman you'll indulge me and let me carry you to the clubhouse." Inside his bedroom, he shut the door behind them with a *snick*.

It was cool and even darker than the living room. Brett slid Francesca down his body, then held her lightly against him. "What do you think of the place?"

"As I recall there was nothing but a dirt floor and the stub of a candle." She was talking about the old clubhouse.

"That's because I'd hid the stack of girlie magazines."

There was real shock in Francesca's voice. "No!"

He shrugged. "Well, I think we had a couple of pages of ladies underwear ads torn from the Sears catalog."

She giggled. "You didn't."

"I'll never tell." The truth didn't matter. What mattered was that Francesca was relaxed against him and laughing.

She sighed. "You were very nice to me, you know."

He drew a forefinger from her wrist to her bare shoulder. "I was, wasn't I? Didn't I even go so far as to spill all the details of our secret ceremonies?" His finger traced across her collarbone and he felt her tremble.

"You even initiated me," she said.

His fingers drifted toward the top curves of her generous breasts. "I did, didn't I?"

Then she went serious and quiet and with calm intent he picked her up again and strode the few feet to his bed. He pushed aside the down comforter and laid Francesca against the cool sheets. He stretched out beside her.

"That initiation rite involved blood," she said.

"Just a little." As he remembered, he'd pricked her ring finger with a pin. "And I didn't hurt you."

"No," Francesca replied. "You never hurt me."

He hoped he wouldn't now, either. He leaned across her. "I'm going to turn the light on."

She grabbed his arm. "I thought you said we needed to be in the dark."

"But we're safe inside now, Francesca." And he needed to be able to see her face. He needed to gauge her reaction to his next move. To his every move. Because he never wanted to scare her again. He only wanted to bring her pleasure.

The bedside light clicked on to provide a dim glow. Brett rolled back into place and then cast a glance at Francesca.

And nearly fell out of the bed.

"Honey..." It came out of his mouth, unbidden, uncontrolled. *Honey.* Honey was the color of Francesca's skin against the white sheets, yards of skin revealed by white, tiny, high-cut panties and a strapless bra.

Honey was the consistency of the thick desire infusing his bloodstream, making his heart beat harder to prevent him from expiring of arousal.

Honey was the sweet, sweet anticipation of having Francesca for himself.

Heart slamming in his chest, he flattened himself against the mattress and stared up at the ceiling.

"Brett?"

"What's the square root of 167? How about 673?" Maybe using his brain would slow down his body.

She sounded confused. "What? I'm not sure I ever knew."

Brett wasn't sure he was going to make it through the night. Not when the woman he was supposed to make a gentle, treasured memory with was turning him on so hard and fast that his hands were shaking and his blood was deserting his brain for his groin.

"Are you...am I...okay?"

He groaned at the tentative note in her voice. "Francesca, you're so okay that I'm bound to forget how in-experienced you are.''

The old sassy Francesca returned for a moment. She smiled. ''So let's forget that and go back to the 'I'm so okay' part.'' One of her fingers reached out and touched a button on his tuxedo shirt. ''There are parts of you that I think are okay, too.''

Afraid to touch her at the moment, he fisted his hands as she unbuttoned his shirt then spread the edges. Her breath sucked in as she looked at his bare chest, and then she swept her palm over his flesh.

His heart and his arousal leaped toward her.

''Honey.'' He rolled to lean over her. His lips found hers, and she immediately opened her lips for him as her arms went around his neck. The heat of her mouth matched the heat of his blood.

The kiss went on, hungry and deep, as one of his hands ran over the silky skin of her arm up to her shoulder. She trembled as he traced the top line of her strapless bra then followed it back again. On his next path he paused at the deep valley between her breasts and then slowly slid two fingers down between them.

She moaned into his mouth.

Her hot, fragrant skin cradled his fingers, and he thrust against the insides of her breasts, echoing the movement of his tongue into her mouth. Francesca moaned again and twisted her hips against him.

The sound of her passion, the sweet taste of her mouth, her soft heat against his knuckles burned all notions of caution from his head. Hooking his fingers into the bra, he tore down the cups to fully reveal her breasts.

He broke the kiss, heaving in air along with her. He looked down at what he'd exposed, her generous breasts peaked by nipples as pink and tight as the rosebuds on the corsage still binding her wrist. The hand with the flowers fluttered up.

"Don't," he said quickly, catching that hand. "Let me look. You're so beautiful, Francesca." With a reverent touch, he circled one nipple.

"Brett?" His name trembled from her lips.

"Yes," he answered. And knowing that she was asking for what he needed, he bent to take her into his mouth, licking the warm skin of her breast. Her body bowed, pressing against his mouth, and when he hollowed his cheeks to suck in her nipple, the scent of roses mingled with the scent of Francesca.

He shivered as her hand stroked his hair and cool rose petals brushed against his heated neck.

Desire pooled hotly in his groin and created an insistent ache at the small of his back. He slid one leg over Francesca's and felt her hands stripping him of his shirt as he moved to her other nipple. He bit it gently—he couldn't help himself—and he shivered again as she moaned, her voice hoarse and needy.

"Brett."

She was aroused, too, and hungry, and now her hands moved insistently over his bare back. He lifted his head. "Soon, baby, soon."

With shaking hands he slid her panties down her legs and then kissed her breasts again as he stroked her belly and thighs, each time lingering longer at the apex. With each kiss, each stroke, he felt the languor overtake her body. Her legs relaxed and inched apart and he didn't hesitate to introduce his touch there. Light and sure, he pressed into her folds.

Hot.

Hot and ready for him. His head began to throb in time with his pulse. Francesca twisted under his touch, trying to get closer. He backed off for a moment, to make her wait, to make her crazy, to make her want him with the same intensity that was burning him.

"What is this?" she asked, her voice uncertain.

He pressed back into her, deeper this time, his finger encased sweetly and hotly, just like her breasts had held him. "This is passion," he said. "Are you ready?"

He knew she was. She was wet and swollen and now her legs were fully open for him. Her thumb brushed across one of his nipples and he jerked.

In a quick movement he withdrew from her body then shucked his pants and boxers, tossing aside shoes and socks and diving right back to Francesca. As gently as he could, he took a breast in his mouth and then touched her between her legs again, stretching her body with two fingers.

Her hips tilted up to his hand. "Francesca." He groaned and reached blindly for a condom from the drawer in the night table. She lifted on her elbows to watch him, her dark eyes heavy-lidded and her cheeks flushed.

Brett burned. His thigh muscles twitched as he kneeled between her legs. He pushed them wide, trying to stay gentle, trying to stay in control, but that darkness in her eyes was heady desire. Passion poured into his body like hot wine, and passion dictated he hold her thighs open with his palms so he could watch as he entered her.

Slowly entered her.

He felt the resistance, heard her quick breath, but then he looked into her eyes and the hot desire he saw there still matched his. "I want you, Francesca," he said. And he spiraled into the darkness as he pushed into her.

She cried out.

But then her body arched upward and the glitter of tears didn't cool the burning passion in her eyes.

"Okay?" he asked, gritting his teeth to remain controlled.

"You're inside me," she said. And there was wonder in her voice as one tear slid down her cheek.

He bent over to lick it away. "And you're inside me," he reassured her gently, not even certain what he meant, but certain it was true. Then he felt her inside muscles squeeze him tentatively, and then he had to move, forcing himself to be controlled and gentle. Over and over he thrust into her, watching closely as she wound tighter and tighter until it took just one quick press of his thumb and one long drive of his body to show them both how to turn Francesca into a woman.

FRANCESCA LAY curled against the cradle of Brett's body, working to catch her breath and trying to ignore a welling feeling of panic.

This wasn't going right!

Just minutes ago she'd made love to the man she'd always dreamed of. She was supposed to feel satisfied and satiated, triumphant and womanly, and she had, for several delicious moments. But now overwhelming her was embarrassment and awkwardness, not the least of which was caused by the fact that she was completely naked except for the strangling twist of strapless bra that was still caught about her rib cage.

There was something else going on, too, something deeper inside her that she didn't want to think about and that she had to get away from.

"Francesca?" Brett went on one elbow and peered into her face. "Are you okay?"

She'd be a *lot* better if she could think of a really clever way of dashing back to her apartment without having to look Brett in the eye. Preferably dressed in an enveloping terry cloth robe.

Her belly-flutters quickened. Darn those women's magazines! They contained plenty of articles on the morning after, but nothing on the *moments* after. Especially not the moments after with the man whose touch tantalized and terrified you at the same time. How was a woman supposed to survive such heartbreaking intimacy?

"Francesca?" he said again, his voice concerned.

She swallowed. "I'm fine," she said, hoping she sounded cheerful and casual. "Right as rain. All in one piece."

One of his big hands stroked her shoulder. "Not quite."

A wash of heat spread over Francesca's face and those panic-flutters became out-and-out beating wings of anxiety. Yes. The irrevocable had happened here. And she wanted desperately to hightail it back in her apartment and hide from all the new feelings.

She eyed the distance from bed to the bedroom door. How was she supposed to manage a dignified exit? With her dress in the living room she'd have to skip out of Brett's room wearing only her bare backside and this devil-possessed bra. Her gaze caught on the bedside lamp. At least turn that off first. Darkness could only help.

She inched away from the warm curve of his body toward the cool expanse of the sheets, her movement rolling the errant bra into a tighter twist.

Brett put his hand on her arm. "Where are you going?"

She froze, his fingers burning her with the kind of heat that sent a field of goose bumps blooming across her body. *Someplace where I can think. Somewhere away from your touch.*

She swallowed. "Just thought I'd turn the light off."

"Let me."

A hope that he'd get out of the bed to accomplish the task, leaving her to remove the bra unnoticed, was born and died in the same instant as he leaned across her. His chest flattened her shoulders against the mattress, then with a click the light in the room changed. Except not to blessed darkness.

No, the golden glow of the lamp was replaced by the silver shine of moonlight spilling through the bedroom's high window.

Oh, great. Because that silvery light meant that when she ran away from him she'd be flashing one bright moon herself.

Her breath strangled again as she tried to come up with a plan. If she could just get the darn bra off! If worse came to worst she'd look better leaving the room naked than leaving it tied up in a piece of underwear.

Inspiration struck. "Could I—could you get me a drink of water, please?"

"Sure."

Francesca held her breath. When Brett disappeared into the adjoining bathroom she could race to the living room for her dress.

Instead, he headed in the direction of the living room himself.

"Where are you going?" she asked quickly.

He paused at the foot of the bed, naked and unconcerned. "Water," he said. "And glasses. They're in the kitchen. Anything else?"

Francesca shook her head because she couldn't speak. The moonlight silvered the angles of Brett's body. Staring at the wide strength of his shoulders and the hard angles of his hip bones caused her mouth to go dry. She kept shaking her head.

After he left the room it took her a couple of seconds to collect herself. Then, with a mental slap to her forehead, she jackknifed into a sitting position and began to attack the bra. At least she could divest herself of that problem.

Fingers fumbling in haste, she tried working the twisted strip of fabric around her body to reach the hooks. The darn bra seemed pasted to her rib cage and she broke into a cold sweat. Which, of course, made the stretchy material stick to her skin even closer.

Just when she was wishing she was limber enough to attack the thing with her teeth, Brett's voice sounded.

"You need some help?"

Francesca froze again, even though she was horribly aware of how she must look, sheets tumbled about her waist, everything above bare and propped up by a twist of fabric that wouldn't let go.

It was all too much.

The anticipation of the evening, the sexual tension, the "lesson" Brett had tried to teach her, the experience he *had* shared with her. All too much. Tears stung Francesca's eyes and to her everlasting mortification she had to place her hands over her face to staunch the flow.

Brett swore.

And even before one tear could roll to her chin, she found herself in his arms. "Baby," he said. He was warm and his heartbeat thumped reassuringly strong beneath her cheek. "Don't cry."

She hiccuped. "Not crying," she said, her face buried against him. "It's just that your shoulder is wet."

He stroked her hair with his hand. "You're right. It's all my fault."

"Yes." From within the circle of his arms, nothing seemed quite so terrible. "You should have taken off my bra."

He didn't laugh. "You're right," he said, and she almost instantly felt relief as he reached down and quickly released the hooks. "Better?" he asked.

She nodded, rubbing her face against his skin to dry the last of her tears.

He continued to stroke her hair and his other palm swept across her back. In a hoarse whisper he spoke soothing words against the top of her head.

Francesca relaxed, melting into the warmth of his body. With the embarrassing bra situation handled, it didn't seem so imperative she go home right away. Though there was still some nervousness, some knowledge, flopping around deep in her belly, she could ignore it as long as Brett touched her with his sure, tantalizing fingers.

She blew out a deep sigh and Brett tilted up her face with a hand under her chin. He kissed her wet eyelashes and then her nose—sweet kisses of understanding.

Francesca's stomach went full-blown panicky again.

"Okay?" he asked, smiling down at her.

Déjà vu. She'd been here before. Or probably dreamed this moment. Naked in Brett's arms, his smile warm and knowing after their night together. But the dream couldn't hold a candle to the sweet burning fire of reality.

Her stomach roiled again, the walls behind Brett tilted dizzily, she put one hand against the mattress to prevent her whole world from toppling over.

Then the movement stopped—stomach, walls, Brett, world settling into a new order.

"Better?" he asked.

No. She smiled back, though, wide enough to show her molars. Because there couldn't be any more tears. Nothing even close.

Brett had given her the night together she'd asked for. The one she said would satisfy her. *I'm not asking for forever.* She'd said those very words.

But here in his arms, warm and comfortable and comforted, she couldn't ignore the truth that had been rolling around in her stomach all night. The truth that had nothing to do with twisted bras or bare-naked embarrassment.

The bare-naked truth was she loved him. She was *in love* with him.

That she wanted forever with Brett.

9

BAM! BAM! BAM! The banging on his front door woke Brett.

Blinking, it took him a few moments to orient himself. Weak sunlight washed into his bedroom. Francesca was in his arms, her face pressed into the hollow of his shoulder.

Morning already. The last he remembered, she'd fallen asleep, all damp eyelashes and warm skin. He'd held her, watching her breathe for hours, vigilant against another flurry of uncharacteristic tears.

Bam! Bam! Bam! More banging. Francesca's eyes fluttered open.

"Yo! Brett!" A deep voice reached all the way to the bedroom.

"Oh, my God." Francesca immediately sat up, clutching the sheet to her throat. "Oh, my God, it's Carlo."

Brett reached out to push a tendril of hair off her cheek. "Don't worry. The front door is locked."

The banging resumed and Francesca pushed on his shoulder. "You've got to go answer him."

"No way." He and Francesca needed to talk about what had happened between them last night. He wanted to know exactly why she'd cried and what they were going to do now.

The banging started again.

Francesca's eyes widened. "Brett!"

"Okay, okay, I'll get rid of him." He slipped out of bed and slipped into his boxers, then tripped over Francesca's shoes on his way to the front door.

Leaning against the cool wood he called through it to his friend. "Carlo! What do you want?"

There was a pause, then Carlo's voice, puzzled. "You're not going to let me in?"

"Give me a break. I just woke up. *You* just woke me up."

More silence. "Fine. Whatever. Want to shoot some hoops? Then we'll go for a heart-attack-on-a-plate breakfast at Judy's Diner."

Brett opened his mouth to refuse. He should take Francesca out for brunch. At a small table in some quiet place where they could talk through what had happened.

From the corner of his eye he saw something move. Francesca, creeping into the living room wearing only her panties and bra. On tiptoe, she dashed over to her dress and snatched it from the floor.

"Brett! What do you say? Hoops and a heart attack?"

He figured he already had the heart attack covered, seeing Francesca in her skimpy underthings again. "N—"

"Say yes!" Francesca hissed. "If you say no he'll suspect something."

Brett continued to stare at her, her words failing to register. Not when her hair was mussed and her lips were red from his kisses and he could see the pink scrape of his beard against her neck.

"Say yes," she whispered.

"Brett!" Carlo again.

He turned his head toward the door. "Give me a second," he called out. Then he turned back to Francesca. "We need to talk," he whispered back, his mind made stupid again by everything that had entranced him the night before. Every bit of her.

Francesca shook her head. "No, we don't. I asked you for last night. End of story."

"End of story?"

"What?" Carlo yelled through the door. "Are you talking to me?"

Francesca bit her lip. "I *told* you I didn't want forever." She stepped into her dress and struggled with the zipper.

Brett started toward her but she waved him off. "Thanks, by the way," she said.

Thanks, by the way? "We've *got* to talk."

"Then talk to Carlo." She slipped on her sandals. "Promise me you can keep him occupied at the front here so I can go out your back door and into mine."

Brett remembered that Carlo's apartment was between his and Francesca's. Thank God he hadn't thought of it until now. Double thank God that his bedroom was on the other side of the apartment and didn't share a wall with Carlo.

"Brett? Are you okay in there?"

Francesca's eyes widened. "Tell him yes."

But how could he when he wasn't sure it was true? He needed to talk things over with Francesca. Think things through. Taste her mouth again before she walked away. "Really, Fr—"

"Shh!" She took a step, frowned, slipped back out of her shoes. "You're invited to that party for Elise and David tonight, right? We can talk there."

"Brett, ol' buddy. My detective antennae are quivering." Carlo's teasing voice came through the door. "You got a body in there?"

Francesca sent Brett a panicked look and then ran barefooted toward his back door. "Let him in and keep him busy for a few minutes," she whispered one last time.

In seconds she'd eased out of his apartment. Brett opened the front door, running his hand through his hair and aware it took zero acting skill for him to appear stupid and confused and like a guy who'd just been woken from the middle of a particularly luscious dream.

"What's going on?" Carlo said by way of greeting, stepping inside.

Brett wished he knew.

FRANCESCA WAS the first guest to arrive at the barbecue Elise's parents were giving for the almost-married couple. When Elise had lost the battle for a small wedding, her parents had promised an early, more casual celebration for them.

In a pretty sundress, Elise took one look at Francesca's khaki pants, plain white blouse tied at the waist and baseball cap, then hauled her out to the far reaches of the backyard beyond anyone's hearing. "What happened?" she asked. "Besides disaster."

Francesca tugged her ball cap lower and shoved her hands in her pockets. "I made a mistake."

Elise narrowed her eyes. "I'm going to kill him. Better yet, I'll tell your brothers and they'll kill him."

"Don't. It's my fault and my fault only."

Elise sighed. "You're head-over-heels, aren't you?"

"And out of my league." Francesca scuffed the toe of her thick fisherman's sandal against the grass. "But it's over with. I'm going back to stick-in-the-mud Francesca. Out of those stupid dresses and back into my jeans."

"That's not going to mend your heart."

"But I'll be a heck of a lot more comfortable." Francesca tried pasting on a grin. "C'mon. Take me to your leader. Your mom will find something to distract me."

Francesca volunteered for pass duty. Wandering through the party, toting large platters of hors d'oeuvres, gave her a good reason to see everybody and linger long with nobody. Bean dip dabs on round tortilla chips, celery packed with cream cheese and salsa, spicy miniature *taquitos,* she blessed them all as she chose who to offer them to and what group to avoid.

When Brett arrived she zipped into the kitchen and spent several minutes refilling the largest platter. After a deep breath she returned to the patio and started circulating again. So what if the group of men Brett was with didn't get a chance at the appetizers. None of them really appeared very hungry.

Well, Brett kind of did. He managed to catch her eye as she made a wide circle around him and the others standing beside the cooler filled with microbrewed beers. The expression on his face, intent and determined, made the little hairs on her neck, the ones right beneath the ponytail she'd shoved through her baseball cap, stand up.

She tugged the brim of her cap lower and ducked in the opposite direction to make another unnecessary platter refill.

As she came out of the kitchen he was there, though, and caught her arm. She pinned on a bright smile. "Hors d'oeuvre? *Taquito?*"

He didn't look down at her proffered plate. "Talk," he said.

She raised her eyebrows. "I've been conscripted to kitchen duty. Can't really desert until, um, after dessert."

He ignored her pun. "When are we going to talk?"

The touch of his fingers on her upper arm tingled—

hot little pinpricks of response that tightened her nipples and made the flesh across her stomach twitch.

He shook her arm a little. "When, Francesca?"

Several months. Several years, maybe. Sometime when remembering Brett's chest under her palms, Brett's mouth on her breasts, Brett *inside* her, wouldn't freeze dry her tongue, making speech nearly impossible.

"I—" She tried moistening her lips. "Look, couldn't we just leave it alone?"

He flattened his mouth. "You mean leave you alone."

She didn't think she should agree. "Do we really need to rehash the event, Brett? I'm fine. You look okay. What more is there?"

He frowned. "I don't like this casual attitude of yours."

Men. Francesca let out a gusty sigh. "Great, then. When are we getting married?"

Astonishment widened his eyes and dropped his jaw.

The full plate of appetizers was getting heavy. "Here," she said, offering the food again. "Stuff something in that wide mouth of yours."

"Francesca—"

"Please, Brett, give me some credit. I was just kidding. I know exactly where you're coming from. I've lived with men my entire life, okay?"

He crossed his arms over his chest. "And what has that experience taught you, O Small-but-wise One?"

"You males put extremely high value on your piles of dirty socks and your meals of microwave burritos and the freedom to drop everything for beers and billiards with the boys. It requires a kind of atomic explosion to blast you out of bachelorhood.''

He shifted uncomfortably. ''Atomic explosion?''

She shrugged. ''You tell me.'' She nodded her head in the direction of Elise, standing nearby with her fiancé at her side. ''With David there, it's clear. He's completely besotted and they love each other in a way that's explosive itself.''

Brett glanced at the engaged couple. ''That might just burn out.''

''I'll lay odds that it won't.''

Brett's gaze sharpened. ''Francesca, you may think you know—''

''Franny!'' A male Milano voice sounded from across the grass. ''We're hungry over here!''

Francesca looked over at the knot of brothers beckoning to her. ''I *do* know, Brett. And you, you're a special case. Rebachelored,'' she said flippantly. ''A guy like you will be eating out of the microwave for the rest of his life.''

Or, Francesca thought, he'll find himself bowled over by some paragon of poised femininity like Patricia. A woman who knew how to dress and how to make love and how not to blubber like a baby when she thought she'd never be held by him again.

''Franny!'' The Milanos yelled as one.

She pivoted obediently toward the hungry-brother bellow, grateful she had an excuse to get away before she said something really dumb. "I'm done with the subject."

Maybe attorneys had to have the last word. Maybe it was men in general. Because Brett called out to her as she walked away.

"Perfect," he said. "Because then you'll just listen when it's my turn."

FULL OF STEAK, salad and corn on the cob, Brett sat back in a cushioned patio chair and watched Francesca wander over to one corner of the deep backyard. A basketball hoop reigned at one end of a cement half court and she unearthed a basketball from beneath a bordering shrub and started shooting aimless baskets.

For a short person, and a girl, she was a pretty good shot. She talked a pretty good game, too.

Bachelors. Rebachelors. He shook his head. She thought she had it all down pat.

But if he knew what was good for him he'd leave things just as she'd left them. He would feel relieved that she was willing to let their one-night stand, well, stand, and not need to take it any further.

But his protective instinct wasn't so easily slayed.

He'd been trying to kill it all evening.

Like a mythical beast, though, it rose again and again, prodding him with sharp talons each time she spoke with another man. Each time he heard her laugh.

And though he cursed himself for all kinds of a fool, while she'd been passing plates around he hadn't been able to get the image out of his head of Francesca passing herself to another man—now that he'd taken the first bite.

He suppressed a groan, thinking of her beneath him the night before. She'd cried out when he'd entered her body, but once the pain had left her face, something had infused him, some *power* that he didn't dare examine.

He scraped his hands over his face. There was a fine line between protectiveness and possessiveness and he *must* keep on the right side of it.

The vow didn't keep him from narrowing his gaze at the man who this minute was approaching Francesca. Brett recognized him as the driver who'd dropped her off a few nights before.

She stopped dribbling. Smiled at the guy.

The other man said something, grinning, too. He pantomimed making a basket.

Francesca pulled a face and put one hand on her hip. They both laughed.

Brett could read their next exchange in the body language. A challenge was issued. A challenge was accepted. A little game of one-on-one.

Innocent. Fun. But still Brett found himself half rising from his chair as Francesca dropped the basketball to start unbuttoning her shirt. He slumped back once he could see the white tank top she wore underneath. Then she completely shed the overshirt to reveal the golden skin of her arms that last night she'd wound around his neck. Brett's blood began to chug heavily through his body.

Her shirt was tossed over a nearby shrub. She let the guy take the basketball out first. Brett realized the other man needed the advantage. He was a lousy shot.

Or maybe just a calculating one. Because he allowed Francesca to control the ball most of their game while he did a foul-worthy job of defending the basket. Chest out, he tried using his bigger size to intimidate her. Or maybe he was using every excuse to brush up against her.

The game ended quickly, though. His tomboy princess won, and acknowledged her opponent's congratulations with a curtsy. Brett found himself smiling.

But then he saw a second challenge being issued and he could tell how easily Francesca rose to the bait. That was her MO, and exactly how Carlo enticed her into that bridesmaid's bet.

Blood chugging hot and heavy again, Brett popped out of his seat. He hustled toward the court, ignoring the stiffness already settling in his muscles from his own play with Carlo that morning. That damned bet couldn't be ignored. And he worried, now that she'd booted him out of the picture, that Francesca would be looking for some way to beat Carlo.

She liked to win.

But so did Brett.

The basketball rested on the cement beside Francesca's feet. He reached it for it, grabbed it up. She stared at him, blinking.

"I'm playing the winner," he announced.

"We just agreed on another game," the other guy said. "You'll be up next."

Brett wasn't in the mood to talk. "My turn," he told Francesca. "Now."

"Hey," the loser protested. "She just agreed to double or nothing."

Brett's whole body went tight. "What're the stakes?" he asked Francesca.

She frowned at him. "I don't think—"

"What are the stakes?"

"For goodness sake, Brett. Pizza. We're betting pizzas."

Yeah, and he could just picture it. An intimate booth in a dark Italian restaurant. Francesca's cheeks flushed and her lips the color of red wine and this...this...*loser* sharing a pizza with her and then sharing her bed later.

"Never gonna happen," he told the guy.

"What?"

"Never gonna happen." Brett eyed him implacably. *"This is my game."*

The guy looked at Brett, looked at Francesca, looked back at Brett again. Then he held up his hands in surrender. "Got it." With a good-natured grin he headed back to the rest of the party.

Smart man. Brett liked him better already.

He turned toward Francesca. Her hands were back on

her hips. Her tank top clung damply to her slender rib cage and lush breasts. Lust pierced him like a sword.

"What's this all about?" she said, her eyes spitting dark fire at him. "You're acting very strange."

He shook his head. Strange would be letting her get away now. With only a few days left until the wedding, she'd be looking for a way to win that bet. And the only one who was going to help her do that was him.

He dribbled the ball a few times. "I don't like playing for pizzas."

"Fine." She crossed her arms over her chest. "We'll play for honor."

Bomp. Bomp. Bomp. The ball echoed the loud thump of his heartbeat. "No. Something else." He didn't want to think about honor right now.

She frowned. "What then? What's going on, Brett?"

A bead of sweat rolled from her temple down her cheek, mesmerizing him. Damn. Tempting him.

Stepping toward her, he caught the drop on his thumb. Then he brought his thumb to his mouth and licked off her taste.

Sweet. Salty. Francesca.

Her eyes widened and she swallowed. "Brett?"

"We'll play to eleven," he said. "When I win, you'll come back to my bed tonight."

It wasn't a bad idea, he thought. It would keep her occupied. It would keep him sane.

FRANCESCA COULD HAVE refused to play under such outrageous conditions. She could have walked off the court.

Instead, she negotiated for a six-point lead.

She hadn't been raised to back down.

But as the game began, she wasn't sure if winning wasn't really losing.

Brett wanted her. It was in the intent look on his face, the harsh intake of his breath, the very real bump he gave her with his hip as she feinted around him.

Shoot. *Swish*. One basket and she had seven points to his zero.

Her lead didn't faze him. He drove the ball toward the basket, and Francesca tried to move in front of him, her heart banging under the triple threat of adrenaline, confusion, desire.

He made four points in a row.

Breathing hard, she still didn't know who she rooted for—herself or her childhood hero.

Though he wasn't playing heroically. Or gentlemanly, either. He grunted when he made another basket and then drilled the ball toward her, a chest pass that stung when it hit her palms.

His intensity was half scary, half exhilarating. Giddy with excitement, her next shot bounced off the rim, but she was quicker than he was and grabbed the rebound. She dribbled, trying to position herself in that personal sweet spot from which she nearly always made a basket.

Brett was in front of her. Between the last points, he'd thrown off his shirt, and the sheen of sweat on his chest distracted her. She hesitated, he closed in and she closed her eyes, shooting blindly.

Swish. Eight to five.

The play turned even more serious. Brett started a verbal—and titillating—form of distraction.

"I'm going to have you tonight," he said.

Her shot went wild.

He picked up the ball and closed the gap in their scores. He had nine. She managed to get her points to ten.

"And there won't be any reason to cry," he said, his eyes glittering blue as she passed him the ball.

She didn't like him assuming she would be so easy—to have and to please. Let him work a little harder for both.

She gritted her teeth and focused on the ball. *Get it back,* she commanded herself. There was pride involved here. More than pride. Her heart. But he was quick and strong, and too soon it was ten points to ten.

She missed her next chance. Brett got the ball again, but she shut out everything but the orange orb and used the last of her energy reserves to bat it out of Brett's hands.

Sucking in air, she lifted the ball for her shot. This was it. Her confidence surged. She knew she could best him. "You're gonna owe me pizza," she said, grinning and sparing him a glance.

He stood back, silent, until the instant the ball left her hands. "I'm gonna make you scream," he said.

Her follow-through failed. The ball sputtered in the air. Brett grabbed it, made his own shot, swift and sure. *Swish.*

He wiped the sweat from his forehead with the back of his hand. "You're mine, baby." His eyes glittered again.

Francesca considered denying it. But she was winded.

And aroused.

And he was right.

Cake was being served when they slipped out a side gate. Under cover of loud laughter, nobody seemed to notice them leaving early. Her wrist wrapped by Brett's hard hand, Francesca spared one backward glance and didn't see any member of her family except Carlo, who stood alone, inspecting the melting ice in a cooler.

A whole bucketful couldn't reduce the steaming temperature in Brett's car. Though he flipped on the AC full blast, Francesca knew it wasn't the air that was so hot, but the desire running between them. His hand moved possessively over her upper thigh.

A shiver edged up her spine. "Brett—"

"No talking," he said. "We'll be there soon."

Her pulse started slamming against her wrists, her throat. She felt it thrumming low in her body, too, in the spot just above Brett's hand.

His tires whined as he whipped into the apartment parking lot. They were out of the car in seconds, and he was pulling her along in the direction of his apartment.

For a moment, just a moment, it reminded her of the

night before, when he'd been so intent on teaching her a lesson. As they reached his front door, her heart leaped into her throat and she coughed.

He halted, looking down at her. That sparkling glitter hadn't left his eyes, and his gaze was hot as he ran it over her. "Okay?"

She wasn't sure. How bad an idea was it to make love with him again? "I'm—sticky," she said, by way of stalling.

His gaze narrowed, and she didn't think he was going to let her get away so easily. "I have soap and water," he said.

Francesca shuffled back, toward her own apartment. "I can—my place—maybe later—"

He shook his head. "No, Francesca." Then without letting her go he unlocked his door.

Still without releasing her, he drew her toward his bedroom. He passed the bed without even glancing at it and pulled her into his bathroom.

In no time he'd adjusted the shower to a steaming spray. Then he looked at her.

"I, uh…" She gestured toward the door. "I'll let you know when I'm done."

He smiled, knowing and certain as his hands grasped the hem of her top. "I'm sure you will." He whipped the fabric over her head, then reached for the waistband button of her pants.

As he stripped her of her clothes he also stripped her of her will to resist. Clothes gone, he ran his hands over every bare inch of her, and then, after removing his own clothing, he stepped them into the shower and ran the soap over the very same paths.

Once her skin squeaked he washed her hair, and she moaned as he massaged her scalp. Then, as the water ran cooler and cooler, he pushed her up against the tiled wall and chased the twin coursing streams of water down her puckering nipples until they became one river at her navel. He navigated that too, following it lower and lower, until, as he'd promised, Francesca *did* scream.

And she screamed with pleasure again on his big bed a little while later, with Brett deep inside her and with all her doubts and fears drowned in the entwined carnal and emotional sensations of loving Brett.

10

FRANCESCA TRIED not to look gift sex in the mouth. That's how she thought of it, each time she and Brett came together after the day of the barbecue—a gift. One that she might have to pay for in heartache at some later date, but a present she wasn't going to regret now.

She wriggled a bit against Brett's mattress, burrowing her head more comfortably against his shoulder. When he'd come home from work he'd found her in the parking lot, making a minor repair to the gate leading to the apartments. He had something to show her in his apartment, he'd said. She'd left her tools behind and followed him, only to end up making quick and passionate love the instant they'd locked the door.

She still had her shoes on and her T-shirt, her bra unhooked beneath it. Frowning, Francesca ran her palm over Brett's bare chest. "Hey," she said. "What was it you wanted to show me?"

He might have dozed off. But then one eye half opened. "What?"

"You got me out of the parking lot and into your apartment because you said you had something to show me," she reminded him.

Both his eyes opened wide. "Francesca. Honey." His hair brushed against the white pillowcase as he moved his head from side to side in amazement.

She pulled her brows together. "What?"

He was shaking his head again. "You are just too cute."

"What?"

"I said that to you because—" He started to laugh. "I thought you knew what I meant." He laughed harder.

Francesca was beginning to feel like the butt of a joke. "The only thing I know is that I'm sitting here half-naked and you're laughing at me!"

He tried to get serious. She could see him drawing the edges of his mouth together, but then it became too much and he was grinning again. "That's because I brought you here to show you my, uh, my…etchings." He hooted again.

It started to dawn. "Etchings?" she repeated suspiciously.

He sobered up, but the laughter was still brimming in his annoyingly bright blue eyes. "Etchings. You know. Tools? Jewels?"

Heat burned Francesca's cheeks. "I get it now," she said, moving away from Brett's side. "I must seem pretty naive to you." Other women he'd known would have understood his innuendo right away. Gotten the joke.

He rolled close. "You're right about *pretty*." One finger stroked her cheek. "And *naive*."

She barely registered his touch, instead looking down at herself. Her oversize T-shirt nearly reached her knees, but had a half-dollar-sized rip at her navel. Then there was the matter of the shoes. Other women would have gone to a man's bed wearing shiny pumps or delicate sandals that could be toed off. She'd broken a lace this morning and had knotted her right sneaker on. In her hurry to be in Brett's arms she'd merely pulled her shorts and panties right over them.

All the gaucheness and awkwardness she'd ever felt about men and romance returned with a vengeance, cooling her skin like buckets of cold water. She shivered and rolled farther from Brett, just wanting to get back to her own apartment.

His hand clamped on her shoulder. "Where are you going?"

"I..."

He hauled her back against him. "What's going on?"

"I just thought I'd go home now."

Brett stroked her hair away from her face. "Did I say or do something to hurt you?"

Mute, she just shook her head.

He squinted at her. "I did. You didn't like me laughing at you."

"I *am* naive," Francesca found herself whispering.

He rolled her over on top of him and held her against his body. "Not naive. Just innocent. And don't think for a moment that I don't like it," he said.

She frowned, and he rubbed at the spot between her

brows with his thumb. "Francesca," he chided her gently. "I do."

But what did he think about her scuffed and still-on shoes? What did he think about the rip in her shirt? The unladylike way she could *almost* beat him at one-on-one? Insecurity tore through her again.

Not that insecurity was a stranger. Even though she and Brett had been spending every night together, she hadn't told anyone, not her brothers, not Elise, that they were even the most casual of items. She'd tried telling herself it was because she didn't want to jinx what felt so right. She'd tried telling herself it was because she didn't want her brothers to interfere in any way.

Lies.

She'd been silent about it because she didn't know where she stood with him.

Yes, she loved him. Yes, she'd willingly gone into his arms because even this little taste of Brett seemed worthwhile. But now she wasn't so sure.

"Francesca." He jiggled her in his arms, turning his head to find her gaze. "Talk to me."

"Maybe we shouldn't see each other anymore." The words popped out of her mouth.

Brett's eyes narrowed. He sat silent for a moment, staring at her. "Why?" he finally said.

She shrugged, trying not to think about the breathtaking feel of his heart beating against hers. "I don't know. I'm going to be busy in the next few days. The rehearsal for Elise's wedding. The rehearsal dinner. The wedding itself.''

Steeling herself, she focused on his raised left eyebrow. "You haven't forgotten I'm a bridesmaid."

In the blink of an eye, he reversed their positions. "I haven't forgotten," he said, his voice almost angry.

With raw power, Brett pressed her into the mattress and insinuated his hips between her legs. "Exactly what about being a bridesmaid makes you too busy for me?"

Francesca could barely breathe. Not because of Brett's weight, but because she wanted him so very much. Wanted him *forever*.

She swallowed. "I just have…things to do." *Such as protecting my heart. Better late than never.*

"Why can't we do them together?" he asked. "I'm invited to the wedding."

Francesca didn't know how to answer. Was he suggesting they attend the wedding as a couple? In front of Pop and everybody? "Well, um…"

"And that rehearsal dinner. Isn't it usually customary for the members of the wedding party to bring an escort?"

Francesca wet her lips. "You mean, kind of like a boyfriend—" She stopped herself hastily. "Or a date?"

"Exactly," he said. "Exactly like a date."

Exactly like a date. In front of Pop and everybody.

She reached up to kiss Brett. If she'd been wearing the rhinestone tiara she couldn't have felt more like a princess.

BRETT SHOWED up at the chapel where Elise and David's wedding would take place three days later. From a side door, he slipped into a pew, taking in that the rehearsal was already underway. David and his four groomsmen, one of whom was Carlo, were lined up beside the white-collared minister. Elise and her attendants were nowhere to be seen.

The minister nodded to the organist, who began playing something soft and soulful. At the back of the chapel a pretty young woman appeared and then walked in measured steps up the aisle. Clutched in her hands appeared to be a paper plate covered with vari-colored gift bows.

He must not be the only dense male in the audience—a pew away a woman whispered to another man that it was a pretend bouquet made from the ribbons on the gifts at Elise's wedding showers. Another young woman started up the aisle with another bow bouquet. Then another woman.

Then, finally, Francesca.

Brett slid forward on the wooden seat. Francesca, making one of her rare appearances in a short dress and high heels, was offering a long drink of her bared legs. His heart rocketed—*slam*—against his chest.

He followed her with his eyes. She'd taken more careful pains with her appearance, her eyelashes sootier than usual and her lips the same rosy color as the soft fabric of her dress.

A primitive, caveman urge rose in him. Brett wanted to take her out of everyone else's sight and take her home. He wanted to peel the dress off her, uncover her golden skin, kiss that rosy mouth and set his blood on fire with the feel and the taste of Francesca.

Bending her head, she looked down at her bouquet and smiled.

Instantly the blood in Brett's veins stopped moving. Something about the sight of Francesca and that bouquet—she held one made up of pure, virginal white ribbons—shut down the pumping ability of his heart. Dizzy, he sucked in a breath.

Why did that damn bouquet terrify him? Why was he suddenly afraid of Francesca?

The rest of the rehearsal passed in a haze. Brett slumped against the hard back of the pew and stared at his knuckles and then his palms and then his knuckles again. He didn't want to watch Francesca. Couldn't.

At the end of the rehearsal the bridesmaids and groomsmen were coupled and filed down the aisle. Still stupid with the weird feeling of dread, it took Brett a few minutes to realize they weren't returning to the main part of the chapel. He finally rose, knowing he had to find Francesca and talk to her.

She was laughing and talking to Carlo. Her brother had that edgy look about him again, but Francesca didn't seem to notice it. "You're going to owe *me* Saturday, big brother," she said. "Don't forget your wallet."

They were talking about that damn bet. A hot bubble rose from Brett's gut. That damn bet was the source of it all. Francesca looking for a man. Francesca in his bed.

Francesca walking up an aisle carrying a white bouquet and looking like everything he'd vowed never to be hurt by again.

Carlo was shaking his head, his mood obviously black. "Give up, Franny. You don't have a prayer."

Her brother's disregard of her feelings, and her appeal, set a torch to Brett's already-simmering anger. He reached them in two strides. "Hell, Carlo. You're the one who should give up. You might as well settle that bet right here and now. I'll lend you the hundred bucks myself."

Two pairs of astonished Italian eyes turned on him. The temperature of Brett's anger instantly dropped. *Uh-oh.*

Francesca opened her mouth, closed it, opened her mouth again. "You know about our bet? How do you know about our bet?"

Brett decided on silence as the best answer.

Carlo narrowed his eyes. "I remember. You showed up at Pop's right after the fact."

With the weight of Francesca's gaze on him, Brett tried shrugging casually. "Yeah. Well."

Another moment of silence, then Francesca looked at her brother. "Go away, Carlo."

His forehead creased. "I don't—"

"Go away, Carlo," she said again.

With one reluctant backward look, Carlo wandered off.

She turned back to Brett, and there was a flush on her cheeks. "You overheard us that day?"

He could hardly deny it at this point. "Yeah."

She rubbed at her temple. She'd painted her nails again, and they were done more expertly now. Brett liked it better when she smeared them a bit.

"You wouldn't—" Her fingers pressed against her temple again. "You didn't do all this because…because of the bet, did you?"

He took a breath. "I couldn't even bring myself to believe you were old enough to date."

She took a step back. "It *was* because of the bet."

"You could get into a lot of trouble out there," he said, frowning at her and defending his logic. "When you're looking for a man to win a bet."

"Rescuing me again, Brett?"

He shrugged.

"Or maybe you felt *sorry* for me."

"No." He shook his head quickly. "I've never felt sorry for you."

Her expression hardened to a coolness he'd never seen before. "What would you call it then? How you feel about me."

In his pockets, his hands balled into fists. "Francesca—"

"I want to know." Still holding that funky bouquet, she crossed her arms over her chest. "Tell me. Or let me try to guess. At first you thought you needed to rescue me. So you asked me out on that date. And then—

and then—'' She halted. "And then I asked you to make love to me. Practically forced you to.''

"I wanted you, Francesca,'' he said quietly.

"In your bed,'' she added.

A long silence welled between them. Then Francesca drew in a deep breath, held it for a moment, let it out. "So what would you call what you feel for me now?'' she asked. "Desire?''

He hated the bitter note in her voice. It made him angry all over again, because from the very beginning, for her entire life, all he'd wanted to do was protect her. From the very kind of hurt he now saw on her face.

"Come on, Brett.'' Her voice taunted him. "Desire? Or should we just call it plain old lust?''

Goaded, he snapped back. "Francesca, what did you expect?''

She blinked. "I thought it might be love,'' she said quietly, then paused. "Just like what I feel for you.''

He thought the top of his head might come off. *"What?"* he said, dread and anger twining in his belly. "What the hell are you talking about?''

She bit her lower lip.

Deliberately flexing his fingers, he forced himself to calm down. "Francesca,'' he said, his voice softer. "You're confused. What we have together—how good the sex is, that's not love.''

He saw her swallow. "So it's just a physical thing?'' she said. "That's what you think?''

"I'm certain.'' He reached out to touch her, but she

backed another step away. "Haven't I always taken care of you? Taught you things you need to know?"

Her face was still a stony mask.

"So let me teach you something else. Don't be so quick to claim love. Love hurts, Francesca. Don't go looking for it."

He clenched his teeth, wishing he didn't need to say it. Wishing she hadn't wanted to change what they had.

"We're through," she said abruptly.

Brett ran a hand through his hair. "Francesca."

"I don't want your pity or your protection anymore."

He shook his head. "It doesn't have to be this way. It doesn't have to end. We're good together."

"But we're not in love with each other."

He shook his head again.

"Goodbye, Brett." As dignified as royalty, she inclined her head in a nod and walked away from him, her back straight and her shoulders square.

She approached the group of people that included Carlo. Putting her hand through his arm, she drew her brother away. Guilt surged through Brett as he noticed her tight hold on Carlo.

Damn if he didn't feel as if he'd just burst the brightest balloon in the sky.

In a booth at a cheesy chain coffee shop, Francesca sat across from her brother, nursing a cup of decaf from a thick white mug. "I'm having a romantic crisis," she said. "And you bring me to a place like this?" Better to complain than to cry.

Carlo raised his brows. "A latte would make you feel better?"

Francesca sighed. "Guess not." She propped her elbow on the plastic tabletop and rested her chin against her fist. "Do you think I did the right thing?" She'd told her brother the entire story, well, not the *entire* story, but enough for him to get the picture.

He shrugged. Beside a few grunts, he'd been pretty silent about the whole thing.

"That's *all* you have to say? I'm giving you a chance for an 'I told you so,' you know."

Carlo smiled ruefully. "If I thought it would make either one of us feel better, I'd say it."

She frowned at him. "I'm not a quitter, Carlo, you know that. Yes, I gave Brett the big heave-ho, but if you think there's a chance, something I could say that would—"

Carlo was already shaking his head. "Forget it, Francesca."

"Forget it?" she echoed. This wasn't why she'd unloaded her troubles on him. In the time that it took to drive to the coffee place, she decided she'd probably acted too hastily. "You're supposed to help me!" Carlo had to help her concoct a plan.

He drained the black and lethal-looking stuff in his mug, then shrugged.

She eyed him with sudden interest, for the first time

noticing he'd lost weight and there were shadows under his eyes. "You've been acting strangely for the past few months. What's going on with *you?*"

"Nothing."

She sat up straight. "Don't give me that. Are you having a problem at work?"

He shook his head. "No, Franny. But I appreciate the concern."

Carlo was really starting to worry her. She'd taken a chance revealing her relationship with Brett to Carlo, especially after that punch he'd given him a few weeks ago. But she needed to talk to someone, and this was not the time to share romantic troubles with her best friend, an imminent bride.

She looked at her brother's stony expression and sighed. "Maybe I *should* have talked to Elise."

Something flickered in Carlo's eyes.

A weird thought entered Francesca's mind, and her heart stuttered. No. *No.*

But Carlo's mood had darkened at the same time that Elise's wedding preparations had really begun. But no. He'd known David and Elise their entire lives. He wouldn't...

"Carlo." She reached across the table and touched her brother's hand. "You—you're one of the grooms-men. David is one of your best friends."

"Correct," he said, in that maddeningly cool, police detective way of his.

"They're very happy," Francesca went on. "Perfect for each other."

"Correct," he said again, his face giving away nothing.

Francesca felt a little desperate. She wanted to believe such a thing couldn't happen. Walking the relationship tightrope with Brett made her want to be certain of a big, cushy, happy-ending net below. But something told her the truth.

"You love her," Francesca said, the words hard to force out. "You love Elise."

Nothing changed on Carlo's face. "With every breath I take."

"Oh, *Carlo*."

His eyes bore into hers. "But that's just between us. Our secret. You get it, Franny? I don't want to burden David *or* Elise with this, ever."

She nodded dumbly. Carlo loved Elise. Elise loved David. No, no, no. Breath shuddered into her lungs. "Why? Why are you telling me this now?"

Carlo raised his brows. "See if you can figure it out."

She had stomped away from Brett half mad, half maudlin. She'd captured Carlo, hoping he would talk some sense into her or at least help her make sense of Brett's distrust of love. Carlo was going to help her forge a plan, she'd thought, because…because…because the simple truth was that she was in love and wanted to be loved back.

Carlo loved Elise. Elise loved David. Francesca loved Brett. Brett didn't want to be in love.

"I thought it was going to be flowers and champagne. Satin sheets and shiny rings."

"I know," Carlo said.

But that's what she wanted it to be! That's the dream she'd always had. The one she'd tossed off her sneakers and her blue jeans to find. It had to be out there!

But Carlo loved Elise. Elise loved David. Francesca loved Brett. Brett didn't want to be in love.

Francesca sighed. "But love's a lot more complicated than roses and rides in limousines, isn't it? Lots more potential for heartbreak."

Carlo gave her another rueful smile. "Isn't that what Brett's already figured out?"

And she'd thought men stuck to bachelorhood because they didn't want to pick up their socks. What a silly fool she'd been. Accepting defeat, Francesca slumped against the back of her red vinyl seat.

WEDGED IN A CORNER of a crowded pew, Brett caught himself craning his neck for a glimpse of the brides-maids. *Damn*. He whipped back around, massaging a cramp in his shoulder.

What was he trying to do? Who was he trying to see? Couldn't be Francesca. She'd made her choice, and he was fine with it. So what if he hadn't slept the past two nights. The problem had nothing to do with the big hole she'd left on one side of his bed.

A hand clamped on his shoulder. He jerked his gaze upward to meet the serious brown eyes of Carlo. Dressed in a dark tuxedo, he was escorting a behatted woman to a seat in the pew behind him.

The woman slid into place, and Carlo squeezed his shoulder. "How you doing?" he asked.

Brett shot him a wary glance, then looked pointedly at the hand still heavy on him. "Fine. Relaxed. Well rested." All lies.

Carlo left his hand where it was and raised his brows. "That so?"

"Yeah." The Milano family had nothing to do with his mood.

"I thought maybe you were...hurting."

Yeah, right. And if he just happened to tell Carlo that his sister was the cause of that hurt and exactly *where* it ached, then Brett could be sure to be reintroduced to at least five of her brother's knuckles. "I'm fine, Carlo."

His only real complaint was sleep deprivation.

Carlo gave one more squeeze to his shoulder, hard enough to make Brett wince. Then he returned to the back of the church.

Brett massaged his arm to loosen his shoulder while the wedding procession began. David and his groomsmen were up front, and just like at the rehearsal, the organist began to play processional music. The first of the bridesmaids passed Brett, wearing a simple white gown.

Did bridesmaids usually wear white? Brett shrugged. Apparently Elise liked the color because the two bridesmaids following wore it as well.

He looked back, just to verify the color of the dress of bridesmaid number four.

Francesca.

The vision of her hit his eyes like a blinding flash. His breath sucked in sharply. Out of his life for two days, and somehow he'd forgotten how beautiful she was. Sleeveless and white, the dress revealed the golden perfection of her shoulders then went on to hug the generous curves of her breasts and the slender lines of her waist and hips.

Closing his eyes, he turned back around in his seat.

Some sensation weighed on his chest, but he ignored it, promising himself a tall beer and a good rest when he got home.

He didn't need to open his eyes to know when she passed his pew. Her perfume, that one she'd had him vet weeks ago, reached him first. The heaviness on his chest increased.

Two beers and a good rest.

The rest of the ceremony went by in a haze. Elise and David must have said the right things, because fairly soon it was over. Brett stood in his pew, shuffling forward as he followed the crowd out of the chapel.

Maybe he'd skip the reception. But what was the likelihood of finding sleep? Gauging the answer as *None,* he dutifully followed the directions to the reception. He didn't hesitate at the receiving line, either, shaking David's hand in congratulations and kissing Elise on the cheek.

Halfway down the line stood bridesmaid number four, and up close he could see someone had performed an elaborate and sophisticated makeup job on her. "Francesca," he said, his voice tight.

"Brett. How've you been?"

No telling what she was thinking behind the dramatic sweep of her eyelashes and the reddened curve of her lips. His hand curled into an involuntary fist. "Great," he said. "I've been great."

She smiled, looking past him to the person following closely behind. He'd been dismissed.

What the hell.

He found the bar and ordered a whisky. Neat.

The reception proceeded as all do. Food. Dancing. Brett drank.

Using the dance band's microphone, the best man made a toast.

Francesca, as maid of honor, grabbed it next. She brought it toward her mouth, and the thing squealed reverb so loudly Brett thought maybe she'd burst his eardrums.

Everyone else laughed, shook their heads and then quieted for Francesca's short speech.

Brett couldn't hear it. His ears were still ringing. That weight on his chest grew heavier by the minute. He thought he was coming down with something.

No wonder he hadn't been sleeping.

Next came the obligatory garter throw. Brett stayed out of the running, instead nursing another whisky.

Elise prepared to throw her bouquet. Jostling and laughing with embarrassment, a whole passel of single women lined up for the chance to be the next designated bride. Veil floating behind her, Elise turned her back, then checked over her shoulder.

Whatever she saw caused her to abandon her position and stamp away. In seconds she was back, Francesca in tow. Rolling her eyes, Francesca broke free and stood at the very back of the grouped women, obviously uninterested in catching the bouquet.

Brett found himself moving forward. Just to get a better view of the action. Then, with a big show of a wind-up, Elise let the bouquet fly.

Obviously the sports gene wasn't going to be passed to Elise and David's future children on the maternal side. The flowers went high and long, flying nearer to Brett than any of the single ladies, who, in their best dresses and heels, didn't have a prayer of grabbing the thing.

But he'd forgotten the one woman raised by four older brothers. Four brothers who'd honed in her a competitive streak impossible to suppress. Four brothers who'd shown a girl how to move, and she sure could do it, since she'd exchanged her high heels for a pair of high-top sneakers.

Francesca faded back, nearly bumping into him. Brett tried to give her more room, but with a table and chairs behind him, his movements were restricted.

The bouquet was still sailing high on a collision course for the wall. Certainly no one could reach it. Then Francesca jumped, her body bowing in the best running back style. The flowers landed in her arms.

Francesca landed against Brett's chest. He went backward.

To save herself from falling with him, she dug her elbows into his ribs.

"Oomph!" With a scatter of crowd and chairs, Brett landed, hard and alone, on the polished parquet floor.

Safely on her two feet, Francesca peered down at him, the flowers cradled in her arms. "Oops," she said.

She didn't look the least bit sorry. But he didn't *think*

she intentionally meant to step on his hand as she turned her back on him and walked away.

Chest heaving, Brett lay sprawled on the floor. His neck cramp was back. His shoulders ached from the Carlo squeeze. His ribs hurt. His back hurt. His fingers, the ones Francesca had crushed beneath her sneaker, throbbed.

But not one of the pains was anything, compared to the pain of seeing her once again walk away. The realization struck him with the force of an atomic explosion.

Carlo reached his side. He clasped Brett's hand and pulled him to his feet. "You okay, pal?"

"I hurt like hell," Brett told his friend seriously.

Carlo frowned. "You need a doctor?"

Brett rubbed a palm over his chest. "I don't think that will help."

He'd called it sleep deprivation. He'd puzzled over the ache in his chest and the strange pain that the sight of Francesca had inflicted on his eyes.

Well, he'd figured it out now.

Somewhere, somehow, some way, the lady in the sneakers, who'd been his tomboy princess, had grown up to become the queen of his heart.

God, it sounded so corny but it felt so true.

He loved her. He was in love with her.

And all the hurt he'd been so afraid to risk by loving her was nothing compared to the pain of living without her.

He looked over at his best friend. "Damn, Carlo. I've been a fool."

Francesca's brother smiled. "My thoughts exactly."

SHE'D DISAPPEARED. Brett forced himself to slowly retrace his steps.

No Francesca on the dance floor.

She wasn't hanging by the wedding cake.

The head table, reserved for the wedding party, was empty.

He walked the perimeter of the large room again, stopping by the bar for another whisky to quell his panic.

He needed to talk to her. Now. His heart was alive and well, and he had to tell her about it.

Stumped, he went outside.

It only took him a few minutes to spot a pair of size-five sneakers loitering around the back bumper of a newly washed car decorated with Just Married signs and tissue paper flowers. A bulging garbage bag at her feet, Francesca stood, frowning at a ball of twine in her hands.

"Need help?" he asked.

She jumped then looked up. *"You."*

"You" didn't think she was feeling very charitable toward him.

He took a breath. "What are you doing?"

"Tying some tin cans together. Then tying them to Elise and David's bumper."

Brett took another deep breath. "Patricia and I never set a wedding date," he said.

Francesca sent him a startled look, then bent her head over the twine.

"I was thinking about that today. Thinking about why we didn't set the date." Brett took a swallow from his glass of whisky. "And it wasn't because it takes five years to plan a wedding."

"I don't think I want to hear any more," Francesca said.

"But I need to talk about it. I need to tell you—to explain."

Her fingers stopped fiddling with the string.

"When she died," he went on, "it was terrible. I couldn't get over what a waste it was. This beautiful, vibrant young woman. I couldn't get over what she *hadn't* experienced. She'd never been a wife. Never held her child in her arms."

Francesca hugged herself. "I *really* don't want to hear any more."

Brett moved closer to her, gripping his whisky tightly in his hand. "And I felt guilty because I didn't regret she hadn't been *my* wife. That she hadn't had *my* child."

There were tears in Francesca's dark eyes. "What are you saying?"

"I'm not sure exactly. I'm just trying to tell you how it was. Patricia and I...we'd been part of each other's lives since we were seventeen. We went to college together. Then law school. When it seemed like it was time to get engaged, we did that together, too."

"But you loved her," Francesca whispered.

Brett nodded. "I did. And I'd give anything to have her back in the world." He inhaled a long breath and then admitted something he'd kept secret for almost two years. "But I don't think I would have married her. And in many ways, knowing that has made her death more painful."

Francesca swiped at her eyes with the back of one hand. Then she kneeled by the bag and started taking out tin cans. "Why are you telling me all this, Brett?"

Whump. Whump. Whump. His heart started a bass drum beat in his chest. Talking about the past was easy. "Because...because I want you to know why taking a chance on the future is pretty hard for me, Francesca."

She lined up the empty cans in perfect rows. Tuna size on the left. Chicken noodle on the right. "I've been disappointed too, Brett."

She didn't have to say that he'd been the one to hurt her. He hunkered down beside her, trying to get her to look at him. "I know it's my fault. And I'm sorry Francesca." *Whump. Whump. Whump.* "But I've figured it out now."

She looked up, her gaze suspicious. "Figured out what?"

"I'd regret it like hell if I let you go. I won't let you become someone else's wife. The only child I want to see you carrying is mine. *Ours.*"

Whump. Whump. Whump. His heart beat so loudly he thought he might have to read her lips. Her head stayed bent over the cans.

"I love you," he said, desperate for her to respond.

She rearranged the cans, and he could see her hands shaking. "You said you wouldn't have married Patricia. But you two were engaged when she died. Why?"

He shrugged. "I suppose because I didn't want to hurt her feelings by breaking it off. And I think she didn't want to hurt mine, either."

One last can plunked to the asphalt. Francesca kept her hand curled over its open edge as she looked at Brett. "But, see, there's the rub."

His heart almost stopped.

"Since I was a little girl, you've been the one to make things better for me," Francesca said. "My protector. My knight."

Brett couldn't deny it.

"And you know I felt bad the other day when you said you didn't love me."

She looked down at the can, and he could see her fingers tighten on it. "How do I know you're not saying this for the same reason you stayed with Patricia?"

Before he could respond, she let out a startled cry. Her hand on the can opened, and he could see a long slice crossing three fingers and welling blood.

"God, Francesca." He grabbed the palm of her hand and pulled her to her feet. "Let's go find a first aid kit and some disinfectant."

She stubbornly resisted him and slipped her hand out of his, her eyes angry. "No. I hate that stinging stuff as much as I hate your pity, Brett."

"Francesca, let's get this cleaned. We can argue later."

She shook her head, her shoes digging post holes into the asphalt, her hand dripping blood. "No. I don't like disinfectant."

Exasperated, Brett moved to run his hand through his hair, only to discover he was still holding the glass of whisky. He looked at the two inches of alcohol in the glass. He eyed the stubborn, sexy, tomboy love of his life. From the top of her sleek dark head to the bottom of her scuffed sneakers she was every chance he needed to take...every bit of life he had to reach out for.

"Let's recap," he said, advancing on her. "You're afraid I said I love you because I don't want to hurt you."

She didn't see it coming. She didn't even try to resist when Brett grabbed Francesca's bleeding hand and in one deft move poured the contents of his glass—whisky, one hundred proof—over the cut.

She gasped in pain. He smiled.

"But now you see, honey," he said. "That point is moot."

"Brett." Tears turned Francesca's eyes to dark crystals, and he knew she believed him. He pulled her into his arms to kiss the tears, to kiss her mouth, to whisper in her ear that he loved her for all time and was never going to let her go.

"Just try," she said, the tears gone and that tomboy gleam back in her eye.

He grinned and held her close to his heart. "I'm afraid."

"Good," she said. "I want you to be afraid. Be *very* afraid."

And Brett was. It scared him that he'd almost turned his back on such happiness.

FRANCESCA automatically moved her feet in the old-fashioned dance steps. Over her father's shoulder, she held out her left hand and admired the wedding band now snuggled close to the engagement ring Brett had slipped on her hand four months ago. She'd only wanted the band, but once they'd shared their news with Pop he'd insisted on giving them her mother's diamond solitaire.

Knowing how happy her parents had been together, it only seemed fitting.

Her veil drifted over Pop's sleeve, and she reached up to adjust her headpiece. Brett had smiled so tenderly when he'd seen it. She'd had it especially made, delicate white tulle attached to the tiara he'd given her that magical night.

Speaking of nights...she sighed. It would be hours before she could be alone with Brett. The reception was going to last *forever*. Her brothers and Pop had turned startlingly romantic on her and sworn they wouldn't feel right if she didn't have a fancy wedding with every trimming known to man, er, wedding planner.

Her Aunt Elizabetta, dear sweet Sister Josephine Mary, had crocheted tiny bags for each guest, which held the traditional Italian good-luck almonds. If those didn't get her great-aunt into heaven, Francesca didn't know what would.

Rising on tiptoe, Francesca looked over her father's shoulders to survey the other dancers. All the brothers had been pressed into Fred Astaire service. Only old Fred never looked as pained as the four tuxedoed men shuffling across the dance floor. She shook her head. They needed women to whip them into shape, but she was sidestepping the job to concentrate on the man who'd taken her heart as easily as he'd taken her up on his bicycle all those years ago.

She loved her husband so very much.

Movement at the edge of the dance floor caught her eye. Brett. She grinned, squiggling her fingers at him in a little wave. He waved back, then pointed to the bowl of sugared almonds on the table beside him. As she watched, he scooped up a huge handful of them and stored them in his already-bulging side pocket.

A little shiver ran down Francesca's spine. Somehow he'd gotten the Italian almond tradition all wrong. Though she'd tried to correct him and explain it was a fertility charm, he insisted it was a sexual charm and claimed he was going to give her a climax for every almond he left the wedding with.

She blew Brett a kiss. It was hard to argue with such a delightful idea.

COMING NEXT MONTH

HARLEQUIN

Duets™

#3

THE COWBOY NEXT DOOR by Laurie Paige

Cybil Mathews bought her ranch knowing exactly what she wanted out of life: serenity and a world free from men! Just her luck to land sexy Mason Faraday as a neighbor. The rancher has an ego the size of Nevada—and a body born to wear tight-fitting jeans. Cybil is determined to stay footloose and fancy-free, but Mason's kisses are branding her heart as his own!

MEANT FOR YOU by Patricia Knoll

Caitlin Beck and Jed Bishop don't see eye to eye on anything—except their inability to keep their hands off each other. He thinks she's too uptight. She thinks he's too laid-back. All the pair has to do is finish renovating the Victorian house they bought together, sell it and they'll never see each other again. Meanwhile, she'll stick to her side of the house, and he'll stick to his. So why do they keep meeting in the hallway?

#4

ONE IN A MILLION by Ruth Jean Dale

Sophie Brannigan—a four-year-old penny-pincher—is the prime suspect in the theft of a one-cent coin. Quint Sterling is hot on her trail, and that of her mother, Amber—because both penny and woman are one in a million. He soon discovers he's no match for the little girl, but Amber is another story...

LOVE, TEXAS STYLE by Kimberly Raye

New York lawyer Suzanne Hillsbury is looking for love in all the wrong places. What she needs is an honest to goodness cowboy, one who believes in hard work, old-fashioned values...and looks good in a pair of jeans. Sexy Brett Maxwell seems to be just the man she's been seeking. Little does she guess that under Brett's Western bravado, he's more of a city slicker than she is...